Division One: Alpha and Omega

by Stephanie Osborn

Chromosphere Press

Huntsville, AL

Table of Contents

Chapter 1

The handsome man in the elegant Suit stood patiently beside his sleek black vehicle, waiting, hidden in the night shadows of the desert. His tall, lean but muscular build nevertheless bespoke power, rendered the more intimidating by his stark black attire and the incongruous sunglasses which hid his dark brown eyes. An observer—had there been one, at that late hour, in that remote location—would have had a hard time guessing Agent Echo's age, but the barest hint of silver just starting to distinguish the dark hair at the temples, and only visible in certain lights, might have placed him as in his mid-to late-thirties. Perhaps.

Given the choice, this wasn't where Echo would have preferred to be, but duty dictated his location, and while he scorned most authority, Echo still understood and abided duty and necessity. Besides, his preference was...no longer an option.

This operation took him back out to the desert Southwest. West Texas again—an area with which he was intimately familiar. The last time Echo had been in this neck of the woods, he'd been with X-ray on that agent's last mission, tracking down a rogue—but very determined—Teludal nicknamed Kenny by the other Division agents, because they'd 'killed' him so many times. Only that time had been Kenny's last death; when the Teludal— believed to be a chupacabra by the locals—had attacked and slaughtered a young family of campers the day before, the "capture, if possible" part of their orders had been omitted. Unfortunately, Kenny had taken X-ray with him.

So Echo had selected and trained a new partner. The process took some time. But the new partner had been a good choice. Within months of the rookie going 'live,' the pair had begun making a reputation for themselves as the premier team in Division One.

Tonight, however, Echo was alone. And looked like being that way for quite a while. Maybe permanently.

Damn, Romeo, he thought as he waited, allowing his mind to drift back a couple of weeks, *gotta watch that clowning around in the gym, kid. Especially OUR gym.* Echo could still hear the sickening crack as Romeo's leg broke in three places. Echo had gotten his howling partner down to the medlab as fast as possible, where a surprise awaited them.

* * *

"Agent Romeo," Fox, the Agency head, introduced, "this is our newest medic, Agent India. India, this is Romeo, and his partner, Agent Echo."

"India!?" Romeo had cried in recognition, as Echo settled him on the gurney and the former ER physician began treating him—the same lovely woman with the silky, short dark hair, almond eyes, and pale milk chocolate skin who, as a civilian, had treated Romeo for an alien acid saliva burn the year before, and for whom Romeo had fallen hard; never, Echo often thought, was a code name more apropos than his partner's. "Aw, never mind! You're he—"

A quick motion from Fox silenced him mid-sentence.

"Hello, Agent Romeo," India had answered, friendly but calm and somewhat impersonal. "I'm pleased to meet you and your partner Echo. You're the two most celebrated agents here, from what I've been told." She paused, a puzzled look crossing her face. "Um, have we met before? You look kinda familiar."

"Uh, aw, psht, girl. Prob'ly passed in the halls, ya know?" Romeo covered quickly, then groaned despite himself.

"Yeah, probably so," India agreed, giving him an inviting smile. "Say hi next time, huh? Now let's take care of this. But first we need to get that pain relieved, or they'll hear you in the Proxima Centauri system." She turned to the tray of medical equipment and prepared an injection.

"Uh, sure thing, yeah, um, good," Romeo answered, glancing at Fox and Echo in embarrassment, then motioning vehemently at Fox behind her back. The gestures translated to, respectively, *what the hell?* and *doesn't she know me?* Fox shook his head. Romeo nodded thoughtfully.

India turned back and administered the injection, a local anesthetic, as Echo and Fox watched. Moments later, Romeo visibly began to relax as the pain subsided. India smiled.

"That's much better," she said with satisfaction. "I'll come back in a few minutes when this is in full effect, and we'll set this leg and get you in a cast, then run some Rejuvic through an IV. That stuff will get you healed up in a third the time. All right?"

"Yeah, sounds good," Romeo agreed, and India left the room. Echo had leaned against the wall and folded his arms to listen as Romeo verbally pounced on the Agency chief.

"Okay, Fox, spill it!"

"Not much to spill. After the Klydonian invasion attempt, we were short-staffed in Medical—hell, we were farkakte short-staffed all over. So I decided to have your old chum brought in, since she'd expressed interest back when. We'd only just gotten her trained on OUR medical technology, and put into active status, when Doctor Zarnix was called out on an emergency. Alien childbirth complications."

"So? I wouldn't die of a broken leg for having to wait a couple hours."

"Romeo," Fox explained patiently, "it was a Gorthonian birth. Labor takes six months."

"Da-yum," Romeo said blankly. "Ouch."

"Exactly. And since we're shorthanded all around after the Klydonian attack, tsu aldi rukhes, I brought India in, and she's running as a full medic now, in Zarnix' absence. BUT—she doesn't remember you."

"What—you mean...I thought you'd have unbleached her by now."

"That's not always standard procedure, Romeo, and you know that. It depends on whether or not the memories would be useful to the agent." Fox shook his head. The men had been quiet for a few moments, thoughtful. Then Fox spoke again. "I AM debating about it, though, I swear. In this instance, it might be good. I'll...let you know, when I've decided."

India re-entered, and the topic was dropped quickly.

"All righty then, let's get that leg fixed now, shall we?" she said, cheerful.

Romeo gave her his brightest smile.

* * *

That had been three weeks ago, nearly four, and Romeo and India had only gotten closer during Romeo's recuperation...which was indeed

3

progressing at three to four times the normal human rate, even for so serious a multiple fracture. It was apparent to Echo that a romance had developed, and rapidly. More, this one looked serious, for a change. He was glad for what he gathered was a renewed relationship, and Fox did indeed decode India's hippocampus, so she would remember the brief affair with Romeo and respond more favorably to his advances—but Echo wondered now if he would soon need a new partner.

He shrugged to himself. *Hell, it's great to see Romeo and India working together so well, personally as well as professionally. It isn't often that Division agents can afford to get close to anybody. I sincerely hope it works out for 'em. And it isn't as if Romeo will be leaving the ranks, after all, and if that's what Romeo wants, I won't get in the way. In fact, I probably ought to just go ahead and step aside, clear the way for 'em to get together. Besides, I can always team back up with Romeo for the occasional mission.*

* * *

So Echo was standing alone in the middle of a cold, dark desert on this one. Yeah, he had backup, hidden in the darkness. But still...it wasn't the same.

He shook himself out of his morose reverie as headlights appeared in the distance, trundling toward him. Same song, umpteenth verse. Just like the last time he'd done it with X-ray, several years ago now. But hopefully with a better outcome for everyone, all around.

"Here we go...again..."

The specially-modified black '96 Corvette hard-top roared up the road toward a specific lone vehicle, executed a hard turn to block the road and screeched to a stop. Echo climbed out. He extracted his carte noir, the standard Division One smart identification, from a Suit jacket pocket; it promptly morphed into an ID. It read:

U.S. Immigration and Customs Enforcement
Agent Jack Alanson

He walked up to the box truck's driver.

"Step out, please, sir."

"What? Why?" The driver climbed out.

"Do you know what your cargo is, sir?"

The truck driver blinked.

"S'posed to be a shipment o' western wear. Yew know—cowboy boots, belts, jeans, shit like 'at."

"Not...quite. Wait right here, please. Whatever you do, don't move from this spot. Your life could depend on it."

The truck driver paled. Echo moved to the rear and opened the back of the truck.

"Come on out. I know you're in there," he called into the rear of the truck. "Don't make me have to burn down the shipping crates. You know I'll do it."

He watched as boxes began to shift, then a large silhouette emerged and moved toward him, wrapped in a cloak.

"Uh-huh...I thought so."

* * *

But when Echo got his suspect off the road, deep into the darkness, and pulled the cloak away, lo and behold, there stood ol' Kenny's long-legged, finned purple hatchmate and sometime collaborator, 'Cartman.'

Uh-huh. There's the same malformed fin that runs in the family, the skull crest...eyes are green instead of orange, though, so we really did take out Kenny...Damn. Déjà vu all over again, thought Echo, checking over his shoulder to make sure the truck driver was safe, and not getting an eyeful of alien—

—Just as Cartman growled something vaguely obscene in Teludal, and grabbed that opportunity to sprint in the opposite direction, into the desert.

"Well, shit," grumbled Echo and promptly laid chase, pulling a pistol that resembled a chrome-plated electrode, or perhaps a 1950's-era child's toy raygun, from underneath his black jacket. Reaching up with his free hand, he tapped the left temple of his sunglasses, and grunted in satisfaction as the high-tech devices—which were definitely NOT sunglasses—switched over to night-vision mode.

"Cartman! Stop! I don't want to have to shoot you like I did Kenny!" yelled Echo, but Cartman just kept running.

Echo was in terrific shape, and knew the terrain better, but Cartman had the slight advantage of a bit more visibility in the infrared range than most humans, even despite Echo's goggle-glasses, and so he could SEE the terrain better.

Mexican standoff, thought Echo. *Damn, it's gonna be a long night. And a long jog. At least I can log it as today's workout, I suppose.*

Cartman glanced back for a moment, to see where Echo was. In that instant, Echo was amazed to see Cartman slam into what seemed in the darkness to be an invisible force field, there in the middle of the desert, and go down in a heap.

A very NOISY heap, Echo thought, wondering why, even as Cartman clattered and crashed. There came a loud smash, as of glass breaking, followed by a prolonged tinkling sound, then all was still for a split-second.

"HEEEY!" came an offended shriek from somewhere very near the source of the ersatz force field. "My 'SCOPE! My data!! What on earth..."

And as Echo ran up, a red flashlight came on and played over Cartman's form, tangled up in the remains of a laptop, a folding table, several cables, and a large black Cassegrain telescope. Then the light turned to examine Echo from head to foot. The light zeroed in on Echo's blaster.

"Hm. Poor choice of words. Wrong planet, too," drily remarked the mysterious figure behind the red flashlight.

"Well, shit," Echo grumbled again.

* * *

Just then, the mop-up team arrived. Some of them began disentangling a dazed Cartman, whereupon they restrained him and led him away. Meanwhile, others began assessing the damage to the telescope, which was severe—the primary mirror lay on the desert scree in no less than half a dozen small and large pieces, not counting the tiny slivers; the telescope's barrel was no longer cylindrical, but vaguely oval...at least in the middle, where it kinda bent a little, too. The laptop, which had evidently been both the controller and the data recorder, once perched on a folding table; both table and laptop with cables were now tangled in a heap on the desert floor, not in much better shape than the telescope. The laptop had a badly cracked screen.

The 'scope's owner observed the damage assessment with concerned interest; occasional muttering and scolding could be heard if the mop-up team did something she didn't like. A sudden angry outburst from the erstwhile astronomer was interrupted when Echo's cell phone beeped insistently, and he retrieved it from his pocket.

"What the hell happened, Echo?" Fox's voice came from the device, audible even over the sound of irate ranting and the occasional curse word. "I just saw part of the chase on sat-vid."

"Y'all got the truck driver taken care of?"

"Yeah, we're on it. He'll deliver his shipment of cowboy boots and will never remember he had a stowaway. Now what happened?"

"Aw, dammit, Fox. I took a second to glance around and make sure the truck driver couldn't see—sudden little instance of vujà dé—and ol' Cartman carpe'd the diem and took off running. Only got 'im when he tripped over our friend's telescope there."

"Which you owe me for, by the way," declared the dark figure in no uncertain terms.

"Which we owe you for," Echo parroted, hearing the soft acknowledgement in his cell that enabled him to deactivate the call. "Sorry about that. But thanks. Who am I thanking, anyway?"

The red flashlight came back on and turned upward to catch the black-clad figure's face. Such illumination was not necessarily the most flattering way to light the human face, but the human being thus irradiated in this instance was attractive enough that it didn't seem to matter much, Echo decided.

"Name's Megan McAllister; I'm with NASA at Johnson Space Center in Houston," she said in a voice more than a little reminiscent of *Gone With The Wind*. She clicked off the flashlight. "Thought I'd do a little observing out here on a pet project over the weekend. Didn't expect to run across—or BE run across BY—anybody."

Echo had already pulled his brain bleach gadget from an inside jacket pocket in the darkness; it resembled nothing so much as an additional smart cell phone. The other Agents slipped on their goggles—which resembled, to the casual observer, ordinary wrap-around sport sunglasses with black matte frames; Echo had never taken his off.

"You didn't run across anyone. A strong freak gust of wind toppled your telescope." And a scintillating, multicolored strobe lit up the desert for two full seconds. When it faded, he looked with satisfaction at her blank eyes.

Saw them blink. Once, twice.

"What in the damn BLAZES did you go and do that for?! Do you KNOW how long it TAKES to get properly dark-adapted for astronomical research? And then this...this CREATURE...destroys my 'scope, trashes my computer! And then YOU come running up and set off a damn full-spectrum flash bomb in my face! My night vision's ruined, my telescope's ruined, my computer with all of my data is ruined, and y'all actually have the unmitigated gall to stand there feeding me some bullshit NONSENSE about WIND GUSTS! Who the HELL do you think you are?!?"

"Well...SHIT," grumbled Echo once again, with feeling.

* * *

As her cousins wound down from chasing fireflies and were gathered up by the aunts and uncles to take home and be put to bed, the girl ran over to her parents.

"Mom? Dad? Can I stay up late tonight, and do some more stargazing? Please? That hill in the back field is just perfect for watching! I'll come back by one in the morning, I promise! I just want to watch the meteor shower." She waved her hand. "I even got an alarm set on my watch! And it's summer vacation! I promise I'll do my chores on time tomorrow! Pleeeeease?"

"Sure, honey," her father said with an indulgent smile. "Go ahead. If you're not back by 1:10, though, I'm coming to look for you. Take a couple blankets. It'll get cool once the dew falls."

"Okay, Daddy! Thank you!" the girl exclaimed, hugging him tight. "See you later!"

The girl caught up the blankets that her mother proffered, and headed out the door at speed.

* * *

Echo led the way out of the elevator and into the Core of Division One Headquarters—31 Division Avenue, Brooklyn, to be precise; the building was shared with a small Jewish school—unbeknownst to the school. A hobbling Romeo on titanium crutches, with a protective India accompanying, brought up the rear, having met Echo in the vehicle hangar, at Echo's called-in request. In between the agents was Megan, who stopped dead in her tracks as she got her first look at the huge room. The others paused, and India raised a hand to push Megan forward. Echo shot India a *no, wait* look, and subtly waved her off, then returned his attention to Megan, continuing to study her, as he had ever since their nighttime encounter some hours earlier.

Megan McAllister was a very attractive woman, somewhat taller than the average—around five feet eight or nine inches, by Echo's estimate, give or take; and with a fair, peaches-and-cream Celtic complexion. Her long, platinum blonde—almost silver—hair was currently in a French-braided updo, wrapped around her head. She appeared to be in her mid-twenties, with a figure that was at once strong and athletic, and full and feminine. *Like something out of a comic book, almost*, the agent thought. *Easy on the eyes, I'll admit.*

And complexion wasn't the only place her Celtic genetics resided. When Megan had discovered the primary mirror of her telescope lying in more than half a dozen pieces on the desert floor, the mop-up team had learned that she also had a bit of Gaelic fire in her temperament as well—in no uncertain terms.

By and large, however, she had handled the whole strange situation remarkably well, never really losing her cool—except for the broken mirror—and maintaining a sort of calm demeanor that Echo, frankly, admired. It wasn't often that someone was dumped into the middle of an alien encounter so suddenly and remained so unflappable. His mind wandered back for a moment, and he remembered he hadn't.

Now Megan drifted forward slowly, until she reached the balcony rail and wrapped her fingers around it, leaning lightly against it to orient herself as she examined the huge open area. Occasionally, Echo saw her lips move slightly, as if talking to herself. Echo noticed, too, that her gaze was systematically taking in every part of the room, even the ceiling, where a couple of aliens strolled by.

* * *

Laid out in front of Megan McAllister was a gigantic room, decorated in shades of black and gray, with the occasional machined-steel accent. Matte black hexagonal tiles covered the ground floor, color-changing lights outlining their edges instead of grout. Whenever anyone, human or alien, walked across the room, the cracks between the tiles lit up like a rainbow... in different colors for each being, in a kind of halo around each person. Most of the humans were dressed in black suits, and paid little or no attention to the floor halos, but whenever an alien entered the giant chamber—which seemed to occur in waves, with up to a dozen or more entering at once—Megan noticed they paid close attention to their halos.

Multiple entryways led from the room, and McAllister observed that each arch had a specific color outlining the tiles near and through it; the halos, she realized, were somehow guiding each person to their desired exit.

"Wow," she mouthed, studying the design, before falling silent. *That sure beats hell outta colored stripes painted on the floor. It's way prettier, too. But how does it pick up where they wanna go...?*

Clusters of seats perched here and there on the main floor, along with several circular rows of desks in the corners, laptops lying on them; a dome-shaped object with a stubby antenna, which Megan took to be a wifi router, sat on a narrow machined-steel pedestal at the center of each circle. It was hard to tell at that distance, but she thought she saw jacks, ports, and pads of various shapes on several of the closer desks, and decided they were probably there for charging personal electronics.

Automated signs—appearing more like flat-screen displays than actual signage—along the walls indicated the route to various departments, such as 'Medical,' 'Customs,' and 'Cargo Check,' and several signs changed into other languages as she watched the ebb and flow of beings through the room. Still another sign, more centrally located and much larger, was headed 'Arrivals/Departures.' In addition to the large archways, smaller rooms opened off the area; McAllister saw a suited human emerge from one with a cup of coffee in hand.

It's a concourse! McAllister realized. *Only for...what? A spaceport instead of an airport? Aliens, after all...*

She let her eyes trail slowly up the pale gray walls, and suddenly realized that they were not ordinary sheet-rock walls, as she had at first thought. Each large panel—some two or three feet high, and at least twenty feet wide, more in places—was in fact part of the lighting; oriented horizontally, they were optimized to provide maximum light about eight feet off the floor, by Megan's estimate. The signs were actually part of the wall lighting as well, and like the tile flooring, the crevices between panels spilled soft colored light.

Higher up, several floors opened onto the area, which was rimmed with balcony corridors and crossed by the occasional catwalk; their railings comprised clear light conduits. Additional doors and corridor archways opened off these. Two hovering platforms shuttled back and forth between floors and archways; occasionally someone would step onto one of these and ride it across the area—straight across, up, down, or sometimes diagonally.

Across the Core from where she stood, a floor-to-ceiling bay window projected into the huge room, an unmarked door next to it. An especially large balcony—equipped with several currently-empty waiting-room-type chairs—led up to the door, but was not connected to any of the other balconies; it appeared to have its own approach via a sweeping, curved ramp from the main floor.

Visible through the bay window, a somewhat older man sat at a desk in a large office, his grizzled head bowed over some paperwork. From time to time he sat back and glanced out the window, over the larger room. His features, visible even at that distance, were chiseled and clean-shaven.

Huh. Wonder who that is? she thought. *Some sorta manager, maybe? Very distinguished-looking guy.*

At last her gaze turned to the ceiling, and she did a patent double-take, then tried not to drool in envy: a huge holographic depiction of the Milky Way Galaxy floated there in all its glory. More, two aliens—tall, bipedal, blue-skinned, with large yellow eyes and straight white hair, their short, stubby antennae gently waving—walked across the ceiling through the hologram, pausing occasionally to point to this or that detail and converse.

"Oh, that is SO cool," she breathed, her voice inaudible. "I wonder if I can get up there to look..."

* * *

Definitely a scientist, Echo thought as he watched her, *trained observer.* But there was something...something in her reaction that was different from anyone else he'd ever seen introduced to Division One HQ. Quietly, he moved up beside her to observe her reactions more closely.

Not quiet enough. She glanced at him, momentarily distracted, then resumed her study of the Core.

"Damn!" whispered Romeo to India, behind them. "Ears like a cat."

But in that split-second look, Echo had seen what made her response different. Her eyes shone with blue fire; her mouth curved in a huge smile. Just as in the desert encounter, she was not afraid; she was not shocked, she was not overwhelmed. No, she was...delighted.

She turned to him then, and fired off one word.

"Immigration?"

"Yes, partly, in a manner of speaking. On average we've got, oh, probably twenty to thirty thousand aliens on Earth. Some are political refugees; some just like it here. Some come here because of their jobs. Some are actually tourists, here on vacation, or for an educational trip; we get a few exchange students each school year. We try to look out for all of 'em—keep 'em safe, keep 'em under wraps; you know what I mean. Now and again we get the equivalent of wetbacks, like our 'good friend' Cartman who took out your telescope." He drew quotation marks in the air with his fingers. "And some...are just trash. We try to throw those back into the garbage can they came from...or take 'em outta the gene pool entirely, if it becomes necessary. And it's our job to keep track of it all."

"Big job."

"We can handle it."

"I don't doubt it. This is fascinating," she responded, returning her attention to the Core, apparently awed by the scope of it all.

Echo studied her for a moment, to see if she was serious. She was. The barest hint of a smile hovered at the corners of his mouth then, as he observed her rapidly changing expressions, which in turn betrayed her racing thoughts. Then he paused for a moment, thinking, and swept his own gaze out over the Core, trying to see it with new eyes, less jaded eyes—her eyes. He remembered she was NASA, and suddenly he understood. And he DID smile, then. For her, the dream was not only alive; it was here, now.

"You should understand: it's not exactly *Star Trek*," he warned her.

"No. I wouldn't expect it to be. This is the real world. But it's definitely pretty damn cool."

"Come on, guys. We gotta talk to Fox about her," urged an impatient India, behind them.

"Who's Fox?" asked Megan.

"The Boss-man," said Romeo.

"The Director," Echo corrected. "At least of the Earth-based part of the organization."

"Oh."

* * *

As they moved down to the main floor and through the Core, Megan felt decidedly conspicuous, but she hid it well, and maintained a cool demeanor.

Just because a bunch of guys in black suits—and aliens—are all staring at me and whispering is no reason, she thought, *to lose my cool. Especially just before going in to see 'the Boss-man.'*

Obviously, she had violated some rule, but she had no clue how, or what; she hadn't done anything of which she was aware—after all, THEY had run over HER...quite literally. She wondered, too, how she had been in NASA for over a decade and had not heard about this outfit.

Heh, she chuckled to herself, *you'd almost think they were the UFO nuts' government...conspiracy...*

Oh, dear Lord.

They ARE.

And I wasn't SUPPOSED to find out.

And the colored lights, and the remarks about wind gusts, and their obvious consternation when I didn't buy it, and the repeated tests of the 'malfunctioning' hologram things that somehow always seemed to go off just as I looked their way...Damn. This could be...bad. Are they gonna make me...disappear?

Echo opened the door to Fox's office, and Fox looked up. Megan

13

boldly walked right up to Fox's desk, hoping the three agents behind her couldn't see her knees wobbling.

"Okay, I get it. This is all a black op, if you'll excuse the pun, and I landed in the middle of one of your 'wetback' retrievals, and your little hologram gizmos don't work on me. So..." she took a deep breath, then sighed. "What are you going to do with me?"

"Well, now," said Fox, raising his eyebrows in surprise.

"Bright one," said Echo, behind her.

* * *

"...And so this is the Earth branch for the Pan-Galactic Law Enforcement and Immigration Administration," Fox continued his explanation, begun some minutes before by McAllister's questions. "Obviously that's an English translation of something that didn't originate on Earth, and equally obviously, it's a damn mouthful to say."

"And the acronym isn't very speaker-friendly, either," McAllister noted, quirking her mouth. "P. G. L. E. I. A? That sure doesn't lend itself to easy pronunciation."

"No, it doesn't," Fox agreed.

"Never tell she's NASA," Romeo chuckled then. It elicited a faint grin from Megan.

"NASA-ese," she noted. "Acronyms R Us. Kinda the rules of the road, there."

"We wanted to try shifting word order until we got something that was easier for humans to say as an acronym," Fox continued, "but the Pan-Galactic Council nixed that. They wanted the translation to be as close to literal as possible, no dinking around, regardless of planet."

"Eh. I guess I can understand that. Oh geez, listen to me," Megan broke off, raking a hand down her face. "As if a body gets picked up every day by some intergalactic law enforcement officers!"

"Some do," India said, grim.

"Not many humans, though," Echo said with a shrug.

"True," Fox agreed. "Once we start getting 'out there' more as a species, that might change, but for now, it's just the occasional hiccup."

"Okaaaaay," McAllister murmured, wistfully pondering that for a

14

moment, then returned to her original topic. "So if the actual name is too unwieldy, what the heck do you call the organization, then?"

"Informally? It's just the Agency, or the Administration," Echo answered. "More formally, though, this is Division One, because we're in the first, uh, I guess you could call it 'precinct,' in the Milky Way Galaxy," he decided. "It isn't a compliment, particularly, but it isn't an insult, either; the Council basically put up a map of the Galaxy and drew a spiral inward, sectioned it off, adjusted the segments until they got reasonably equal population sizes in each precinct, then assigned numbers to 'em. This part of the Galaxy isn't heavily populated, though, so Earth is actually the Administration headquarters for most of our precinct."

"Are there other offices on Earth, or is it all headquartered in the Big Apple?"

"Oh, hell no," Fox replied, having dropped much of his formality early on, in order to set Megan at ease; a couple of quick nonverbal communiqués from Echo told him what he wanted to know, anyway. "There are major offices on all of the continents, including Antarctica, and several across the larger continents, such as Eurasia and Africa—usually in the larger cities, though the Antarctic office is at, or rather, near McMurdo Station. This office is the biggest, however, and is essentially the administrative headquarters for the planet, and to a lesser extent, the precinct, as Echo told you. The main branch, I guess you could call it. And we have departments within the Division—Legal, Immigration, Import/Export, Transportation, Medical, Science and Engineering, Facilities, Supplies, Special Operations...you get the picture."

"Yeah. Pretty cool. And so...the hologram thing was..."

"The Cerebellar Holographic Mnemonic Re-Encoding Induction System," Fox finished for her. "Again, a mouthful to say, and not much way to abbreviate it."

"So most of us just call it 'brain bleach,'" Echo continued.

"Okay. Only...it doesn't work on me."

"No, and that's a puzzle," Fox admitted. "If you don't mind, our Medical department would like to run some non-invasive tests, to see if we can figure out what's going on there."

"I...suppose so," McAllister agreed. "But...what are you gonna do with me?"

"Given that we've already run a preliminary background check on you, and you've been with NASA for some few years," Fox said, patting a folder at his elbow, "I believe we have a serious proposal that we'd like to put before you."

McAllister blinked.

"Um, okay," she said, uncertain. "I'm listening..."

* * *

"Are you sure she'll be safe, Honey?" the mother asked from the living room window of the old farmhouse, where she watched their daughter scamper off. "Maybe you should go out there with her."

"She'll be fine," the father replied, confident. "That back field is miles from anybody. Who's gonna mess with her?"

"I dunno," the mother wondered, anxious. "Somebody could sneak through the woods. And there's bobcats and coyotes, and you KNOW that neighbor said he saw a cougar. I got a bad feeling about it tonight, and I'm worried."

"Baby, you worry too much," the father said, taking his wife in his arms and holding her close. "She's twelve, smart as a whip, and knows every critter and every sound on this farm. And I'll still be up anyway, to know she made it home safe. Everything is gonna be fine. Trust me. Trust HER."

"It's not either of you I don't trust," the mother protested.

"Quit worrying. She's fine," he reiterated.

"I guess..."

He kissed her.

* * *

"Fox, let me talk to her," Echo offered quietly, glancing at the corner of Fox's office where a slightly pale Megan looked out over the Core. "No one around here knows better than I do what she's going through right now, or what's in store for her."

Fox looked Echo over, then nodded.

"All right. Fair enough. Especially since, if she checks out, you'll be training her. Identify with her, huh?"

Echo shrugged.

"I just know what it feels like to have your life co-opted by a bunch of people you've never seen before," the agent told Fox. "Remember, we didn't have cerebellar re-induction systems yet when I accidentally ran across y'all in the First Envoy, so...I've been where she is right now. And I get where she's coming from. I know what she's feeling, what she's thinking. Completely and totally."

Fox nodded permission, then waved Romeo and India to the door and exited with them, leaving the pair alone to talk.

Echo moved over to stand behind Megan, looking over her shoulder into the Core, careful not to touch her. He was concerned that even a sympathetic shoulder pat might be misconstrued as coercion, in her current frame of mind.

And in the circumstances, I wouldn't blame her, he thought. *I wish there was an easier way. Or at least, some options for her.* Finally he broached the silence.

"Still as fascinating as you thought it was a few minutes ago?" he asked her.

She nodded an affirmative, but didn't speak.

"Do you think it's something you would enjoy doing?"

A more vigorous nod this time.

"Are you saying yes because it's true, or because you don't have a choice?"

"...Both..." she replied in a very subdued voice. She turned her head ever so slightly, to take him in with peripheral vision. "So...I really can't go back?"

"No. It's policy, because it's considered a security risk. Mind, none of us are saying YOU are a security risk; we wouldn't be discussing what we're discussing if you were. It's just that it's all too easy to forget, to slip up and say something that turns out to be way the hell more revealing than you meant it to be."

"I understand."

"What we do with those in your position—which, I might add, is about as rare as finding a live T. Rex these days—is dependent upon our analysis of them, though. Not everybody gets the offer we just made you. And that was BECAUSE we trust you. And our preliminary check indicates to us that you'd be really good at it."

Somewhat to his surprise, her head bowed in grief.

"And I was so close..." she whispered. "Just one more test...that's all I had...just one more..."

Echo looked at her quizzically and shifted position subtly in order to study her face, but Megan didn't elaborate. So he decided to try to help her change her perspective.

"Look at it this way," he said, voice quiet. "You've already accomplished, just by being here, what other NASA personnel are still dreaming of: You've made contact." He pointed at the various aliens wandering about the floor of the Core.

"That's true..." she acknowledged, turning toward him at last.

"You've heard our proposal. If you accept, it WILL be hard. The hardest thing you've ever done, or will do, in your life. And the hours are long. One Division day is really forty-eight hours—we work one Earth day on, one day off. ALL day AND all night. And there will be times you'll think you're going to die...and you might. I won't lie to you about that. This can be a damn dangerous job. But I promise you this: It's worth all the effort, all the fear, all the hard work...or I wouldn't still be here. And I think, in the long run, if you have 'the right stuff,'" he grinned at the deliberate joke, "if you have it in here—" he lightly tapped her temple, then the top of her breastbone, "—like I think you do, then this job will give back to you more than you ever dreamed possible."

"How do YOU know what I have inside?" There was a hint of anger in her voice, a blue flame in her eyes, and she turned away, resuming her surveillance of the Core.

"A hunch. You...remind me of someone. Someone I...used to know." *Someone I used to BE,* he added silently.

* * *

Megan absorbed his spoken comment, and accepted it at face value.

"And...if I refuse?" She looked up at him. Echo's face tightened marginally. She nodded in full comprehension.

"Then...I accept."

Chapter 2

McAllister sat in the Medical department, alone with Zebra, the adjunct chief of the department. She had started out being examined by staff physician Whiskey, but had, much to her surprise, been quickly handed off to the current department lead; Zarnix was still attending the Gorthonian birth. Zebra was now studying Megan's charts, her brow furrowed in puzzlement.

"Is something wrong?" Megan asked politely, not sure whether to be concerned or not. "My NASA physicals all showed clean..."

"NASA doesn't have the sensory capabilities we've got," Zebra replied, in a somewhat absent and curt tone, and McAllister blinked, mildly offended. Zebra looked up then, and apparently saw the expression on Megan's face. "Oh, no no, no offense intended," the other woman added hastily. "It's just that NASA is still running on Earth-originating tech, and we've got access to diagnostic equipment from across the Galaxy and beyond. We've reaped the benefits of civilizations that are not just millennia old, but literally millions of years old, with science and engineering achievements commensurate."

"Oh, I see," Megan said, mollified. "Yeah, that makes sense. So is there something wrong? I don't have...I dunno, some fatal disease coming, or something?"

"No, no, nothing like that. But you do have some interesting data, here."

"How so?"

"Oh, it's just unusual for us to encounter a human in such good health," Zebra said, waving a hand. "Then again, you were an astronaut candidate in the final phases, according to your file, so it stands to reason you'd be in the top percentile for most things."

"Um, yeah, I guess," Megan answered, feeling her cheeks heat with the flush; she had never gotten used to the notion of being in an elite group.

As far as she was concerned, she was who and what she was, which was nobody especially important or unusual, and she was as well aware of her shortcomings as her gifts. She was confident in herself and her abilities, but unlike some of her colleagues—*former colleagues now,* she thought— she had no untoward egotism in her being. She just wanted to explore the universe. "You know, I've heard that sort of thing before, lots of times, but I still can't get used to it. I'm just me. So have I passed your physical and mental criteria?"

"With flying colors," Zebra said with a smile.

But Megan thought the smile seemed guarded, somehow.

* * *

"...Flying colors?" Fox parroted.

He was in his private office overlooking the Core, discussing the medical data of the Agency's latest recruit with Zebra; the bay windows were opaqued to maintain patient confidentiality.

"Exactly. And the very level of those flying colors is..." Zebra broke off. "'Unusual' is too mild a term. 'Unheard-of' is more like it."

"Explain."

"Well, the best way I know of to put it is that she's a statistical outlier for the overall human population," Zebra explained. "A way-the-hell-out-there outlier."

"Give me details."

"You can read the medical charts, right?"

"I can. After all these years, I would hope so."

"Here, then." Zebra handed over a file folder, flipping it to a certain page. "Look at this. To say she's a prime physical specimen is an understatement. The only other agent I know of with that level of...health and fitness...is Echo himself, and even he had a couple of bad habits when he first came into the Agency that are apt to bite him in the ass, down the road."

"The cigs."

"Exactly. Glad we finally broke him of that."

"Didn't really take long, as I recall," Fox noted, thinking back.

"No. But given the chemicals they put on that shit when it's growing, if I could wave a wand and instantly break people of the habit, I would," Zebra said with distaste. "I think it's the way tobacco is commercially grown."

"Too many chemicals in the mix. Pesticides, fungicides..."

"Exactly. Which then get heated when the stuff is cured, so everything reacts and recombines into all KINDS of nasty shit, and then it's burned, which makes MORE nasty shit, and finally inhaled. So the fact that Echo smoked at all is a black mark in his charts, in my book. Zarnix agrees. We're keeping an eye on him, though, and we've already given him a few... eh, I guess you'd call it 'preventative treatments.' And we can fix it once it starts manifesting, so don't worry."

"But...SHE doesn't smoke."

"And never has; nor did her parents, according to her recollections. So in that regard, she's actually got a cleaner chart than Echo. Which puts her at the top of the Agency in that respect." Zebra leaned over and flipped a couple of pages in the file. "Now have a gander at this one."

"What?" Fox said, startled, staring at the varicolored printout. "That's...weird. What the hell am I looking at?"

"Brain scan. It shows up best if you look at the recording. Pull up file...uh, lessee..." She consulted a note on the printout, "MEDREC 2021A 05091218A and initiate it, and you'll see what I mean."

Fox turned to the small computer display on his desk, swiping an area of the desktop to activate the virtual keyboard. He quickly typed in the file name, hit enter, and watched as the networked system brought up the requested file almost immediately. A couple of quick keystrokes initiated the recording, and Zebra watched over his shoulder.

An image of a human brain appeared, in virtual 3-D, and various regions sparkled in different colors.

"This is the scan of cerebral activity during the testing. Where it lights up and sparkles indicates brain activity. The colors denote the type of activity; yellow is cognitive activity, green is sensory processing, blue is autonomic, red is memory transfer, and so on. The brighter the sparkle, the more intense the activity. What we want to look at here is principally the yellow, though there are interesting things going on with most of the others, as well. You'll see in a couple seconds, when she gets to the problem-solving section, exactly what I mean."

The brain image on the screen abruptly lit up in yellow. It did not merely sparkle, it fairly glowed—for all practical purposes, all over. Brighter, almost-white flashes blipped from region to region.

"Oy! Holy shit!" Fox exclaimed, shocked. "I've never...have YOU ever seen anything like this?"

"No, I haven't. Nor have any of the specialists I've consulted, on- or off-world, at least not in humans."

"What does it mean?"

"It means..." Zebra shrugged. "The woman thinks really, really well. I'm talking...Do you remember that old cartoon about the coyote and the running bird?"

"Yeah?"

"Well, she's Dr. Megan McAllister, Super-Genius."

"Damn!"

"You gonna tell Echo?"

"I dunno. Not yet. I need to think about this. You run the DNA profiles?"

"Not yet. I got the samples, and they're in work. That'll take a while, like usual. Running a full codon sequence determination ain't easy, ya know, even with our tech."

"Get on it as soon as you can. He's gonna be the department lead, and she'll be his trainee and probably eventual second, so I gotta tell Echo at some point. But I'd like to have a complete package, and a better understanding of what's going on, before I say anything."

"Gotcha. I'll get right on it," Zebra noted. "Anything else, hon?"

"No. You're dismissed, if you need to head back to Medical."

"Thanks. Yeah, I do. I'll ping you as soon as we get anything else on Dr. McAllister."

"Roger that. Drinks on Tuesday, like usual?"

"I'll be there, Fox." Zebra smiled warmly at the head of the Agency, just before she left his office.

* * *

The girl threw the blankets over her shoulder as soon as she got off the front porch of the farmhouse, and broke into an excited run. She ran all the way to the back field, to the base of 'her' hill.

There, she slowed to a walk and trudged up the hill, out of breath. Near the top was the perfect spot; it was flat, just slightly inclined, and faced south. And as the hill had no trees and was high enough to place her above the other trees in the area, she had a clear, gorgeous view all the way to the horizon.

Once she reached the spot, she stopped and turned in a circle, gazing over the darkened landscape for miles upon miles, in delight. Then, after checking for rocks, she spread one of the blankets over the grass and stretched her length on it—a length that was long for her age; she was going to be a tall woman when the growth spurt stopped.

Gazing deep into the cerulean night sky liberally spangled with diamond dust, she sighed, smiled, and relaxed. The core of the Milky Way was easily recognizable, off to the south-southwest; its configuration as a spiral galaxy, viewed edge-on, was just as obvious. She pulled out a note pad and pencil, checked her wristwatch, and scribbled down the time. Then she folded her arms behind her head and returned her attention to the heavens south of her position.

"Ooo! There's one...that's two..." she began to count, annotating her page with hatch marks.

However, so intent was the girl on counting meteors in her field of view—periodically scratching down the tally and the time—that she neglected to watch the sky behind her.

* * *

"I don't get it," said Romeo from his seat in the training observation room. "Y'all didn't put ME through all this testing crap. Creativity testing and obstacle courses and puzzles an' junk. I know we're shorthanded an' all, but...what gives? It'd be way simpler an' quicker to just put her through the old testing."

"We're getting ready to start up a new department," answered Fox, across the small conference table from Romeo; next to the younger agent sat his new partner, India. "Echo's already agreed to head it up, while you were laid up with the leg. Good to see you off the crutches, by the way."

"Damn good to be off 'em. Still hobblin' around a little, but that'll go away eventually; 's why I'm keepin' a cane handy for a while. So tell me about this new department. If you can, yet."

"I can. It'll be a kind of combination SWAT team and commando unit. Teams from this department will take the point whenever we have the really dangerous situations—the interstellar terrorists, the galactic invasions, things like that. We think, with her background, she may have what it takes to make it in this department. We sure as hell can't send her back where she came from. She seems intrigued by the idea, at least. And no family complications to worry about. Single, only child, birth family gone in a car accident."

"But, Fox, what if she can't hang?"

"I don't know yet, Romeo. We'll cross that bridge—"

"We won't have to," interrupted Echo, coming into the testing observation room and moving past the table around which the others were seated, directly to the observing window. "She'll make it."

"But how do you know?" asked Romeo. "'Got a feeling'?"

"Yup. Same one I had about you, junior."

"WELL, the lady'll hang, then." Romeo sat back in his chair, satisfied.

"Damn," muttered India.

Echo shot her a hard look, then returned his attention to the observation window overlooking the course.

"Have we started yet?"

"No," Fox answered. "We're still getting set up. And we were waiting for you."

"I'm here. Let's get rolling."

"Done." Fox hit a button on an adjacent control console.

Romeo, Echo, and India watched as the observation window, as well as a hooded monitor on the command console, showed several aliens of various types entering the obstacle course. Romeo gasped as he recognized a Betelgeusian giant arachnoid, possessing, by his estimate, a good fourteen- or fifteen-foot leg span—accompanied by several Division One agents sporting flamethrowers, lasers, blasters, and disintegrator rifles, entering the course. Two heavily-armed guards in black armor moved into position at the entrance. Romeo and India noticed then, with a shock, that they were FACING the course, as if the concern was from something inside.

"Hope she's not afraid of spiders," Echo remarked offhandedly.

"Hope she's not afraid of death," Romeo murmured to India. "Shit."

* * *

Megan came into the observation room just then. She was wearing black workout leggings and sports-bra top, but the rest of her attire was somewhat odd: menswear-style black lace-up dress shoes, a black tie, a dress leather belt, and a pair of the special goggles-cum-sunglasses strapped to one hip. An unusual device, like a large plastic bangle bracelet, was fastened around her right ankle. Sensors attached to her head and torso connected to a small transmitter pack on her back. Echo met her and led her to the command console.

"All right, Megan," Fox began, waving a hand at the view in the monitor, which now only depicted a door and two guards, "this is the obstacle course. When you go through that door," he pointed to the image of the guarded door on the monitor, "you will enter the first of a series of six rooms, each of which has various...impediments...to your progress. Your objective is simply to reach the exit of room six as quickly as possible. The tracking device on your ankle will enable us to monitor your progress. You may make use of anything on your person, as well as anything you find along the course. In addition, you may select from one—and only one—of the items on this side table."

Megan eyed the monitor display in detail before Fox led her over to the table. On it was an eclectic collection of items: a Phillips-head screwdriver, a small glass bottle, a pair of wire cutters, a coil of rope, a pen knife, a jar of cheese spread, a pocket-sized Winchester & Tesla Mark II death ray, a packet of facial tissues, and a chocolate bar.

Megan was in no rush. She scanned the table carefully, considering, as the four Division One agents watched. She looked herself up and down, fingering the items she already carried. Echo watched as she flipped over the tie and checked to see what was on the label. He smiled inwardly, pleased as he followed her mental processes, realizing he understood how she thought. Finally she reached out, picked up the pen knife, and clipped it to the belt at her waist.

Echo raised an eyebrow in carefully-hidden surprise and looked at Fox, who returned his gaze unemotionally. Romeo and India watched the whole scene in amazement.

"Ready, then?" Fox asked Megan.

"As I'll ever be."

"All right. Follow me."

As Fox led Megan out, Echo turned to the console, put on a headset, and began entering commands. Romeo and India walked up to the observation window, and Echo hit a button. Blast shutters on the window began to close.

"Sorry, kids. Can't watch this one; you'll have to go through this yourselves soon enough."

"Oh, joy," India muttered.

"You can monitor her progress on this schematic." Echo hit another sequence of commands, and a panel opened on the wall. It showed the layout of six variously-shaped, interconnected rooms, a number on each room.

"How are you gonna evaluate her if you can't see what she's doing?" Romeo asked him, as he and India sat back down at the table, across from the schematic.

"I didn't say Fox and I couldn't watch. I've been through it. You haven't. Yet."

Fox re-entered the room. "She's ready, Echo."

"All right, then." Echo handed Fox another headset, then keyed the microphone switch. "Megan? GO!"

* * *

The door opened, but Megan was in no hurry to charge through it. Any obstacle course that had a funky-looking little weapon like that strange pocket-sized ray gun as one of the equipment options was not one into which she intended to go running headlong. Let alone the armed guards stationed around it. So she eased around the left side of the doorframe, surveying the room from the threshold.

How odd, she thought, as she scanned the room; *it looks like an ordinary study: hardwood floors, bookcases lining the walls, cozy fireplace on the far side, with a wing chair and decorative wrought iron side table next to it.*

A heavy walnut desk with granite top stood in the center; a lamp and crystal decanter sat on one corner. *Waterford crystal, it looks like. An EXPENSIVE study, then.*

The door into the next room was in the far wall, to the right of the fireplace.

She stepped forward into the room.

* * *

Romeo and India watched the display as the first block lit up with a big red '1.' Echo and Fox leaned together over the screened closed-circuit monitor.

"She's in," Echo observed.

"Aaannd the timers have started," Fox noted. "Both of 'em."

India and Romeo exchanged glances...and thoughts. *BOTH of 'em?*

* * *

Megan had taken no more than two steps into the room when she heard a faint, almost inaudible click off to the left. Quickly spinning, she saw bookcase holograms fade away to reveal a blank wall with horizontal slits halfway up. *Oh shit,* she had just time to think. She dropped flat on the floor as a flurry of projectiles whistled through the space she had occupied fractions of a second before.

Suddenly the fireplace roared, belching a tongue of flame into the room. She rolled to her right, out of its reach, in the barest nick of time. Another projectile barrage opened up. Scanning the room, she swiftly combat-crawled over to and under the desk, where she caught her breath as she analyzed her situation.

* * *

"She actually heard that," Echo remarked in surprise. "Damn. I knew her ears were pretty sharp, but wow."

"Pulse, one-twenty and steady; blood pressure, 130 over 90," Fox read off the sensor readouts. "Respiration, twenty-three. High left hemispheric encephalographic activity. Trigger the plasma jet, Echo."

Romeo and India spun around and stared in dismay at the two calm men. *Plasma jet?!*

* * *

A faint whine was the only warning Megan got before the plasma cannon behind the right-hand wall opened up. She crouched farther back, under the desk, until its initial salvo was complete. Then, in a momentary lull between projectile bank, flame-throwing fireplace, and plasma cannon, she reached up with her right hand, over the desktop, and grabbed for the decanter she had seen there. Miraculously, it was unbroken, having been below the level of the projectile barrage. She unstoppered it and sniffed the decanter mouth. *Brandy. Perfect.* She put on the special glasses.

She timed her next move carefully. In the split-second after the projectile weapons fired, while the plasma cannon built to discharge again, she emerged from her cover and flung the stoppered decanter with all the force and accuracy she could muster, straight at the plasma gun, then she turned and pushed with all her might against the back of the desk.

The desk slid across the polished floor just as the crystal decanter crashed into the now-firing cannon...and exploded. The improvised Molotov cocktail melted the circuitry and ignited the fuel tank, sending a geyser of flame out into the center of the room. But the desk was no longer in the center. Instead, it was now overturned, with its substantial polished granite top largely blocking the flame-throwing fireplace.

Megan held her breath, closed her eyes, and crouched in the desk's opening until the flames from the plasma cannon subsided and the current round of projectile barrage ceased. Then, slightly singed, she scuttled on elbows and knees behind the wing chair. She overturned the marble-and-iron side table, heedless of the useless trinkets which tumbled off it, and caught it up in her left hand, holding it by the wrought iron pedestal. Using the tabletop as a shield, she moved up into a crouch, ducking behind it when the next round of missiles opened up.

"Aahh! Dammit!" A ricochet off the nearby marble mantelpiece winged her right shoulder. But she had reached the exit door. Still shielding herself with the table, she tapped the door handle warily with her right hand; no booby traps. She opened it; stepped sideways to her right...

* * *

Block 2 of the schematic lit up.

"Pulse, one-thirty and rising; BP, 135 over 92; respiration twenty-five. Hemispheric activity high and equally dominant," Fox called out.

"Staying calm, thinking fast and getting creative. Great. Fox, did we get the fumes vented properly?" Echo asked, glancing over his shoulder at the two younger agents, so very intent on the largely-blank schematic, with a grin. *Good idea Fox had, letting them see only a small part of the test. Ups the ante for 'em, and gives us a chance to see how THEY react to the pressure.*

"Yeah, no problem," Fox responded. "Didn't want it building to potentially dangerous levels, anyway."

* * *

Fumes? What kind of fumes? Romeo and India sat staring, unbelieving, at the schematic while listening to the two men. *WE'RE gonna have to go through this?*

"How's she doing?" Echo asked.

"If she maintains this pace, she'll equal the record," Fox responded.

"Dayum! Who set it?" exclaimed Romeo.

"I did, about six months ago," Echo remarked, offhanded, his attention never wavering from the lithe figure going through its paces on the monitor.

* * *

This room was a formal dining room, of all things, complete with chandeliers and elegantly-set banquet table. *Funny notions they have about obstacle courses,* Megan thought. Whatever she had been expecting, so far this wasn't it.

Megan discarded the side table and moved cautiously into the room, on the lookout for booby traps now. Her nose caught it first: an acrid, pungent odor. Then she saw the wisps of vapor rising from the floor.

"Acid!" she cried out in horror. The flooring was being eaten away underneath her.

Do they really want to kill me? I didn't think that Echo-guy would've... but at least they would be rid of an eyewitness. Damn. Is this all just a set-

up, then? An excuse for knocking me off? I am in such trouble...

An adrenalin-propelled standing leap took her to the near end of the banquet tabletop, irrespective of china and crystal, which tumbled this way and that, shattering. The way out, an open archway, was at the opposite end of the long table, but the opening was far out of reach of her ability to jump. The floor was now out of the question; large holes were starting to appear in it, a bubbling fluid underneath. She looked up.

The row of chandeliers ran almost the entire length of the oblong room, and were of the ornate Victorian candelabra style. Jumping up, Megan caught onto the one overhead and swung on it, tugging, testing. *Strong enough, but not far enough,* she thought, easing back down to the tabletop. *If they only hung a little bit lower...*

Abruptly, the table dropped out from under her, lowering by a full six inches, as what was left of the floor gave way. Megan lost her footing and fell, smashing china and sliding across the polished wood, over the edge. Digging her fingernails into the wood, she halted herself, her bent knees mere inches from the acid that now pooled around the bottom of the table. She slowly clawed her way back onto the tabletop. *At least now I know how deep the acid is...*

Suddenly, she whipped off her tie and belt. She threaded the leather belt through its buckle, making a loop, then used the pen knife to enlarge the last belt notch. Replacing the pen knife securely on her hip, where it clipped to the waistband of her leggings next to the glasses case, she quickly threaded the small end of the silk tie through the hole in the belt and knotted it firmly, jerking it hard to test it. Then she ran to the far end of the tabletop. She didn't know if it would hold, but there was no time to change her mind. The table legs were starting to disintegrate now.

"Hope the farm skills are still with me," she muttered as she swung the makeshift lasso.

The leather loop caught a prong of the chandelier, and Megan jerked it tight. Backing up as far as her improvised rope would allow, she made a running start, then swung forward.

No time to check the next room, she thought as she swung through the air. *I just hope I hit the door opening straight, or this is gonna hurt bad...*

"BANZAI!" she yelled as she reached the top of her arc and let go, flying head-first, arms stretched out in front, hands fisted, through the open doorway.

* * *

"Wow. Nice Superman jump," Echo noted with a grin.

"Yeah, I liked it too," Fox agreed, nodding.

Romeo and India just stared at the two men in consternation.

* * *

As soon as she was well through the opening, Megan realized she was in a bad way. Landing hard, she rolled, looked up, and blanched. At the far end of the room crouched a giant, hairy, black spider-like creature, with a leg-spread of at least fifteen feet, in a huge cage. To Megan's horror, the front of the cage began to slide slowly up.

"Spiders. Dammit. I hate spiders. Why did it have to be spiders?" she muttered.

* * *

"3," read the bright red number on the schematic block.

"Hm," Echo remarked. "Not good. Looks like she IS arachnophobic."

"Heart rate just shot up to 140—no, 150, Echo. Blood pressure 151 over 102. Encephalographic readouts are almost maxxed," Fox informed him.

"Good. We're giving her a workout," Echo decided. "Mental AND physical."

"You have no idea," Fox murmured.

"And my heart rate's about 200," Romeo muttered to India just then. "The poor kid."

"Poor her? What about us? We gotta do this next!" India shot back.

Fox and Echo glanced over their shoulders at the two younger Division One agents, now with chairs huddled around the schematic, and grinned at each other. As Fox looked back down at his readouts, he blinked and did a double-take.

"Echo—I've lost the data stream."

The big red '3' on the schematic flickered and died.

"I've lost the video lock," Echo added.

Romeo and India came up, out of their seats.

"What's happening?" Romeo exclaimed.

"Did—did something—?" India stammered.

Fox and Echo looked at each other. Echo jerked his head toward the door, and Fox nodded, then spoke sternly to Romeo and India.

"You two will stay here until we return, and while we are gone, you will not leave this room UNDER ANY CIRCUMSTANCES. Only a Maximum General Emergency declaration overrides this order. Failure to comply is grounds for brain-bleaching, or worse. Is that clear?"

They nodded.

"All right, Echo, let's go see what we've got."

* * *

As Echo and Fox approached the course exit, they encountered the two heavily-armed guards in black body armor that were stationed there, facing the course, near duplicates of those at the entrance.

"Anything escape?" Fox asked one of the guards.

"No, sir," she replied.

"So Megan is still in there too?" Echo asked.

"Test subject has not yet exited, sir," the other guard replied.

Fox and Echo folded their arms and waited.

Just then, the door opened from the other side.

"I am NOT a happy camper," declared Megan with a scowl.

* * *

She was a sight. Disheveled, bruised, bleeding from the shoulder graze, belly cuts, and a scratch across one cheek. Her fingertips were swollen and raw, with splinters under the nails. Her leggings were torn, with small acid burn holes; her sport top was held up only by the left shoulder, the right strap having been severed by the bullet ricochet. Her frowning face was bright pink, except for the outline of the special glasses, which had protected her eyes from both the Molotov cocktail in the first room, and the acid in the second.

"I notice your ankle tracer is gone," Echo pointed out.

"Yeah. Along with the sensor transmitter." She turned to show them the loose wires dangling down her back. "I finally realized that nothing triggered until my right foot—the one with the ankle bracelet—crossed the threshold. So I took apart the transmitter with the penknife, got out the electromagnet, and disrupted the magnetic lock on the ankle collar. Then I threw it all back into the acid. After that, I just walked out."

"Not quite, I should think," remarked Fox. "How did you get past the Betelgeusian arachnoid?"

"The giant spider?"

Fox and Echo nodded.

"You ever read any Tolkien? *The Hobbit, Lord of the Rings*?"

"A long time ago..." Echo acknowledged, remembering.

She pulled out the penknife. It dripped a sticky black liquid.

"I call this, 'Sting,'" she said.

* * *

"...And remember, don't tell Romeo and India any of this," Fox admonished as Megan limped behind Echo and Fox back to the observation room.

"You're sending THEM through that torture chamber, too?" Megan wanted to know.

"We are," Echo noted. "Don't worry. The course has been very carefully designed. Even if somebody gets killed, it's nothing we can't patch up down in Medical."

Megan just stared at him.

* * *

Romeo and India were pacing when the trio entered the observing room. As soon as the pair got a good look at Megan, India sat down suddenly, and Romeo's jaw dropped open. Echo pushed it closed as he passed.

Fox met Echo off to one side of the room, as the two young agents tried to quiz Megan.

"Megan didn't hurt Charlotte badly. Just gave her a few painful cuts, to force her back. She's already in the medlab, being treated. She'll be fine. How'd Megan do?" Echo asked.

"Less than three seconds behind you, Echo."

"Well...good," Echo remarked succinctly. "At least she'll be able to keep up with me."

* * *

She had passed the obstacle course test rather admirably, Megan gathered, even though no one had said anything to her: She had gotten a good look at Echo's face in the observation room and accurately read his satisfied expression.

After Echo provided her with a little first aid, gently scraping the splinters from beneath her nails and swabbing a topical anesthetic on the worst of the boo-boos before bandaging anything that was oozing, she retired to a nearby locker room. There, she changed into a fresh set of black workout gear...and it was on to the next test.

* * *

Echo set this one up for her. He led her into a wide, high-ceilinged room with four stations; various pieces of equipment lay on and around each station.

"We're gonna check your targeting accuracy on this test, Megan. Four stations; four solid holographic clay pigeon targets from different parts of the room—"

"Sounds a little like indoor sporting clays."

"Yeah, a little bit. The big difference is, you're gonna use a different weapon at each station. Let's walk through it." He moved to the first table. "Station one: know what it is?"

She picked up the pistol, popped the safety, checked the magazine, pulled the slide, and re-engaged the safety. "Beretta, model 71, .22 caliber long rifle. Plinker. No longer manufactured. Small, easily concealable, but capable of some serious damage in the hands of a pro; that's why the Israeli Mossad likes it."

Echo glanced up at the one-way observing window, hiding his surprise.

* * *

On the other side of that window, Fox sat watching. He started in shock as McAllister identified the weapon, and detailed its make. But it was the reference to the Israeli Mossad that took him by surprise.

Hell YES, the Mossad liked it, Fox thought, dumbfounded. *That particular firearm was my personal-issue concealed weapon! I offered it to Echo for her testing specifically because I knew it was no longer being made, and thought it might provide her a moment's pause. What does she know, HOW does she know, and what does she intend to do with the information?! I need to find out more about this woman, and fast, otherwise we could end up in a world of hurt.*

The Director of the Agency extracted a tablet from a pocket and set to work, accessing networks and searching files.

* * *

Echo paused briefly to see if Fox intended to message him. When nothing happened, he mentally shrugged and moved to the next station.

"And this?"

"Standard Remington pump-action 12-gauge. Doesn't appear to have recoil damping."

"Right. This one?"

Her eyes lit up with interest.

"I got no clue. But I think you had one, the other night."

"Very good. You're right." Echo raised one eyebrow at her observation. "It's a proto-cyclotron blaster. This one's designed to be 'hot,' supercharged, so be careful with it. Mine is, too, for that matter, but that's personal preference, not standard issue."

"Oh. So this coil must be the magnet, and this is the particle source, and...hmm..." She bent over the table, fingers hovering fractions of an inch over the sophisticated weapon as she studied it, but never quite touching it.

Echo threw another quick glance at the window.

"And how about this?"

"I'm waiting," she responded, blue eyes sparkling with fascinated interest. "Looks kinda like the thing I blew up in the obstacle course, only smaller."

"Right. You're observant. It's a plasma rifle."

"Aha. Hydrogen?"

"Yep."

"Storage tank?" she asked again, pointing under the table to the large canister sitting there.

"You got it."

"Hm. We called them ETs in the Shuttle program."

"Come again?"

"ETs. External Tanks. The Space Shuttle Main Engines were fueled with liquid hydrogen, and used LOX—liquid oxygen—for oxidizer. Is this one of y'all's regular weapons?"

"Not particularly. Why?" Echo asked.

"Good. Ever see what happened to *Challenger*?"

"...Yeah. That's why this isn't a regular."

"After this is over, can I take a closer look at it?" Megan requested.

"I don't see why not. What for?"

"I got a couple of ideas. If I could make some modifications, we might be able to avoid the kablooie problem."

Echo blinked, then shot another look at the window. "That...would be useful."

* * *

Back in the observation room, Echo moved past India and Romeo to the window and picked up a microphone. Fox stood beside him and entered several commands into the console. Romeo and India jockeyed for position.

"Stopwatch sensors zeroed, Echo," Fox noted. "Whenever you're ready."

"Copy that, Fox." He keyed the microphone. "Only one round per station, Megan, so make every shot count. Ready?"

Her hand went up. It grabbed an imaginary handle, and pulled down on it.

"Go!" Echo called. The stopwatch clicked, and began scrolling hundredths of a second.

Megan raced forward, grabbed the pistol firmly in her right hand as she popped the safety with her thumb, steadied the gun with her left hand, squared off in a wide-leg isosceles stance, and fired at the solid holographic clay pigeon as it flew through the air from the back of the room, directly at her. The clay broke apart in midair, and Megan was already at station two, pumping the shotgun.

This time her stance was appropriately forward-and-back, Echo noticed, to help absorb the 12-gauge's recoil into her shoulder. The clay came in high and wide from the side this time, but before it could get

37

halfway across the firing room, it turned into so much holographic dust.

Megan grabbed up the proto-cyclotron blaster, analyzed it swiftly, and flipped the switch that began the particle accelerations. She assumed the pistol stance, and fired at the clay emerging from the far back left corner of the room. The clay 'smoked,' as the hyped-up blaster's recoil lifted an unwary Megan into the air and carried her backward a couple of yards. She managed to land on her feet, however, and easing the blaster to the floor, headed for the final station, where she shrugged her way into the harness of the plasma rifle.

A moment later, a lethal jet of white-hot plasma shot into the air, and the clay just...vanished. Megan laid the barrel down and began working back out of the harness. The digital stopwatch readout froze; it read 18.82 seconds.

"Holee..." Romeo exclaimed. India simply stood there in amazement.

"She just tied you, Echo." Fox looked intensely satisfied. Echo glanced at Fox, raising an impressed eyebrow.

"When she said 'sporting clays,' she knew what she was talking about," he commented.

"Yes, she did. I do believe I'm glad she's working for us," Fox agreed. He leaned over, producing his tablet to show Echo, murmuring, "And she IS. When she came out with that comment about the Mossad, I dug in deeper, just to make sure no one had sent her after me. And she's clean. Turns out she's a bit of a weapons buff."

"Well, she DID grow up on a farm," Echo pointed out. "And judging by that little show she just gave us, learned to be a damn fine shot somewhere in the process. I'd lay odds I see her daddy's hand at work."

"Probably," Fox agreed. "But she had me going for a second, there."

"I'll bet," Echo acknowledged.

* * *

Echo led her next to a new testing room; this one had a central table, complete with holographic projector and virtual reality equipment. A powerful computer, reminding Megan of a desktop supercomputer, sat on one side of the room, hooked into the tabletop equipment. A single chair sat by the table. A networked standard laptop computer sat on a console in one corner, a compact printer nearby.

"This last test measures spatial perception and problem-solving skills," Fox explained as Megan sat down at the special table. "It's basically a puzzle. Have you ever heard of a tesseract?" He picked up a handheld remote control device.

"More commonly called a hypercube by astrophysicists..."

"Okay, hypercube then. I take it you have."

"That's an affirmative." Megan unconsciously dropped into her NASA lingo.

"Well, this computer will generate a four-dimensional hypercube jigsaw puzzle."

Her eyes widened.

"You have to assemble it. Put on the gloves. They'll enable you to 'touch' the pieces."

"Ooo-kaay. Give me a second." Her eyes began to defocus slightly, as if she were concentrating on something that wasn't there.

"What for?" Fox asked, startled by the unexpected request.

"Oh, to shift gears. I'm ready now." She donned the gloves.

"Go." Fox initiated the test with the remote.

Holographic pieces abruptly covered the tabletop, shifting and morphing as the four-dimensional structure tumbled through spacetime. Megan used the VR gloves to pick up and move the pieces. Echo, Romeo, and India watched as she began assembling those pieces. She looked carefully at the holes, scanned quickly over the table, and selected another piece.

Echo casually moved over to the terminal in the corner, where he began bringing up files and scanning them, while still keeping an eye on Megan's progress. He found what he was looking for and printed it.

Megan dropped the last puzzle piece into position. The hypercube and all of the readouts froze in place.

Fox picked up the computer's remote chronometer and motioned Echo out of the room.

* * *

In the corridor outside, Fox showed Echo the time; the chronometer read 19:33. "Dammit, Echo," the director said, "I've never seen anyone do it in under an hour before, and she did it in less than twenty minutes."

"And here's why, Fox." Echo handed the printouts to his superior.

One was a paper from a recent technical journal. The title read:

On Hyperdimensional Wormholes and the Space-Time Continuum.

The author's name was Dr. Megan McAllister.

The other printout was an evaluation form out of the NASA astronaut office. It read, "Subject possesses quick reflexes, extreme visual acuity and spatial perception. Appears to have the capability to not only mentally visualize three-dimensional objects without aid, but possibly those of higher-order dimensions. Advanced in cosmological astrophysics, relativity, and unified field theory, having published several cutting-edge research papers in each field. Recommend as excellent candidate for development and testing of advanced drive project.

"Subject name: Megan McAllister."

"We've got an Einstein for an agent here," Echo said.

"I thought he was from Gamma Lyrae 11."

"He was. SHE'S human."

"Hm. THAT explains a lot."

"Explains what?"

"Tell you later, in my office. I was hoping to have a complete package for you first, but after seeing all this, I think I've changed my mind."

* * *

Back in the observation room, after Echo returned from dropping her off at the medlab for a post-testing physical, the agents began discussing Megan's performance in her absence.

"What makes her so...so..." India searched for the right word.

"Capable?" suggested Fox.

"That's...not exactly what I had in mind..." muttered India.

"Turns out, she was in line for astronaut," remarked Echo, shooting India a sharp glance. "Had one last round of medical tests left in the selection process."

"So?" Romeo said.

"Well, see, Sparky, sometimes they don't let on, but that last round of tests isn't necessarily for screening. It's often to establish the individual's baseline norms. For all intents and purposes, she WAS an astronaut."

As he spoke, Echo suddenly remembered Megan's grief-stricken remark, *"So close,"* in Fox's office, and understood. *One last round of tests...for NASA, too. And then she'd have been assigned her mission. Shit. She'd made it. That kind of accomplishment is nothing to sneeze at, even here. And then we come along. Damn, but timing sucks sometimes.*

"Wow. 'S way cool. Astronaut. She just didn't know, huh? You told her yet, man?"

"No."

"What?! Come on, Echo, why not? Astronaut, that's a big deal."

"You're right, it is. Look, Romeo, it's like this. Most people that become astronauts these days, they spend their whole lives working toward it, preparing for it. They eat, sleep, and breathe it, usually since they were kids. Their education is geared toward it, their hobbies are geared toward it, and their careers are chosen for it. It's their life's goal and their life's dream. So stop and think about what that means for Dr. McAllister. See, I think that's one reason nothing about this setup shocked her. She's been dreaming about it, about discovering aliens and exploring outer space, her entire life.

"Now, adjusting to being an Agent is hard enough without being told that your lifelong ambition, your childhood dream, was in your hands and the Agency took it away. It's even harder when you don't have a choice in the matter. I've been there, at least. Trust me on that."

There was a long silence. Then Romeo asked quietly, "You gonna tell her? Ever?"

"Probably. She deserves to know that she did it...fulfilled her childhood dream. But I think I'll wait a while until it's less likely to be so painful."

* * *

"Well. So..." Megan began as Echo led her to a locker room to change and get cleaned up.

"So?" Echo echoed.

"Sooo...how am I doing?"

"You're passing."

"How well?" she pressed.

"Pretty damn well, all told. New record on the hypercube puzzle. Tied the record on the targeting test. Two point seven seconds behind the record in the obstacle course."

"Hm. Well...good. But what did I do wrong in the obstacle course?" she queried.

"Nothing. I just figured out the tracer was the trigger as I was leaving the second room, and you figured it out right after entering the third."

"Oh..."

* * *

Echo sat across the desk from Fox in his office. The bay windows overlooking the Core were opaqued so they could talk over their newest recruit in privacy. Echo had just finished looking at the medical records, and nodded comprehension.

"Yeah, I see what you meant about the hypercube test explaining a few things," Echo noted.

"She is one more unusual woman," Fox decided.

"She is, that. But I 'get' her. You figure maybe she's some sort of mutant? Like those comics?"

"Dunno. Could be, I suppose. Or maybe just a really exceptional standard human. I'm still waiting for the DNA analysis to come back. That's what I was waiting on, before showing you the med files. Then I changed my mind, because those things take way the hell too damn long, and McAllister is moving through our selection process like a wildfire through prairie grass. Oy! By the time the full, detailed DNA analysis comes back, you two would have been working together for weeks, at this rate. I figured you needed to see this, before making up your mind on her."

"Oh, okay. Yeah, keep me posted on all that. I'm curious as hell now."

"You and me both. Well, anyway, she checks out. How do you feel about working with her?" Fox asked Echo. "You saw the brain activity scan. She too egghead for you?"

"No, don't call her that. It doesn't fit. Besides, I can keep up with eggheads just fine. I've encountered a few in my time, and trust me, she's not one of 'em. She may be one of the smartest humans we've encountered yet—okay, maybe THE smartest human we've encountered—but for one thing, she's got common sense; she's very matter-of-fact. She doesn't seem to think her gray matter's any big deal. It's just something she's good at, like target practice or riding a horse. She's not egotistical about it, but actually gets embarrassed if somebody points it out—though you can tell, she's used to expecting a lot out of herself. I mean look, Fox, working in this new Line, you never know when that level of brainpower may come in handy. Look how quickly it enabled her to pick up on two advanced weapons she's never laid eyes on...before encountering us."

"You've got a point there."

"And like I said, she doesn't have an ego about it, either. She totally gets that she's not omniscient, and there's things I might know that she doesn't, for instance...things she needs to learn. And not only is she willing, she seems eager to learn 'em. Sometimes she's almost childlike in her eagerness to learn something new. And that lack of ego and willingness to learn from another, as much as anything I can think of, is what makes her different from your stereotypical egghead."

"That's very good to hear. I really hate it when we get a rookie with an attitude. The first thing you gotta do is take 'em down a peg or two before you can even get 'em to listen, let alone train 'em."

"I'm with ya there, and I'm glad not to have to do it with her. So no, I think she'd be pretty damn good to have around. And I'm more than willing to train her and work with her. I think we'll end up making a good team."

"Go bring her in, would you, Echo?"

* * *

"Well, lady, it looks like you're an Agent now; congratulations," a cheerful Fox announced as Megan and Echo sat across from him in his office. "You'll be working with Echo as the prototype team for our new Line. Now we need a code name for you." He typed her first name on the keypad of his tablet; it lit a small screen on the wall behind him:

M.E.G.A.N

"Hm," said Echo.

"Exactly," said Fox.

"What?" said Megan.

"Well, we already have a Mike," explained Fox. "And nearly had two, at that. And a Mary, and a Monkey, and a Madrid. And several other M's..."

"Fox, I have an idea," Echo said after a moment.

"Go ahead."

"Okay, try this on for size. Lemme see that tablet a minute."

He took the device from Fox, and began moving the cursor:

M.E.G.A.N

M.E.G.A

O.M.E.G.A

"...And we can call the new department, 'Alpha Line,'" he finished. "The last word in agents, in our first line of defense."

Megan and Fox looked at each other, then at Echo. And smiled.

"Go get Omega's Suit," Fox ordered.

Chapter 3

"First things first. Omega can't wear the Suit until Megan McAllister vanishes," Echo said, pulling up her records on the PGLEIA computer system from a handy desk in a conference room off the Core. As she watched, she saw all her files appear, from birth records all the way down to her most recent NASA astronaut evaluations. Despite herself, she winced. Echo noticed it.

"I'm sorry. It has to be done. I know it's hard."

"I know it does. And I know now that you do understand. Romeo told me the other day, over a quick bite to eat in between all my testing and training, a little bit about how you got to be an Agent."

"Yeah." He resumed his computer work then, and she watched in silence as he steadily, inexorably deleted her records, her history—her life. The life she had so carefully constructed, so thoughtfully engineered to make the perfect astronaut candidate, the supreme space explorer. The pain that shot through her in that moment seemed nearly unbearable.

Megan McAllister is dead, she thought, swallowing hard. *As dead as the rest of my family. The McAllisters of Madison County are no more. And for all that, I'm still stuck on this watery blue rock. Dammit.*

"Does it get any easier?" she asked, suddenly hoarse.

* * *

Echo heard the hoarseness and knew what it meant. He hit the delete key—one last time; Megan McAllister was indeed no more—and turned to look at her. He saw the bleak look in her eyes, heard the rawness in her voice, and let his expression soften slightly. He understood that look, in spades. He remembered it all too well, staring back at him in the mirror, morning after morning, when he had first joined the Agency.

Maybe...just maybe, I can make it easier for her, he thought.

"You may not believe me now, but it does get easier. It'll take a while, but it'll get better," he promised. "And in the meantime, I'm a good listener, if it helps. And..." he shrugged, glancing down for a moment. "I know what helped me. I can at least offer suggestions."

"Thanks; I'll take—" she said, breaking off when her voice cracked; for a moment, she looked as if she might try to say more, but swallowed hard instead, and he grasped that she didn't trust her voice sufficiently to try to force anything else out. He ignored the broken statement, easily able to fill in what she had not been able to say; he nodded his acknowledgement and understanding of the aborted statement, and stood.

"Come on, now. One last thing before we get the Suit."

He led her into an adjoining room and over to a special console, fitted with slight hand-shaped recesses. Below it, and directly in front of it, was a pad containing depressed areas in the shape of very large feet. Extremely large feet. Feet so big that clown shoes would have fit inside them.

"Take your shoes and socks off and stand on that platform, put your feet in the prints, then put your hands in the recesses. I know they're way the hell too big for you right now, but don't worry; it'll adjust to the sizes of your hands and feet as soon as it feels your contact. But when it fully activates, it'll remove the prints from your hands and feet. Oh, and grit your teeth. It's not exactly without sensation. But don't worry—it won't leave scars."

"Well, this should be interesting. Can I ask how it works?" She smiled then, curiosity patently evident as she pried her shoes off with her toes, then grabbed the toe of each sock and tugged until they came off.

"Mmm. You can, but I can't answer."

"What, I'm not cleared high enough yet?"

"No, I just dunno how it works. I'll pass your question on to the Science and Engineering department, and let you know what they say."

"Okay. How often do you have to re-do this? I mean, I know that fingerprints grow back and all, so I figure it ALL does..."

"Yeah. Not as often as you might expect, though; maybe once a year or so. Depends on the individual. Now stand there, put your hands in the thing and hold everything as still as you can. Whatever you do, don't start hopping around once the thing starts, or we'll have a mess."

She obeyed, standing on the warm platform and placing her hands into the obvious depressions, and Echo saw her jaw tighten as she followed his instructions. A moment's pause, then he watched her eyes widen, and her jaw tighten further, but she never uttered a sound. A moment more, and it was done.

"Okay?" Echo asked.

"Um, yeah." She sat down on a nearby bench and commenced replacing her socks and shoes. Echo noticed that the skin of her palms and soles was slightly pink. Then he remembered her reddened skin after the obstacle course, and realized that her pale blonde Celtic complexion had resulted in somewhat sensitive skin.

Makes sense, he thought. *I'll see to it she gets sunscreen from Medical, and actually uses it. Some of the stuff we're around could make for nasty burns otherwise.*

"All right," he decided, as she stood. "Now the Suit. And your new home."

"Hmn?"

He led her down the corridor and stepped into an elevator. As soon as the doors closed behind them, it took off at a high rate of speed, moving up.

"Well, since we have no outside identities, it's not like we can get houses or apartments very often, so most of us live here. I'm one of the senior agents despite being some bit younger than the rest of 'em, so for a while I had an outside apartment, but it didn't...um, the whole cover story issue turned out to be more trouble than it was worth, so I moved back here."

"Wow. I bet."

"We do have safe quarters and safehouses in various places, though— several around the various boroughs, and in other cities, too, all over the world. Even a few in the country, here and there. You'll need to learn the sites and memorize them, in case a mission goes south. If we were to get split up, or something happened to me, you'd need to know how to reach someplace where you could get additional equipment, first aid supplies, food and water, and where you can hole up until backup arrives."

"Oh. Sounds interesting...in the ancient Chinese curse sorta way."

"Something like, yeah. But there's a few that most often get used by agents on vacation, island getaways and stuff. Even a ski lodge. It makes for a safe place to take a break, really. We can look into that on down the road, once you have some time built up, if you want to. Anyway, right now I'm taking you to your new quarters—similar to an apartment. It's next to mine. Romeo and India are around the corner. The Agency likes to put partners as close as possible. Sometimes they connect, like a back door."

"Do ours?"

"Dunno. Didn't this morning. That's a while ago, though."

"So...am I your partner?" she asked, somewhat diffidently.

"You're my trainee. Same as. Probably will be, once you go fully active."

"Didn't Romeo used to be your partner?"

"He was, but...it's a long story."

"I got time if you do. I figure we're all on the same team, so I wanna know enough not to put my foot in something."

"That's reasonable. Yeah, he and India go back a bit. I think they mighta known each other before the Agency, but I'm not sure. Then I brought him in, and he got separated from me and injured on an early mission, and she patched him up. We brain bleached her, but she'd expressed interest in the job, and when we...lost some agents...during a recent invasion attempt, Fox decided to bring her in. Then the kid busted—"

"Wait," she interrupted. "'Kid'? How old is he?"

"Romeo? Oh, I think he's maybe 25, 26. Might be a couple years younger; I don't remember offhand. Acts like he's about ten years younger than that, sometimes. India's a few years older than him, actually, but it seems to work. I think she keeps him grounded, to tell the truth. Anyway, he busted his leg but good while he was clowning around in the gym, and India ended up the physician of record..."

"Aha. And they rekindled the old spark."

"Pretty much, yeah. And just so you know, Romeo didn't ask to be assigned a new partner. I saw what was happening and offered to step aside, and he was...appreciative."

"That was awful nice of you."

"I...look after my partners. The best I can, when I can."

"I can tell. I think I'm gonna be glad of that pretty soon, too."

Echo snorted, then threw her an amused glance, to find she was grinning. He met her eyes then, and grinned back; her grin grew even broader.

"I'm serious, you know," she told him. "From all I've been told—which, I'll admit, is mostly hearsay and rumor, though from your ex-partner, I'm inclined to listen—if I had to get sucked into this organization, I probably hit the jackpot for a trainer-slash-partner. Romeo says you're a damn good trainer. AND I've been told you're the most respected, most daring, toughest agent in the entire Division. You're Numero Uno. So I'm as happy as the proverbial shellfish about it."

Echo felt his cheeks grow warm. He had known he had an offworld reputation as the toughest of the Division One agents; he was proud of it, and tried hard to cultivate it. Not out of any sense of ego—rather, it proved beneficial when he had to go up against certain insterstellar criminals, who often became a lot more cooperative upon finding out who he was. But he hadn't known that he was so respected WITHIN the Agency.

"Ehrm," he said, searching for words. "If you say so."

"Wasn't me said it, it was your colleagues. I'm just reportin' it."

"Okay. You might regret it in the gym, though. I chewed Romeo a new one for horsing around, even while I towed his ass to Medical to get his leg unbusted."

"I'm no slouch in the gym myself," she allowed. "I don't think we'll have a problem."

Eventually the elevator stopped moving up, and the doors opened. They stepped out of the elevator and walked down a corridor. They turned a corner into yet another corridor. A thoughtful expression developed on her face as they progressed into still another corridor.

"This building," she began, as they walked, "is way bigger..."

"Bigger on the inside than the outside?"

"Yeah. A lot. What gives?"

"You're perceptive. Most new recruits don't figure that out for a couple of weeks, and tend to get lost all the time as a result. It's a simple dimensional warp. We can continue to expand our operations on the inside, as required, without anyone on the outside being the wiser. On the outside, this building has something like two or three stories, four if you count the basement. Inside, we have over a hundred floors, above and below ground."

"WOW! You're kidding."

"Nope."

"Can I..."

"Eventually."

* * *

After a few moments and yet another corridor, she glanced up at him. "Echo?"

"Yeah?"

"Just listening to you talk...you're not from New York. Not originally."

"...No."

"You sound more Southern than anybody else around here—except me, I guess. Which is nice. I feel a little less...alone..."

He shot her a single glance, but remained silent.

"In fact," she mused, "I think I'd guess...Texas?"

Echo stared straight ahead as they walked.

"Well?" she pressed.

"Well what?"

"Am I right?"

He gave her a sharp, stern look.

"Division One Agents have no past, Omega." His voice was brusque, brooking no further questions, and she glanced at him, startled not only at his tone, but his mode of address—it was the first time she had been truly addressed by her new code name. "If he volunteers it, that's one thing. But you never ASK a fellow agent about it. Remember that. I told you information about Romeo and India that pertained to their history HERE, and which is a matter of record within the Administration. However, you'll notice I barely touched on anything that came before. You're new at this, so I'll let it go. This time."

"What?!" she responded, confused. "I'm just trying to get to know my new partner. You mean I can't even ask you where you're from??"

This time he didn't even look at her. She halted abruptly.

50

"Now wait just a damned minute!! YOU just pulled up ALL of MY records. You know who I am—well, who I WAS—where I'm from, what I d— used to do, even how much I made. But I can't even know what STATE you're from?? Yet you expect me to trust you, maybe even put my life on the line for you? Not just no, but HELL no! That's unacceptable, 'Agent Echo.'"

"I don't see that you're in any position to decide what is or isn't 'acceptable,' Omega." Echo had stopped a few paces in front of her without turning, and stood there, simply waiting.

She spread her feet, folded her arms, cocked her head, and looked at him, refusing to budge from where she stood.

"I always decide what is or isn't acceptable—for ME, Echo," she said quietly. "I'm not trying to be difficult, or to break any rules. It's just how I stay true to myself. How I know who I am...on the INside. No matter who or what I am on the outside. Whether you call me Dr. Megan McAllister, or Agent Omega."

Echo's eyes narrowed consideringly as he listened.

* * *

After several stalemated minutes, he spoke.

"You know," he remarked, "I noticed in the obstacle course that your sense of hearing seemed unusually...sensitive."

She pondered the apparent non sequitur for a moment, studying him. Finally she nodded, and he grasped that she intuitively understood what he'd just communicated. Then she silently moved forward until she was standing beside him again. His head tilted slightly as he surveyed her with peripheral vision, and he saw her shrug.

"So when do I get the right to—"

"I'll let you know."

They continued walking.

"Romeo and India are around the corner, you said?" she verified.

"Yup."

She was silent for several moments, and he waited, suspecting what was coming next.

"I...get the impression India doesn't care for me very much."

Yup. Expected that one for a while, now. Still don't have a good answer, dammit. Think fast, Echo.

"Oh. That. See, when you came aboard, she had to move to the apartment on the other side of Romeo, so you could be next door to me," Echo lied smoothly; he didn't want discord between the two, because he fully expected them to be working together in the near future. "She was settled in pretty good where she was. She really hates to move."

"But I thought you could adjust the parameters for more space," she pointed out.

"Well, we can—to a point. It gets complicated when you start shuffling individual apartments around. Sometimes things don't go quite where you put 'em. And THAT...gets...interesting."

He shook his head, remembering a particular case in point—a toilet on the ceiling, the Agency had discovered, was neither useful nor convenient. *And flushing was hell,* he thought.

"Oh," she said then, interrupting his musings, but her tone was filled with doubt.

Echo dared a surreptitious glance at her. She was wearing an expression that was half-scowl, half-frown; one eyebrow was raised. The overall effect was skepticism in the extreme.

Nope. Didn't buy that one. Not one word of it. She knows something's wrong as far as India is concerned. This one's as sharp as a Jovian diamond-bladed knife. Training her is either gonna be one hell of a pain in the ass, or a hell of a lotta fun. And after the last five minutes, I'm laying my money on the ass. He sighed inwardly, and told her the truth.

"But the biggest thing is, I think your immunity to the brain bleach threw her off a bit. Spooked her—kinda bad, actually, if I had to guess. Remember, her background is medicine, so when they brought her in, she got briefed on how all of that stuff works. It's pretty rare when we encounter someone like you, who's immune to it. In fact, I'm not sure if it's ever happened before. So India more than half thought you were an alien in disguise, I think. Don't worry, though; she'll get over it, soon enough. One way or another, I swear to you, we—emphasis on we, because I'll be right there with you—we will get her over it."

Omega considered that without speaking, then nodded silently. Echo noticed her shoulders slump a bit. Then she squared them again, and grinned as a thought struck.

"I would guess she and Romeo share a 'back door.'" Omega smiled mischievously.

"Ohhh, yeah." He shot her a quick look, letting a hint of a grin show on his own face. "I gathered you picked up on them right off, huh? I mean, I kinda figured, judging by your earlier questions?"

"Yeah, I did. Well, look, let's face it—whenever they're together, the chemistry practically oozes into puddles on the floor around 'em! I think it's great, under the circumstances. Fact is, I thought maybe that was the problem between us, so I've tried to be very...um, circumspect... around Romeo, in particular, if you catch my drift. I didn't want her to think I was trying to flirt with him, 'cause I'm not. I like them already, and wouldn't want to mess things up for them just on account of a simple misunderstanding."

"I know. That's why I stepped aside after his accident, especially when I only just..." he caught himself, then finished, "came back."

* * *

"'Came back'?" Omega looked at him, her curiosity engaged again.

"...Around here." He turned the corner abruptly, and she changed direction quickly—in several senses of the word—to keep up.

He REALLY does not want to talk about himself, she thought. *I don't think he meant to say THAT much. Which, to me, is odd, because he seems like a very impressive sort of guy, the kind you're glad has got your back. Surely he hasn't got any, like, BAD stuff in his background. Could he? Or is he just that withdrawn? That introverted? Or maybe only massively reserved...yeah, I could see that. Especially after years in this job.*

Echo led her down another hallway, past a door. "This one's mine. Here's yours."

On the nameplate was a lone Greek letter. Ω. Omega. Her.

Not Megan. Not Dr. McAllister. Omega. That's who I am now. It's ALL I am now. This...is gonna take some getting used to, she decided, feeling a wave of decidedly indigo despondency wash through her being.

"Is there a key, or a card swipe, or something?" she asked, hoping her voice didn't sound as flat as she felt.

"Nope. Door has a sensor. It recognizes you. It'll unlock automatically for you, and it'll let in anyone you tell it to." Echo shot her a penetrating, mildly concerned glance, and she realized she hadn't fooled him. "It also recognizes me and Fox, just in case something comes up. Oh, and your Supplies delivery person, who'll probably be the same one I've got. You can password it if you want to, but most agents don't bother; it's kinda hard for anybody but Agents to get this far into the building. After you've been with us for a while and built up some seniority, we can look at getting you an apartment off-site if you want to. Like I said, I had one for a little while. Kinda nice, sometimes, to get away from work, you know? Have some down time. But you don't have to, if you don't wanna fool with it. Like I said, keeping up the cover story for it—and you—can be a real pain in the ass."

The door opened, and they entered. She looked around, and her eyebrows shot up.

Huh, not too bad. Not bad at all. Rather nice, really. Light, open, and airy. Good-sized rooms. No windows, though. But I guess that's to be expected. If I can't see out, nobody else can see in. Besides, I got no idea how that would work, with the space warp thing and so many floors inside, but not outside. Might come across from the outside looking like giant insect eyes or something. She followed along behind as Echo led her about.

"This is what's officially called 'the living area,' aka the den...aha, back door...kitchen...we can take turns cooking, or cook together if you want to, or do it separately, it's your call. I'm a pretty good cook, though, if I do say it. This is the dining area, breakfast nook, or whatever you wanna call it...here's the study..."

"Lots of bookshelves. Good."

"I thought you'd like that. Requisitioned 'em especially for you. The laptop there is yours now; it's permanently assigned to you. It's networked to the Agency system. You can web surf if you want to, no problem; but it all routes through the Agency servers, so security is maintained. Bedroom and bathroom are through that door there. That's your private space, so I won't go in. If you're sick or injured, partners can sometimes be expected to check up on each other; otherwise, it's off-limits unless and until the Agent it belongs to invites you in."

"I bet it's not off-limits for India and Romeo," Omega muttered to herself, restraining a smirk. Echo made a soft sound, suspiciously like a snort of amusement, but otherwise showed no reaction, continuing his tour of her new quarters. He moved to the door of the bedroom, but did not go in.

"...Both the bedroom and bathroom are good-sized, and I gotta admit the beds are awful damn comfortable—which is good, because you'll be ready for yours by the end of shift every day. Frankly, Agency quarters are some of the nicest—and largest—apartments you'll find anywhere in the Big Apple. And they come with the job." He pointed. "Another thing: I had Facilities install a small night light in your bedroom—see, over there—and another one in the bathroom. You'll find they're useful, at least for now, until you get used to the place. Since there are no windows—for obvious reasons—it gets pretty dark in here with all the lights out. There've been a few broken toes and worse among new recruits who think they're too tough for a 'sissy night light' and then try to get up in the dark. Hell, I got one, AND a flashlight on the nightstand, just because on the rare occasions when I get up in the night—for ANYthing, and sometimes 'anything' is a midnight snack—I'm probably not awake enough to know WHERE the hell I am. It isn't about bein' tough. It's about being able to navigate in the pitch dark, when humans don't have infrared vision."

"Okay. Makes sense to me. I appreciate it."

"Hope the furnishings are all right with you. We don't have a whole lot of options, but we do have a few—upholstery material, style of chair, wood finish versus chrome or brass and glass, stuff like that. I tried to pick what I thought you might choose."

"Truthfully, it looks pretty damn good, Echo. Comfortable. I like your assessment of my taste. Thanks. Um, hey, listen...is there a snowball's chance in hell of getting any of my personal stuff back? Books, pictures, mp3 player, and junk like that?"

"Recruitment team's already on it, actually. It's part of erasing you from the outside world, too—get rid of your personal effects, and then you're out of sight, out of mind. Since you signed over the family farm into our trust as a safehouse when you came aboard, they'll even run through there and pick up anything you want 'em to, then install security and a caretaker. All your stuff oughta be delivered here in a day or so. Let me know if you want help hanging pictures; I'm good at getting things level. Your Suit's already laid out on the bed there, if you want to go ahead and change. I'm gonna check the fridge for a drink, if you don't mind. It'll be stocked for you by now."

"Huh? Stocked FOR me? I thought I'd have to, like, go to a PX or something."

"No, that's all part of the recruitment team's duties. They go to your old place, check what you have in your cabinets and pantry and bathroom vanity and shit, then relay it back here, and Supplies replicates it in your quarters, at least initially. Your preferences get added to the supply stock, and when you need more of something, you send in an electronic requisition and it'll be sitting on your dining table when you get off shift—unless it's perishable, then it'll be in the fridge or freezer already. They do prefer you compile a grocery list, rather than doing it in dribs and drabs, though. The delivery guy gets pretty annoyed if he has to keep coming back up here every other day; I can tell you that first-hand."

"That sounds like it has a story behind it."

"Uh, not so much, but a little, I guess. The delivery guy before this one was a real prick. Left some notes about my food and drink selections, especially the quantities and how 'unhealthy' they supposedly were. Now, the thing you'll soon realize, Omega, is that when we're in the field, chances are, we're gonna be burning serious calories. Even on a stakeout, because your adrenaline is up. But Agent Pencil-Pusher didn't get that, and had the presumption to tell me what, and how much, to eat...and then started substituting my orders for things HE thought I should have. Like after all this time, I don't know how to feed myself to stay in shape." Echo shrugged in mild disgust. "So I started ordering smaller quantities...every two days."

"Ahhh!" Omega exclaimed, and doubled over in laughter. "How long did he stay in the job after that?"

"About a week," Echo said with a grin. "Not quite, actually. Fox was puzzled why the guy insisted on an immediate transfer, especially after I had a little private chat with the Supplies chief. Now run put on your Suit, in case Fox calls with something. I doubt he will, but shit happens, especially in this job."

"Okay. Out in a minute."

"All right. You want me to come see about you if it takes longer?"

She threw him an exasperated look over her shoulder, and he grinned.

* * *

He was popping a can of Diet Coke when her muffled voice came through the door.

"Trousers. Not a skirt. Good." She sounded satisfied.

"Another case of picking up on your personal preferences. Besides, it's far more practical for Alpha Line field work," he said as he sat down on the black leather couch and relaxed.

"That sort of thing is the reason I prefer 'em. Can't really see me trying to chase some bug-ugly across the countryside in a skirt and high heels, anyway."

The statement painted a mental image for Echo, and he cocked an eyebrow and drawled, "Weell, might be kinda interesting to watch, though. Awkward as hell, but interesting. In a comic sorta way."

A snort emerged from behind the door. So Echo decided to push it, and see how she reacted.

"I dunno, maybe you could, you know, sharpen the heels," he suggested. "Then you could use 'em as a weapon."

Silence.

"You suppose they're shaped enough like a boomerang to come back to you if you throw 'em?" he added.

More silence.

"We could always have special ones made up so they morph into blasters or something, I guess. I dunno how comfortable they'd be, though."

Towering silence.

"You'd have to be careful if you tripped, but...wow, damn, waitaminit, I'D have to be careful if you tripped. Maybe we better not go that route..."

That finally got a response.

"Echo?"

"Yeah?"

"Shut. The hell. Up."

But he heard the grin in her voice, and it evoked an answering grin in him.

Yep, we are going to get along perfectly fine, Omega and me. She just threw the meter from 'ass' back to 'fun.'

A few moments later, she emerged in The Suit and stood in the doorway, arms akimbo on her hips, feet spread. He sat up straight and looked her up and down, as she reached into a pocket and withdrew the special wraparound goggle sunglasses, donning them. The Suit fit her to a tee, easing over her curves, nipping in at her waist, emphasizing her long legs and highlighting the silver in her white-blonde French-braided hair. Her chronometer gleamed brightly on her left wrist. Her high, sweeping cheekbones were prominent beneath the wraparound glasses.

Damn! Now THAT, Echo thought, impressed, *is the epitome of a female Agent. Do Not Mess With Her.*

"Good," was all he said.

* * *

It was several weeks into her training, and Echo and Fox had started to consider sending the Alpha One pairing out on some basic field missions, but had yet to do so. Omega and Echo were in the Agency gym that morning, where they started at least every third day. Echo insisted on weight and resistance training, aerobic conditioning, flexibility, and explosive power.

"...Because you never know, in the Agency, what's going to happen next," he had told Omega on their first day in the gym, only two days after her induction. "Especially the way Fox and I envision Alpha Line. And you and I are the prototype team. We need to be ready for anything, or we could end up dead pretty quick."

"I can see that, and I don't have a problem with it," Omega had replied. "I worked out pretty hard in the gym when I was gunning for astronaut, so I'm on the same page with you."

And it turned out that she really could keep up with him in the gym

58

fairly readily. There were a few techniques he had to teach her, and a few workout styles she needed to learn, but after a couple of workouts to feel out her abilities, he even let her spot for him whenever they were lifting weights.

"Not meaning to put down women in the least," Echo said, mopping sweat from his face with a towel as he sat up on the bench, dressed in loose black mesh shorts and a thin black sports jersey. His feet were shod in high-topped athletic shoes, designed to give his feet and ankles maximum support and stability while lifting heavy weights. "But I've generally found that they have more leg strength, and men have more upper body strength. There are exceptions, of course, on both sides, but on average, that's what I've observed. But you've worked hard to build upper body, too."

"Well, I have," Omega admitted, swapping places with him for her turn at the Olympic-style barbell, after knocking off a couple of weight plates. She wore shoes similar to Echo's, but her body was clad with black leggings and sports-bra top; her partly-bare midriff showed more than a few hints of a six-pack. "I can't lift as much as you do, but I never will—I'm not as big. You're, what, six-one, six-two?"

"Six-three and a half. And around a hundred and eighty pounds, give or take." Echo moved into position to spot her.

"Oo. Taller than I thought. And I'm only five-foot ten inches," she replied, "and about a hundred and forty-three pounds."

"You told."

"Huh?" she panted, shoving the barbell upward.

"Your weight. You told me your weight. Most women are sensitive. I don't think I've ever heard a woman admit to her weight before."

"Most women don't have a body fat ratio of 16%, either." She racked the weight after her set and sat up. "But the way I always figured, space exploration is kinda dangerous. Just because a thing is weightless in space doesn't mean it hasn't got any mass, 'cause it still has inertia."

"True." Echo replaced the weight plates, and stretched out on the bench, as Omega moved to his head and prepared to spot.

"So I wanted to be ready for anything. Besides, pressurized EVA suits—what most people know as 'space suits'—are hard to manipulate,

BECAUSE OF the fact they're pressurized. It's like trying to work inside a human-shaped balloon, and make it bend where you want it to."

"Well, it sorta IS...a human-shaped balloon." Echo spoke between exertions as he pressed the barbell.

"Yeah, it really is. But anyhow, that's how come I can spot for you. I can't press as much as you can, but I know I can keep that weight from landing on ya if something slips."

"And that's appreciated. I told you about...what happened with Romeo...horsing around..."

"Yeah." Omega cringed in sympathetic pain. Echo abruptly racked the weight before he'd finished his set, and sat up, twisting around to look at her.

"You okay?" he wondered, concerned, reaching for his water bottle; the gym was rather warm that morning. "You just looked like somebody walked across your grave, stomping in combat boots the whole way."

"Yeah, I'm okay. I just feel for Romeo. I dropped a small plate on my foot once and cracked a bone, and I remember how much it hurt. What happened to him hadda hurt like hell."

"Judging by the way he screamed, yeah, it did. It started off as a howl on the first break, broke into a falsetto by the second, and I guess he went ultrasonic at the third—'cause when his voice cracked FROM falsetto, I couldn't hear him anymore, but he was still screaming. I kid you not," he swore, then somewhat impulsively reached for the hem of his shirt.

* * *

"What?" Omega wondered, seeing the gesture.

"Too hot." He whipped his shirt off over his head, revealing broad, muscular shoulders, a powerful chest, and chiseled abdominals, a sheen of sweat over all. "Lay this over there on the weight rack, will you? Spread it out so it'll dry off a little, if you don't mind. And hand me my towel. I'll spread it on the bench so you don't have to do your next set lying in my sweat."

Without another word, Omega took the shirt, exchanging it for the towel, and Echo lay back to finish his set.

* * *

He glanced up at her, to see her staring at him with raised eyebrow. "What?" he wondered.

"Nothing. I just never saw you without your shirt before."

"Something wrong with the way I look? I know I got a couple scars from some fights with alien big bads..."

"Not at all. I was just debating how you'd take it if I made a 'beefcake' comment. You got good definition, there, Echo. Seriously. You look good."

"Thanks. I don't really think about the appearance all that much. I guess it's just a side effect."

"It's a good side effect," she agreed. "I hope I don't offend if I say I have no objections to the view right now. I'm not comin' on to ya, I'm just sayin'."

"Oh. Uh, okay." He felt his skin grow even hotter and knew he had probably flushed at the comment. He gave her a quick glance to see if she'd noticed, but she said nothing, and if she had seen, her expression didn't betray the fact.

* * *

Aw. I made him blush, Omega thought, watching with a hidden smile. *I didn't mean to embarrass him. I better pretend I didn't notice.* She made a business of lifting the barbell out of the rack and easing it into his hands, and he resumed his set. *I guess I figured, a handsome guy like him, he'd be used to the compliments. Then again,* she considered, watching him work out with all the intensity of a tiger stalking prey, *I'm not sure how much opportunity Agents get for, uh, that sorta thing. Maybe not. Maybe that's why the relationship between Romeo and India is such a big deal—because it's so rare.* She sighed noiselessly. *That doesn't bode too well for me. I think, Meg, you put things off too long, girl. That ship done sailed.* She shrugged mentally. *Oh well.*

As she continued to watch, endeavoring to ensure her partner and trainer didn't have an accident, a tiny puddle of sweat grew on Echo's chest, then spilled over his ribcage in a rivulet as he lowered the barbell to his chest. He flinched slightly, apparently at the sensation, and shoved the bar back to the top of the press. The motion set off another rivulet, followed by another flinch.

"Here," Omega offered, grabbing her own towel, "lemme get that for ya." Before he could respond or react, she swiped her towel across his ribs, blotting away the sweat.

"Umph!" he exclaimed, flinching even harder and quickly racking the weight. "Give a guy some warning next time! I was concentrating on the lift!"

"Oh! Damn, I'm sorry, Echo," Omega apologized, smacking her forehead with the heel of her hand. "I was just trying to make you a little more comfortable, 'cause you were dripping. But yeah, I shoulda waited 'til you'd racked it."

"Meh. I was about done anyway," Echo declared, sitting up and grabbing his own towel off the bench to wipe down.

But Omega noticed that the skin over his ribs was still rippling in reflex, and the hairs were standing up, almost in goosebumps.

What? she thought, puzzled, watching as he removed plates for her. Then the understanding hit. *Oh, oh, oh! Echo is ticklish! Mr. Big Tough Super-Agent is actually TICKLISH! Aw! And he doesn't want anyone to know,* she noted, seeing the heightened flush as he moved past to give her access to the bench. *So okay, I won't tell anybody. But that doesn't mean I'll forget,* she decided, hiding her grin as she began her set. *One of these days, that knowledge is gonna come in handy. Probably not any time soon, but if I survive in this job for any length of time, and stay Echo's partner, I'll just betcha...*

* * *

"Anybody seen Omega?" Echo asked a couple of days later, as he walked into the Agent break room off the Core for coffee. "She wasn't around when I got ready to come in this morning, and it's gym day again." He made a fresh cup of the brew as he spoke, and added two sugars.

"Yeah, Echo," Romeo replied, as he and India sipped from steaming cups at a small table in the corner. "I saw her go into Fox's office a while back, and leave with Madrid."

"She'll be training in the weapons lab, then. Thanks, buddy."

* * *

Echo headed for the weapons lab with his coffee. As he pushed open the door, he heard a by-now-familiar feminine voice, coming from the research lab proper. He slipped just inside the door of the weapons facility, and listened.

"...And so I was thinking, if we replace the hydrogen with helium, it'll make for a much more stable configuration—"

"Yes," Madrid's British voice replied, "but the energy required to ionize the helium atoms versus the hydrogen increases to the point that the rifle's power pack becomes very unwieldy."

"No offense, Madrid, but it isn't exactly pocket-size now."

"You do have a point there..."

Echo slipped up to the partly-open lab door and leaned against the wall just outside it, listening, fascinated and unwilling to interrupt their inventive brainstorming.

"Now look at these calculations I did last night, Madrid. This proto-cyclotron blaster is significantly smaller than the plasma rifle, yet it has the energy not just to ionize the atoms, but to split the nuclei. So I was thinking..."

"Oh! I see where you're going with it! If we take the power pack from the blaster...let's see..."

Echo heard large equipment being moved and shoved about. The clinks of tools in use reached his ears. *Damn,* he thought, *I knew she was gonna be a great fit for this job. And now she's learned enough to get inventive.* He smiled to himself.

"We're gonna need an adapter to make the jack compatible...mm... okay...yeah, that oughta do it. That looks good. You got any helium around here?" Omega's voice queried.

"Yes, over here."

"Fill up the fuel tank for me, then, would you?"

"Righto!" Madrid's voice suddenly sounded like a British version of Donald Duck, and Omega emitted a long, musical peal of laughter. Echo stifled his own laughter with an effort and grinned, still listening.

"Stay outta the helium, Madrid!" she chuckled.

"Spoilsport."

"Are you SURE you don't know any British secret agents?"

Echo heard the two dissolve into laughter, and chuckled silently himself. *If you only knew, Meg.* He smiled again.

"Okay, this oughta do it. I'm taking it into the test room. You handle the control panel," Omega's voice continued.

"Got it."

There was a click, then a whirring sound as the latches of the blast-proof weapons test room engaged. Echo silently eased around the laboratory door and leaned up against the back wall in order to watch, a very slight hint of what might have been pride in his demeanor—she was, after all, his protégé. Through the observation window, he could see Omega thoroughly checking out the newly-modified plasma rifle, then putting on the harness. Madrid set up a short sequence on the control panel, then leaned over to the microphone.

"Omega, are you sure about this?"

"You double-checked my numbers, Madrid. It'll be fine." Omega's voice filtered through the speaker.

"But if it doesn't work—?"

"You ever see that film footage of the *Hindenburg*? 'Oh, the humanity!'"

That galvanized Echo into motion, then. But before he could reach Madrid, he heard Omega call, "Pull!" and saw Madrid's finger come down on a button. A brilliant light filled the window of the testing room, and a blood-curdling scream sounded over the speaker as he was temporarily blinded. His gut clenched in horror.

* * *

The spacecraft, a small classic saucer, came in low over the trees of the farm. Faint starlight glinted off its metallic hull; its yellow running lights chased each other around the rim of the saucer. It was silent and slow, but other than the direction it took, and the fact that it was barely above the treetops, it made no attempt to hide itself.

It approached the hilltop from the north, gliding in silence, unseen by the lone inhabitant of said hilltop.

* * *

When Echo's vision cleared, he pressed against the window, scanning the room beyond. There stood Omega, still in the plasma rifle harness, whooping enthusiastically and doing a kind of end-zone dance. He slumped for a moment, leaning heavily against the window frame, as he waited for the adrenaline surge to diminish and his heart rate to return to normal.

"It worked! It worked!" rang out her voice on the intercom. "But, wow, Madrid! We gotta remember to make the settings lower for helium. I scorched the far wall with this thing! Whooah!"

"Aaand so much for the surprise..." Madrid muttered to himself, glancing at Echo. Ignoring Madrid, Echo leaned over the microphone and keyed it.

"Omega, it's Echo," he said flatly.

"Oh. Uh, hi, Echo. Did you see?! Did you SEE that!!" Omega skipped like a child in her enthusiasm.

"I saw." He paused, considering wording, finally settled on, "Come out here. Now."

"Oh. Um. Okay. Be out in just a sec. Lemme get outta the harness."

Madrid cycled the door, and Omega emerged, still in process of removing the plasma rifle and its harness. Echo took it from her, handed it wordlessly to Madrid, and turned back to Omega.

"Let's go."

* * *

Omega glanced in some little puzzled consternation at Madrid, who shrugged. Then she fell quietly into step beside Echo, subdued, her enthusiasm quenched like a disciplined child. She glanced at his impassive face, then down at the floor, following him down the hall and into the hangar-slash-garage as they prepared for their second-ever routine patrol as a team.

Blew it already, she thought, discouraged and disappointed. *But I was trying to help...I thought he'd be pleased when he found out...*

Echo put her into the black Corvette's passenger seat, then climbed into the driver's side and started the engine.

They were several blocks away from Headquarters when Omega finally got the nerve to break the silence.

"Um, so...where are we headed?"

"Standard routine patrol. Like today's schedule said. Part of your training."

The car fell silent again. They drove for almost a dozen blocks in absolute quiet; Echo took the ramp onto the Brooklyn-Queens Expressway, headed for the Brooklyn Bridge into Manhattan, and still the car's interior remained silent. Finally, she couldn't stand it any longer.

"Echo, just chew me out and get it over with."

"For what?"

She looked at him blankly.

"For monkeying with the plasma rifle. For taking risks..."

"Did Fox know what you were doing?"

"Yes. He's the one who called in Madrid to oversee it and help me put it together."

"Was it an unacceptable risk?"

"In my considered opinion—AND Madrid's—no."

"Did it succeed?"

She grinned.

"Fantastically." *Maybe everything is all right after all.*

"Then there's only one thing to chew you out for."

Uh-oh. "What?"

"Not telling ME."

* * *

"Telling YOU? To be honest, I wanted to surprise you with it. What's the big deal? I was gonna tell you...later...once I saw if it worked. I told Fox. He's 'the Boss-man,' right?"

"Technically, yes."

"And he gave me permission, and called in Madrid to supervise."

"True, though as head of Alpha Line, I'm your direct supervisor, and should have been involved in that call. Then again, Alpha Line is just us two for now, so I'm not gonna stand on that kinda formality."

"Then why are you so bent out of shape—"

"Omega, I'm your partner, remember? And you're a rookie. I'm responsible for you." He kept his voice brusque, clipped; his face was equally stern.

66

"'Responsible'? Oh, I get it!" The Celtic fire began to flare; her face flushed. "Anything happens to the 'rookie,' the poor little dumb blonde, you get your hide nailed to the wall by Fox! Nice to know where *I* stand! And I'll have you know I don't need anyone holding my hand—"

"Meg," he used the familiarity of the nickname deliberately, "Fox isn't gonna nail my hide to the wall. Not for that, or anything else—except a flagrant violation of regs. But did it ever occur to you that I might manage it on my own?"

* * *

"Huh?" She stopped, startled, her anger and disappointment fading as rapidly as it had come. "What...do you mean?"

"You're a rookie, Meg. That's not an insult. That doesn't mean stupid, doesn't mean irresponsible, doesn't mean expendable. You are none of those things. What it means is inexperienced. There's a reason why some of our agents refer to rookies as 'baby agents,' because, like a baby, you have to learn to walk before you can run. You have to learn the ropes. It's my job to SHOW you the ropes. And to make sure you stay alive until you get the experience necessary to do that for yourself." Echo paused. "I take my job very seriously."

She stared at the floor of the car for a while, mulling that over.

"I'm...sorry, Echo," she finally offered in a low voice. "I...guess I never thought about it quite like that."

"That's okay. And apology accepted...baby." He shot her a mischievous look to lighten her mood. "You did great, by the way. Just let me know next time, before you go running off with another idea. I appreciate the thought, but I hate surprises. Plus I spent all morning hunting for you to hit the gym with me, so I missed my workout."

"Aw—I forgot all about the gym! Dammit! I'm sorry. I don't quite have this weird shift down yet, and my days of the week...what passes for 'em, at least, what with 'days' that last TWO days...are all screwed up. Besides, I woke up with the idea about the power supply, couldn't go back to sleep, and ended up brainstorming half the night, scribbling plans, running calculations, and junk. So all I could think about while I was getting dressed this morning was the plasma rifle."

"Aha. So that explains the non-regulation tie knot today. Look, Meg, it's cool; I understand. That's the sign of serious inspiration, and that's a good thing. But...do we have a deal, or not?"

"Do what, now?"

"Will you let me know next time, first, before running off with an idea? In exchange for my unqualified help, if it's needed," he threw out the full measure of the compromise he was offering.

"Oh. Yeah, I'm okay with that. It's a deal."

"Good. Now let's head up to the Bronx and go see Jerry the Packrat, and see if he has any offworld gossip for us that we can use."

"Okeydoke."

"You don't mind?"

"Mind what?"

"That we're going to see Jerry."

"No, why should I?"

"India thinks he's creepy. As in 'dirty old man' creepy."

"Well, she's right on that one. The first time you took me over there, the bastard tried to cop a feel, while you were in the back, looking at his files."

"Shit, Meg! Why didn't you tell me?!"

Omega shrugged.

"No need. I took care of it."

"HOW?!"

"I grabbed his hand, pulled the thumb back until it hurt, and told him if he wanted to keep all ten digits, he'd never lay a hand on me again. And he hasn't."

Echo's laughter rang out as he drove down the street.

Chapter 4

"...I don't care whose trainee she is, Romeo, there's something wrong there. Really, really wrong. She's...too good to be true, or something. I dunno how to explain it."

"You sure you're not just jealous, India?" Romeo asked, as they sat at the table in the corner of the otherwise-empty break room. "You've got no reason to be, you know. You're just as good as she is. Aaand, you've got the coolest 'partner' in the whole damn place." He grinned suggestively.

Omega overheard the conversation in the break room just as she and Echo came through the door looking for coffee.

* * *

Romeo and India both broke off as Echo gave them a hard glare. Omega continued on to the coffee pot as if she had heard nothing. Only the faint flush in her face betrayed her awareness of the conversation.

India scowled and left abruptly, and a glum Romeo shrugged at Echo in a semblance of apology before following her out. He was still limping a little bit on his cast, but no longer needed crutches, or even a cane, to support his weight.

Once they were out of the room, Echo glanced over at Omega's back and watched her shoulders droop in dejection.

* * *

Outside, in the Core, Romeo and India continued their argument as they walked toward Customs, the security for which lay just past the archway.

"Can't you at least try to give her the benefit of the doubt, girl? She's Echo's trainee, for cryin' out loud! He knows what he's doing."

"Oh, give me a damn brea—" India broke off, staring.

"What?"

"Look over there. In the customs security line."

Romeo scanned the line of aliens. "I don't see any—"

India was already in action.

"FREEZE!" India's voice rang out across the Core as she lunged for one of the aliens, who was drawing something shiny out of a pocket. "Drop the weapon!" she shouted as she knocked a small, metallic, pistol-shaped object out of the alien's tentacle.

With a roar, the alien lashed out. The force of the blow sent India flying back through the archway and across the Core, where she struck the wall and fell to the floor, stunned and seeing stars.

Meanwhile, the alien dived for the object. Romeo, reacting quickly, ran forward and kicked the device out of his reach with a cast-encased foot, drawing his own blaster.

"No, you don't! Now put your hands—er, tentacles—in the air, sucker!"

The alien roared again, and wrapped all four tentacles around Romeo's neck, lifting him clear of the floor. Romeo began to kick frantically, clawing at the tentacles, and then gradually to go limp, as the pressure of the tentacles around his neck increased.

On the far side of the room, a dazed India slowly sat up, to see Romeo being strangled. Still groggy from the dual impact, she struggled to get to her feet.

* * *

Echo and Omega came running out of the break room at India's first shout. Taking in Romeo's situation, Echo drew his weapon and ran forward to try to assist him. The Core was in pandemonium as other agents worked to lock down the entire area.

Omega, meanwhile, chose to focus on the object that Romeo had kicked out of the alien's reach, since as a trainee, she had not yet been issued her own personal sidearms. She ran over to confiscate the weapon. But when she picked it up, she looked at it curiously, studying it, puzzled. She moved to one side, unnoticed in the general hubbub and thinking fast.

She pointed the weapon carefully at a nearby wastebasket, and depressed the obvious trigger. A hiss came from the device, but the wastebasket remained intact. A faint whiff of...something chemical... reached her nostrils, and her eyebrows flew upward as the light dawned.

Omega ran over to where India struggled to get up. She handed India the alien object, and whispered something in India's ear, gesticulating urgently at where Echo and several other agents were trying desperately to rescue Romeo. She mimicked her attempts to destroy the wastebasket. Then Omega asked her a question. India's mouth formed an 'O' and almond eyes grew wide as she stared down intently at the alien device in her hand, and she nodded vehemently, then whacked her forehead with the heel of her hand in annoyance. Omega pulled her to her feet and gave her an encouraging shove in the direction of battle. India began to run.

* * *

The alien was getting ready for the kill. Romeo's breath was already coming in weak gasps. If this kept up much longer, Echo knew, Romeo's windpipe would collapse, and his neck would snap. But the alien was using Romeo as a shield, and Echo couldn't line up a good shot. Suddenly, India ran right past him, directly up to the alien.

"India!! Wait! What the hell are you doing?!" Echo shouted. "Get away from there!"

"Here. I'm sorry. I didn't know," India said as she looked up at the alien and offered him the device.

A universal translator hanging around the alien's neck converted India's apology into a cacophony of grunts and squeaks. The alien unceremoniously dumped Romeo onto the floor and frantically grabbed the object that India proffered, raised it, pressed the trigger, and...inhaled. After a moment, the alien emitted another burst of grunts and squeals, and the translator rendered it in English.

"Thank. You. When. You. Knocked. It. Away. From. Me. I. Thought. That. The. Agents. Of. The. Supreme. High. Council. Had. Caught. Up. To. Me. And. Were. Trying. To. Kill. Me."

"You're safe," India replied, in a soothing tone. "I just misunderstood." The alien nodded and turned away. India ran to Romeo then, and the other Agents gathered around. "Are you all right, Romeo?" she asked, kneeling beside him and checking his throat.

"Yeah, I'm fine—or I will be," he answered in a very, VERY hoarse voice. In fact, he was so hoarse, Echo decided that he sounded like he'd

71

been gargling gravel.

"What the hell happened?" demanded Echo then.

"I goofed—big time—and it nearly cost Romeo his life," India admitted shamefacedly. "I saw the alien drawing something that looked like a pistol, and instantly assumed it WAS a pistol."

"You mean it wasn't?" Romeo asked in that same gravelly voice.

"No."

"What was it?"

"An asthma inhaler."

"Whaaat?! You mean I was almost killed by a damn asthmatic??"

"How did you figure that out?" Echo demanded to know.

"I didn't, exactly. I should've—I'm a doctor! But I was in field agent mode." India glanced into the Core at Omega, and smiled gratefully. Omega smiled back, put her index finger over her lips, and gave her a little surreptitious thumbs-up. "So a little bird...suggested it to me."

"A little bird, huh?" Echo followed India's gaze. "A pretty quick-thinking little bird, I'd say."

"Thanks, India," Romeo growled, hugging her.

"Let's get you to the medlab where I can treat you," India said, returning the embrace.

Echo could see the wattage of Omega's beaming smile from across the room.

* * *

"Echo, would you and Omega come over here, please?" Fox called as they walked through the Core.

"Sure thing, Fox. What's up?"

Fox pointed to the map he had displayed on one of the big wall screens. To Omega's surprise, it depicted Central Park.

"We have a situation, on several levels," Fox explained. "A newly-arrived Dendroid family went to Central Park to 'ground' after their flight, and their youngest slipped off and got lost. The parents have two more young children, and are having trouble looking for their smallest with the others in tow. If we don't find little Preeg soon, there's no telling what could happen to the kid. Plus, it's our understanding that Preeg is too young to understand that he isn't supposed to tell humans that he's not from around here."

"Whu-oh," Omega murmured.

"Exactly, Omega," Fox agreed. "So we could lose a child...which is bad in itself, but then it also creates a potential diplomatic snafu...but we could also end up with a security breach that we'll need to clean up. OR, we could have a mass panic occur in the middle of the Park."

"I take it that Dendroids don't look like us," Omega observed.

"Not much, Meg," Echo confirmed. "'Dendroid' is what we call 'em; root word comes from the Greek 'δενδριτης,' which is where we get the word 'dendrite,' and it means—"

"Tree, or tree-like," Omega finished for him.

"Right," Echo agreed. "So that probably tells you about what they look like. Their own name for themselves is Tentweein, as best I was ever able to pronounce it. The diphthongs get a little tricky."

"And Echo is about as good as anyone around for picking up proper pronunciation," Fox commended, "so that's awful damn close."

"So they're plants?" Omega asked.

"Pretty much," Echo said. "Plant-based sentient lifeforms."

"What on Earth are they doing in New York City, then?"

"What is anybody doing in New York City?" Echo asked, raising a quizzical eyebrow. "They just arrived, and haven't had a chance to get farther out yet. They have to 'ground' periodically when they're away from their homeworld, though. Basically, that just means that they need to sink their feet into some dirt someplace. On a spacecraft, they bring along boxes of dirt from home."

"Like vampires," Omega said with a huge, mischievous grin, and the unexpected simile caused both Echo and Fox to chuckle.

"Yep," Fox averred. "About like. But since it was getting close to time to ground, they bundled up in their human gear and decided to sightsee while they were about it. They were enjoying Central Park when they turned around and realized that, not only was their littlest sapling gone, he'd left his human disguise behind."

"So we have a tree sapling running around naked in Central Park?"

Omega said, the corners of her mouth twitching.

"You got it," Fox noted, his own lips quirking in amusement.

"Y'all behave," Echo commanded, eyes twinkling. "I'm trying to teach Meg to take this shit seriously, Fox. You're not helping at the moment."

"Farkakt! Sorry, old friend," Fox said, as a full grin spread across his face. "But your trainee there has a gift for pointing out the levity in any given situation, I think."

"Can't argue that one," Echo agreed. "I've nearly bloodied my lip a couple times now, trying not to laugh when she comes out with something in the middle of a serious situation. Have you got details for us?"

"Yeah. Hang on a second." Fox pulled out his electronic tablet, activated it, and issued a couple of quick commands. Instantly the smart phones in Alpha One's pockets both dinged. "There you go. All the details. Omega can read it to you while you're en route. Take the Corvette airborne, and activate the passive cloaking system; you'll get there a lot faster, this time of day."

"We're on it, chief. Let's go, Meg." Echo turned and headed for the hangar garage at speed.

"Right behind ya, Ace." Omega jogged along hard at his heels, since Echo's longer legs outdistanced hers at a swift walk. Echo shot her a withering look over his shoulder. She grinned, then shrugged. "Hey, I think it fits."

"...Right."

"Maybe you'd prefer 'Tex'?"

"Maybe I'd prefer 'Echo'..."

* * *

"And we're supposed to meet 'em over by Harlem Meer, whatever that is," Omega noted, reading from the files Fox had downloaded to her smart phone in the passenger seat of the Corvette. Echo was in the driver's seat, as they headed across the East River, angling north toward Central Park. Echo had activated the 'Vette's radar and automatic sensor alerts to detect any local air traffic and avoid, not only accidental collision, but an inadvertent sighting—the passive cloaking mechanism was good, but it wasn't a full cloak, and unfortunate silhouettes and the like were possible.

"Oh, that's a kind of a pond on the north end of the Park," Echo said, as he banked the 'Vette to head farther north. "It's pretty big; where around the Meer?"

"Over by something called the Huddlestone Arch, on the Loch walking path?" Omega read.

"Oh, okay, that'll work. We'll put down by Lasker Rink and park, then walk over," Echo decided.

"You know way more than I do about where we're goin', hon," Omega deferred. "I'll follow your lead."

"And that's as it should be, for now," Echo agreed.

* * *

"...And you didn't see which way he went?" Echo pressed the parents, Tumeer and Yaewen Spleekanus.

"No sir, we didn't," Yaewen averred.

"What about your other children?" Omega asked. "Did they see him run off?"

"No madam, we didn't," Eerlav, the eldest, declared. "We were all excited about the big artificial pond that the humans are swimming in. Then Preeg was...gone."

"But this was the last place you saw him?" Echo tag-teamed.

"Yes, Agent Echo," Tumeer confirmed, pointing. "Right about here. We were actually across the road, over there."

* * *

Alpha One paused and both turned in a slow circle.

"Gotta be the forest," Omega concluded. "We'd have heard a ruckus if Preeg had gone into the rink area."

"That matches my assessment," Echo said. "It's possible he headed up or down the road, but again, we'd have heard reports of an ambulatory tree sapling by now, if he had."

"So how do we handle this?"

"You got your spectral imaging scanner?"

"Yep."

"Okay, have a look at that grid map Fox gave us with the packet of data," Echo said. "I'll take the even grid numbers, you take the odd. Set the scanner for Dendrite, at a height of..." He turned to the Spleekanus family. "How tall is Preeg?"

Tumeer held his hand about two and a half feet above the ground.

"There we go. Now, what tree morphology does your family closest resemble?"

"Probably elm," Tumeer decided.

"Got it," said Omega, busy programming her scanner. "So if I run into a copse of, say, cedar, I can just keep going."

"Yeah. Run a quick scan just in case, but chances are, he won't be there. Mr. and Mrs. Spleekanus," Echo gave instruction, "keep your other two children close, and just stay here. We'll bring your son back as soon as we've found him." He turned to Omega. "Ready, then?"

"Yup. When one of us finds him?"

"Can you whistle really loud?" Echo asked.

"If I use my fingers, I can," Omega averred. "So give a loud whistle?"

"Yeah. A long single whistle means you've found him. A series of three short whistles means you need help. If it's repeated, it means you need help NOW. An SOS means you're in trouble and need backup fast."

"Roger that. See you in a bit," Omega said, and they set off.

* * *

Omega was astonished by how quickly she effectively left the city behind. Soon she was surrounded by a patchwork quilt of variegated greens and browns. She swept each grid block in a strip search pattern, steady and systematic in her approach.

But, even with the imaging scanner set for a proximity detection alarm, she didn't find the alien toddler. She reached West Drive and turned farther north.

Omega began to worry.

* * *

Echo also set up his imaging scanner for a proximity detection alert, and alternated strip and spiral search patterns. He generally paralleled the walking path to the Loch, but did not himself walk along it, preferring to stay off the path to avoid attracting attention.

As he marked off each grid on the interactive map on his cell phone, he noted Omega's progress as well.

She's getting along nicely, he thought. *But she hasn't found the kid either. That's not good.*

He pressed on.

* * *

But as he approached the waterfall along the Ravine, he heard children's voices. Just then, his scanner alerted.

"Bingo!" he muttered to himself as he started after the voices.

As soon as he reached the edge of the clearing around the rocky waterfall, Echo saw four small children playing—and one of them looked like a tiny tree sapling, little more than two feet tall. He glanced around quickly; no adults were in sight, though he had passed a group chatting near the Haswell Green Bench a few hundred feet away, and knew that the human children belonged to them, based on what had been said.

He put his fingers to his lips, and delivered a loud, single whistle, to let his partner know he had found the lost Dendroid child, then he started forward.

"There you are!" he addressed the sapling. "Preeg, your parents told me you were lost—"

Preeg let out a shriek that sounded like green wood splintering, turned and ran.

"Well, damn," Echo muttered, and laid chase, as the human children screamed and scattered.

* * *

Omega heard the distinctive whistle of her partner floating from somewhere to her south. She turned in relief, and, paying close attention to the annotated terrain on her cell phone's map, started cutting cross-country toward the sound.

Just then, she heard a series of three loud whistles, and she paused.

"Oh, that ain't good," she decided, speeding up her progress...

...Just as another series of three whistles sounded.

"Aw, DAMN!" she said.

Omega broke into a run.

* * *

"Wait!" Echo called as he ran. "Preeg, stop! I'm here to take you back to your parents!"

But the little sapling ignored him and ran like the wind, scurrying straight across the stream, headed south.

"STOP RUNNING, dammit!" Echo yelled, putting on a burst of speed.

They crossed the road at the intersection of the 102nd Street Crossing and East Drive; fortunately there was no automobile traffic on either street in that moment, though Echo was shocked—and relieved—that there was also no pedestrian traffic.

* * *

Omega crested the rise behind the Green Bench, and saw a beehive of activity, as agitated children ran up to adults.

"Daddy! Daddy! The bad man was chasing our friend!" she heard one child cry.

"Yeah, he was a talking tree!" another boy exclaimed.

"David, how many times have I told you? There are no such things as fairies," the boy's mother replied.

"But he was still chasing him!" David protested.

Immediately Omega dropped out of her run and detoured to the group, thinking fast.

"Did anybody see a man in a Suit come running by here?" she called. "Our son ran off, and my husband and I have been trying to find him..."

"Yeah," said the father of the crying child. "My Julie says she was playing with a stranger child, when a man came outta the woods and started chasing him."

"That'd be them, all right!" Omega exclaimed. "Which way did they go?"

Little Julie pointed across the road to the south, and Omega turned, breaking into a sprint.

* * *

Echo finally managed to trap the sapling at the base of a rock outcrop a couple hundred feet west of the Conservatory Garden. The area was a bit rugged, and looked as if it were intended to be storage for the landscaping crews, given the odd discarded landscaping timber, remnants of half-decayed mulch piles, and the like. A poor, frightened, confused Preeg saw the detritus, spun and stood at bay, facing Echo and crying softly.

"No no no no," he whimpered. "Don't. P'ease don't."

"Son, don't what? I'm not gonna hurt you," Echo said, keeping his voice level and calm. He held his hands out, holding them low and open, fingers spread, to show he held nothing in them.

"No no no. No no no," was all Preeg would say.

But every time Echo stepped forward, the sapling would start to keen in terror, and he backed off.

Just then, Omega burst through the foliage over Echo's right shoulder, and ran toward him, panting.

"Echo? You got—there he is!" she exclaimed. "Preeg!"

Preeg let out a relieved shriek, and ran straight to Omega, as fast as his little limbs would take him—which, as Echo already knew, was plenty fast. He didn't stop until her arms were around him. Then he tried to all but burrow into her body, apparently wanting to hide. When Echo came toward the pair, Preeg screeched again and cowered against Omega, vine-like tendril arms clutching frantically at her. Echo stopped dead at the obvious sign of the child's fear.

"Look, we gotta get him and get outta here," Echo noted. "The parents of the human kids he was playing with are gonna descend on us like the wrath of God, judging by the way they all screamed and ran off when I showed."

"No, I took care of that. I said my husband and I were hunting for our son, who ran off, and did they see a man in a Suit running after him. They pointed me straight at you."

"Oh, great job, Meg. That's a relief. I was half-expecting to get lynched or something. C'mon, little guy, let's go," Echo said, taking a step forward. "We gotcha now."

"NOOOO! No no no," Preeg whimpered again, pressing into Omega's body and trying to hide from the senior Agent.

"What the hell? I don't get it," Echo wondered, puzzled and more than a little dismayed. "He ran from me, but he came right to you. Am I that scary to kids?"

"I dunno." Omega blinked in surprise, as she crouched next to the little Dendroid. "You shouldn't be scary at all, Echo. Not like this. Not to him." Her brows drew together in concern, then she bowed her head and murmured something in what passed for little Preeg's ear, as Echo watched, stymied.

Preeg's leafy head bobbed; he tucked his face into Omega's neck, and Echo could just barely hear the alien child murmuring something to his partner. From time to time, Omega nodded in understanding. When little Preeg finally finished talking, Omega turned her head slightly, whispering to the child, who gradually seemed to relax.

Finally Preeg lifted his head from Omega's shoulder and gazed at Echo with large green eyes, scanning him up and down. Then Preeg looked back at Omega.

"Pwomise?" he whispered, sounding like a breeze in the leaves.

"Promise," Omega said with a soft smile. "He's here with me, helping your mommy and daddy look for you when you ran off. He would never— EVER—hurt you."

"Never," Echo avowed. "Meg, what's wrong?"

"It seems that the little girl he was playing with had been very sick recently, and her mommy took really good care of her. Preeg saw me, recognized me as an adult human female, and assumed I must be a mommy, too..."

"Ah. That explains THAT." Echo offered her a slight, gentle smile. "But why's he afraid of me?"

"Well, I'm workin' on that. But I found out that one of the OTHER kids is from outta town. And his daddy, of whom he was very proud, is a big, strong lumberjack..."

"Aw shi— Aw, shoot," Echo hastily corrected himself, suddenly understanding exactly what had happened. *'No no no, don't,'* he remembered. *Don't—what? Cut him down and chop him up? Damn.* He glanced around. *Dead timbers, chopped-up wood mulch, and everything. This place is a horror movie set to a sapling Dendroid. And this is where I caught him.* He sighed. "So...all adult human MALES got equated to lumberjacks, in his mind."

"Pretty much, yeah. I've just explained that you're not a lumberjack, you're a Pan-Galactic Division One Agent, and you're my partner. That seemed to help a lot. And when he asked if you and I were friends—well, um, actually, he asked if we were a mommy and daddy. I, uh, I told him we were best friends. Was that...okay?"

"That's fine, Meg. Did it help?"

"Yeah. He's ready to try to meet you now. Just go slow."

"Okay. Um...what now?"

Omega gestured to Echo, waving downward with her hand. He immediately took her meaning and crouched down, putting himself more on the child's level. Then he duck-walked a few steps closer, and held out a tentative hand, palm up, fingers spread. Preeg reached out a gingerly vine-arm, and very slowly moved his tendril hand toward Echo's. He started to pull it back several times, uncertain and still a little afraid of the big human male, but Omega shushed him gently, soothing and encouraging, and finally Preeg's fingers brushed Echo's. Echo let his own fingers curl slightly around Preeg's, making sure that the little one never felt trapped or caught, and after a moment, Preeg smiled shyly.

"This is Echo, Preeg," Omega introduced them. "He's my partner. He's a very good man. And very nice."

"You Meg's fwiend?" the little one asked in a soft voice.

"Yes, I am," Echo replied in kind, offering the child a slight smile. "And so are you, it looks like."

"Hope so," came the answer. "Make us fwiends?"

"Yes, I think so. You're Meg's friend and I'm Meg's friend, so I think that makes us friends."

"You not chop down fwiend?"

"Never." Echo was as solemn as he knew how to be.

"Okay. Where Mommy-Daddy?"

"They're not far. We'll take you to them, all right?" Omega stood, and Echo eased himself slowly back to his full height. It no longer seemed to bother the little Dendroid, who now reached up with his top limbs, indicating Omega should pick him up.

Without hesitation, Omega took the slim little sapling in her arms, cradling it gently and resting it on one hip, as she and Echo turned to head back to the road.

* * *

The tiny child waved its vine-hands at the female agent, and instinctively she cooed at it as they walked across the road and back into the woods, where they were less likely to be observed. One tendril-finger reached up and lightly brushed her face, and she took the extremity and tenderly shook it. The sapling rustled its pleasure, and wrapped the tendril around one of her fingers. Moments later, the rest of the tiny boneless hand followed suit.

"I like you, Meg," the little one sighed.

"I like you, too, Preeg," she replied with a smile.

"Good." Big green eyes blinked slowly. "I s'eepy."

"Lean against me and go to sleep, then, honey. Echo and I will take you straight to your mommy and daddy."

"Okay." A tired Preeg rested against Omega.

Omega smiled as she looked up at Echo, a tender light in her eyes.

"I never saw a little anything that wasn't cute," she murmured.

Echo moved closer and tentatively stuck out a finger, gingerly rubbing the drowsy sapling's smooth cheek-bark with his fingertip. Preeg rustled again and smiled as he wrapped another tendril-hand around Echo's finger.

"Oh, he likes you now, Echo."

"Yeah, well..." Echo carefully disengaged his hand. In his experience, dreadlocked alien monsters, man-eating red globs of goo, and vicious giant mechanical lizards were one thing. But a child, especially a very small one, was something else entirely.

"Here, you wanna hold him?"

"Uh, no, I..."

Omega deposited the sleepy sapling in his arms. Echo held the child at full arm's length away from him, worried it might somehow soil his Suit, and struggled to keep from dropping the suddenly-squirming sapling.

"Hold me," Preeg murmured, trying to get close to Echo's body. "I s'eepy. You big like Daddy. Daddy hold. Me s'eep."

"We'll be back to your Daddy soon, and he can hold you," Echo told

82

the youngling.

"Daddy no here. You here. You hold. Me s'eep."

Eventually, despite his best efforts, it got one of those vine-like limbs wrapped around his neck and pulled itself in, close against the warmth of his chest, whereupon it snuggled in, settled down, and promptly went to sleep...just as they emerged back on the road near the rink, where the Spleekanus family waited anxiously. Omega made a beeline for them and began explaining what had happened.

Now that the sapling was quiet, Echo's attention focused back on Omega; he was entirely ready for her to finish talking so he could give the baby back to her...or Mrs. Spleekanus...or anybody, really, as long as he didn't have to hold it any longer than necessary. After all, he had a reputation as a tough agent—one of the top human agents, if not THE top agent, according to Omega—one that he'd worked hard to achieve; and if anybody got a photo with a cell phone, he hated to think what would happen the next time he walked through the Core.

But giggles, raspberries, and catcalls would just be the start, he thought, grim. *Never mind what would happen the next time I had to confront a perp.*

Abruptly he realized Omega was talking, and focused in on what she was saying.

* * *

"Everything is fine," she told the Dendroids. "Preeg is unhurt, and the little kids he was playing with think he was a fairy child; their parents are just going to assume it was all make-believe. Get him back in his disguise as fast as you can, out of sight someplace, and I'd recommend heading straight for your final destination. Oh, and explain about lumberjacks, and the difference between Dendroids and Earth trees."

"All right," Tumeer Spleekanus agreed, mildly confused by the addendum.

"Thank you both," Yaewen Spleekanus added. "We...don't know what we'd have done without you two."

"Oh, it's not a problem. We were glad to help." Omega smiled. Yaewen and Tumeer glanced at each other, then Yaewen met Omega's gaze.

"One more thing. We're curious..."

"Yes?"

"Did the Agency make sure Echo's partner was a lifebearer? For situations like this?"

Omega looked over at Echo, to see him—entire body stiff, verging on steely rigid—being hugged by a sleepy baby alien. But she also noticed that her partner's arms gently cradled the infant Dendroid, despite his body's rigidity.

Now THAT is adorable, she thought, and grinned. *There's a soft spot in there, all right. So much for tough agent.*

"Kinda looks that way, doesn't it?" she replied.

* * *

After Echo had disentangled the sapling, who was quite comfortable on his chest and didn't in the least want to be disentangled, he and Omega sent the Spleekanus family on their way. They got back in the Corvette and Echo thoughtfully cranked the engine before putting it in gear and driving back to Headquarters in normal automobile mode.

"Do you have...um. How do I put this? You didn't—leave anybody behind when we found you, did you? I mean, anybody important? Someone we would've missed seeing? What I'm trying to say is...you were REALLY good with that kid. He came right to you. You don't...have...?"

"Oh!" Judging by her startled reaction, Omega suddenly picked up on his train of thought and blushed, looking down. "You mean, do I have a significant other, or a child, or...or something like that? Oh, no. In fact, I, um," she blushed deeper, and intently contemplated the changing view out the side window, "never even had time for any...romantic involvements; I was too busy pursuing those astronaut wings. Always figured there'd be opportunity for that kind of thing—romance, a family—later on. Guess I was wrong, huh?" There was a pause; Echo hid his wince, but said nothing. Finally she continued.

"Anyway, to answer your real question: I don't know. I just...did. I... well, I like kids, and Lord knows, I babysat enough when I was a teenager, earning money for college and junk. It isn't like I haven't had a ton of experience around kids, and I don't think the Dendroids really were that

different from us, where it counts, so I could relate. There's a certain...
instinct, I guess."

He watched her carefully out of the corner of his eye as he negotiated
the freeway traffic. He worded his next statement cautiously; he wanted to
evaluate her reaction, not hurt her. But it had nothing to do with Agency
policy, in any event; he simply wanted to understand his partner better.

"Looked to me back there like you would have made a good mother."

She shrugged, and tried to act nonchalant. It didn't fool Echo.

"Thanks. But I suppose it's a moot point now."

He got directly to the point then, but gently.

"Do you ever miss it...family...children?"

"Echo, I haven't had a family in a long time now. Not since the
accident. And children? I don't think you can really miss something you've
never had." She looked down at her tightly-interlaced fingers for a moment,
and then said, somewhat diffidently, "Truth is, at the risk of sounding silly,
I guess now I kinda feel like I have a family."

He blinked in surprise, and shot her a sidelong glance.

"Really? Who?"

"Their names are Echo, Romeo, and India."

Echo had no answer to that.

* * *

"Echo! Omega!" Fox called, urgently motioning them over to the foot
of the ramp leading to his office, as they entered the Core together. Around
their feet, a deep red color lit the spaces between flooring tiles, pulsing
imperatively. As they hurried up to him, Fox continued, "Good timing!
We've got a craft jacker in a stolen saucer, headed for upstate New York.
It's probably one of the guys from the chop shop that's been giving us
problems for the last six months, and it's high time we nailed 'em. Go bring
'im back."

"On it, Fox!" Echo sprinted for the elevator, Omega close behind.
Once inside, he hit 'SB2,' uncovered a hidden panel, and keyed a code. The
elevator shot downward. A long way downward.

He turned to Omega as she said, "But the Corvette—"

"I thought we'd take the T-Bird this time," he interrupted.

85

The elevator doors opened onto a huge, bustling, terminal-like area. Omega looked around in curiosity as she followed Echo quickly through the area.

"What's all this? I haven't been down here before..."

"This? Oh, we call this 'Grand Central Station.' We've got maglev subways connecting Headquarters to all the other offices and the various landing sites." He pointed up.

"One floor up: Main computer servers. One floor down: Facility maintenance—mostly automated."

"Maintenance? You mean, like, trash and stuff?"

"Waste management, water, recycling, heating, cooling, electrical, general utilities—all that stuff." He nodded, then stopped in front of a single maglev car. "In we go."

Inside, he pointed at the heavily-padded, five-point-harnessed seats. "Sit. Face forward and strap in, as fast as you can."

Buckling herself into the seat, she asked a similarly-occupied Echo, "Why straps? I never heard of a subway with seat—WHOOAAAA!!"

"Because we're in a hurry," Echo deadpanned as the maglev shot off at high speed.

* * *

"How the heck fast are we goin'?" Omega asked, scrambling to get the last of the buckles fastened against the g-forces.

"Oh, average cruising speed on these short-range puppies is around a thousand miles an hour, so we'll be at the pad in about five more minutes, give or take," Echo noted with a shrug. "'Fast' is more like twelve hundred. In a pinch, they can go fifteen hundred, but that's dangerous; it gets hard to slow 'em down at the end. The long-distance trains cruise at twelve hundred, and emergency speed is...mm, eighteen hundred miles an hour? Yeah, I think that's right."

"But...but..." a patently-shocked Omega stammered, "but the bullet trains in Japan only go—"

"That's because the so-called bullet trains are exposed to the air," Echo explained. "Our subway tunnels are evacuated to near-vacuum. Did you note how the entryway looked a little like an airlock?"

"Oh SHIT!" an obviously excited Omega exclaimed, practically bouncing in her seat. Echo strongly suspected that if she hadn't been tightly strapped in, she WOULD have bounced. "I've seen science fiction-y plans and designs, but I didn't know anybody had actually DONE it!"

"There's a lotta stuff that Division One has done that nobody knows about," Echo pointed out. "Like made contact with extraterrestrials, for one thing."

"This..." Omega ran a distracted hand through her hair, dislodging several wisps. "This job is way the hell cool."

"Glad you're enjoyin' it," Echo replied, blasé.

But he hid his grin.

* * *

Within moments, the maglev arrived at their destination: a Division One landing site well outside New York City. Waiting there for them was a group of agents with gear in hand.

"Alpha Team?" their leader queried, stepping forward.

"Affirmative," Echo replied. "Alpha One."

"The foo fighter is on a heading due west-northwest, sir."

The Division One agents quickly helped Echo and Omega into black hyper-aramid flight jumpsuits, then handed them helmets and oxygen masks.

"Your T-Bird is fueled and ready, Alpha One."

"That's a roger..." and Echo and Omega were sprinting across the tarmac toward a sleek black aircraft.

* * *

Echo kicked in the standard, stage one afterburners as their highly-modified T-38 raced down the runway, taking off and then banking sharply, setting a bearing west-northwest.

"You all right back there?" Echo spoke into the mike.

"YEESSS!" he heard in his headset. "WAAHOOOO!"

He grinned beneath the oxygen mask.

"Never been in a T-38 before, huh?"

"Uh-uh!"

"That's 'negative.'"

87

"What?"

"Remember your comm protocol."

"Oh, copy. I know better. Sorry, Echo; I got a little carried away, there."

"Literally." He grinned again.

"What's the plan?" Omega's voice sounded in his ears.

"Force him down. Gently, if possible; if not, our discretion."

"How much of an advantage have we got? I mean, the T-38 is a pretty old aircraft..."

"This is just a T-38 frame. And even the frame is made out of a... special alloy, if you get my drift. Nothing else about it is anywhere close to Earth standard. And MY T-Bird isn't even a Division-standard aircraft. I've made a shit-ton of mods to it over the years, and I keep it updated. We got strategic advantage and to spare, no problem."

* * *

They were coming up fast on the rogue saucer now; evidently, the shipjacker didn't yet know they were coming. *Stealth mode must be one of those non-standard options,* Omega considered. *And maybe some passive metamaterial cloaking, like the 'Vette has.*

Just then, the saucer's pilot appeared to become aware of their presence.

"Oops, there he goes," Omega said into the comm set as the saucer suddenly took evasive action.

* * *

"I'm on it," Echo said as the T-Bird smoothly arced across the sky in pursuit. He flipped a switch to change to an outside frequency and activate a universal translator.

"Unidentified flying object, this is Division One team Alpha One. You are outside of your authorized region in a craft that has been listed as stolen. Please land immediately. Repeat, please land immediately."

The saucer's pilot ignored the warning.

"Echo," Omega's voice sounded in his headset, "what if we ascend 500 feet—come in on top of him? Maybe we can literally force him down."

"Copy. Good plan. Wilco."

Echo eased the jet upward. Now they were pacing the saucer just above its trailing edge.

Unexpectedly, the saucer came to a full stop, hovering, and then darted back along its previous trajectory. The black jet overshot.

"Shit. Hang on, Meg, we're gonna pull some g's. I'm up-and-over."

"Roger that. Up and over."

Echo pulled back hard on the stick as he simultaneously kicked in the decidedly non-standard stage two afterburners. The T-Bird shot almost straight up at a dizzying speed.

"Ughn...mff...huh...huh..."

"Meg, you okay back there?"

"Yeh...huh..."

"Color or gray vision?"

"Gray..."

"Peripheral vision?"

"...Nuh-uh...huh...huh..."

"Meg, tighten all your leg, butt, and ab muscles. As hard as you can. Right now. You're grayed out. It'll keep you from blacking out."

"C-copy...wil-wilco...huh..."

Meanwhile, Echo pulled the jet up and over in a loop so tight, standard Earth aircraft could not have withstood it; his face underneath the helmet's visor was set in a grimace against the g-forces, his own body rigid. He could still hear Omega panting in his earphones as she resisted the powerful centrifugal force.

As he came over the top of the loop, upside down, he rolled the plane 180 degrees and nosed into a dive, in a half-Cuban eight maneuver. Rapidly, they caught up to the fleeing saucer as Echo punched the afterburners again. Omega's panting had stopped.

Either she made it through fine, or she's blacked out from the g's, Echo decided. *Given her astronaut training, I sure hope it's the former. I better check.*

"Meg? You alive back there?"

"Affirmative...ACE."

Echo grinned at the nickname this time. *Good. She's gonna do just fine.* He flipped the external switch again.

"Unidentified spacecraft, this is Echo of Division One team Alpha One. If you refuse to land voluntarily, you will be shot down." He flipped the switch off.

"Echo, are you really—? I mean, it's STOLEN, not..."

"Stay cool, Meg. Trust me."

* * *

She waited in suspense as he powered up the weapons and checked his radar for stray aircraft.

Abruptly, Echo fired. Twice.

Two dark purple beams lanced from the black aircraft. One went past the saucer's port side, the other to starboard, diffusing in the distance. He flipped on the external frequency again.

"Unidentified craft, that was a tachyon smasher cannon firing to your port and starboard. This is your final warning. The next shot comes down the middle."

The spacecraft began to slow down. A chittering came over the headsets, and the translator rendered it.

"Surrender. Landing in field below."

Fox's voice came over the air then.

"We copy, Alpha One. We'll take 'em on the ground. Escort 'em down, then bring it back to base."

* * *

"Roger, Fox." Echo dropped his port wing long enough to look down and see the landing saucer surrounded by black Suits and black vehicles. "Alpha One handing over to ground control. Returning to base."

Echo heard a soft, disappointed, "...Aww..." in his ears, and wondered if Omega knew she had a hot mic. He smiled to himself underneath his O2 mask.

Yeah, I like this kid. It's gonna be a helluva lotta fun working with her. Well, damn, what am I saying—it already is.

"Echo?" Omega asked tentatively.

"I read you, Meg. Go ahead."

"Any chance I can get rated on one of these?"

"Alpha One to base."

"We copy, Alpha One. This is base; go ahead," Fox's voice answered.

"Fox, is there any rush to return to base? I've got somebody up here who's dying to be properly introduced to the joys of TRUE high-performance aircraft."

There was a pause. Then Fox's voice replied, a hint of pleased amusement in it.

"Alpha One, you have a go on that introduction."

A lone afterburner plume, blue diamonds scintillating, executed a perfect barrel roll as it shot through the darkening sky.

* * *

The girl lay on one blanket, not yet chilly enough to wrap up in the other, and happily counted meteors, intending to submit her numbers to the online archive. She had just made the latest annotation in her note pad and laid it and the pencil on the blanket beside herself, when darkness loomed overhead. She looked up...to see the leading edge of the saucer, pale yellow running lights blinking, moving over her, slowly blotting out the stars.

She gasped in amazement, then smiled in excitement. But when she tried to push up to a sitting position, she found she was unable to do so.

No, no. Naughty girl! Lie still. I have plans for you.

You're talking inside my head! *the girl thought, shocked.*

Indeed I am. Now shut up.

As her body floated up, away from the blanket into the air, the girl began to struggle...

...But she could not move.

* * *

Omega was sitting at a desk in the Core, studying case histories on the laptop there, when Echo and Fox walked up.

"Meg, you know your way around the NASA field centers..."

"Yeah, Echo, sure. After all this time, I'd hope so." She grinned.

"Which ones?"

"Well, Johnson Space Center, of course...Marshall Space Flight Center, in Alabama—that's where I started...JPL...Goddard..."

"What about the Cape?"

"Not a problem. Spent time working there, too. Mostly on travel, but I know my way around it."

Echo gave Fox a meaningful look; Fox nodded.

"That'll do," the chief concurred. "Get on it yesterday."

Echo turned back to Omega.

"Let's go, then."

* * *

"So, let me get this straight," Omega said as the morphed black Corvette cruised at speed along—or rather, high above—the Beeline Expressway through central Florida. "We have word that someone has tampered with the Phoenix deep space probe, for reasons unknown, and that this someone is not a...'native,' shall we say?"

"Correct. We suspect sabotage."

"Why?"

"The list of possible motives is too long to go into. Let's just say that deliberately spreading the contents of the plutonium power supply along the entire East Coast might not be too healthy for the residents."

"Well, actually, that would dilute it so much, it wouldn't be anything much above normal background, if at all."

"Hm. Probably so, now you mention it."

"Yeah. People get all upset about these 'huge nuclear power packs' the space probes use, and in reality the bulk of the pack is electronics and stuff. The fissile material is only a very small amount—MAYBE as much as a few hundred grams, depending on the isotope—all in a pellet no larger than a marshmallow, if that."

"How do you know all that?"

"Worked on a probe, about five years back. So I know this stuff."

"Yeah, I guess you do. But you have to admit, the political ramifications sure wouldn't be great."

"No, they wouldn't. Mostly because people that don't know any better would be scared of it. And panic, we don't need." Omega looked around, checking their immediate vicinity. There were no vehicles along this stretch of road. She tapped Echo on the shoulder. "Pull over. Um, down. Uh, what I'm tryin' to say is, can you land this thing on the road shoulder?"

He glanced at her, hit the appropriate switch, and eased the Corvette down and over to the side of the road. It settled gently onto the gravel with a soft crunch as it transformed back to an apparently normal automobile.

"What's up?" he asked.

"Swap places with me."

"Why?"

"This is my turf. I can get us where we need to go."

"Without flying?"

"As close as we are, we were gonna have to land pretty damn soon anyway; the NASA facility is in the middle of an air force station, and it's restricted airspace. We're driving from here, one way or another."

"That'll work."

* * *

As they drove north through Kennedy Space Center along the Kennedy Parkway, Omega turned to her passenger.

"Well?"

"Well what?"

"Pretty smooth entrance, huh?"

"We're past the gate," Echo acknowledged noncommittally.

"Hmph."

The carte noirs they wore on their lapels now morphed from VIP visitors' badges into NASA Headquarters personnel badges. Ahead, the huge Vertical Assembly Building loomed, with its patriotic Stars and Stripes and giant NASA logo.

"That where we're headed?" Echo asked.

"Yeah. The VAB. With the launch scheduled for late next week, they'll be getting ready to stack the probe on the bird."

They pulled up to the VAB visitors' parking lot.

"Remember, Echo: KSC is one of the more laid-back field centers as such things go, so we can't afford to be too 'by-the-book,' or we'll stick out too much. Here, we can pass for top brass easily. 'Suits,' literally. That's what I've got in mind. We're from NASA Headquarters in D.C."

"Got it."

They entered a door on a side wing of the building, the barest hint of pride in Echo's eyes as his trainee confidently took the lead. In the foyer, they stopped and quickly scanned the list of rooms and offices. Omega looked over a checklist posted nearby, then tapped it with her finger.

"Here. The probe's in a clean room. Follow me."

* * *

Setting off down the corridor toward the main wing, they headed for the indicated clean room. Walking in lock step, they barely noticed as the workers they passed along the way deferred to the powerful couple in the black Suits. *Wow. Grand High Poobahs. Must be from Headquarters.*

As they turned a corner, they came smack upon a large observation window looking out into the high bay. The new Orion space plane loomed before them, shining white, already mated to her SLS external tank and booster rockets. Beyond it stood a smaller, multistage rocket. Omega stumbled to a halt.

Echo watched silently with narrowed, pain-filled eyes as she moved, almost trancelike, to the window, wordlessly put out a hand, and traced the outline of the spacecraft on the glass. Her expression was that of one who saw her life's dream within sight, but forever out of reach. That same hand, splayed against the glass, abruptly formed a fist and withdrew. Unexpectedly, an impassive mask slid over the yearning face, and Omega deliberately turned her back on the observation port and headed down the hall.

With a noiseless sigh, Echo fell back into step with her. She pointed ahead, and in a crisp, almost brittle voice, said, "Down here."

They entered a room with lockers, and Omega moved to a series of shelves, pulling down two paper jumpsuits, paper booties, gloves, and surgical-type masks.

"Here." She handed one set to Echo. "The mask goes on first. Make sure the hood covers all of your hair completely. And grab a hard hat."

* * *

Inside the momentarily-deserted clean room, Echo looked up at the Phoenix probe and grunted underneath the mask.

"Huh. Bit bigger than I would've thought."

"Yeah. You don't get a real perspective until you're standing next to 'em."

"I meant it's bulky compared to the spacecraft I'm used to."

She frowned beneath the mask. Echo pulled out some diagrams.

"Okay, here's the schematics. Let's get down to work."

A clean room worker entered the room and came up behind them.

"May I help you?"

"Hi. I'm Dr. Meg...Black, and this is...my colleague, Dr. Reflète. From Headquarters." Omega shook his hand as she spoke. "The project office had some questions that didn't get resolved in the FRR, and we were the lucky ones who got the action items."

"Been there, done that. Lucky you." The worker grinned. "I'm Matt Forrester. What can I do to help?"

"Well, there were a couple of places where the schematics didn't seem to be quite accurate, and we just wanted to be sure of some things." Echo waved the schematics. Forrester looked over Echo's shoulder while Echo pointed out several pertinent sections of the spacecraft.

"Okay, so you just want to remove a panel and take a look? Match the schematic?"

"Right." Omega nodded. "Verification by visual inspection."

"Okay, that's not a problem; you caught us early enough in the countdown checklist that we can just open 'er up and have a look. I'll go get the tool kit. Be right back."

As Forrester walked away, Echo fixed Omega with a stern look.

"You almost blew it just now. Don't tell me that nobody around here would recognize the name Megan McAllister."

* * *

Omega looked down at her paper booties so he wouldn't see the pain in her eyes. She was thankful the surgical mask hid half her face.

"I know. I'm sorry. This...is a little harder than I thought it would be. Just being here, I mean."

* * *

Thinking about her unanticipated encounter with the Orion spacecraft, Echo watched her for a moment, reading her expression despite the mask and her averted gaze. But he remembered his own pain, the first time a mission had taken him back to west Texas, and recognized her emotions.

More, he understood—possibly as no one else could, in that moment—and could not fault her for them. So rather than continue reprimanding her, he decided to change the subject.

"What's an FRR?"

"Flight Readiness Review. High mucky-mucks have a final approval meeting, usually in the launch minus two-to-four-week timeframe. It's another go/no-go on the launch checklist. Usually it's a rubber stamp, but it's not unknown for concerns to come up."

Forrester was already across the room, removing the indicated panel, and Echo and Omega walked over just as he lifted it off.

"Ho-lee shit!" Forrester exclaimed in astonishment.

"What is it?" Echo and Omega asked in unison.

"Lemme see that schematic," Forrester said, taking it from Echo and looking it over. Omega glanced over his shoulder, then knelt to look inside the probe. She caught her breath just as Echo whistled.

"What's that doing there?" Echo asked.

* * *

'That' was a large titanium box with rounded edges, about three feet by two by one, sealed, and connected into the main power bus.

"That's not one of the experiments..." Omega murmured.

"No, it's not," Forrester replied. "You guys wait here. I'm gonna go get Joe—my boss."

As soon as Forrester got near the door, Echo whipped out a small optical device, held it to his eyes, and scanned the box.

"Aha," he said, sounding satisfied.

"What is it?" Omega asked. "Is it a bomb?"

"Quick—help me disconnect it from the power bus."

Carefully, they removed the unit from its power source inside the probe, and lifted it out of the spacecraft. At a gesture from Echo, Omega sealed the power connection and replaced the probe's panel.

"Now, give it a minute," he said.

Echo folded his arms and waited. Omega gamely stood her ground, not knowing what to expect.

Suddenly, one side of the box retracted, and a small, furry biped with enormous ears, not much bigger than a large rat, emerged.

"We've got a stowaway," Echo declared. "From a previously undocumented species, no less."

Omega reached for the creature, and it promptly dived under the Phoenix. She lunged after it. Echo knelt beside the titanium pod, studying it carefully.

"Echo," Omega called, from where she chased the little alien around the room, "I could use a hand here! Preferably before we break something!"

Echo continued to survey the alien's life-support capsule.

"Echo, Forrester and his boss will be back any minute!"

"Hmm," Echo said, probing the capsule's interior.

"I'm trying to catch a greased piglet, and all he can do is study the damn box. Aha, gotcha cornered now, you little furball-with-ears."

Omega advanced on the tiny creature, who had nowhere left to run. Suddenly she staggered, grunted in surprise, then dropped to her knees with a moan, holding her temples and grimacing. The 'furball' took that opportunity to dart around her, toward the clean room door.

* * *

Echo looked up in concern when he heard Omega's moan, and saw the alien hotfooting it for the exit. He jerked down his surgical mask, raised two fingers to his mouth, and let out a shrill, ear-piercing whistle.

The Furball stiffened in mid-stride and toppled over. Omega covered her ears and scowled, groaning louder. Echo calmly replaced his mask.

The senior agent walked over, scooped up the paralyzed Furball, and placed it back into its capsule, sealing it in with a magnetic lock he produced from one pocket. Then he bent over Omega.

"You okay?"

"Ugh. NO. I'm not okay. I think...I'm gonna be...sick..."

"Migraine?"

"I don't know. I've never had one before."

"Put on your special glasses. It may help if you cut out some of the light. Can you stand?" he asked, offering a hand as she fished out her sunglasses.

"Yeah, I think so." She shoved on the glasses, took his hand, and stood carefully. Just then, Forrester came back with his boss.

"Look, Joe! There it is, on the floor! They must've disconnected it while I went to get you. What the hell is this thing doing in the Phoenix?"

Echo pulled out his own sunglasses.

* * *

"...And estimating from the supplies inside his habitat, we think the Furball intended to be picked up by another craft once the probe got well away from Earth," Echo reported to Fox.

"And you brought him down—with a whistle??" Fox asked. "Oy."

"Yeah. Judging from the Furball's features and the amount and type of soundproofing in the habitat, I figured he might be sensitive to nervous system disruption by high-frequency, high-decibel sonics."

"How's Omega?"

"I...don't know. She hasn't returned from her CAT scan and MRI yet."

Omega entered the Core just then, and Echo nodded a greeting as Fox motioned her over to where they stood.

"How's the head?" Echo asked as she walked up.

"Fine now. I don't understand it."

"What did the doctors find?" Fox queried.

"Nothing. Not one damn thing. I'm as healthy as a horse. Healthy as I ever was. Go figure."

"So what caused the headache?" Echo asked, puzzled.

"We have no idea whatsoever. The medics did say something about an unusual EEG, but they seemed to think that was normal for me."

Fox and Echo glanced at each other. Then Echo told Omega, "Well, let me know if it happens again."

"I don't think you could miss it," a wry Omega replied.

* * *

Much later, Echo walked into Fox's office alone and sat down across the desk from him. Fox looked up from his paperwork, leaned back, and nodded.

"Thanks for stopping by, Echo. I know it's almost end of shift. Well, what do you think?"

"It's been—what?—a couple months now? Omega's catching on fast.

Really fast. She did great on the mission to KSC; you should have seen the way she slid us right past base security and straight on into the VAB. It was a thing of beauty, Fox."

"So she did good, huh?"

"Oh, hell yeah. Fortunately, it's been relatively quiet, so she hasn't had to dive in right at the deep end of the pool like Romeo did, what with the invasion and all; so I've had a chance to train her properly, instead of her learning entirely on the job the way he did. Speaking of Romeo, that situation's going well. He's back on his feet, the cast is gone, and he's in physical therapy; you've probably seen the reports, but India was worried some tendons might have torn, what with all those breaks. And it seems there were some problems, but he's getting better fast. Oughta be ready to hit the streets again soon. India got over her mad at Omega pretty quickly after that little episode with the inhaler, and the four of us have been working really well together in training scenarios. I think we could even eventually trade out partners if needed, with little or no ill effects on our teamwork. Not so much two teams of two, as one team of four."

Fox nodded in approval.

"That's excellent news to hear. And a medic is always good to have in the field."

"And the knowledge and skill spread among the four of us is REALLY good. Once we've validated Alpha Line, I'd like to bring Romeo and India into it, with your approval. Romeo proved himself against the last of the invasion force already, so we know he can handle it. After all, dammit, Navy SEAL. And India's record shows not only was she a damn good ER physician, she even put down a gang riot in her ER—twice."

"Well, if anyone knows vulnerabilities and kill zones, it's an ER medic," Fox pointed out. "Did she do it with or without medical equipment in hand?"

"A little of both, according to the reports I read. She took down two with martial arts moves, and three more with strategically-applied medical equipment within reach. One of which was a syringe full of anesthetic! I think she'll handle the 'heat in the kitchen' just fine. So I wanna put 'em through the formalities and get 'em in as soon as possible."

"I think it's a good idea. So you figure you and Omega are ready?"

"Close. Couple things I want to check on first. We've gone out on some routine patrols, glommed a few jackers. Nabbed the stowaway. No really big stuff yet."

"All right. I trust your judgment, Echo. Let me know when you're ready."

"Anything out there you need Alpha Line for?" Echo queried, concerned by the conversation.

"No. I'll just be glad when you're fully on-line. I've had...a feeling... the last couple of days. And I've been in this business long enough to trust my instincts."

"Okay, Fox. We'll keep our eyes open. Yell if we're needed."

"Will do."

Chapter 5

A fully-dressed Echo stuck his head through the back door between his and Omega's quarters just before the beginning of the next shift.

"Hey, MEG!" he called, not seeing her.

"Yeah, Echo?" her voice floated out of the bedroom.

"You ready yet?"

"Um, workin' on it. Tuckin' in my shirt, so don't come in the bedroom unless you want an eyeful. Still gotta put on my tie and grab my jacket."

"Make it snappy and let's go. Fox called. There's a situation, and we drew the short stick."

"Coming!"

* * *

As they headed for Fox's office, Echo glanced over Omega's attire, then frowned.

"Your tie is wrong. Again."

"Um, yeah," Omega said, flushing. "This is the knot I can tie quick and easy. You were in a hurry, so I used it."

"It's not regulation."

"I know. Sorry. I have a hard time with the regulation knot."

"I've noticed, but that doesn't give you the excuse to use something else. I'll let it slide this time, but get it right."

"I'm workin' on it."

"Work harder."

She threw him an irritated glance. He ignored it.

"Get outta bed on the wrong side this morning?" she asked, voice crisp.

"No. C'mon," he said. "Shake a stick. Fox is waiting."

* * *

"...And the requested negotiator was the Vice-President of the

Ke!endarian Coalition," Fox explained in his office. "Which makes sense given Ke!endarian reputation, and normally would be an excellent choice. But out of the blue, there's a coup attempt occurring on the home planet RIGHT NOW, and there's already been at least one crack at taking out the Vice-President here on Earth, during negotiations."

"Which, if the coup is successful, means that the line of succession is destroyed, and the coup leader takes over unopposed," Echo noted. "And the leader of the coup is hostile to the Pan-Galactic Council, and every system in it." He turned to Omega. "Think, um...think an alien version of Daesh. Only maybe worse in some respects. They're not suicide terrorists—at least, not yet—but they ARE nonaligned, and expansionist. And any sentient who doesn't agree with 'em is considered NOT sentient, and worthy of elimination. They call themselves, as nearly as it renders in English, 'H!nar kre Naese!en!Re,' The House of the Gods' Wrath."

"Oh, okay. Wow, they don't get along with anybody, huh? And that's the group running the coup?" she asked.

"Precisely," Fox confirmed. "Half religious cult, and half terrorist organization, as near as I can figure. Naese!en!Re is a fairly new movement in the Coalition, popped up all of a sudden a little over a year ago, but it's gained power and momentum fast. The strange thing is that our analysts can't get a handle on it. It seems like, given the general Ke!endarian culture, it shouldn't exist, at least not in such a radical form."

"Interesting," Echo murmured.

"What he said," Omega agreed.

"The Coalition itself is in a different Galactic Division," Fox continued, "so the coup itself isn't our responsibility, and we won't have any say in what happens...unless the whole mess blows up, and then EVERYBODY gets called in. You better pray that doesn't happen; a galactic war is a major disaster, and damn hard to keep secret."

"I can see that," Omega murmured.

"But we'd still be mandated to try," Echo added.

"Shit," she whispered.

"...It IS our responsibility," Fox pointed out, "right now, to try to keep the Vice-President alive. Not to mention, it's a personal friend—I've known it for decades—so I'd like to get it extracted and taken somewhere safe."

"Roger that," Omega remarked, still trying to organize and collate the data dump of a mission pre-briefing.

"While the cogs are turning over there, Fox," Echo shot Omega a slight smile, so she'd know he was teasing, "I'm just curious—think this was what triggered your 'arachnid sense' last night?"

Fox snorted his amusement, and Echo's half-smile morphed into a grin, containing more than a hint of mischief. They both sobered within seconds.

"I dunno, Echo. It might well be; it sure has the potential ramifications for it. But I think your trainee's cogs have finished turning. Got a question, Omega?"

"Um, yes sir, sorta."

"Let's hear it."

"Okay, to start, I just wanna make sure I'm remembering something correctly, 'cause it's been a while since I read the summation in training. This is that long-tailed, ongoing negotiation between the Caltorians and the Ulyffon Alliance, right?"

"Right, Omega," Fox confirmed. "It's gone on so long, it's a running joke in diplomatic circles. But it's still fairly serious, in that if it goes wrong, we're back in that galactic war scenario; plus both sides have threatened to destroy Earth if anything happens to their envoy staff. All things considered, I didn't want it here to begin with, but there wasn't much I could do about it. This MIGHT just give me an excuse to move it off-world, and get us out of any potential backlash. It's going to put the negotiations on hold regardless, but that's no more than they do themselves on a fairly regular basis, so I'm not overmuch worried about THAT. But I WOULD like to see to it that everyone—especially Vice-President Zhaejoh kre Ranan—gets out of it intact."

"...Kre Ranan?" Omega parroted.

"Yeah," Echo explained. "It means House of Ranan. Sort of like how Germans use 'von,' or Celts use 'Mac' or 'Mc' to mean 'son of.' And Ranan means..." he pondered for a moment, searching his memory, "Reason, if I'm remembering right. House of Reason."

"Oh, okay. Interesting. Pretty cool name, too."

"Yeah, it is. Where are the negotiations being held this time?" Echo asked Fox.

"At the McMurdo Office."

"Antarctica?!" Omega exclaimed.

"That's the one," Fox said with a nod.

"Is the office near the American research station?"

"He's told you about it once before, Meg," Echo issued the mild reprimand.

"It's all right, Echo," Fox noted, as Omega's face flushed. "If I remember the incident you're referring to, it was early on, when Omega was still scoping us out."

"Yes sir," Omega murmured, "and at the time, you didn't say exactly WHERE it was in relation to the research station, just that it was in the general vicinity."

"True. So your answer is yes and no," Fox said. "The research station is on Ross Island. Our office is on the mainland, on the opposite side of the Sound from Ross Island, in the remnants of an old mountain range along the coast of what's called Marie Byrd Land—there's a reason why it's unclaimed territory, and we're that reason. Which location also puts it east of the International Date Line, and in the same time zone with Hawaii. It's not as well protected by the mountain range, though, so it gets colder." He paused, and studied her for a moment. "Have we assigned you a personal sidearm yet?"

"Not yet," she replied. "I took a laser pistol with me to the Cape and for a couple other assignments, but that's all I'm allowed yet, and that's only on an as-needed basis."

"Echo, take care of that before you two leave."

"Right, Boss. Standard issue, proto-cyclotron blaster?"

"Yeah, and a Winchester & Tesla Mark II as backup. She knows how to use one, right?"

"Yeah, Fox; I've trained her on everything up to and including a trans-warp boson cannon. If it points and shoots, she can nail the target. She's a damn good shot."

"Daddy taught me to shoot his guns on the farm when I was a little girl," Omega observed, pleased at the compliment. "I've been takin' out groundhogs and rodents in the fields for years. Until..." she paused, then continued, "until the accident." She shrugged.

"...Good," Fox commented, apparently choosing to ignore the addendum, though he did offer what seemed a sympathetic nod. "You're experienced. Let's make the weapons assignments permanent, then. Alpha Line's first team is going active, as of right now."

"Yess!" Omega cried in delight, punching a jubilant fist into the air as they rose to go. "Finally!"

Fox raised a vaguely amused eyebrow at her reaction; Echo remained impassive.

"Echo," Fox called as they went through the door, "make Omega redo her tie before you two meet the Ke!endarian Vice-President."

Echo threw up an acknowledging hand. Jubilation evaporated in an instant, as Omega stared at them both in consternation.

* * *

"Echo! Where are you going?" Omega wondered, astounded, as she followed Echo, who was making rapid time along the corridor into the Agency residences. "This is the way back to our quarters!"

"Damn straight," Echo agreed. "We're going to Antarctica. Gotta go back and put on our winter-weight Suits."

"But—"

"Hurry up and change," Echo said, opening his front door. "Dig through your things and find all the thermal layers you've got, and put those on, too. Oh, and fix the knot on that tie."

He went inside and closed the door.

"Damn," she muttered into the air as she walked next door. "I don't got any of that. But they oughta have some good stuff for us at the hangar... or pad...or, or wherever. Well," she decided, opening her door, "at least I can try that knot again."

* * *

Support agents met them in Grand Central Station, proffering hooded parkas with advanced alien insulation, and gloves and balaclavas of a similar, but thinner, material. All of it was black, of course, not that Omega was surprised at the color scheme. There was, after all, a reality behind the many urban legends, and she was living that reality.

Moments later they were on a maglev tube train with several extra cars headed south...way, way, WAY the hell...

South.

* * *

"So, the extra cars are for the various diplomatic teams?" Omega asked, as they traveled at speed, and Echo briefed her on procedure and protocol. They sat facing each other in a small compartment in the foremost car.

"Right." Echo nodded affirmation. "The fact that the coup's terrorist is out for the Ke!endarian vice-president doesn't negate the fact that he puts the other diplomats in danger. We'll evacuate each diplomatic corps in its own car, which also will obviate any infighting, and kre Ranan and its entourage will be in the forward car with us."

"Entourage?"

"Yeah—it's a politician, after all. It's got a personal chef, three diplomatic advisors, one of which serves as a liaison and aide, and two bodyguards."

"Oh. Crap. Now I get why the cars are so big on this train. The one we took to the airstrip was a lot smaller."

"Yeah, that one was designed for only a couple paired agent teams, max. But we'll be cramming several dozen aliens of various sizes and persuasions on board this one, along with probably a couple more agents from the McMurdo office, to help us out. If nothing else, those guys should know how to keep the peace among the diplomats by now."

"Then...why are we even going down? Do they really need us, Ace? They got agents there to handle things."

"Because there are agents, and then there are Agents, Meg. And Alpha Line—of which you and I comprise the prototype team—is intended to have Agents with a capital A. You'd lived in Texas for some time when we found you, right?"

"Yeah...?"

106

"So you know about the legends surrounding the Texas Rangers? 'One riot, one Ranger,' stuff like that?"

"Yeah!"

"Well, consider us the Division One equivalent. One situation, one team."

"Oooh. Badass R Us."

"Yeah. That's the intent, anyway. Think you're up to it?"

Omega gave him a wolfish grin.

"Watch me," she told him, and it was his turn to grin.

They were silent for a few moments.

"Hey—do we need to go ahead and put on the parkas and junk soon?" Omega wondered then. "This maglev train really moves..."

"No, we have plenty of time yet," Echo informed her. "Even straight-line like this—"

"Straight-line?! We're taking a chord through the Earth? A geometrical chord? Like, skipping through the top of the mantle?"

"Oh. No, we're still actually moving in an arc, just down deep. I meant straight line in terms of following the meridian straight south, although we'll curve west for a bit just before arriving. I think they originally tried to dig chord tubes, if memory serves. But since the mantle is plastic, it kinda flows a little, and it did weird shit to the tube, so they decided to stay inside the crust, where things are reasonably solid."

"What about crossing tectonic plate boundaries?"

Echo held up his hands.

"Whoa, Meg; I'm not a geologist like you are—among other things. When we get back, if you want me to, I'll introduce you to some of the structural engineers who maintain and expand the tube system. And then you," he grinned, "can teach ME for a change."

"Sounds cool. Yes, thank you, please...and I'd be happy to. Go on."

"Okay, so the gist of all that is, we aren't moving at anything like orbital velocities. The entire trip will take a little over six hours."

"Oh. Wow." Omega frowned.

"Yeah. We're still an hour from crossing the equator, yet. And McMurdo is another four or five hours past that."

"But that's...shouldn't we have taken something faster, Echo? If we took the T-Bird into the stratosphere, we could..."

"Ever been to Antarctica, Meg?"

"Uh, no..."

"How about northern Alaska in winter?"

"Southern girl here, remember?"

"Okay, so you don't have any first-hand experience with it, so it won't come to mind, even though you probably have been taught it. You DO know what season it is down there right now, don't you?"

"Um, yeah. I'm an astronomer; I know that. We're in summer, so they're in winter...oh. Duh. I have been SO stupid. Is that it? It is, isn't it?"

"That's it. And in the Antarctic winter, temperatures can go as low as 140 degrees below zero."

"Fahrenheit, I assume..."

"Yeah, Fahrenheit. I guess I should start using Celsius and metric and junk, but old habits die hard. You can bug me about that, and I'll bug you about that tie. Which looks good now, by the way. Here's the thing, though: at those temperatures, most metals become really brittle. Now think about what that would do to, say, the T-Bird—especially when we hit the afterburners on takeoff. The best we could hope for would be that it tore itself apart; worst-case scenario, it blows itself to Kingdom Come, and us with it. Either way, you and I go bye-bye. That's why the standard researchers at McMurdo STATION—the people who aren't Division One—tend to clear out for winter, and those that are left batten down the hatches, stow the equipment, and don't venture out unless they have to."

"Ooo, ick. I get it. But what about a spacecraft?"

"Where would we stow it when we landed?"

"Don't we have some underground hangars or something?"

"No, not there. It isn't like in New York—or any other place we have a field office—because in New York or wherever, the underground structures are only holding up the weight of the ground over 'em, and maybe a building or two. In Antarctica, it would have to support the weight of the ground plus the buildings, PLUS all that ice. AND, like I'm sure you know, the ice is moving. Slowly, I'll admit, but it does flow. And that flow tends to set up very long-wavelength harmonics in any structures built under it, which adds even more stress. We actually ended up building McMurdo mostly out, not up OR down. It has a way bigger footprint than any of the other offices, by several times. And even the Pan-Galactic Council tries not to send anything directly to the McMurdo Office during its winter, Meg. So what condition would a spacecraft be in, if we had to make an emergency exit? No, this is the safest way because, since it's underground, the temperatures stay pretty constant throughout, especially with the evacuated tube insulating it all. It takes a little longer—not THAT much—but we can get there and back in one piece, no matter what."

"Surely there are ice worlds in the pan-galactic...whatever. They gotta have equipment for that."

"Pan-galactic government. Not as many as you'd think," Echo noted. "There's actually more hot worlds than ice worlds. Life seems to prefer warmth. And the life that develops on ice worlds has a completely different chemistry, and uses completely different architecture and structural materials. It turns out that the two forms of structural engineering don't hand off that well, and are next to impossible to merge in one structure."

"Then why on Earth—literally—are they holding the negotiations THERE?"

"Because we thought that the very conditions we're talking about would make them safe, or at least, difficult to reach. Evidently we were wrong."

"But Fox's friend..."

"Fox ordered this transport mode; he knew the risks. It's cool, Meg." Echo looked her over for a moment, seeing the tenseness she was trying hard to hide.

Hm. I hope she's up to this, after all, he thought, concerned. *She's got the attitude...at least for now. But it isn't like she's got combat experience, though she does have that martial arts training. A black belt ain't no slouch. But she's no Navy SEAL. I don't need her spazzing on me right in the middle of a gun battle or some such shit.*

What he told her was, "Try to relax, baby. I know this is your first official, really serious mission, but don't get all bent out of shape before we even arrive. Trust your partner, trust your trainer, and trust your training—that's me, me again, and yourself, in that order. You can do this. Kick back and take a nap or something. Or pull up an ebook on your phone and read a while. Kitchenette's in the next compartment if you get hungry; there's one in each car, stocked appropriately for the race expected to be in it, but the one in this car has human food and drink as well as Ke!endarian. The booze is for the diplomats on the return trip, but if you get anxious, I won't bust you for ONE drink to help you settle. Don't worry about the cold gear for now. As long as we're in the tube, we won't need the stuff; like I said, the temperatures in the tube stay pretty constant, since it's underground. We'll only need those once we reach McMurdo."

"Well...okay. But..."

* * *

"But what?" Echo jumped on the word, eyes ever so slightly narrowed.

Omega started to tell him about her lack of heavy clothing, but there was something about his expression and tone of voice that told her he wasn't as confident of her as he made it sound, and she hesitated. She felt the blaster snuggled in its shoulder holster under her left arm, and the Winchester & Tesla nestled in the small of her back.

They wouldn't have given me these if there wasn't going to be significant danger, she thought. *And if Echo could handle it by himself, Fox would have only sent him. But Fox DIDN'T. He sent me, too. Which means Echo needs backup on this. And if they didn't think I was ready to BE that backup, they'd have sent Romeo with him, not me. But if I tell him I'm not dressed for Antarctica, he'll probably make me stay in the train. And then, when I'm not there AS that backup...he might get killed.* She hid the wince and the way her gut clenched at the thought, and made her decision.

"Nothing," she lied, regretting the need. "I'm just...a little hyper, that's all. Excited."

"Understandable in the circumstances. Unlax, baby. We got this, I swear."

"I know. I'm not worried. We got each other's backs." She pulled out her phone and brought up the library app. "I think I'll take you up on that 'read a book' suggestion, though. So what are you gonna do while we wait?"

"Me?" Echo hit a button in the armrest, and the seat promptly reclined, a footrest extending as a pillow extruded. "Hand me that throw. I'm gonna take a nap."

* * *

Upon arriving at the maglev station for the McMurdo Office—which station was small, Echo had explained in advance, to help maintain the integrity of the evacuated tunnel, the ice being prone to sublimating into the near-vacuum—the pair were met by a small local contingent of Division One agents, all dressed similarly to Alpha One—hooded parkas, thin, face-conforming balaclavas, matching gloves, and what appeared to be special, heavy-weight wool-blend Suits under that. Earlier discussion with Echo had revealed to Omega that, due to the extreme conditions, specialized wardrobes and equipment were issued to agents stationed permanently at McMurdo. This included a very unusual, high-tech fiber blend of wool and several off-planet materials, intended to ensure safety in the frigid temperatures; the blend of fibers in the threads lent a distinctive matte sheen and appearance, and a considerably heavier hand, to the Suits of McMurdo Agents. The differences were only noticeable to an experienced, knowledgeable observer, however. Since the cold was already making itself felt in Omega's legs and feet within seconds of debarking, she decided she was mildly jealous.

As the two groups came together, they all pulled their balaclavas down under their chins to allow for facial recognition. In the lead was a petite woman agent with long chestnut hair spilling down over the shoved-back hood of her parka, green eyes and a sultry smile...all directed at Echo. Omega's eyebrows rose, and she held back, watching.

"Ah! Agent Echo, welcome!" the other woman said, beaming and stepping forward. "Your reputation precedes you! We appreciate Headquarters taking matters so seriously! I'm Agent Tango, acting chief of the McMurdo Office, and head of the diplomatic security team. Thank you for coming. I'm sure you'll have things straight in no time."

"Hello, Tango," Echo said, taking her proffered hand and shaking. To Omega's knowledgeable eye, it looked like the female agent held on just a fraction of a second longer than was strictly necessary. "This is my partner, Agent Omega."

"Oh—hi, nice to meet you," a suddenly-curt Tango said, nodding briefly at Omega before sidling in close to Echo, effectively cutting out Omega from her rightful position at Echo's side in the small space. Omega raised an eyebrow again, but said nothing, merely nodding in response to the other woman; she saw when Echo's eyes narrowed slightly, before Tango continued. "Echo, this is the lead team I put together for security on the negotiations. This is King, Ocean, Able and Baker." She pointed to each agent in turn.

The four strapping, handsome young men nodded courteously to Echo, shaking his hand. But when Omega stepped forward to shake hands, they smiled and became a bit more effusive in their greetings. Tango's face grew hard.

"Who's in charge of McMurdo these days?" Echo wondered, glancing around the carved ice cave and seeing no sign of the usual plaque designating Office leads. "Didn't I see where Pip retired a few months back?"

"That's right. Like I said, currently I'm interim Office chief." Tango preened a bit. "We've been expecting that to be made permanent any day."

"Are the five of you armed?" Echo continued.

"We are," Tango averred, raising her head proudly.

"With what?"

"Standard issue blasters," Tango informed him, and looked like she was about to say something else.

"Great. Are the negotiations taking place now?" Echo pressed on, not giving her a chance to say more.

"No, after the third attempt on Ranan's life yesterday, they retreated to their respective quarters," Tango replied. "They—er, we felt it was safer that way."

"That's 'kre Ranan,'" Echo corrected. "Calling it just 'Ranan' is like calling someone named McIntosh just 'Intosh.' And it's good to hear they returned to their quarters. Split up, it's harder to get 'em all. Send out word—as of right now, negotiations are suspended until the situation is resolved, likely to resume in a different location at a later time, possibly off-planet. We are evacuating the diplomats, effective immediately."

"But do you really think that's—" Tango began.

"On it, Agent Echo," Baker noted, pulling out his cell phone and drawing several patterns on it with his fingers. "I'm the comm chief for the Office...there. Done."

"Baker!" Tango exclaimed. "I didn't give you authori—"

"Did Fox explain Alpha Line to you, Baker?" Echo interrupted.

"Yes sir!"

"What about you, Tango?"

"He said he was sending his top agent." The woman shrugged, dismissive.

"Agents, plural. Which would be us," Echo said, indicating himself and Omega. Omega knew that Echo was stretching it a bit in calling both of them the top agents, seeing as Omega was still just a rookie, but given Tango's attitude, she understood why, and tacitly agreed. "The Alpha team on site outranks all other field agents, and Alpha Line missions take priority over all others. And Omega and I are the Alpha One team." He turned to the other agents. "Until further notice, you answer to us. All of you. Omega?"

Omega stepped to his side, pointedly going around Tango, who scowled.

"Right here, Echo."

"Let's go. Baker, you're our liaison. Contact the envoy liaisons for the Caltorians and the Ulyffon Alliance and have 'em meet us in the most secure room in the facility, then take us there. And pop me the location of the known attacks, and any suspected ones, while you're about it." He waved his cell phone. "Ciphered, please."

"Wilco, Echo," Baker replied and pulled his own phone again.

"I really think—" Tango began, as Baker carried out Echo's orders.

"Let's go," Echo said, heading out, Omega at his side.

* * *

Omega was fascinated to see the layout of the McMurdo Office—which Baker had sent to BOTH members of the Alpha One team, and it included not only the attack locations, but the locus of their upcoming meeting. The facility was a bizarre combination of carved ice tunnels,

113

caverns, and palaces; and gigantic, ancient Maya-like pyramidal stone structures which were largely buried under the ice cap, save for a few larger ice caverns which exposed significant portions of certain pyramids, including the central one which housed the Office proper. All of it was well below the surface of the ice cap.

As they headed down the ice corridor for Echo's intended meeting with the diplomatic teams' representatives, the group of agents fell into an order. Baker led the way through the maze of corridors, Echo right behind, Omega beside him. Hard on Alpha One's heels was Tango, with Able, King, and Ocean guarding the rear. However, Tango kept trying to usurp Omega's position, pushing her way up next to Echo and attempting to carry on a running conversation with the senior Alpha team member, even though Echo was fixated on what needed doing—which included studying the map of the facility, in order to determine the strategies being employed by the terrorist.

But when Tango openly body-checked Omega into the wall of the tunnel and Omega slipped and nearly fell on her face as a result, Echo stopped dead.

"All halt," he ordered, and everyone stopped; the younger male agents assumed defensive postures, but their expressions were knowing—and mildly disgusted. Echo knelt beside Omega, who had landed on one knee. "You okay, Meg?"

"Yeah, I'm fine. Just slipped on the ice when I lost my balance." She didn't tell him that her feet—clad only in leather shoes and several pairs of lightweight summer dress socks, which she'd layered—were already so cold they were starting to go numb. *Otherwise Ms. Gimme Attention would have gotten as good as she gave,* she thought, in intense annoyance.

"I would have expected a member of our 'top team' to be a bit more graceful," Tango muttered, and Echo and Omega locked eyes for a moment. He held out a gloved hand, and Omega took it. Then he stood, drawing her back to her feet, and turned to the other woman.

"Tango?"

"Yes, Echo?" The woman all but simpered.

Abruptly Echo grabbed the petite agent by the upper arms, lifting her bodily off the ground as she squeaked in surprise, before pivoting and depositing her back on her feet...two steps behind his position.

"Stay. There," he said, in a tone that was nearly as cold as the ice around them. Then he leaned in, scowling right in the woman's face. "And if you EVER do that to my partner again, I will PERSONALLY see to it that you are brain-bleached back into infancy. And while you're at it, shut the hell up. I'm trying to analyze the situation, here."

"And what are YOU doing?" Tango asked Omega, expression bordering on—but not quite daring to cross over into—an ugly, truculent glare.

"Getting my partner's back while he analyzes the situation," Omega answered. Echo turned and started the group moving forward again with a few hand gestures.

"Well, I guess that tells me all I need to know about the Alpha One team, then," Tango muttered. "Especially given the blonde hair."

"Actually not," Echo noted, overhearing. "Just because she's the junior partner, don't make the mistake of underestimating her gray matter. DOCTOR Omega has degrees in five sciences, AND one field of engineering. She was an astronaut when we recruited her."

"Ooo," came a male voice, sotto voce, from the back; Omega couldn't tell which of the three agents guarding their rear had reacted. She threw a quick glance at Echo's face. That worthy cut his eyes sideways at her, then just barely raised an eyebrow. She tucked her head, worrying her chin into the collar of her parka to ensure her grin was hidden, even despite the balaclava.

"Shit," Tango grumbled under her breath, and subsided for the time, much to Omega's—AND Echo's—relief.

* * *

Soon, an ancient rock wall appeared in the distance: they were reaching the main pyramid, where most of the Office's facilities lay. As they drew near to the main pyramid, Echo called another halt.

"What's up, Ace?" Omega wondered.

"His code name is Echo, not Ace," Tango corrected...very clearly.

Echo and Omega both turned and stared her down, blue gaze and

115

brown perilously hard. Tango shut up.

"You and I don't need to have a big escort into the facility proper, Meg," Echo explained to his partner then, emphasizing his use of her nickname for Tango's benefit. "It draws too much attention to us. So here's the plan, folks. Baker, Omega, and I are going to remain here, well down the corridor from the main entrance proper. Tango, you're the acting Office chief."

"Right," she said, beaming him a smile.

"Then go act."

"What?!"

"Go. Back. To. Your. Office," Echo reiterated with gritted teeth. "Do whatever you have to do there, but GO. NOW."

Tango affected a sultry pout, but it had no effect on Echo, who barely noticed it. Finally, and reluctantly, she meandered off in the direction of the pyramid ahead.

"Able, King, Ocean, you're next. Chat casually, like nothing's wrong, and you haven't seen two new agents show up at the facility." Echo held up a staying hand, watching down the corridor until Tango's distant form vanished; that meant she had entered the open cavern in front of the pyramid entrance, which was slightly offset relative to the tunnel. "Aaand...go!"

They went.

"I assume you'll want me to precede the two of you by some distance, as well," Baker presumed.

"You assume correctly," Echo told him, watching the trio.

"Tell me when."

"About the time you see your buddies get to the end of the tunnel; little before, actually. We don't want y'all to look regularly-spaced. So... okay, go now."

Baker sauntered nonchalantly down the ice tunnel as if he hadn't a care in the world.

* * *

"He gets it," Omega noted, as soon as the McMurdo agent was out of earshot. "He's a smart one."

Echo noted that she watched Baker all the way down the tunnel, and

116

wondered with some trepidation...and annoyance...if he was about to lose yet another partner to romantic interests. *Then again,* he considered, eyeing her surreptitiously, *judging by her expression, maybe she's got something else on her mind.* He felt oddly relieved at the notion.

"He does," the experienced agent replied then. "And he'd make a helluva lot better acting chief than that...that..."

"Bitch?" Omega offered.

"Well, I wasn't going to call her that, but..." Echo shook his head in bemusement as he tugged down his balaclava. "What is her deal, anyway?"

"I'm kinda glad you brought it up, Ace," Omega said, a little hesitantly, Echo thought. She pulled down her own mask.

"What's up, Meg? Can you tell me what's going on under that brown hair of hers?"

"The color's properly called 'chestnut,' it comes out of a bottle, and yes I can," Omega answered, somewhat to Echo's amusement.

"Then tell me."

"It's simple, Echo: She wants you."

"WHAT?!"

"She thinks you're handsome, she knows your reputation, and she wants you," Omega repeated and elaborated. "Chances are, she met you at some Division function that you probably don't even remember. Normally, I'd expect her to drop the meeting into casual conversation, but that doesn't seem to fit her intent, which apparently is to push the impression that you've come down here to help her out of a jam. Compared to you, she's pretty much a junior agent, probably not too used to doing real field work—I'd figure her for being in Supplies, or maybe Facilities, something like that—and you impressed her. You're good-looking, strong, smart, and you're essentially the best field agent, arguably the best overall agent, on the planet. But we've discusssed all that before." Omega shrugged. "The upshot is, you're a catch among those men and women who think like that, and she wants to land you before anybody else does. Which also explains why she was trying to cut me out—evidently she considers me a threat. Exactly why, I'm not sure. I don't THINK I did anything that could be interpreted as coming on to you. But maybe it's only because you have a female partner. She might just assume that opposite-sex partners all become lovers or something, I dunno."

Echo felt his face flush in embarassment as a consequence of several ego-boosting things his partner had just remarked, but he carefully considered what Omega had to say anyway. She had, after all, duplicated his assessment in several points, and introduced several more potentially-valid points. It was the notion that the woman might be after him that caught him off guard, for while he had had lovers in the past, he was not used to being pursued, himself. But Omega's analysis made really good sense of Tango's behavior, and he decided it was worth keeping an eye out, in case Meg was right.

"I did notice that the MALE agents seemed to approve of you," he offered mildly.

* * *

"Um..." Omega felt her own face heat—except for her nose, which was cold. "If you say so, I guess."

"And she didn't like that, either. I thought, based on that, maybe one of those guys was her main interest, and she was jealous of the attention they were giving you."

"Which is still a possibility," Omega pointed out. "But I had a different interpretation of that same behavior. I think she just wants to be the center of attention. Some women are like that. You know the type—all male eyes on her, all other females subservient."

"Hm."

"Yeah."

"Wait...are you into guys, or girls, Meg? Or both? I don't wanna offend..."

"Um, guys," she admitted, cheeks getting hotter. "You?"

"Girls. I thought you'd have that figured by now, after all the movies we've watched and shit."

"Yeah, I figured. Just makin' sure."

They were silent a moment, thinking.

"This...brings up a whole new problem," he decided.

"Yeah, it does," Omega agreed. "Which is what I wanted to talk to you about, but not in front of everybody. I'm glad you cleared 'em all out."

"Yeah. So. Is this even a legitimate mission, or did she kluge something up to get me down here..."

"...To glom onto you. Right. And that, I dunno. We don't have enough information." Omega chewed her lip in thought. "We might wanna call Fox and see if she specifically requested you, though that's not absolute proof there's nothing serious going on, even if she did. I guess once we talk to Fox's alien friend, maybe we can figure something out. I don't THINK she's dimwitted enough to have faked an attack on a foreign diplomat, let alone several..."

"Damn." Echo ran a distracted hand through his hair.

"Yeah. Sorry. Thanks for defending me, though."

"Damn bitch tried to knock you down. Did knock you into the wall. You're my partner. I don't stand for that shit."

"Me neither. Unfortunately, in my case, 'not standing' was the operative term. But I also appreciate your countering her 'dumb blonde' crack. I was working out how to do it myself without sounding like a hyper-egotist, but you saved me the trouble, way the hell smoother." Omega paused, as a thought struck. "Hey, waitaminit. You said, when we got here, that the previous head of the Office had retired recently. You don't suppose that was an unwilling retirement, do you? Y'all brain-bleach most retiring agents and set 'em up with a nice new life, right?"

Echo stared at her for a moment, wide-eyed in shock at the idea. Abruptly his eyes narrowed, then closed.

"Well, damn it to hell," he finally cursed with feeling. "Keep your eyes peeled for any evidence to that effect, and I'll go to Fox when we get back if we uncover anything. Oh, the hell with it! After the events of our first half-hour here, I'm gonna go to Fox anyway. We do NOT need that hell-cat running an entire Office. Especially if she really is as incompetent—or careless, at least—as she came across to me."

"Eh. Good point. Yell if you want me to provide backup on that 'mission,' too."

"Backup is always good, partner," Echo told her with a grin. "Baker's been out of sight for several minutes. You ready?"

"You bet. Let's go."

* * *

When they emerged from the tunnel into what Omega decided to think of as an ice plaza, she was fascinated by the gigantic, ancient stone structure before her. It towered upward, ascending in large tiers of some fine-grained, golden stone before disappearing back into the ice high overhead, and aside from the stone's color and the much larger size, it looked very much like similar structures she had seen on Mexico's Yucatan Peninsula.

Conversation with Echo, as they eased down the rest of the tunnel, had revealed that there had once been a fairly advanced civilization on Antarctica before it froze, and these structures were the last remains of it—restored and upgraded by Division One.

* * *

"...Though there are some interesting little quirks, apparently left over from the original builders," Echo told her. "Some are things nobody has figured out to this day."

"Such as?"

"Doors that seem to go nowhere, corridors with NO doors, shit like that. And there's supposed to be..."

"What?"

"A bottomless pit someplace in the complex, in what looks to be a ritual center, or an altar, or something. I'm not sure where, or in which structure, though I've seen maps..."

"Wow. How far down does it go?"

"No, Meg, I don't mean it's just really deep. I mean truly bottomless. According to some reports Fox showed me, they've even sent agents down there with antigrav boots on, and never found the bottom. It's...like a," Echo shrugged, "a 'desktop' black hole, only without the extreme gravity field. A singularity of some sort. The Division archaeologists speculated it was part of some sort of ritual sacrificial altar, based on the items found at its mouth."

"You're pullin' my leg."

"Nope. I can dig up the reports when we get back. Actually, they may be in the files packet Fox transmitted to our phones." He extracted his cell phone and leafed through the files. "Yeah. It's in the last of the background info on McMurdo Office. Third from the last file." He held up his phone to show her the display.

"Wow. Human or extraterrestrial?" she'd asked.

"Nobody knows for sure. If I had to bet, though, I'd say alien..."

* * *

Just before they exited the tunnel, they both pulled up their balaclavas and put on their special sunglasses, pulling their hoods down low, in an effort to obscure recognition if anyone was watching. Then they wandered across the relatively large open space, being as nonchalant as they could, chit-chatting for good measure.

Inside the 'front door' of the pyramid was a large atrium-style reception area; it was a long way from being as large as the Core, but it was a good-sized room, the size of a typical hotel lobby. Baker waited casually in a rectangular arch on the far side. A few other agents passed through, evidently on business of their own, but in another variant from the Core in Headquarters, no aliens were anywhere to be seen. As soon as Alpha One spotted Baker, they headed toward him—being careful to work around the perimeter, rather than walk through the center, where they would have presented a much more obvious target. Once they reached him, he turned toward a corridor.

"This way," he murmured, and they followed.

* * *

Moments later they were in a small room with three alien beings. Omega found herself scrutinizing them with interest, as Baker introduced the Alpha One team.

"Milords and lady, may I introduce the team sent from Earth Headquarters to assist us in our...dilemma," a tactful Baker announced. "This is Agent Echo, the premier field agent in Division One, and his newly-recruited partner, Agent Omega, whose background is impressive in its own right. They are the first team in a new department, the Alpha Line, our special missions unit." Baker stepped over to the first alien being; it appeared male and more or less humanoid, despite being only about half Omega's height, with an oversized, bulbous head, thick, stocky body, and nearly nonexistent neck.

"...And Agent Echo, Agent Omega, this is Lord Erutil, our liaison to the Caltorian envoy," Baker continued the introductions.

"The Caltorians are from a super-Earth in a Jovian-type system, Meg," Echo said to his partner. "Their bones are a couple times denser than ours, and they have large resonating chambers on the backs of their heads for speech."

"So they talk outta the backs of their heads?" Omega tucked her head to mutter.

"Yup." Echo responded in kind, then raised his voice and moved forward, bowing deeply. "We are honored to meet you, Lord Erutil." Omega, beside him, followed his lead, remaining quiet.

"Ah, you continue to train your partner, even now," Erutil noted with a smile, vibrating his excitement, as what passed for hair wavered in the breath of his voice.

"Yes, I am," Echo confirmed, standing upright once more. "I would like to request that, if possible, none of you become offended by any exchanges of information you may overhear. Omega is quite capable, but as she is new to the organization, she hasn't yet had the experience—or pleasure—of meeting your races, and I'm still in the process of familiarizing her. It's a good opportunity for training, and I hope you don't mind."

The three aliens glanced at each other as variants on a nod were exchanged between them.

"No offense is taken; we appreciate your thoroughness," Erutil declared. "The more she knows of us, the more effective she becomes at your side. I believe I speak for all three of us when I say that we will also forgive any diplomatic misstep she may commit by accident, and inform our...teams...of the same." A chorus of agreements met his statement. "I am pleased to meet you, Echo, Omega. I tremble with pleasure. Your people are like angels, so tall and slim."

Baker moved to the next entity; this one looked like nothing so much as a six-foot-long rat, or perhaps a mole. It seemed to alternate between a bipedal stance and quadripedal, with long slender limbs and a short, fat, mostly hairless body, which was loosely clad in a toga-like garment to cover its nakedness. The head was snouted like a rat, with large floppy ears similar to those of a rabbit or a lop; the hands only possessed four digits each.

"And this is Ecaracor, the kraduk of the Ulyffon Alliance," Baker noted. "Milady, Agents Echo and Omega."

* * *

"The honor is ours, kraduk," Omega offered, bowing deeply. As Echo also bowed, he shot her a sideways glance, raising his eyebrow, pleased. "From my studies, I gather you represent one of several different races in the Alliance?"

"I do," Ecaracor answered in a high-pitched, almost squeaky voice. "There are twice eight species in the Ulyffon Alliance, youngling; my people are Vandana. I am pleased with this installation; when you visit us, you will see it is very much like my home world. The Alliance welcomes your and your partner's help in this dangerous situation."

"We are glad to provide it," Omega responded with a smile. She glanced at Echo, who pressed his lips together to hide his own smile.

That was as smooth as Fox could have done, he thought, unsure whether to take pride in his training, or simply in the fact he had so astute a pupil. *Or maybe a little of both,* he added to himself.

* * *

The third entity, beside whom Baker now stood, was a seven-foot-tall avian with lurid red eyes; brightly-colored feathers not unlike a giant rainbow lorikeet; clawed, birdlike feet which were at that moment shod in insulating booties; a beaked mouth; and a large red crest on its blue head. Instead of wings, however, it had densely-feathered arms, and long, spindly fingers on slender hands. Omega noted that the feathers extended onto the backs of the hands up to the first interphalangeal knuckles, with tiny down feathers extending past that. Each finger ended with a sharp, almost claw-like nail.

"This is Throtlama kre Meorn," Baker said. "It is the chief advisor to Vice-President Zhaejoh kre Ranan."

"Our honor, Chief Advisor," Echo said, bowing a third time. Omega, beside him, mimicked the gesture. "Omega, kre Meorn is, like Zhaejoh, a

Ke!endarian. The Ke!endarians are known across the Pan-Galactic Council for fairness and impartiality, and are often negotiators between species, as a result."

"I can understand why," Omega responded, giving the giant bird-being her nicest smile. Throtlama clacked its beak in response. Then it fluttered its wing-arms in what appeared to be distress.

"Hold on, Throtlama," Baker said, searching his pockets. "I should have one here someplace. I try to keep one handy in case somebody forgets, or one goes on the fritz."

"What's up?" Omega wondered, voice soft, even as Baker came up with a small device.

"I think kre Meorn forgot its translator," Echo noted. "And the Ke!endarian language is a combination of what we would consider bird song and beak clacking. Only a few have learned any human languages because it's so hard for them to shape the sounds, and humans can't speak Ke!endarian at all. The names and words we use for them are just approximations of the real Ke!endarian language."

Just then, Baker managed to get his translator activated, and the clicks and trills Throtlama was making emerged as a voice from the device, speaking English. "Do call me Throtlama, both of you. Yes, I fear I am one of those who cannot, Agent Echo, though I understand you well enough. Forgive me for the oversight; I was so anxious to meet you that I left our compound without thinking of the translation device. Our mouths and voice boxes are very differently configured from yours, and while I have tried very hard, I have not yet achieved human speech. My good friend Zhaejoh has managed it, however. He is quite fluent in numerous languages."

"Does he know Fox, too?" Omega asked Echo in an undertone, but Throtlama answered.

"I do, but not nearly as well as Zhaejoh, for we have only met twice. Please give Fox my greetings when next you see him."

"You might see him yourself, soon," Echo said, then addressed the room. "Gentlebeings, can you confirm for us that there have been attempts upon the lives of any of you or your diplomatic teams?"

Heads bobbed all around. Baker compressed his lips and stood back, watching with bright eyes and a knowing expression.

"There is no doubt, Agent," Erudil noted. "The target seems to be the honorable kre Ranan, but one attempt at its assassination nearly took out three members of our staff. Another almost killed the entire Alliance staff, in addition."

"Agreed," shrilled Ecaracor. "There have been three attempts upon Vice-President kre Ranan of which I am aware, but Advisor Throtlama may know of more."

"No," the translator spoke for Throtlama. "There have been only three to date." Then the befeathered alien cocked its head. "Well...three that we have recognized. There WAS that bout of avian flu which swept our nest... in retrospect, perhaps it was more...serious."

Echo raised a considering eyebrow.

"Are you..." Omega broke off before glancing deferentially at Echo.

"Go ahead, Meg," he said softly. "You had an idea, there. I saw it in your eyes."

"It isn't gonna be very diplomatic," she murmured.

"Neither are at least three attempts on ambassadors' lives. We need to get to the bottom of this and put a stop to it. If you've got an idea, chase it."

"Well, are we sure that it isn't a faction of one of the NEGOTIATING parties, trying to stop the proceedings? And just using the cover of the Ke!endarian coup?"

There was a pause, as everyone glanced at everyone else, startled by the question. Finally Ecaracor spoke up in her squeaky little voice.

"Of course one can never be certain," she said, obviously thoughtful. "But our team stays in close contact with the Alliance Hub, and there has been no word of anything other than relief that a war may be avoided."

"Likewise," Erutil agreed. "We want war no more than the Alliance. And our people are unusually united behind the negotiations this time. Nor have we heard intelligence information that there is a schism in the Alliance."

"On the other hand, we all know the situation on Ke!enda!ar," Throtlama pointed out.

"Plus," Baker interjected, "I think we had an identification by an eyewitness."

"Oh really? Who got pegged?" Echo asked.

"Klu!vit, of the Ke!enda!ar House Molcren," Baker informed them. "Kre Ranan's personal chef recognized it from their mutual home town. It's a known member of the insurgency, along with most of its house, according to kre Ranan."

Echo and Omega gazed at each other for several minutes, then nodded at each other nearly simultaneously. Baker raised an impressed eyebrow as he watched the wordless interaction. Echo turned and addressed the room once more.

"In that case, Alpha One will proceed with our original plan," Echo declared. "Effective immediately, and for purposes of safety, negotiations are suspended. How many of you are in each party of diplomats?"

"A round dozen for the Caltorian embassage," Erutil noted.

"One and a half eights for the Alliance," Ecaracor said.

"And our intel shows that the Ke!endarians have seven beings in attendance, right?" Omega asked Throtlama.

"Correct," the translator said for Throtlama. Echo turned to Baker.

"I want two teams of four agents guarding the ambassadorial groups, one on the Caltorians and one on the Alliance," he told the younger agent. "You will be on one of those teams, reporting directly to Alpha One; choose from your own staff for the rest. Also designate someone in your stead to remain here at McMurdo. Evacuate the two embassages to the maglev, effective five minutes ago. Omega and I will round up the Ke!endarian staff and meet you there. Rendezvous in..." he glanced at his wrist chronometer, "not later than one hour. The maglev is programmed to depart in one hour and fifteen minutes, regardless of who's on board. Don't be late. Each team will report to me as soon as you're aboard. If there's a delay, I wanna hear about that, too."

"Roger that, sir."

"If something happens and we don't make it aboard, it is your personal responsibility to use the comm system on the maglev to contact Headquarters and tell Fox to send the backup maglev he and I arranged, ASAP. Got that?"

"Yes sir!"

"Get on the horn and then GO," Echo ordered. He turned to the aliens. "Lord Erutil, kraduk Ecaracor, go with him, please. Get your teams together—don't bother packing anything except essential life support. We can and will ship the rest to you later. The important thing is to get everyone out of here alive and in one piece."

As the three sentients left the room, Baker in the lead with weapon drawn, Echo threw a couple of gestures at Omega, and she nodded, pulling her own proto-cyclotron blaster at the same time her partner did. With her other hand, she took gentle hold of what passed for Throtlama's shoulder.

"Sir, uh, ma'am, milord, um..."

"Your Excellency," Echo tossed over his shoulder.

"Oh. Sorry. Your Excellency, please come with us."

Throtlama clacked and whistled.

"Yes, we'll make sure to grab the translator along the way," Omega reassured it.

* * *

Thirty minutes later they were in the Ke!endarian suite, several stories up in the pyramid, and Zhaejoh and its team scurried about grabbing translators and the essentials. Echo's cell rang. He pulled it from his pocket.

"Echo here."

"Echo, this is Baker. I have the Caltorian envoy and his staff aboard the maglev. We took them to the rear car; it appeared to be best outfitted for them."

"That's correct," Echo verified. "Stay there and wait for us. Remember—if we're not there by the time the maglev departs, contact Fox and tell him to send another immediately."

"Roger, sir!"

Omega touched his shoulder as he replaced the cell in his pocket. "We're ready, Ace."

"Let's go."

Echo took the point; Omega took the rear, and the nervous Ke!endarians crowded in between. They set out.

* * *

Twenty minutes later, Echo's cell rang again, as they crossed the pyramid's entrance atrium.

"All halt," he called.

"Can we not continue, friend Echo?" Zhaejoh asked.

"Afraid not, Your Excellency. I wanna be able to concentrate on what's around us, to make sure I spot and counter any threats we may run into. So either I answer the phone or we move forward; as ranking agent, I can't afford to miss something. And since the call is likely to be one of the other agents reporting in about whether the ambassadors made it to the maglev safely, I have to take it, in case they need backup or assistance." So the group stopped while he retrieved his phone and answered it. Omega kept a watchful eye out in all directions, as best she was able.

"Echo. Yeah, Able. Middle car. Yeah, we're on the way. Yeah, cutting it a little close. We should be there in time. Make sure Baker calls Fox immediately on the maglev comm if we don't." He deactivated the cell and returned it to his pocket, just as the nearby elevator dinged and disgorged...

...Agent Tango.

"Oh great," Omega groaned under her breath. "Just what we needed."

* * *

"THERE you are! How is it going?" Tango sang out cheerily across the open space...which, Echo noticed, was uncommonly open; there were now no agents passing to and fro. There was, in fact, no other sign of life. His hackles went up.

"We don't have time for this, Echo," Omega murmured as Tango drew near.

"YOU shut the hell up, rookie," Tango growled, scowling at the other woman. "You don't outrank me."

"She does right now; she's Alpha Line, on assignment," Echo corrected, and Tango's scowl deepened. "Why are you here, Tango?"

"Why, to escort you and our esteemed diplomats back to the maglev, Echo," Tango fairly lilted. The scowl disappeared, to be replaced with a coquettish smile. "I thought, what with only a rookie backing you up, you might want an agent with a little more...experience in the Division."

Omega rolled her eyes, and Echo simply gazed at the woman, with an expression on his face that Fox had been known to term his 'Yellowstone stare'—because, if the recipient continued in his or her current behavior, it heralded an event that was every bit as dangerous as that supervolcano's eruption...at least for the recipient.

"And you have a good bit of field experience?" Echo asked, voice crisp. Of all the agents in the facility, only Omega would be able to recognize the irony in his tone. Cutting a swift glance at his partner, he saw her tug her balaclava up nearly to her eyes, and nudge her chin into the collar of her parka, twinkling gaze dropping to the floor. *Yup. She caught it, all right.*

"Oh, yes! I've got nearly a decade in the field. I'd say that's plenty of field experience, wouldn't you? I was recruited when I was young," she added, obsequious.

"Where have you put in all this field experience?"

"Why, right here at the McMurdo field office, silly. I've been here eight years."

And I can just bet I know why, a scornful Echo thought. *A more cold-blooded...bitch...I've seldom encountered among humans. Thank God I don't have to work with her on a regular basis.*

"Before Pip retired, what department were you working in, and what were your assigned duties?" he wondered.

"Oh, I was an accountant in Supplies," Tango said, waving a dismissive hand.

Echo glanced at Omega, meeting her eyes. *You were right, Meg,* he thought. *Called that one like an expert. Which I guess you are, now especially.* Somewhat to his surprise, she nodded, pressing her lips together underneath the balaclava to hide a smile. *Damn. Does she read me like a book, or what?*

"Are you armed?" Echo pressed, returning his attention to Tango.

"Why, of course," Tango sang, patting under her left arm. "My blaster is right here."

Tell everyone including the terrorist's dog, why don't you, Echo considered, trying not to shake his head in disgust. *And show 'em right where you've got it into the bargain.*

"Backup weapon?" he barked.

"No need." She smirked. "I don't miss."

"When's the last time you were cert'ed on it?"

"Um...don't recall offhand," she murmured vaguely. "Couple years ago, maybe?"

"Last time you practiced?"

"Echo, time," Omega muttered, sounding impatient.

"I know, Meg. Hang on. Tango, answer the question."

"Uh, I don't remember off the top of my head. But it's like riding a bicycle, you know."

"How. Long?"

"Um. Six months?"

"Then you aren't carrying it," Echo said, holding out his hand. "Turn it over. Now."

"I don't think so." She smiled.

* * *

Abruptly Tango found herself staring down the muzzles of two proto-cyclotron blasters pointed at her chest—Echo's draw was smooth as silk, with a slight flourish, and Omega had drawn so fast the other woman hadn't even seen it. More, the rookie agent had simultaneously herded the small diplomatic contingent behind her, where they were shielded from Tango by a huge stone column...and Omega's own body.

"The man said," Omega growled, "Turn. It. Over."

"NOW," Echo appended. "Slowly pull it from your holster, and hand it to Omega."

Tango blinked.

Two blasters came up, unwavering, aimed at her head. She blinked again, then reached inside her Suit jacket and gingerly grasped her weapon, pulling it out slowly as Echo had instructed. It hung up partway; she wrestled with it for a moment before finally freeing it of the holster, mute testament to her lack of skill.

"Good. Hand it to Omega. If you try anything at all, I swear you will not have a head left to be brain-bleached."

Frightened and offended, Tango obeyed.

"You're gonna regret this," she castigated, as she relinquished her blaster to Omega's spare hand. "I'm reporting you to Fox!"

"We have Fox's full authority," Echo pointed out, his blaster never shifting an iota from Tango's face.

"To hell with Fox! I'll go over his head!" the woman shrilled. "The Pan-Galactic Council won't like hearing about two rogue agents threatening an Office chief!"

"ACTING Office chief," Omega muttered. "Emphasis on acting."

* * *

A sound emerged from behind Echo's balaclava that might have been, "Snrk." Simultaneously, cheeping from several avian throats came from the other side of the stone column.

"What are they saying?" Tango demanded. "What are the Ke!endarians saying?"

"Nothing," Echo noted. "They're not talking, they're laughing. Meg, did you wear that spare holster like I suggested?"

"Sure did, Ace." She slid Tango's blaster into the empty holster under her right shoulder. "There we go. I like the way these parkas give us holster access."

"Good. Consider that blaster yours, for now, and don't be afraid to use it. You now have two backup weapons; feel free to use whatever comes to hand first. Check her for additional weapons, then use a set of force cuffs and hook one of her wrists to that railing. She's right-handed, so cuff the right wrist. I'll call once we're well out of here and have one of her people come take her into custody for refusing a direct order from an Alpha Line agent."

"Meanwhile," Omega said, obeying orders, "we're gonna have to hoof it to reach the maglev in time."

"I know. Round up our feathered friends, and let's haul ass."

"We are here and ready, friend Echo," Zhaejoh declared. Then it chirped, "Make that tail feathers, and we shall haul them right behind your ass." Cheeping erupted again, and both Echo and Omega laughed as well. Tango merely scowled impotently.

"Tail feathers, then," Echo said, balaclava wrinkling slightly as he grinned beneath it.

And they set off at a run, across the atrium and out the door into the ice plaza, toward the tunnel that led to the maglev station, herding the Ke!endarians between them.

* * *

Inside the saucer, her body floated through the darkened cabin, over to a metal table and down onto it. The metal was cold, and the girl tried to shiver, but her body still wouldn't move.

What are you doing? *she asked.* Are you keeping me from moving?

I am, *came the same voice.* I have need of your...services. I believe you will be the perfect subject. Or one of them.

There's more people like me?

Not just like you. Which is why I have chosen you. You are rather unique, girl.

Who are you?

You have no need of that knowledge.

A dark hulk moved through the shadows. She jumped mentally, but her body still refused to move. An odd squelching sound reached her ears and she puzzled over it; it was like no sound she'd ever heard, and yet it somehow seemed familiar.

What's that? *she asked then, having gotten no answer to her previous query.* What's happening?

Hush, child. I have work to do, and your incessant babblings are distracting me.

But why? What are you going to do? Why am I on this table? Can I help?

You can help by being silent. *This time the voice sounded menacing.*

Abruptly several large hypodermic syringes with long needles shot into her fixed field of view, wielded by some half a dozen or more robotic remote arms. Before she could even formulate a thought, they jabbed deep into her torso in several places and disgorged their contents. Fire seared through her body, pain such as she had never before known. She tried to gasp, but even that reflex action was denied her.

* * *

Handcuffed to a brass rail in the apparently-empty atrium of her own building and left alone, Tango cursed under her breath. "It would be my right hand, too," she grumbled. "Damn the man. And the bitch. Especially the bitch." With an effort, she managed to reach her cell phone—in a right-hand pocket—with her left hand. She activated it, then clumsily managed to key in a special code and hold it to her ear. When the other end answered, she murmured into it.

"Clack, this is Number-cruncher. Yeah, I'm stuck in the entrance; force cuffs. No, it didn't work! Not at all! I thought they said he was unattached, and liked brunettes! YES! That's what I was told, dammit! I wasted all that time dying my hair and everything! Do you have any idea how hard it is to get HAIR DYE in this place?! Yeah, dishwater blonde. No, it's his partner; I couldn't pry 'em apart with a crowbar! Look out for that bitch. She's fast. Yeah, either he's got a heart of ice, or they're lovers, I couldn't tell which. But they're awful damn protective of each other, which kinda argues against the icy heart, so I figure they're lovers already. You can do that? Yeah! Let's keep him a while; maybe I can break down his defenses. If it comes to it, a couple rounds of brain bleach will take care of him. He'll make a nice, docile little pet when I'm done. No, I don't give a damn WHAT happens to HER, just make sure Tall, Dark, and Sexy is okay. Thanks, Klu; you're a pal!"

She deactivated the phone and slipped it into the left pocket of her Suit jacket, to wait for eventual rescue.

Chapter 6

As the group pounded and fluttered their way across the ice plaza, Omega found she was having a hard time keeping up. It wasn't that she was aerobically challenged by the sprint; she and Echo worked out hard enough in the gym that this was little more than a fun run. No, the problem was that she could no longer feel her feet, so it was becoming hard to tell when they were contacting the floor, or if there were any nonuniformities in that flooring. Worse, as her body heat escaped through her shoes and socks, it tended to melt a thin layer of the ice beneath her shoes, making the ice floor far slicker for her than it was for Echo. The fact that her shoes were much newer, and the soles much smoother, only added to the problem.

So she slipped, stumbled, and slid—but somehow never actually fell.

She was, however, starting to lag behind a bit.

"Meg, COME ON!" Echo urged from the front. "Get your ass in gear and keep up!"

"Coming!" she called, just as her partner led the way into the tunnel to the maglev station. She put on a burst of speed, hoping and praying she could maintain an upright stance, and caught up to the rear of the Ke!endarians moments later.

At least the parka and gloves are keeping my hands and body warmer, she thought. *But running like this, the hood won't stay up. Guess they figured the hood would protect my ears, 'cause the mask sure doesn't. I wish I'd left my hair long and not put it up in a braid today; it'd cover my ears, at least. They're freezing. Gotta keep going, though. No time to take it down and re-do it. The train will be warm. We'll be there soon. Hang on, gal. Just hang on. Not long now.*

They didn't slow down as they entered the tunnel; dealing with Tango had wasted precious time, and they now had less than eight minutes to cover the distance to the maglev station and get the negotiating team aboard.

"Aw shit!" Omega heard Echo exclaim from his position on point.

"ALL HALT! BACK UP, BACK UP, BACK UP! GET BACK!" And she watched in astonishment as he scrambled to backpedal on the ice, shoving the Ke!endarians unceremoniously behind him with outstretched arms.

"ECHO! What's wrong?!" Omega yelled forward...

...Just as a loud *BOOM!* sounded in the close space, and the roof of the tunnel caved in before them.

* * *

"Everybody okay?" Echo called, when the glittering ice crystals settled.

"Fine in the rear," Omega declared; she didn't consider it a complete lie, because the cave-in hadn't hurt anyone. The fact that she was starting to shiver a little, despite her physical exertion, was beside the point in the circumstances. "Y'all okay up there?"

"Fine," Echo said. "But that did it. We won't be making this train."

"Shit. Surely there's an alternate route?"

"Yeah," Echo agreed, checking his wrist chronometer, "but look at the time. We got four minutes before the tube train is IN MOTION, and this was the direct route. By my estimate, the quickest we can make it to the station now is about six minutes."

"Damn," Omega murmured. "Two minutes too late."

"Right." Echo pulled his cell phone. "Baker, this is Echo. We've been cut off by a deliberately-set cave-in, and a detour won't get us there in time. Yeah, I saw the device just in time to avoid it. No, nobody got hurt. We're just cut off. Use the comm in the maglev and contact Fox NOW; tell him everything that's happened, and get him to send that other tube train as fast as he can get it here. Omega and I'll keep the Ke!endarian negotiations team alive, and meet the second tube at the prearranged time. Good. Yeah, might as well go ahead. The first thing we gotta do here is figure out how to disappear. Yeah, your erstwhile leader may be part of this. Oh, really? That's interesting information. Yeah, tell Fox about that, too. The maglev is programmed to take you to a safe site that's so secret only Fox knows where you'll be. Yeah, get everyone strapped in, then go call, and brace yourself—the tube's gonna really haul ass on the way out. It's programmed for emergency speed evac." He deactivated the phone and returned it to his pocket, a deep frown etched on his chiseled features.

"What is wrong, Agent Echo?" Zhaejoh asked; it had a high, singsong voice, precisely what Omega would have expected from an intelligent bird speaking English, and she enjoyed listening to it.

"There's a good possibility that the woman who took charge of the McMurdo Office—the one we left cuffed in the lobby—is working with the terrorists, Zhaejoh," Echo explained, "whether knowingly or not, we're not sure yet. But regardless, the end result is the same." He looked around. "We gotta get this lot someplace out of sight until the next maglev arrives in a few hours. Meg, how closely did you study the layouts Baker sent us?"

"Pretty close, Ace; why?"

"Do you remember the secondary passages marked in yellow?"

"Um...yeah?"

"There should be one pretty near here, only through some ice. Help me locate it."

"Oohh-kaaaay. How we gonna— Oh, duh. I really gotta get used to a different way of thinking. Blasters. They must make nice emergency excavators, huh?"

"At least where ice is concerned. Gets a little trickier with rock and dirt..."

* * *

By the time they located where the secondary passage was in relation to the one they were in, the sweat Omega had broken in their all-out sprint—and which had soaked the layers of clothing next to her skin, to include her bra, panties, and shirt—had turned cold, and she was becoming badly chilled.

"Um, Echo?" she finally said, trying to keep her teeth from chattering.

"Mm?" He was busy studying the wall. He pulled out his proto-cyclotron blaster and started adjusting the settings as he did so.

"I, uh, I'm really gettin' pretty cold..."

"It's Antarctica. It gets cold. Move around a little more and you'll warm up."

"Um, well..."

"Hey, I'm gonna cut us a door here, so I need you to get Zhaejoh and its people and move 'em down the tunnel a little ways. It should be stable, but as old as this ice is, you never know. If there's a density change between seasonal layers, it could fracture."

"O-okay..."

Omega followed instructions and took the alien contingent about fifteen yards back, then stood in front of them, close enough to Echo to be able to aid him swiftly if needed, but out of range of any flying ice chunks that might dislodge. Echo fine-tuned the blaster to a tight beam, then aimed at the wall and calmly depressed the trigger. In seconds he had carved a large rectangle in the ice; the experienced agent widened the beam and began brushing it back and forth across the block, sending meltwater gushing across the floor...a matter which did not help Omega's poor frigid feet.

But moments later, they had a nice, neat passage into the side tunnel; the meltwater was already beginning to refreeze.

"Everybody through here," Echo ordered.

* * *

"Meg, take 'em down that way," Echo urged, gesturing left. "Take the point. I'll close this off behind us; that way, hopefully nobody will know where we went."

"Okay. W-where am I g-going?"

"This is one of the old tunnels, from before we built the maglev. It leads down below sea level, to...well, let's just say that, whatever it was originally, the Agency didn't build it. But we used it as a submarine docking facility for years. Just keep bearing right."

"Wilco."

"Now go. I'll catch up to the rear in a few."

Omega turned, made her way to the front of the group, and told the Ke!endarians, "Follow m-me."

She headed off at a steady trot, Zhaejoh's team right behind. Moments later, well behind them, came the sound of a large cave-in.

"Oh damn. All halt!" she cried, turning. "Echo?!"

No answer. She whipped out her cell phone, initiating a short-distance direct comm to her partner.

"Echo? You there?"

"Yeah, Meg, I'm here."

"You okay, Ace?"

"Fine."

"I heard a roof collapse. Need me to come back and dig through to you?"

"No. Zhaejoh and Company take priority over my welfare. I'm on your side anyway. Get moving, if you're not already."

"What happened?" Omega pressed, waving the Ke!endarians to follow her as she started back down the tunnel.

"I caved in our opening, to make it look like it was one job with the terrorist's collapse. Just gotta smooth out the wall here, and I'll catch up."

"Warn me next time, okay? I thought the perp got ya, for a second, there."

She heard a slight chuckle. It sounded grim...and just possibly annoyed.

"I did, but evidently not with enough detail to suit you. Now GO."

Omega deactivated her phone, shoving it in a pocket with some annoyance of her own, as she ordered, "Move out at speed," then followed her own orders, breaking into a long-distance trot. The Ke!endarian negotiations team fluttered close on her heels.

* * *

Two right turns later, Omega discovered Echo at her side.

"Why aren't you moving faster?" he wondered. "I expected you to have 'em two corridors down by now."

"I'm having some trouble with my shoes on this ice," Omega confessed. "I'm sliding all over. I can't take a full stride, else I'll either fall down or pull something. And it's not helping that the floor is slanting down." She didn't admit that part of the problem was because her feet had no feeling in them at all any more, to at least ankle level.

"Mm. Probably your shoes are still too new. Slick soles. Damn. We shoulda grabbed some PolarKlawz for you."

"What are those?"

"Stretch things that go over your shoes, with metal cleats to grab the ice."

"Oh. Yeah, that woulda been good. Oh well. 20/20 hindsight. And damn, my feet are cold," she finally dared. "Which isn't helping the slipping shit at all."

"It's Antarctica. It's cold. Here. Lemme take the point. You drop back and guard the rear, and keep up the best you can without falling down. Try to stay close enough not to get separated, if you can, because if you get captured I can't come rescue you until the Ke!endarians are safe. So we can't afford to get split up."

* * *

Half an hour later, they entered a huge domed structure that appeared to have been carved from the same golden, fine-grained stone of which the pyramid was made; extending all the way to the far wall was a large body of water—salty ocean water, by the tang in the air. Several quays, evenly spaced, extended out some thirty yards or more into the water, which splashed and lapped softly at the rock.

Given the floor, walls, and roof of the giant room were one unbroken expanse of stone with no seams visible, Omega concluded that the steep slope of the tunnel flooring, combined with the fact that they'd taken no less than fifteen complete right-hand turns, served in lieu of a staircase, which made sense if equipment and cargo had once moved back and forth. *Which it would almost have to,* she thought, *or it negates the whole point of having a sub dock. But I think we're still a considerable distance under the level of the maglev station—and that was already way underground.*

So Omega adjudged they were now well below ground—and sea-level, for that matter. *And way, WAY the hell under the ice surface,* she concluded, running one gloved hand over the unpolished but smooth stone surface. *Hm. Pretty rock. Probably a rhyolite of some sort, given where we are.* The chill of the frigid surface came to her fingers even through the sophisticated insulation of her Division-One-issue gloves. *And damn cold! Brr.*

"Meg!" Echo called. "You take the right half of the complex, I'll get the left. Look for any signs the terrorist has been here."

"What about the Ke!endarians?"

"The place isn't THAT big, and it's pretty open. They'll stand here in the middle, where we can both see 'em while we're scoping things out. Back in the center in ten."

"Roger that."

She moved to the right and began a careful scrutiny of the submarine dock.

* * *

Minutes later they met back in the center.

"Nuthin'," Omega declared.

"We're clear then, because nobody has been in here in decades, according to what I'm seeing," Echo determined, then turned to the group of aliens. "Your Excellency, you and your contingent may now find comfortable locations and rest. Yes, your bodyguards may verify our assessment of the area. We have about three and a half hours before another maglev train arrives."

"Very good, friend Echo," Zhaejoh agreed. "We shall do as you suggest."

The avians spread out across the area, the two bodyguards scoping out the room for themselves while the rest busied themselves finding places to roost reasonably comfortably. Echo and Omega moved to one side.

"We got-t over three hours, th-then?" Omega verified. She was shivering more frequently now; it was causing her teeth to chatter, and she had hard work to cover up the fact.

"Yep. I didn't figure this would go down easy. So I made sure Fox arranged backup transport in advance, and had it waiting in the nearest side tunnel—which, unfortunately, is still a good distance away."

"Have we got a quick way to get t-to the t-tube station from here?"

"Yeah. Study your facilities map and you can probably figure it out on your own, pretty quick. If I have to, I can send it in a ciphered message. Rather not show you openly, in case somebody's watching. I doubt it, but you never know. Especially if Tango is involved."

"Okay. Is there s-someplace I can go and get warm while I do it?"

Echo's eyes narrowed and he stared at her in palpable irritation.

"What about 'This is Antarctica' don't you get, Meg? We're under an

140

ice cap. We raise the temperature, the ice melts. The ice melts, the facility floods AND gets exposed. I'm sorry this isn't a nice sunny tropical vacation for you, but that's the way this works! We don't get to pick and choose our missions. It might help if you'd keep the hood of your coat pulled up; I'd have thought you knew already that most body heat escapes through the head. Now suck it up, quit complaining, and go study that facility map!"

He spun on his heel and went to check on Zhaejoh, leaving a shivering Omega to stare after him in aggravated dismay.

* * *

After tugging her parka hood over her head, Omega managed to find an alcove with a bench where she could sit down and get her cold feet off the frosty floor, but it didn't seem to help much; her feet remained too cold to feel anything. It was not unlike, she decided, trying to walk with both feet in the clunky old-style plaster casts, but with no crutches to help stabilize.

Worse, the longer she sat still, the colder she got all over—and the stone of the bench was as cold as the rest of the place, which was odd in itself. Since they were so far underground, Omega fully expected the place to be more like a cave, and have a moderated 'underground' temperature, like the maglev tube. *But,* she considered, *that also connects to warmer climes, so maybe the fact that THIS room only connects to ice tunnels has something to do with it. And it's way the hell down, so all the cold air drains down here.* Fortunately the parka she'd been issued was long enough that she could halfway sit on its tails, else she would have had a much more serious problem; but it still made for a chilly seat.

So periodically she got up and paced, while studying the plans of the facility. She had long since worked out the most direct route from the submarine dock to the maglev station, as well as several backup routes; now she was trying to determine the most likely hiding places for the terrorist.

She spotted something.

"Hey, Echo," she said, wandering over to where he stood, alert and ready. *He's standing guard,* she realized as she pulled down her balaclava to talk easier, *and giving me a chance to rest and warm up, even if he did tell me to suck it up. He wants me to be tough, but realizes that I've never experienced this kind of cold before and need to get adapted. Which I*

141

maybe could, if I actually had socks thicker than a millimeter, and a heavier wool Suit, instead of this wool and linen summer blend. DAMN, I'm cold!

"Yeah, Meg? I've seen you studying the map and pacing periodically. You've either got a question, or an idea. Which is it?"

"Both, actually."

"Shoot."

"Bang."

He just stared at her, blinking, and she offered a rueful grin. He didn't return it.

"Never mind," she murmured, feeling discouraged; she had thought she had a good rapport with Echo during her training, but was beginning to consider the possibility that they might not mesh well during a mission. She dropped her gaze so he wouldn't see her disheartened state, and thereby missed the mischievous twinkle that finally appeared in the brown eyes at her joke and his deliberately-deadpan response. "I gather..." she broke off, glancing back down at the map on her phone's display to verify her deductions, not wanting to say something stupid and risk annoying him again. "Okay. I gather that there are...I'm not sure how to put this...multiple 'time levels' to this office complex, probably relating to different stages of building...right?"

"Yeah, I get what you're saying, and you're right. The oldest layer, of course, is the neo-pre-proto-archaic Maya...whatever." He waved a hand at the giant room around them. "It's way the hell old, like I've told you—the Maya themselves went back at least four millennia before the present day, and this is at least a couple thousand years older than THAT. Given that, as best anyone can tell, these pyramids were built when Antarctica had a temperate to subtropical climate, and it iced over around fifteen million years ago, you do the math."

"Damn."

"Then there's different stages of modern building by the Agency, which you can sorta tell apart by the levels of sophistication of construction; we didn't start out with a lot of fancy galactic tech."

"Mm. Okay." She continued to study the map. "I can see that."

"You got the route to the maglev station figured?"

"Yeah, and three backup routes, just in case."

"Three?! Damn, Meg, not bad. I bet we picked the same three backups, too."

"Probably. You taught me, after all."

"True. So you've asked your question, and you've passed my pop quiz. What's your idea?"

"Look here." Omega held up her screen for him to see, then pulled off a glove and tapped a location with only her fingernail, ensuring he could see the place she referenced without throwing off the reactive screen.

"Ooo, yeah, nice snag. Have you been practicing our covert codes?"

"Yeah. Go into 'em?"

He nodded and tugged down his balaclava so she could read his face, as she deactivated and shoved the phone in a pocket and hurriedly replaced her glove over a now-reddened hand.

Tell me what you think, he told her, *using those same covert codes.*

I'm thinking that might be where our baddie is hiding, or one place, at least, she communicated. *Unfortunately, it's between us and the maglev. And it's not that far from here, which ain't good.*

No, it isn't. Any of it. More, chances are, he has an inside ally.

Tango?

Yep. She knew well in advance that I was coming, according to Baker— like, weeks before—but NOT that YOU were coming with me. Which goes along with your hypothesis that she was wangling to get me down here...to suck up and seduce, I guess. Pardon me while I throw up at the idea. And cross my legs into the bargain.

Can't blame you there. Do they make chastity belts for men?

Echo snorted.

Yeah, I dunno. But there's more. I contacted King, who is still in the facility with the rest of the Office's staff, to go fetch Tango from the lobby and put her in stir...only she was already gone when he got there. Now, because of the potentially dangerous conditions down here, all of the agents have locators in their chronometers, so at any given time, Security can find them if somebody gets in a bad way, maybe lost outside on the icepack or something. So not only could King verify that no agents came through the atrium after we left it…Tango has disabled her locator. She's gone. Nobody knows where she is.

Well, shit. Omega shook her head in disgust.

Exactly.

Do they have any ideas as to where the terrorist is holed up?

Not a damn clue. Unlike someone I could name. That was good strategic analysis, there, baby.

Thanks. Listen, Echo, I was thinking…as close as that possible hideout is to us here…and given how the bomb nearly caved the roof in on all of us…

Wait. You knew it was a bomb, from the back of the pack?

Kinda hard to miss, Ace. Ice goes "crack-pow." Bomb goes "boom." The first roof collapse went boom. YOUR roof collapse went crack-pow.

Echo raised an impressed eyebrow at her logic and observation.

Good job. Okay. You're thinking we should take the fight to it, while the Vice-President and its contingent are safe, and we have some time to kill?

Well, one of us, anyway. I was sorta figuring… She drew a deep breath, and plunged in. *Look, Echo. You're top dog in the Agency, at least where field agents are concerned. I've seen the chain of command, and I know that you're probably next in line to be Director if something happens to Fox. Me, I'm just a rookie. If we time things right, I can probably keep it busy while you get Zhaejoh and its people to the maglev…*

While what happens to you, exactly?

Does it matter?

Damn straight it does. Aside from the time and effort I put in training you, you're my PARTNER, Meg. That isn't how this shit works. If we didn't CARE whether or not our agents came back, we'd send 'em out individually. Now, I'm all for taking the fight to the perp, but we'll set up a protective perimeter here for the Ke!endarians, and BOTH of us will go, or neither of us will. Is that understood?

Yes sir.

Right now I'd rather hear, "Yes, Ace."

Yes, Ace. She threw him a half-smile, and he returned it in kind. *When do we leave?*

In a minute. Round up all the Ke!endarians, over there next to the big column. We got a perimeter to set. He reached into a pocket—Omega was never sure where he got all those pockets—and pulled out a silver device.

* * *

Moments later, the Ke!endarians were clustered around a small silver hemisphere that Echo had placed on the floor, some ten feet from the column he'd pointed out.

"Okay, everybody crouch down and keep your hands and arms pulled in; it's gonna be a little tight," he commanded, taking several steps back. "Meg, come get behind me; you're too close right now, and I don't want you caught in it when it activates."

When she obeyed, he aimed a small remote at the hemisphere and depressed a button.

A force dome materialized around the alien contingent, glowing a soft, pale yellow.

"Perimeter set," Echo declared. "Y'all wait here, where you're safe; Omega and I will be back shortly. Meg, c'mon and let's go tie up a loose end."

* * *

When he was certain they were out of eye- and earshot of the Ke!endarians, just inside the corridor opening and around a corner, Echo ran a quick scan for bugs and other electronics, then turned to his partner.

"You worried we'll get overheard?" she wondered.

"Yeah."

"Just use our codes."

"No, I wanna make sure there's no possible mistakes about what I'm gonna tell you."

"Sounds serious."

"It is. Just in case something happens to me," he murmured to Omega, who frowned in obvious concern, "here are my emergency instructions for you: You are to return to the sub dock, get the Ke!endarians to the maglev using whatever means necessary, and once aboard, activate security code Alpha One Red Priority Max-1. Then enter departure code, 'Godspeed, John Glenn.' Three separate words."

Omega desperately stifled a sudden snort of unexpected mirth, clapping one gloved hand across her masked nose and mouth.

"I take it, you approve of my choice," Echo said, raising an amused eyebrow. "You oughta; it was chosen in your honor. First full-up mission and all."

"Yeah, I do, and thanks. I'm not likely to forget it, either."

"Good. All right, lemme finish those instructions. The second maglev isn't programmed like the first; it won't leave until one member of Alpha One gives it a voice print AND a retinal scan, THEN enters that code into the onboard computer. So DON'T forget it."

"I won't. I couldn't if I tried." Her eyes twinkled. Echo noted the fact with some satisfaction, but pretended to ignore it.

"You still got Tango's blaster?"

"In the spare holster you instructed me to wear this morning...which seems like a week ago already."

"Yeah, it does, and that's typical of a mission like this. I swear, I spent a month on Io one day..." Omega opened her mouth, and he knew she was about to ask about the Io mission. They didn't have time for it, so Echo made a mental note to tell her later, then cut off her attempt. "Okay, so far, so good. From this moment until we get back to Headquarters and report to Fox, you are officially authorized to use both weapons as needed, your discretion. We've trained on it enough that you oughta have it down. If you do well with it, I'll enter permanent authorization for you to carry tandem plus backup on your own cognizance, AND we can then discuss modifying your weapons to run 'hot,' like mine. Just be careful not to shoot your partner in the process."

"Not gonna shoot you, Ace. I'd never do that." Omega's face assumed a configuration that was somewhere between a scowl and a pout, readable even through the balaclava. He grinned, then reached into the hood of her parka and ruffled her hair with affection.

"I know. That was supposed to be a joke. I thought I'd try to lighten the mood between us a little. I know this mission is rough on you, not being used to the cold and all. I guess you HAVE lived all your life in southern climates. But I really need you to grit your teeth and tough it out with me, if you can. This mission is a lot more like what you can expect as an Alpha Line agent than any of the stuff we've done before. It's gonna be tough, dirty, dangerous work. Just like this. If you can't—or don't want to—handle it, I need to know, and know soon."

Omega stared at him with an expression that was hard for even the experienced agent to read, especially given the fact that the lower half of her face was covered. He finally concluded that it was blank surprise.

"...If I said I couldn't, or wouldn't, what would happen?" she asked then.

Echo felt a lump of lead form in the pit of his stomach.

"Then I'd get with Fox about it, and we'd transfer you someplace you were more suited. Maybe one of the scientific departments. And I'd be looking out for another rookie to train as a partner."

"Well, hell with that," she declared, to Echo's intense gratification. "C'mon, PARTNER, we got a perp to...um."

"'Um' what?"

"Are we supposed to catch him, or uh, take him out? Oh! It, I mean, not him."

"It's okay. You'll get used to the pronoun conundrum eventually. And this one's simple, compared to some of the gender combos you'll encounter."

"Huh?"

"The Xemlon have FOUR genders," Echo explained patiently, "all of which are required to reproduce." Then he watched with a grin hidden under his mask as her eyes grew wide, then her brows drew together and her forehead wrinkled, as she tried to figure out how THAT all worked. She opened her mouth, and he knew she was about to ask something he didn't particularly want to have to answer, so he diverted her train of thought again, back to the original conversation. "I'll overlook your choices of pronoun, as long as it's only us, 'cause I know you're still learning; just try not to let one of the Ke!endarians hear you again," Echo said, turning to ease farther into the ice corridor.

"Again?"

"Yeah. You called Throtlama 'he' back when we first met it, though

I don't think you realized you did it. Fortunately, we'd just got done explaining you're a rookie, and it ignored your gaffe. So they're aware of your learning status now, and will overlook most errors, but that might be more than the rest of 'em are willing to overlook. As for your question: that depends on what this Klu!vit kre Molcren does. We're basically cops, but we're closer to being like a SWAT team...or those Texas Rangers we were talking about on the ride down...than your average beat cop. Or maybe like a secret agent. You know, 'license to kill'? Still and all, we're not executioners, Meg. A peaceful resolution is always preferable to a shootout. But it isn't always possible."

"Have you had to kill somebody?"

"You should know that from your studies."

"I do. That was sorta an invitation to talk about your missions. I'm still curious about Io."

"Not now. Maybe later, when we have the leisure. For now, let's focus on the mission." He turned right, out of the main corridor into the tunnel Omega had noted—and which lay between the submarine dock and the maglev station, along the main route. "Okay, here we go. Weapon—or weapons—out. Standard leapfrog procedure, kiddo."

"Right behind you, and ready. I got our six."

"Good. Stay close, and stay alert."

* * *

The tunnel they now followed, which Omega had scoped out on her cell phone, was dimly lit and poorly maintained, if it was maintained at all; it appeared to have been largely forgotten by the Agency, being merely a legacy of bygone days, when it had been used as a corridor to a storage warehouse. Its walls were irregular, the floor rough; odd curves and abrupt shifts in direction denoted overall movement of the flowing ice cap. Gigantic icicles reached down from the ceiling in places, connecting to the floor in some instances, and the overall effect was more like that of a limestone cavern than an ice tunnel—except for the cold, which was still taking its toll on Omega. They took their time working their way through; they didn't have far to go, and still had nearly a full three hours before the second maglev arrived, so they chose caution over speed.

Whenever they had to change their relative positions in the tunnel, they leapfrogged, the one in the lead providing cover as the one in the rear swiftly crossed the passage to assume the point. The transitions were smooth, having been honed in repeated practice sessions through the obstacle course, the Training department varying its configuration each time through. They stayed low and behind cover as much as they could, as they progressed down the agéd ice corridor, which the map showed dead-ended in the old, unused storage room up ahead.

* * *

When they neared said storage room, Echo held out a staying hand, and Omega stopped, moving close at his gesture. They crouched behind a thick row of ice stalagmites. He tugged down the fabric swathing his face and began another unspoken, coded communication, as she followed suit.

You stay here, he told her. *Cover me while I scope this out. If ANYTHING happens to me, you head back to the dock, deactivate the force field, and immediately take the Ke!endarians TO THE MAGLEV STATION to wait. As fast as you can.* He handed her the remote to the force field; she tucked it into a pocket.

What about you?

I already told you. The mission takes precedence. If Fox sent anyone down on the maglev to meet us, you can put the Ke!endarians aboard, then come back to look for me, if you want to. Otherwise, you go with them, and notify Fox of what went down.

But Ace—

No buts. You WILL do what I say, Omega. Just trust me. I'm tough. I've been pretty easygoing with you, so you haven't seen what I'm really capable of, not yet. But there's a reason I'm one of what's sometimes termed The Originals...most of whom are no longer with us, one way and another. But I am. Which should tell you a lot about me. Now, he met her eyes with a stern, hard gaze, *are you gonna follow orders?*

Yes sir. Her shoulders slumped and her brows drew together.

Yes what? He let the corner of his mouth quirk. When he saw her grin in spite of herself, he relaxed.

Yes, Ace, came the familiar, affectionate response, as she squared

149

her shoulders in obvious determination. It hit him then that she truly was fond of him, and her apparent near-insubordination was only because she was honestly worried about him. The squared shoulders told him she had decided not to LET anything happen to him, so as to render his emergency orders moot.

He abruptly remembered the time she had once referenced him, Romeo, and India as her new family; at the time, he hadn't been sure what to make of it, and had wondered if it indicated she was too soft for this line of work. He now decided that this was probably a good thing in general, and he could live with it.

Mama Bear, he suddenly thought. *Meg is a mama bear. And mama bears don't take shit when their family is threatened. And I'm family now.* He almost laughed aloud. *I pity the perp that tries to take me out, if she's around. 'Cause she will be pissed.* Echo allowed himself to feel that 'warm fuzzy' for a moment before getting serious again.

All right. Weapons ready? he asked in code.

For answer, she pulled out both blasters. He pulled his own.

Cover me.

He stood and moved forward.

* * *

As Echo entered the abandoned storage room, he stopped long enough to examine and finger an old, corroded plaque beside its entryway, nodding to himself before stepping through. Once inside, he glanced around, carefully surveying the area. It was an ice cavern, not in any better shape than the tunnel had been; more, it still had old crates and boxes stacked about, here and there. Consequently, it had plenty of places for someone to hide.

I'm gonna have to play it right, or mama bear Meg will end up having reason to worry, not to mention one fewer 'family member,' he considered briefly, before returning his concentration to a scrutiny of the room. Instinct kicked in suddenly, and he ducked—

—Just as a high-intensity particle beam shot through the space where his head had been.

* * *

He stayed low and dove toward the nearest cover, which happened to be a stack of decrepit wooden crates, rolling behind them and coming up in a crouch; he intended to ascertain where his quarry was before doing anything else. Just then, a blaster shot came from the corridor he'd exited moments before, knocking a big hole in another crate along the far wall.

Meg saw her chance, and took a shot, he determined, just before spotting movement behind her targeted crate. *Aha, there you are, you feathered little bastard. Wow, you've bleached your feathers into shades of gray and brown, for camo! Thanks for pointing it out, Meg.* He decided he'd imagined hearing her say, *"You're welcome,"* in his head. He grinned to himself. *It's what she'd say.*

* * *

Omega spotted the Ke!endarian rebel—oddly drab of plumage, compared to the other Ke!endarians she'd met, who were all brightly-colored—as it emerged from cover to take a shot, and saw Echo dodge that same shot.

DAMN! she thought, aghast. *That was close!*

She promptly brought around her right blaster, took swift aim, and fired.

Shit. I missed. But not by much. With any luck, Echo saw where I was aiming.

Just then, she could have sworn she heard Echo's voice in her head, saying, *"Thanks, Meg."*

You're welcome, she thought before she caught herself, and chuckled noiselessly. *Well, he is.*

But to her surprise, kre Molcren now abandoned its hiding place, slipping from cover to cover, always keeping something between it and the last place Echo had been seen.

Wow. He's headed MY way, Omega observed. *It, I mean. I wonder if it thinks it killed Echo. I...wonder if it DID kill Echo. Nah. That was a clear miss. I heard the blast hit the wall, off to the left. So what the hell DOES it think...? Tango. Shit. I get it now. They ARE working together, and it intends to capture Echo...and kill me. Or just kill us both, then kill the Vice-President, and to hell with Tango. Well, not if I can help it.*

151

She glanced around. *Damn. Where kre Molcren is now, I can't sneak back through the tunnel to get to the Vice-President. There's just not enough cover. It'll see me, and pop off a shot in my back. Then Echo'll have to train a new partner all over again.*

But where IS Echo? she wondered. *Does he see what's happening? As much junk as there is in there, maybe he hasn't realized it yet. I better be ready for anything.*

Grim of face, Omega crouched farther back into her hidey-hole, and readied both blasters.

* * *

Echo slipped cautiously, silently, from crate to ice stalagmite to columnar ice flow and back to crate, flanking his quarry. The tunnel where Omega crouched remained silent, and he knew those bright blue eagle eyes were watching.

She gave away that I'm not alone, he thought, *but our perp probably figured that anyway—and she knows that. AND she showed me exactly where it was. My rookie has some serious strategic street smarts. I wouldn't have credited her with that. About every OTHER kind of smarts, but not that. That's...really good.*

Even as Echo moved, he noted that kre Molcren was moving, as well...toward the tunnel in which Omega hid.

Now why would it be doing...Tango. It IS working with her! In exchange for access to the Vice-President, it kills Meg and delivers me. Shit. He paused, planning swiftly. *Well, that ain't happenin' anytime soon. Any of it.*

As silent as any ninja, Echo continued to flank kre Molcren, coming in behind it. Since it kept throwing glances at where Echo had been, and always maintained cover between that location and itself, Echo concluded that it believed him injured.

This might just work, then, he decided.

* * *

Echo moved in behind kre Molcren, angling himself carefully so that any stray shots wouldn't hit Omega where she crouched down the corridor, or equally bad, collapse the corridor around her ears. Then he holstered his blaster, jerked down his face mask, stood, and stepped from behind a large crate, giving a loud whistle followed by a tongue clack—the closest humans could come to a Ke!endarian, "Hey you!" and Echo's rendition was particularly skilled—then waited.

Kre Molcren spun in surprise, and its beak gaped as it saw the experienced male agent, hale and hearty.

"What?!" kre Molcren exclaimed in clear English. "You should be injured and nursing your wounds in the corner!"

"You're not as good a shot as you think you are, and I'm faster," Echo noted, calm. He was deliberately baiting the Ke!endarian to draw its attention away from his partner, and hoping—expecting—Omega to be watching, waiting for an opportunity.

* * *

Omega WAS watching, most intently. She was also shocked; she had seen Echo deliberately holster his weapon as he stepped from cover.

Are you TRYING to get killed, Ace?! she wondered in horror. You must be expecting ME to do something, but what? I can't shoot him—it—in the back, not when it hasn't drawn down on you...that's against regs...though if it so much as waves its weapon in your direction, with you unarmed, I'm probably gonna say to hell with regs.

* * *

"It matters not," the terrorist decided, bringing its weapon around. "I have you now. At this range, I cannot miss."

"Maybe," Echo said, "and maybe not." Abruptly his hands blurred, and suddenly both were filled with proto-cyclotron blasters—a dual wield, both aimed at kre Molcren.

Kre Molcren squawked in horrified surprise, and fired instinctively.

* * *

Omega, who had aimed one blaster at kre Molcren's back just in case, had all she could do not to gasp and cry out as Echo drew his weapons.

Holy shit! she thought, startled. One nanosecond his hands are empty, the next, he's wielding dual! No wonder he didn't seem worried! AHH! she added, gut clenching as kre Molcren fired.

* * *

Echo didn't even flinch. The Ke!endarian's shot went wild, as the experienced agent knew it would; behind him and to the left, a rotting wooden crate gave its life to the cause. Echo lowered his weapons slightly, scanning the alien rapidly.

The weapon kre Molcren was using was a standard proto-cyclotron blaster, intended for human use; Echo had been debating whether kre Molcren stole it, or if a certain suspected accomplice had provided it. In any event, it was not well-suited to Ke!endarian hands, which possessed long, webbed fingers studded with pinfeathers near the knuckles. Echo had noted several of these appeared broken and stained a dark golden brown with blood. Echo made his decision: He lowered his blasters.

"I'm offering you a chance to give up peacefully, kre Molcren," he said, his voice carrying clearly, even down the corridor to his partner... which was his intent. "Put your blaster down and surrender, and you won't be harmed. Resist, and I won't be responsible for what happens next."

Fully expecting Omega to be watching the whole thing, and facing her, he sent her a coded message without ever taking his eyes off kre Molcren.

Maneuver Alpha-One-23 Left, Omega. Be ready for my signal.

He stood, calm, cool, and composed, but at the ready.

* * *

Omega saw the message from Echo, and eased down below the row of ice stalagmites, bringing her personally-assigned blaster to bear on kre Molcren.

And waited.

* * *

"NEVER! We are H!nar kre Naese!en!Re! We are the House of the Gods' Wrath! The Old Ones will return! Ke!enda!ar shall be cleansed! We shall triumph!" kre Molcren cried, and brought its blaster around again.

Gotta time this just right, and hope my memory of twelve years ago is correct, Echo thought. He leaped into action as kre Molcren shot, bringing up his dual wield and firing both weapons even as he ran to one side, out of the Ke!endarian's line of fire, vaulting over a crate.

One precision shot took out the barrel of kre Molcren's blaster, causing the weapon to explode in its hand; kre Molcren screamed, a high, shrill sound, as several fingers disappeared and abruptly-truncated pinfeathers bled profusely. The other meticulous shot nicked kre Molcren's thigh, and it stumbled. The next half-dozen shots were intended to miss, but closely enough to unnerve his opponent and throw the avian farther off-kilter. Echo's intent succeeded; several more decomposing crates died on the far side of the warehouse, what was left of their contents bleeding onto the icy floor.

As kre Molcren scrabbled to recover, Echo spun, leaped onto the nearest crate, and fired both guns at the back wall, even as he allowed his momentum to carry him over the crate to the next one, several feet away.

A large figure-eight-shaped hole appeared in the ice, and the wall began to crumble, exposing a small room or alcove composed of the same golden stone as the rest of the proto-Maya structures. A kind of open altar stood there, a carved golden sun disk featured in the center, flanked by bas relief carvings of what appeared to be Kukulkan—Maya god of war—and Cum Hau—god of death. Gold-inlaid inscriptions wreathed the sun disk, and shadows crowded close about its base, which appeared to be a cylinder of dressed stones, some two layers high.

At sight of the altar, the feathered serpent Kukulkan beside it, kre Molcren shrieked again, in righteous triumph this time, as Echo deliberately bounced off a taller crate, leaped down and ran in front of kre Molcren.

"TULSSAS APPEARS!" it screamed. "The old gods return! Praise be to Tulssas! I am justified! I shall defeat these infidel enemies of the true gods!"

The Ke!endarian rebel lunged toward Echo, stumbling forward on the hamstrung leg to grapple with the agent, clutching at Echo's throat, attempting to throttle him, though somewhat hindered by the missing fingers. Its claws, however, presented some danger of puncturing jugulars and carotids, which was apparently part of its intent; but Echo was a skilled enough combatant to prevent it, at least for a time. The taller alien overbalanced, and despite being much lighter in weight, Echo went down on his back beneath it, dropping both blasters to grab kre Molcren's shoulders and hold the murderous being away from him.

"NOW, MEG!" he yelled, just as he kipped with all the strength of his powerful legs, flipping kre Molcren up and over his head. Kre Molcren went flying through the air toward the altar—

—As a blaster beam lanced out, swinging like a scythe. Two booted, birdlike feet fell to the icy floor with a mushy thud, severed from their owner. Kre Molcren screeched in excruciating pain as it left two pulsing streams of dark yellow blood behind it. The blaster arc changed, and a pinfeathered hand joined the feet; a third arc of blood joined the first two—

—While kre Molcren hurtled forward, shrieking in agony. Looking down, it added an additional scream of fear into the mix. It bounced off the sun disk, desperately and ultimately futilely grabbing for it with the remaining, maimed hand, scrabbling frantically—

—And plummeted into the yawning black pit at its base, still screaming.

* * *

Echo picked himself up off the icy floor as Omega came running, vaulting over several obstacles at full speed and nearly sliding down twice. He retrieved one blaster and returned it to its proper holster as she grabbed his arm.

"Are you okay?" she fired off without preamble.

"I'm fine," he said, cocking an eyebrow at her. "Fetch my other blaster, would you?"

She turned and picked it up off the floor, having to tug on it a bit; the residual heat from its firing had melted a small puddle of water underneath, which was now freezing back. The gun finally popped loose, and she held it up, checking it for damage.

"Aw, shit," Echo grumbled, seeing what she was doing. "I'm gonna have to strip it and clean it when we get home. Here. Gimme."

"Looks okay, Ace."

"Yeah, and these things work pretty much regardless of conditions— unless you remove some vital parts, like what I did to kre Molcren's—but I'll still probably want to dry out its guts as soon as I can."

Omega handed it to him, and he shoved it in the other shoulder holster, then turned toward the altar. Omega followed, staring at him in what he decided must be astonishment. He was puzzled by her reaction...until he heard her next words.

"You...you know gun fu."

"Yep." He shrugged.

"I...didn't think that was possible. Not in real life. What you did, I mean. Dual-wield firing while running, vaulting, jumping...it looked like a movie special effect. But...you were DOING it. For real."

"Lotta things in Division One that people think are impossible. Toldja that you hadn't seen me in full action yet. Now you have." He gingerly leaned through the opening into the altar room. "Combine the right tech, way the hell more practice than most people would even consider, and plenty of field experience, and there's not much we can't accomplish. Stay back, Meg."

"From what?"

"Listen." He pointed at the cylindrical pedestal, which turned out to be a short, well-like enclosure for a very dark hole, some four to five feet in diameter.

* * *

The pair fell silent. Kre Molcren's screams could still be heard, very faint and distant, coming from the pit at the base of the altar.

"Aw, shit," Omega whispered in horror, remembering Echo's earlier discussions on the history of the facility. "Is that...?"

"The purported bottomless pit? Yeah. See this inscription?" He pointed to some neo-Mayan language carved around the sun disk.

"Uh-huh..."

"Best our linguists could figure when we discovered it, it reads, 'Here lies the Mouth of Mitnal. Woe unto all those who enter it.'"

"What's a Mitnal?"

"It's what Dante would have termed 'the ninth circle of hell.'"

"Ooo, shit." Omega winced. "Kre Molcren better hope it IS bottomless."

"Yeah. Or that he bleeds out along the way...which he might. Good shooting, by the way."

"Now I understand why you called the maneuver you did," Omega murmured with a shiver, staring at the opening of the pit in a kind of appalled fascination. Kre Molcren's terrified shrills of pain and desperation could still be heard, just faintly, as it continued to fall...and fall. "You already basically took out one of its hands when its blaster exploded. Then you hamstrung it, so it'd be off-balance when it jumped you."

"Right. So by the time you were done and it got to the mouth of the pit, it didn't have a way to stop itself from falling in," Echo finished, nodding. "This way, it's not dead, so it isn't a martyr to the cause, but it sure isn't gonna be helping out that cause any time soon. In fact, it's something of a sacrifice, according to...whoever built this thing." He patted the sun face, then walked over, picked up both severed feet, and casually tossed them into the pit after their owner. Then he produced an evidence bag from a pocket, stuffed the amputated hand inside, and shoved the lot back into his pocket.

"What on earth is that for?" Omega asked, scrunching her face in distaste. "Surely you don't keep some sorta disgusting trophy room that I haven't seen yet."

* * *

Echo eyed her for a moment, wondering if she really thought him that macabre...until he saw the balaclava shift as the corner of her mouth twitched.

Imp, he thought with a hidden grin, pulling up his own mask. *Damn, does she have an offbeat sense of humor. I like it.*

"Proof," Echo finally said, "that we got the guy who tried to assassinate Zhaejoh. Ke!endarians leave latents, same as humans. A Ke!endarian latent print isn't quite the same as human fingerprints, but the end result is. We match this to the latent evidence left at the assassination attempts, and bingo." He put a hand on her shoulder and pulled her back; in her intense curiosity, she was leaning entirely too close to the unguarded mouth of the pit for his liking. "Back up there, baby. Reports said we lost a couple agents down it initially, poor bastards. The whole reason the warehouse was originally put here was to cover the damn thing up—that ice I blasted out wasn't glacier ice, it was artificial. We—not me personally, but the Agency—brought in fire hoses and covered the whole mess, after making sure there was nothing above it BUT ice, then carved the store room in front and put a warning plaque up at the door, so nobody would come back in and unknowingly dig through to it. Ergo we—as in, you and me—can't just go off now and leave that damned hole yawning open like this. So...you wanna help me bring the house down?"

"But don't we need the room, like you said, as a marker it's here?"

"Nah; the rubble of the collapse oughta do that, especially if we leave the entrance and warning plaque intact. Gonna help, or not?"

"Sure!"

"Wanna do it all by yourself?"

"If I can, yeah, I'd like to try."

"Yeah, you can do it. It's all about finding the stress points, and I'm betting you'll be good at that. Big as this place is, you're going to need both blasters, though. And you're gonna need to boost the beam intensity. Lemme show you how to set the things to do this..."

* * *

Moments later, they were standing in the old corridor, and flakes and shards of ice were settling in the doorway. In the area that used to be the storeroom, little was visible but a wall of white rubble.

"That. Was. COOL," a highly satisfied Omega declared, and Echo grinned under his balaclava.

"You have a singular ability to choose appropriate descriptors," he decided. Omega looked startled, then thoughtful, as she reviewed what she'd just said. Suddenly she squinched her face.

"Ooo," Omega groaned then. "That pun was NOT intended."

"Like hell it wasn't!"

"No, really!"

"Meh. The only person I know who likes atrocious puns more than Romeo is you!"

"Echo, I swear!"

"All right, all right, if you say so. Okay, we got that done," he said with a grin, turning. "Let's go. We can make some speed now."

* * *

Fifteen minutes later, they were escorting the Ke!endarian diplomatic contingent to the maglev station. Twelve minutes after that, they'd arrived.

"We still got nearly an hour," Omega noted, pulling back her coat sleeve to check her chronometer.

"We do, but if we're already here, we can load as soon as the tube arrives," Echo pointed out, "and we don't have to worry about Tango, or some 'present' that kre Molcren left us, or something like that."

"True," Omega agreed. "Do we know where Tango even went?"

"No, but King and Ocean were gonna light a fire under McMurdo Security, and see if they couldn't scare her up." His cell phone rang just then, and he fished it out of his pocket and glanced at the display. "Aha. Speak of the devil." He activated it, shoved his hood back, and held it to his ear. "Echo. Yeah, King. Really? Good. She WHAT?! Oh HELL no! Not if she were the last human female on...well, you get the picture. Absolutely not. No, when Omega and I get back to Headquarters, we'll report the whole mess to Fox, and he can figure out what to do with her. No, I am NOT taking her back on the train with us. Keep her in the brig until you get instructions from HQ. Yes, on my authority. I don't care what she thinks she is. I'm officially leaving you in charge until such time as you are relieved of command by your Director-assigned successor. Yes, because I'm Alpha Line. In fact, I'm the Director of Alpha Line. Yes, I report directly to Fox. Right. Echo out."

"I gather they got her?" Omega wondered. "And she still won't shut up?"

"Yes, and yes," Echo said in disgust, shoving his phone back into a pocket and jerking up his hood in annoyance. "Turns out she was holed up in her quarters—which King says were tricked out like a harem, and even had manacles on the walls...apparently waiting for my delivery."

"Ugh!"

"My sentiments exactly. Okay, partner, look over there."

* * *

"What?! Where??" A startled Omega spun, dropping into a slight crouch and checking out the area like a hunting hawk. Echo, impressed, noticed her arms instantly floated into position, ready either to block or throw a punch. He noted, too, that either hand—or both—was in position to draw a weapon.

"Calm down, baby, everything's fine. Look over in the alcove, in the corner of the station. There's several rows of benches, and unlike the ones in the sub dock, they're made of wood, so people can actually sit on them without literally freezing their asses off. If you go sit down, huddle up, and tuck your feet up under you, it might help you get a little warmer. I know you've been kinda chilled. That oughta help."

"Ooo!" Omega exclaimed, and made a beeline for the nearest bench. Her enthused reaction amused Echo, and lifted his mood.

Yeah, training her is proving to be a lotta fun, he concluded. *Been a few times I wasn't sure, but she hasn't let me down once so far. And I don't see that starting, any time soon.*

He decided to join her, sitting beside her and tucking his own feet under himself, before wrapping an arm about her shoulders in a companionable sharing of body heat. When he heard her sigh and felt her snuggle in under his arm, he smiled absently to himself beneath his balaclava, and relaxed.

Then he turned his attention to his surroundings, and watched the Ke!endarians milling restlessly about the maglev station.

* * *

All right, *the cold, emotionless mental voice spoke again, when the lava in the girl's veins finally cooled.* That much is done. Now to begin the more difficult enhancements.

What? What enhancements? *the girl tried to query, but she could not formulate the thought. Or perhaps was not allowed to do so.*

...I believe I shall start...with the sensory apparatus, *the voice returned.*

Up until this point, the girl had not been afraid. Concerned, even anxious, certainly. But not afraid.

But now she saw those same robotic arms that had injected her with she knew not what, approaching her face with various sharp implements.

Fear gripped her then. One word formed in her mind, powerful, insistent, managing to get past whatever the creature was doing to shut down her ability to think.

Anesthetic, *she thought.* Anesthetic! ANESTHETIC!!

No, *came the chilling response.* It will interfere with the cognitive feedback. I must know that the enhancements are working.

But I'll FEEL it! *she cried.*

So?

It was only when the robotic arms started wielding a laser scalpel on her eyes, delicately dissecting them, that she finally began to scream...

...But she made no sound.

* * *

By the time the maglev was on approach—discernible by a distant rumble; the tube wasn't a complete vacuum, and the train's movement tended to set up propagating compression waves in what air there was in the tube—Echo's relaxed attitude was less so.

Something's wrong here, he thought, watching the Ke!endarians interact, and trying to puzzle out what was up. *I can't quite put my finger on it, but something isn't right.*

"Meg," he murmured, still watching the alien contingent, "do you see..."

"Hm?" she said, looking up. "Damn! Sorry, Ace, I nodded off for a second, there."

He stared at her in intense disapproval.

"You fell asleep on duty?"

"No, not entirely," she admitted, and he saw her face flush. "I kinda zoned out. I was aware of what was going on around me, I just sorta shut down for a bit."

"Well, wake up now," he grumbled. "I was hoping you were watching shit like I was."

"I'm awake," Omega averred, then glanced around. "I hear the train coming."

"Yeah. Pay attention to our wards, only don't LOOK like you're paying attention."

Omega sat silently, watching surreptitiously, for a minute or two.

"They're anxious," she murmured. "Ready to get outta here."

"Keep looking."

As the rumble of the approaching maglev grew louder, her brows drew together.

"Something's wrong," she muttered to her partner. "What's going on...?"

"I'm not sure," Echo said under his breath, "but watch yourself as we board the train. It could be as simple as an argument between team members, or...it could be a LOT more complicated. We may not be done with this yet."

"You think...?"

"No, I suspect," Echo corrected her terminology. "The word 'think' implies knowing, and I wouldn't go that far yet. If I'm right, though, I want you to take Zhaejoh straight back through to the rear car. I don't care who goes with it or doesn't go with it; it's your priority. I'll handle what I suspect. Your job is to keep Zhaejoh alive. Got it?"

"Got it."

The train hissed into the station.

"Up and at 'em, partner," he said, rising and offering his hand to Omega. She stood, and the pair moved forward.

Chapter 7

This second train also had multiple open-layout passenger cars, but whereas the previous one had only three, this one had four: a pre-mission briefing between Alpha One and Fox had concluded a possible need for an extra prisoner car on the backup train; the only reason Echo had refused to take Tango aboard was that he hadn't wanted a possible collaborator placed in such close proximity to Zhaejoh...or himself. Also, unlike the first train, whose cars were specialized for the individual alien groups, all four cars of this train were intended to serve regardless of species. As the avians boarded, they milled about in restless unease. As she watched, Omega had an idea how she might be able to settle them.

"Meg," Echo murmured as they boarded, "go ahead and lead 'em back to the last car right now. It's the farthest away from the door into the station, and probably the safest, if something else goes down. I'll lock down the entryway and guard the rear. Which is actually the fore, being the front of the train, but you know what I mean."

"All right. Hey, these guys have any clue about commercial airlines here? Like, on Earth?"

"Uh, yeah, we've had to put 'em in disguises and send 'em commercial once or twice. It's not optimal, but it happens sometimes. We usually replace out the flight crew and attendants with our own people, though. Why?"

"Nothing important. Just wondering."

"Okay. Take 'em on back. I'll get the door."

"On it, Ace," Omega replied, hiding a smirk, and moved to the front of the group. "Hey y'all! Okay everybody, follow me," she said in a cheerful tone. "All the way back."

The anxious group bustled on back to the rear car; as usual, one of the Ke!endarian bodyguards immediately followed the point Alpha One agent, and the other immediately preceded the rear agent. Zhaejoh was in the center, surrounded by its advisors and personal chef. Echo brought up the rear as promised, after triple-locking and pass-coding the entry door.

"Everybody please find a seat," Omega ordered once Echo had firmly closed the special door between cars; since the tube was evacuated to near-vacuum to enable the swiftest possible transit, the passage between cars was enclosed in a flexible shaft and pressurized. But the doors were still airlock doors, just in case the fabric of the passage ruptured. "Now, we request your full attention as your flight attendants demonstrate the safety features of this aircraft."

The Ke!endarians all blinked, bemused. Echo stopped dead where he was and simply watched, brown eyes narrowed. Omega threw him a mischievous glance and continued, even mimicking the demonstration with hand motions.

"...Please follow along on the card located in the seat pocket in front of you. Whenever the seat belt sign illuminates, you are required to fasten your seat belt. Insert the metal fittings one into the other, and tighten by pulling on the loose end of the strap. To release your seat belt, simply lift the upper portion of the buckle. You seat cushion doubles as a flotation device in the event of a water landing; slip your arms into the straps and hold it against your chest. In the event of a cabin decompression, an oxygen mask will...No, sorry, wrong transport mode. My bad."

Echo snorted; it sounded more than a little like a redirected guffaw. The Ke!endarians cheeped their enthusiastic laughter. Several doubled over, trilling giggles. The group's stress diminished instantly.

"Seriously, though," Omega continued, grinning, "we will be departing the station momentarily at high speed. Please sit, strap in, and get comfortable."

"Very, very good, friend Omega!" Zhaejoh applauded. "A perfect rendition! One would almost think you had been a flight attendant, before coming to the Agency!"

Echo raised an eyebrow in commendation as the Ke!endarians, all signs of anxiousness gone—at least for the moment—sought seats immediately and began buckling themselves into the safety harnesses. Omega jerked her head back, wordlessly querying if she should sit in the rear; Echo nodded, then pointed at a seat near the front for himself as he pulled down his balaclava. Then he moved to the command console nearby, where he murmured into the mic, submitted himself to a retinal scan, then murmured something else; a watching Omega read his lips and saw, "Godspeed, John Glenn." It was her turn to stifle a laugh; it came out as a strangled cough instead. He cut his eyes around at her to see what produced the reaction, saw her trying to hide her laughter, and grinned.

Then both members of the Alpha One team sat down and buckled into their chairs.

Moments later the maglev departed, accelerating to its maximum emergency speed of over 1,800 miles per hour within seconds.

* * *

Once the maglev reached emergency cruising speed, Echo unstrapped and stood, peeling out of his parka, gloves, and balaclava, tossing them aside into an empty seat. Omega followed suit, being a bit slower to remove the warm outer layers; she was still badly chilled from so many hours in the Antarctic environs.

"I think it's about time we all had something to eat," Echo declared. "Zhaejoh, perhaps you'd like to have your chef prepare a bit of a meal for you and your staff. There's plenty of appropriate food in the kitchenette stowage, and more in the other cars if we need it. Meg? What say we cobble together some soup and sandwiches? You'd probably like something hot to eat, about now."

"Sounds like a plan, Ace," Omega agreed without hesitation, as everyone unfastened their restraints and got to their feet. "Although," she directed her addendum to the Ke!endarians, "if you're not actively doing something, it would probably be best for you to stay seated and in the seatbelts. Not all of these tunnels are completely straight. And if for some unlikely reason we had to emergency brake, it could be bad for anyone unsecured."

"That's true," Echo threw his weight behind her warning.

"We shall do so, Agent Omega, Agent Echo, right after we have stretched, and obtained food," Throtlama said through its translator, as the chef—one Unc!nar by name as Omega had discovered, a highly friendly sort—rummaged the cabinets and cupboards in the train car's

166

kitchenette. The two bodyguards spread out and explored the entire train car, familiarizing themselves with it as they had both the submarine dock and the maglev station after Alpha One had given the all-clear sign.

"Agent Echo," the senior bodyguard asked through its own translator, "might I fulfil my duty and examine the rest of the train?"

"Can't you take our word for it?"

"Would you, in my place?"

"No, I wouldn't. Okay, you can come forward with me. Meg, the human food is in the lead car," Echo noted, "so I want you to stay here and keep an eye on things, and I'll go slap together some sandwiches while I nuke us both some soup."

"Okay, Ace. Sounds good," Omega agreed.

"Ergev, you will remain here, even as Agent Omega does, to aid her, and keep the Excellency and its staff safe," the bodyguard told its companion.

"I shall do as you say, Zembir," Ergev agreed.

The lead human agent and the lead Ke!endarian bodyguard headed forward, through the inter-car passage.

* * *

A few moments later, Unc!nar came to Omega, as most of the rest of the alien creatures sat down and buckled their seat belts, save only a couple, who appeared to be stretching their limbs and fluffing feathers in the welcome warmth of the maglev car. Omega decided Ke!enda!ar must be a warmer planet, maybe more so than Earth overall, and regretted that she hadn't been able to do more than read a summary about the system prior to the mission.

"Madame," Unc!nar began, directing its speech into its electronic translator, "for the dish I should like to prepare, which is what you might call Ke!endarian comfort food, I do not have quite enough of one ingredient; the sunflower seeds are only stocked in snack packages, rather than in bulk. May I be permitted to check the storage of the other cars for more?"

"Sure," Omega agreed, "but we have a problem. I need to go with you, to keep you safe, but I need to stay here with the Vice-President and its advisors, too..."

"Allow me," Ergev offered. "If you will stay here with the Excellency, I shall attend Unc!nar; it should not take long, I think. And that way, all will be well protected, though I cannot think what danger we are in, to require it."

"I think that'll work, Ergev," Omega said, offering the avian a smile. "Go on ahead."

As the two Ke!endarians exited the car, Omega sat down in a chair across from Zhaejoh and Throtlama.

"Your Excellencies," she began with another smile, "would you do me the honor of telling me a bit more about your home world? I have studied the mission briefing files, but it isn't the same as having full access to information about it. And I haven't had any off-planet missions yet, so I'm really curious. But if it would offend, or, or breach security or something, please forget I asked."

"No, no, not at all, Agent Omega," Zhaejoh said in a cheerful tone. "It is only to be expected, and we are honored by your interest. I hope that once you do begin to go off-world, you will come to visit our lovely home and the coalition of worlds it represents. You and your partner shall be ever welcome in my House."

"Though perhaps waiting until the current unrest has died down would be advisable," Throtlama murmured.

"True, true," Zhaejoh agreed. "And now is as good a time as any to get to know one another! Your partner Echo, whom I have known for as long as I have known Fox—though not quite as well—tells me that you were a member of Earth's space exploration corps when you were recruited to work for the PGLEIA. So your interest is understandable, especially in one trained to be an explorer of the universe."

"Yes, I—"

A resounding *BA-BOOM!* reverberated through the air, popping Omega's ears painfully in the confined space of the maglev tunnel. It was accompanied by a violent shaking of the railcar, followed by a sudden hard deceleration and an ear-splitting, continuous shrieking noise. The combination was sufficient to fling an unsecured Omega out of her seat to the floor, even as several large dents and depressions noisily appeared in the car's ceiling and the car began to vibrate, a large-amplitude, relatively high-frequency motion. One of the secondary advisors, Daeshev by name, who likewise had not yet strapped back in, flew across the aisle and fell hard. Despite her own bruises, Omega scrambled to her feet and scurried to its side...just as the lighting dimmed to emergency mode.

"Are you hurt?!" she asked, concerned.

"N-no," the avian murmured. "Only shaken."

Swiftly she helped it to its feet and into the nearest chair, pulling the straps across its torso and securing it.

"There. Everybody else okay?"

"Indeed, Agent," a concerned Zhaejoh agreed, glancing around. "I and my three worthy advisors are all intact. Do what you need to do."

"Thanks," she said absently, and broke into a sprint to the front of the car.

* * *

Omega ran to the door and entered the airlock. It automatically cycled shut behind her, but the door into the next car showed a red light for its status, and refused to cycle open.

"Oh shit," she muttered. "That can't be good."

Leaning over the tiny control panel, she studied the readouts, spotting another small blinking red light.

"Oh, that's not good either," she grumbled. "Dammit. Our car's cabin has a slow leak. We're depressurizing. But why...?"

She punched in several commands, and the door in front of her turned transparent. Omega sucked in a sudden, deep, horrified breath.

Well, THAT sure explains it, she thought, staring. *What the hell?!*

On the other side of the door, for many tens of yards, she saw little but shredded metal, scraping the tube walls and throwing brilliant white and yellow sparks, which comprised almost the sole light source. The only thing left of the two middle cars was their bed frames, their track runners... and shrapnel. Far in front, she could just make out the slightly battered rear of the lead car, which also served as something of an engine, though the magnetic motive force ran through the bottom of all the cars. Fortunately, it seemed, said electromagnetic drivers were installed into the bottoms of the car frames, which were, at least, all intact, though not undamaged—the ongoing vibrations she'd felt since the apparent explosion were caused partly by the fact that the electromagnetic 'wheels'—the runners which wrapped around the sides of the track—had been warped. However, the status readout on the control panel indicated that they had dropped to well less than a third their previous speed—they were now traveling at only 528 miles an hour.

Dear God! What happened? she wondered, shocked. *Is everybody okay? Is ECHO okay? Damn it, after enduring all that cold, have I lost my partner—my best friend—anyway?!*

Just then her cell phone alerted. She jumped, startled, but jerked it out of her pocket and activated it. To her surprise, it displayed a video image of Echo, instead of merely his voice. He was pale, and looked alarmed.

"MEG! You okay?"

"Yeah, Ace, I'm fine. So's the Veep and its advisors. I'm not sure about the bodyguards and the chef, though."

"They're dead. Well, one of the bodyguards is. It and the chef were in the third car when the whole thing blew. I think I was supposed to still be in one of the middle cars, too, but I wasn't. The other bodyguard is the bomber. It's up here someplace in the front car with me. The whole 'search the train' demand was evidently nothing but a pretext for setting grenades."

"Well, shit."

"Exactly."

"Are YOU okay?"

"Yeah, I'm good. I was already in the lead car when things blew. Listen, this Zembir is obviously trying to commandeer the train; it's probably looking for the master control panel right now. What it doesn't know is that it's keyed only to you and me, so that'll slow it down a bit. And I think the bombing was meant to detach the rear car—this cat's the one who said something to me about the rear car being safer, if Tango or somebody was still after us, back at the station. Which I'd already been considering anyway, but still. So that means there's something or someone waiting for it, intending to off Zhaejoh. And while the bomb didn't quite do the job, the intervening cars—what's left of 'em—are in pretty sorry shape, per my eye of experience. They might just detach on their own. Which leaves y'all sitting ducks back there."

"Ugh. Not good. Bad pun, too." She stuck out her tongue, trying to lighten the mood a little. She saw Echo's eyelids flutter slightly and knew he got and appreciated the joke, but otherwise he ignored the off-topic editorial remark.

"Nope. And if it's a concerted attack, I doubt you have the firepower to hold 'em off, not by yourself. Only it gets worse."

"How so?"

"There were at least two grenades that detonated, by my count and estimate of effect—probably one in each car," Echo explained. "Does that match your count?"

"Yeah. It wasn't BOOM, it was BA-boom. Two explosions."

"Right. So those made for some damn big forces, all confined inside—"

"The tunnel," Omega realized. "Aw, hell. We could have a cave-in. Granted, it's behind us. But..."

"Right. It could break the circuit in the rails," Echo pointed out. "But it gets even worse than that."

"Aw. Don't tell me. We're under ocean, aren't we?"

"Yeah, and I dunno how deep the tunnel is, down in the crust," Echo admitted. "There's some places that it gets kinda shallow, but I dunno just where those are. So if we have a tunnel collapse, back there where the blast occurred, the tunnel could flood. But I got my hands full up here with the traitor Zembir. So I need you to do something. It's gonna be damn difficult, and even more dangerous."

"Oh no. You don't mean..."

"Yeah. I need you to figure out how to get the Ke!endarians up here, into the lead car, alive and intact. If we can consolidate that way, we can cut the rest of the train loose, and probably regain some speed, maybe even get away and out before anything bad happens to the tunnel."

"Well, we can't stay back here, anyway," Omega pointed out. "Judging by the little control panel here in the airlock, we got a slow leak."

"Damn! Debris?"

"That'd be my guess, yeah. We literally ran into it, so the closing speeds musta been substantial. It was LOUD! We got dents and dings all over the roof and the nose of the car."

"Yeah. Okay. Get everybody up here as soon as you can, then. Keep in mind that, while we no longer have a near-vacuum in the tunnel, which combined with all the shit scraping the walls is why we slowed down so much, it's still damn low pressure for human or avian lungs out there. And we're still traveling at over 500 miles an hour, with not very much in the way of clearance around the cars, so falling off would be a Very Bad Thing."

"Ew. I reckon so."

A bumping sound came from somewhere behind Echo, and the background on the screen whirled dizzyingly as his gaze went past his phone and he spun into a crouch. She could just see the butt of his blaster in a corner of the screen, though his draw had been so fast it was effectively invisible.

"Gotta go, Meg," he murmured, gaze still averted, glance darting here and there. "Be careful, stay safe, and watch your six."

The video image cut to black.

Omega deactivated her phone and shoved it back inside her jacket.

"Hoo boy," she said, running a distracted hand through her hair and dislodging several silvery-white strands, as she stared out through the transparent door at the nearly-airless devastation she now had to negotiate with no partner...and four alien diplomats in tow.

* * *

Echo shoved his phone back into a pocket with one hand, holding a blaster in ready position with the other. He hated to leave Omega with such a daunting task to handle all on her own, but they had to get the Ke!endarian envoy out of the rear car and into the only one that Echo was certain could make it to their destination—assuming the tunnel didn't flood, else all bets were off—or the entire team of avians was most likely dead, Omega along with them. She was good, but she was inexperienced, and would likely be outnumbered and outgunned; she was exceptionally handy with weapons, but two or three weapons against a dozen or more was still a damn unequal firefight, in Echo's book. And it did her no favors if he tried to return to assist, only to get himself shot in the back by this new threat.

My best bet is to take care of this piece of trash as fast as I can, then get back there to help her, he decided. He considered what he knew of Ke!endarian physique, sensory abilities, and non-human capabilities. *Which means...*

He slipped on his special sunglasses and eased over to the airlock control panel, trying to study its controls while still keeping a wary eye on his surroundings.

* * *

Omega stood in the airlock, thinking hard. She wasn't willing to go back to Zhaejoh without having a plan for proceeding in hand, and at the moment, she was empty-handed. Unfortunately, she was also tired, cold, and hungry, which did not make for easy brainstorming. So she closed her eyes and took several slow, deep breaths, letting them out in a long sibilance, and let her mind go blank.

"In the event of a decompression, oxygen masks will automatically drop from the overhead panels. To start the flow of oxygen, pull the mask toward you..."

As the standard patter of a commercial airline flight attendant, which she had mimicked earlier, floated through her brain, Omega's eyes suddenly snapped open. *Of course! The safety manual for the maglev SAID...now I just gotta find 'em.*

She cycled the rear door into the last car, and headed straight for the stowage bins.

* * *

Most avian species, including the inhabitants of Ke!enda!ar, had visible spectral ranges comparable to humans. So Echo knew that if he couldn't see Zembir, the Ke!endarian couldn't see HIM.

Which was why Echo located the lighting switch—for the entire car— on the control panel for the airlock, shut it off...

...Then broke it away entirely.

The car, possessed of no outside windows anyway since they would only open onto the tube, instantly plunged into pitch blackness. The Division One agent heard a soft, surprised squeak in the darkness, and knew exactly

173

where it had come from.

Aha. Gotcha, you murderous bastard, he thought.

He tapped the left temple of his sunglasses, and their night-vision capability initiated. Taking three swift steps to the right, he scanned the area...just as a pale blue ray shot through the space where he had been and made what Romeo sometimes called 'mounds of coleslaw' out of a seat.

Just in time. Thanks, asshole. You gave me the angle and path right to you.

Echo visually followed the remembered track of the ray backward until he spotted the dim, fuzzy infrared outline of the avian, crouched between two seats and a table; the cover was sufficiently effective that Echo suspected he couldn't nail the Ke!endarian before it got off another shot. The avian also wore its armor, and the blue ray beam had come from its Ke!endarian weapon, a pulsed impulsive kill rifle currently still in hand as it peered ahead; Zembir was obviously attempting to determine if it had wounded Echo.

So Echo obliged. He leaned over in the general direction of the shredded seat and let out a faint groan, turning his head to disguise the sound's direction but never taking his peripheral vision away from Zembir, making full use of the wraparound property of his special sunglasses. The avian immediately jerked a fist in satisfaction, and eased upward from its crouch. Echo could just see, then, that the corrupt bodyguard had no flashlight or other artificial light source clipped to its armor...anywhere, that he could see.

Now THAT was a damn big oversight. Then again, we did hustle 'em out in a hurry. Either way, I'll take it. Okay, then. Time to go, and take a different path in the going, Echo thought, fingering his pocketed cell phone in the darkness, until he had a good grasp of its orientation. Then he tapped the dark screen in a certain sequence, holstered his blaster, waited a couple of seconds, and turned to the side wall behind him. He reached out and placed the palms of both hands flat against the wall, then raised his right foot and planted his toe firmly against the wall as well—

—And crawled straight up the wall and onto the ceiling.

* * *

In the rear car, Omega was frantically scrabbling through the emergency equipment stowage bins, searching for the items she needed, as the now-frightened Ke!endarians peppered her with questions, which she ignored for the moment. Finally she came up with a length of thick, elastic fabric. Next to it was a small full-head helmet and a rebreather.

"Bingo!" she said, digging further. "How many have I got...?"

She quickly came up with the lot, and counted.

"Twelve," she said in enthused relief. "I've got twelve! Bless you, Fox!" Omega spun to the alarmed, and now mildly-exasperated, Ke!endarian envoy. "Listen, folks, here's the situation, and here's what I need you to do..."

* * *

Echo stole silently across the ceiling of the maglev car like some futuristic ninja, even as the traitorous avian, Zembir, crept along the floor toward the place Echo had been. Within moments, Echo had flanked Zembir as the avian groped about in the dark, seeking what it assumed was Echo's wounded body so it could finish off the Agent. *And then go after Meg and Zhaejoh,* the Agent thought in cold anger.

As Zembir poked blindly among the remains of the railway seat, Echo stood upright, hanging from the ceiling by his feet, Suit jacket tails flapping loosely behind him, staring down at the Ke!endarian and pondering how best to do what needed doing.

I really don't want to start a gun battle, he considered, *because we need this car to stay intact, or we'll have twelve kinds of atmosphere problems. Not to mention, I'll have to deal with surviving explosive decompression, which ain't fun, and try to stay conscious, let alone not-dead, or only slightly dead. Either way, I got a feeling my partner isn't gonna be very happy about it.*

On the other hand, Zembir's back is to me, and regs aside, it isn't exactly sporting to shoot a fella in the back, even if he did shoot at me first. Okay, then. I do this the hard way. Or...I could let it take itself out for me. He patted his pockets down. *No, dammit, I forgot—I gave the force field generator to Meg to keep as we left the sub dock for the maglev station, in case she needed to defend Zhaejoh. Okay, the hard way it is.*

175

He glanced down at the plain gold signet ring on his hand; in its center was a simple script letter E. *Well, this thing better work,* he thought, *or this is gonna be one damn short and REALLY painful gunfight,* and he touched two hidden buttons simultaneously, one on each shoulder of the ring. A faint yellow circle formed, centered on the face of the ring, then faded into invisibility. He nodded to himself, satisfied.

Then he let out the loud whistle and tongue-clack characteristic of the Ke!endarian, "HEY, YOU!"

* * *

Now clad in a skintight compression suit, a clear helmet encasing her head, her sunglasses underneath in automatic-toggle night-vision mode, a rebreather on her back—along with an additional suit, bundled for Echo, in case he needed it—Omega donned her various holsters and equipment belts over the pressure suit, and turned to see if the four remaining Ke!endarians needed assistance donning theirs. Given their body feathers, it was only slightly more difficult for them than it had been for her to don the thing over her Suit, and about as uncomfortable. But helping each other, and with Omega's urging and assistance, they managed it relatively quickly. She keyed her helmet microphone and initiated the voice activation.

"Everybody ready? Let's go," she said, turning toward the forward airlock. "Stay close to me, and be careful. We're still moving pretty fast, and the car bed is an open frame, so falling is not a plan, and will likely get you killed."

"Should we not simply stay here, friend Omega?" Throtlama asked, and as best the rookie agent could tell, the alien's face looked worried. "It seems to me that it would be much safer to remain where we are and await your partner's rescue, as well as backup by your organization."

"We don't dare," Omega demurred. "If the train car detaches, we could be dead meat for any members of, um, I can't quite pronounce the words in your language, but the faction that's trying to kill your Vice-President, here. And I don't know what happens to the power if we end up stranded, either. We could end up sitting in the dark with no life support. Plus, the cabin has a leak, so we're losing air—AND the tunnel behind us could collapse at any time and flood the entire tunnel. So this car is now a death trap, several times over. No, we need to follow Echo's orders and get ourselves to the lead car as quick as we can."

"Very well," Zhaejoh agreed, game, following her forward, as its advisors trailed behind. "Lead on, friend Omega, and we shall haul tail feathers behind you!" It cheeped, and Omega grinned back, but its laughter sounded as weak as her grin felt.

"Okay, let's try to all cram into the airlock," Omega suggested, stopping before the forward door. "It'll be a tight fit, but it's better than my leading only one or two of you at a time onto the car bed in front of us, then having to leave you alone to go back for the rest."

"True," Daeshev, one of Zhaejoh's junior advisors, agreed.

They all squashed into the airlock together, and Omega cycled it, then brute-forced the outer door into opening.

* * *

Zembir spun, seeking the sound, and fired its weapon. Echo leaped into gun fu mode, blocking the shot with the experimental force shield on his fist as he ran across the ceiling, preventing the shot from punching a hole in the car's bulkheads. The shield wasn't very big, only about a meter in diameter, but while it was in development, he'd been training with an actual steel shield of the same size, and could already do a good bit with it. *I'm not as good as that comic-book character,* he decided, *but I'm still no slouch.* So it was no problem for him to catch the wild shot near the rim of the shield with an outstretched hand.

But the shield flickered slightly, a soft yellow glow, and Echo felt a vibration in his hand. *Uh-oh,* he thought, as Zembir spun toward the agent, an expression on the beaked face that Echo recognized as the Ke!endarian equivalent of a smirk, and he realized the very device that he'd hoped would protect both him and the railcar had, in fact, given away his position.

He crouched on the ceiling, allowing the small force shield to screen him as much as possible, as he surveyed his situation in the fractions of a second before Zembir unleashed a barrage.

* * *

Once Omega managed to manually open the far door of the airlock, she stepped out gingerly, looking for footing, as the night-vision capability

177

of her glasses initiated. The car bed was not solid, but rather a structural support framework, fairly sturdy, but not intended to withstand a force of the magnitude of the blast that had wiped out the car it supported. More, the entire area was still being showered with sparks from shrapnel that dragged against the walls of the tunnel; from time to time, a shard of metal ripped away and flew backward through the space where the cars had once been, and it became necessary to duck or dodge.

But the engineers, in their wisdom, had seen fit to ensure that the area around each coupling was fairly substantial, and this meant that directly in front of each airlock door was the structural equivalent of a solid, oblong platform of reasonable size. So Omega led the Ke!endarian contingent out onto this platform, where they stood, tightly clustered together. Daeshev, slightly braver than the rest, stood in front, close to Omega. It was followed by Zhaejoh, then Khaeoza!ak, and Throtlama brought up the rear.

"All right," she said through the comm, "we made it this far, y'all. Stay here a couple minutes while I scout out a safe route to take to the next coupling platform."

"I swear to you by my sire's crest that we shall not move from this place until you tell us," Zhaejoh said, sounding more than a little anxious. Omega suspected it was now badly frightened but was refusing to openly admit the fact, and she didn't blame it one bit.

This is not gonna be any kind of fun, she decided, *especially with these ice cubes I got for feet. So much for finally getting warm.*

She moved forward, measured and cautious, ducking out of the way of flying metal shards from time to time, and testing each step as best she could before putting her full weight on anything.

* * *

Echo continued to shelter behind the small force shield, as Zembir fired barrages in his general direction. At every opportunity, Echo fired back with one of his blasters, but that wasn't as often as he would have liked, since Zembir seemed to have its weapon set on something approaching a machine gun's automatic fire, and kept firing in long bursts.

Unfortunately, each time the shield took a hit—which was now pretty much every time Zembir fired—it glowed faintly yellowish; Echo could feel the increasing vibration in his hand, but it was inaudible. Zembir, he knew, could only see the shield's glow, and that barely and intermittently, but the avian was a highly trained bodyguard, and had not only zeroed in on Echo's location, but was gradually finding the extent of the field. And since it didn't fully cover Echo, it was only a matter of time before the Agent was hit.

And that'll be bad. So I can't wait around for it, he thought. *Gotta take some pre-emptive action, here. But damn, am I gonna have some things to say in my test report!*

Just then, a pulsed energy projectile caught the heel of his shoe, nearly knocking him off his feet and gouging a groove in the bottom of the heel. The next shot, fortunately, struck the shield.

Then, in timing so perfect—and perfectly bad—that Echo briefly wondered why the Almighty had it in for him, the shield mechanism evidently decided it had had enough—literally. It seemed to fairly explode with the excess energy it had absorbed and could no longer contain. Lightning bolts leapt from its edges to the nearest conductive objects, illuminating the entire area like a giant van de Graaff generator, at least briefly, and Zembir gave a caw of jubilation audible even over the sizzle of the plasma arcs. The Ke!endarian assailant opened up a continuous fire on Echo, attempting to get past the shield and at least injure, if not outrightly kill, the human wielding it.

However, Echo decided the Almighty was on his side after all, for the unexpected light show had its pluses as well as minuses: the lightning bolts were bright enough that Zembir apparently had difficulty seeing past them to target Echo. Some of the plasma arcs were striking the Agent, as well, but as he was essentially 'in the circuit,' they did no harm, though they did tickle more than a little.

Which is all I need, he thought, trying not to laugh, as one plasma arc caught him in the ribcage. *Aside from the distraction, I do NOT need it getting out that I'm ticklish. Meg would never let me hear the end of it. And if Romeo found out, I hate to think. Let alone the galactic news media; my reputation as Earth's toughest agent wouldn't survive it.*

On the other hand, anywhere else in the car that the plasma struck, it left long, dendritic scorch marks, burning off paint and emitting showers of sparks.

Which isn't good for the system keeping me on the ceiling, Echo realized, as a smoky stench rapidly filled the air. *I better get down from here, fast, and I think I know just what will soften the landing...if I can time it exactly right. Zembir has to change the cartridge at some point.*

He readied himself for an opening, and watched.

* * *

When she had almost reached the far coupling platform of the third car, a horrified cry sounded in Omega's helmet speakers, followed immediately by a terrified scream, abruptly cut off by a crash and a fading gurgle. Spinning, she saw Throtlama, Zhaejoh, and Daeshev, grappling. Khaeoza!ak was gone, with a splatter of golden blood on the nose of the rear car to tell its tale, and she realized she'd heard its death cry as it fell beneath the train.

"Kill it! KILL IT!" Zhaejoh screamed. "Omega, kill it! It is the assassin!"

"WHICH ONE?!" Omega shouted back. "WHO?? DAESHEV?"

"NO!" Daeshev screeched.

Just then, Throtlama managed to produce a pulsed impulsive kill pistol from somewhere, aimed at Omega.

Throtlama?! she had just time to think. *I thought it was one of the good guys!*

Throtlama fired.

* * *

Echo eased across the ceiling, feeling its grip on his feet lessen as the system started to weaken, when Zembir's rifle stuttered, then stuttered again.

Low battery—finally, Echo thought, watching closely, shuffling a little closer as several more energy projectiles impacted on his shield, which continued to arc wildly across the cabin.

Just as Zembir's weapon faltered again, Echo started to leap—

—And the ceiling let go.

He found himself falling rather than leaping, so he tucked into a somersault instead, the shield on the outside of his tuck. Echo landed on his feet in a low crouch, force shield over his head, still arcing from all sides of the circular edge. He tapped the hoop of his ring, and the circular shield morphed into a classic arrowhead shield shape; simultaneously Echo aimed the point of the shield at his adversary.

Instantly the plasma charges shifted to the tip of the point, and arced to the nearest conductive object...

...Zembir.

The alien being let out the barest grunt as every feather on its body ignited, filling the air with the unpleasant stench of burnt feathers, and Zembir dropped to the floor, unmoving. The rifle slid from long limp fingers onto the deck.

A wary Echo crept over, wielding the now-calming shield on his left hand, one blaster in the other hand, and kicked the rifle out of Zembir's reach. The Ke!endarian didn't move. Echo poked the being with the toe of his shoe; it still didn't move. Finally he reached down and put a hand on the side of the avian's ribcage, then behind its knee, seeking a pulse.

"Huh," Echo muttered, standing up and deactivating the force shield before holstering his blaster. "It's only supposed to be defensive, not offensive, but given the way the damn shield design hosed up everything else, I'll take it. At least we don't haveta worry about this one."

He searched the body quickly, removing all the weapons he could find and dumping them, along with the pulsed energy rifle, into the stasis bin, before extracting a body bag from emergency stowage and stuffing what was left of Zembir into it, then back into stowage.

Then he fished out a pressure suit and hurried to don it.

I've left Meg to her own devices far too long as it is, he thought, as he locked the helmet in place and initiated the rebreather. *She'll need help.*

Just then, he heard a dispersing pulsed energy round ricochet off the rear of the car. It was followed by the faint hum of a blaster firing.

"Oh shit, too late," he muttered, and sprinted for the aft airlock.

* * *

"GET DOWN!" Omega yelled, flinging herself onto her back along a narrow beam, as Throtlama's shot flew by overhead. Both blasters appeared

181

in her hands as she drew quick as thought, and Daeshev shoved Zhaejoh to the platform and covered its leader with its own body, keeping as low as it could. Omega opened fire, alternating hands.

Throtlama was not without its own skill with weapons; the avian grabbed a warped strut overhead with both hands and swung upward, out of the way of the shots.

But Omega, even from that distance, could see the focus of those red eyes, almost glowing with malevolence, and she knew that, when Throtlama landed, the Vice-President would once more be its target, even if it had to shoot through Daeshev to kill it.

And that ain't happenin', Omega thought, determined. *Not on my watch. And that means I gotta...well, shit. Time for the magic word: OmigoshIhopeitworks.*

Swiftly analyzing the layout of persons and what she knew of Ke!endarian physiology, Omega brought up her blasters. *If I miss,* floated through her brain as she targeted, *we're all dead. Zhaejoh, Daeshev, and me.* She opened fire with both weapons simultaneously, not waiting for Throtlama to get into position, but firing where she calculated he ought to end up, in order to accomplish his intended mission of killing Vice-President Zhaejoh kre Ranan of the Ke!endarian Coalition.

* * *

"MEG!" Echo yelled into the comm as he emerged into the low pressure of the open tunnel and ran aft, hopping nimbly from strut to beam to platform, knowing the design of the cars, and just which parts would be structurally sound. "MEG, ANSWER ME!"

"I'm b-back here, Ace," Omega's calm voice replied. There was a slight tremor in it, however, and Echo caught it.

"I can't see you..."

"All t-the way back. It's pretty dark. Except for the sparks."

"No shit..."

Echo crossed the linkage between nonexistent train cars, took two more steps, ducked under a huge piece of twisted metal...

...And stopped dead.

Omega stood before him in the skintight compression suit, feet akimbo, both blasters in hand, heat waves rising from them in the rarified atmosphere of the tunnel. The weapons were leveled at Advisor Daeshev, who had both hands in the air and a worried look on its face. Advisor Throtlama lay dead at her feet, holes in chest and head. Khaeoza!ak was nowhere to be seen, but the golden-brown blood spatters on the nose of the rear car told the experienced Agent a great deal.

"Where's Zhaejoh?!" Echo demanded. "Omega, where's Vice-President Zhaejoh?"

"H-here, friend Echo," Zhaejoh murmured, emerging from behind Omega. "I...am unharmed. Your partner has destroyed this emissary of my demise."

* * *

"Sorry about holding you at gunpoint," Omega apologized to Daeshev, as Echo escorted the group forward, across the framework of scaffolding that comprised the beds of the two destroyed railcars. "I had to be sure."

"As long as you did not fire, I was all right with that," Daeshev said, somewhat nervously, Echo thought. "And I can see why. With no less than two traitors embedded in our midst, you had no way of knowing there were not more."

"Exactly. If you hadn't been able to pass Echo's field polygraph, and if Zhaejoh hadn't vouched for you..." Omega shrugged. "You'd be in force cuffs right now, if not dead. I'm glad you're on our side."

"So am I," Daeshev replied simply.

"Okay, in you go, you two," Echo said, ushering the two Ke!endarians into the open airlock door.

"Um, Echo?" Omega asked.

"Hm?"

He watched as she resorted to their special codes.

Uh, shouldn't we go in first, and check in case the guy you took out left more bombs?

No need.

You already did?

No. But it planned to escape in this car. So it didn't plant anything that might backfire on it.

But...Throtlama stayed behind.

And was probably very well known by anybody who might have been waiting for the disabled car. Or might have been the backup itself, after killing all the others. It only had to claim it hid from the assassins until rescue arrived.

Well, that actually explains why he quit trying to convince me to stay after I mentioned the air leak, and the possible flooded tunnel.

Yeah, that'd do it, all right. So relax. Everything's fine.

Are you SURE?

Yeah. But you're not, and I get that, and you're being a good agent in pointing it out. So let's do this.

* * *

Echo fished his cell phone from a pocket—*how the HELL did he manage a pocket in the COMPRESSION SUIT?!* Omega wondered—activated it, and launched an app. Seconds later a readout flashed up, and he glanced at it, then showed it to her.

'All clear,' she read the display. *Okay, I'm satisfied, Ace. Thanks.*

No problem, partner. It's how I realized what happened to the middle two cars, just not in time to rescue the other two Ke!endarians. Good shooting, by the way.

'Preciate it. Omega turned her attention to the two Ke!endarians, who waited anxiously in the airlock. "Go ahead, guys, it's clear," she told them.

"Zhaejoh, you know how to cycle the airlock, right?" Echo asked.

"I do, friend Echo."

"Go ahead and get inside, then. Meg, stay here with me. We got a little work to do first."

As the two remaining Ke!endarians entered the lead car, Echo knelt to look down at the coupling connecting the car to the remaining train, then grunted.

"Huh. 'S what I figured. The coupling is too damaged to do much with. We'll need to cut it loose. And that'll be a little tricky."

"Blasters, I assume?"

"Yeah, but we gotta angle 'em just right, so we don't cut the maglev rail underneath. That'll break the circuit and we stop having magnetic

184

levitation."

"And come to a screeching halt," Omega noted.

"Emphasis on screeching. It wouldn't be too healthy for any of us, but it'd be especially bad for you and me, out here on the platform. But we need to get rid of this shit," Echo waved a hand at what was left of the train behind them, "so we can go faster. We won't reach emergency speed, not with all the gas in the tube now, but we might get close to nominal speed." He eyed her. "It isn't hard, really, you just gotta maintain the same angle through the entire cut. I can do it all myself, but it's a little like cutting a tree; past a certain point, things need to go fast, you know? But if two people work on it, and come from opposite sides, it's practically a cakewalk."

"Okay. Show me what I need to do, and I'll start on this side, and you start on that side."

"Good girl. Get down here and lemme show ya, and we'll have this done in a couple minutes..."

* * *

Inside five minutes the matter was done. The Alpha One team each held tight to a platform rail with one hand as they cut through the last of the coupling. Within seconds the remaining car accelerated away from what was left of the last three cars, while the two Division One agents hung on for all they were worth.

"Wow, this is fast," Omega murmured. "Hangin' onto the back like this, you really get a feel for it."

"You okay? Not getting vertigo, are you?" Echo wondered, concerned.

"No, I think it's neat," she declared. "Wannabe astronaut here, remember."

"Okay, so you like your speed," Echo said with a grin. "Shoulda known, after the whole thing with the T-Bird. C'mon, let's get inside, outta these compression suits, and see about some food. Probably just cold sandwiches at this point, but it's better than nothing. I dunno about you, but I'm hungry."

"Deal! Let's go!"

* * *

The remainder of the trip took longer that it was originally supposed to, but it was also uneventful; to their knowledge, there was no tunnel collapse of significance—Division One engineers had built the thing to last, and it did. A few hours after they deposited Zhaejoh and Daeshev in the safe house prepared for them, Alpha One was back at Headquarters, in Fox's office.

"...And in the end, only the two members of Zhaejoh's envoy team survived," Echo reported to Fox. "But since one of those was Zhaejoh himself, and two of the five dead were embedded assassins from H!nar kre Naese!en!Re, and the REST of the dead were killed BY the assassins, we should be okay diplomatically, at least." He glanced to his side, where his dejected partner stood, downcast. Then he looked back at Fox, who nodded subtly.

"I agree," Fox declared then. "I've already notified the Ke!endarian government, and sent a cleanup team to clear out the remains of the maglev cars and retrieve the bodies in the tunnel. Forensics has the other various bodies and body parts?"

"All except for Khaeoza!ak," Omega offered softly, and rather sadly. Her gaze dropped to the floor. "I'm r-really sorry I couldn't save it."

"Not your fault, Meg," Echo murmured, attempting to console his partner. "I doubt you could have stopped Throtlama pitching it off the car bed any more than I could have stopped the train car bombing. We can't prevent what we don't know about."

"Don't beat yourself up about it, Omega," Fox said in a gentle tone. "'A mensch tracht und Gott lacht.'"

"Huh?" Omega said, looking up, puzzled.

"Yiddish, baby," Echo said quietly.

"Yiddish? Are you Jewish, Fox? Oh!" Omega broke off, flushing. "I'm s-sorry. I know I'm not s-supposed to ask stuff like that. I just f-forgot for a sec. I'm...kinda t-tired."

"No offense taken, Omega," Fox replied, keeping his voice and manner soft. "And yes, I am."

"He doesn't make a secret of it, Meg," Echo added. "We have a rabbi in the chaplain department, and Fox attends synagogue services when he can."

"Which probably isn't nearly often enough, but I stay busy...as the two of you have reason to know." Fox shrugged.

"Oh, okay. What's it mean? What you s-said?" Omega wondered.

"It's an aphorism," Echo said. "Correct my translation if I'm wrong, Fox, but I think it means something like, 'A person plans and God laughs.' Kinda the same idea as, 'No battle plan ever survives first contact with the enemy.' Not that the Almighty is the enemy. It's just the old concept of, you can plan all you like, but things are gonna do what they're gonna do."

"You got it, Echo," Fox confirmed, "but I think it sounds pithier in Yiddish." He turned back to Omega. "Though I'm betting, with your ancestry, you're more familiar with Robert Burns' 'The best laid schemes o' mice an' men gang aft agley.' Right?"

"Um, yeah. Okay, I get it."

"I'll be sure to send your personal condolences to the family, Omega. You done good, Agent. I couldn't have asked for better. I know that sounds... harsh...to you right now, and I know you may feel as if the mission was not totally successful. Loss of innocent life is always regrettable, and I am glad to see you know that. But we none of us are übermenschen. Now, it's been a damn long day for you both. Go fill out the reports, then go crash." Fox laid a light hand on Omega's shoulder, then frowned.

"No arguments there, Boss," Echo agreed, already turning for the door. "C'mon, baby, let's go."

* * *

After that quick report to Fox—not even taking long enough to sit down—the Alpha One team left the Director's office, headed across the Core to the side room just off the hallway leading to the gym, where the Agents generally filed their post-mission reports. As they crossed the large, open area, Omega espied Romeo and India, coming out of the break room. She touched Echo's arm, and he glanced down at her.

"I need t-to talk to India about something real quick," Omega murmured, nodding at the agent under discussion. "I'll catch up."

"Okay. See you in a couple." And Echo headed on, out of the Core.

As soon as he was out of sight, Omega made a beeline for the physician-agent.

187

"Hey," she greeted the couple.

"Hey, there!" Romeo replied, cheerful.

"Well, hi," India said with a smile. "How'd the mission go?"

"India," Omega said without preamble, "I n-need your help. I c-can't feel my f-feet."

Chapter 8

"No, absolutely not," India decreed once she and Romeo had gotten Omega back to her quarters and seated on her own couch. The pair had quickly stripped her of jacket, tie, shoes and several layers of socks, and India fairly gasped once she saw the condition of Omega's feet. They were almost dead white—except for her toes: three of those were bright red, one was deep blue, and one was nearly black. Her hands and ears were better, but not by a lot. "You are not going anywhere until you get warm, and I treat all this! No wonder you couldn't feel them! You're just before losing digits, girl! Romeo, run back to our quarters and fetch my medikit, would you, honey? The big one, not the little one. And hurry."

"On it, babe."

He was gone and back by the time India could finish her examination of Omega's extremities, and the former physician promptly got out an electronic thermometer and stuck it in Omega's mouth before Meg could protest. Seconds later it beeped, and India grabbed it and looked at the readout.

"Damn, damn, damn," she muttered. "Romeo, run into Meg's bedroom and grab all the blankets you can find, and start wrapping her up. Oh, and crank up the thermostat in here. Set it...set it for 80 degrees Fahrenheit, heat. I've got to get moving, glopping meds on this."

"Right."

"What I'd like to know," India grumbled, selecting several items from her kit and kneeling to better reach Omega's feet, "is why Echo let you get in this state."

"H-he, um..." Omega tucked her head, as Romeo commenced wrapping her in blankets. "Oh, th-that-t f-feels b-b-better."

"Answer the question," India insisted.

"He d-didn't-t know," Omega admitted, barely able to speak through chattering teeth. "Th-things w-were m-mov-ving f-fast, and w-we didn't-t have t-time...I, I t-tried to t-tell him I was-was c-c-cold, but..."

"He toldja to suck it up, didn't he?" Romeo finished for her, with a knowing nod.

"Y-y-yeah. How'd y-you...?"

"It was a damn serious mission, wasn't it?"

Omega gave up trying to talk through her teeth chattering, and just nodded.

"Earth in danger an' all?"

She nodded again.

"Anybody die?"

Her face crumpled, but she didn't cry.

"Uh-huh. He gets really focused when things 're like that," Romeo explained. "Doesn't like a lotta distractions, and he'll take you at your word. He assumes 'is partner is competent enough to handle things, and will TELL him if he—or she—is in a bad way. Which you shoulda done," Romeo chastised, but gently.

"I...w-was af-fraid to," Omega admitted.

"Why?" India wondered, as she treated the other woman's feet. "Was he mean, or hateful, or something?"

"No! N-not that," Omega protested. "S-stern, yeah, but...L-look, guys, b-blonde hair not-notwithstanding, I'm not s-s-stupid. An' I got more c-common sense th-than most f-folks credit t-t-to people with lo-lotsa deg-grees. S-s-so I kn-know h-how it w-works. He n-needed backup, or he'd h-have gone al-lone. He a-and F-Fox figured I c-c-could h-handle it, or they'd-d have t-tapped R-rom-meo. So wh-when I r-realized how b-b-bad the c-cold really w-was, it was k-kinda t-too late to d-d-do much. I...I thought if-if I back-ked out, he m-might not come b-b-back. Excep-pt in the p-proverbial p-pine box." She swallowed hard. "And I...d-don't think I could-d have lived with m-myself, if th-that hap-pened."

Romeo and India glanced at each other, telegraphing their mutual concern.

"Meg," India began a delicate inquiry as she treated Omega's hands, "you and Echo...you don't have a...a 'special' relationship, do you? Like Romeo and me?"

"Oh!" Omega blushed deeply. "You m-mean, are we l-lovers or, or something? No, no. Nothing like th-that. But we ARE good p-pals...at least, I think w-we are...I mean, he's the-the best f-f-friend I've g-got, maybe t-that I've ever had, I j-just dunno if..."

"You dunno if it goes both ways?" an astute Romeo finished her statement. "Because th' man's so reserved?"

"Y-yeah." She shrugged, and the mound of blankets about her shifted, then seemed to slump inward.

"It was a pretty damn rough mission, huh?" India murmured in sympathy, sensing the other woman's depressed exhaustion before picking up a different topical medication and starting on Omega's ears.

"Yeah." It was a sigh.

"But successful, right?"

Omega nodded. "Sorta, I guess."

"Sorta what? People really did die?" Romeo asked, and Omega nodded in response to that question asked a second time.

"Wait. The Vice-President survived, didn't it?" a suddenly-worried India tag-teamed.

Omega nodded again.

"And Echo's all right?"

Another nod.

"Well, just relax then. You're both home and safe. Do what I tell you, and everything will be okay."

So Omega tried to burrow as deep into the blankets as she could, while India worked on her hands.

* * *

Omega didn't show up to help Echo fill out the day's reports, so he did the paperwork by himself. This annoyed him; he had made it plain early on in her training that the reports were an important part of the job, even going so far as to explain why and what purpose they served, and she was expected to participate. He made up his mind to give her a thorough reaming-out the next time he saw her.

I guess I spoke too soon, he thought, disappointed...rather more than he had expected to be, actually. *She sure let me down on this one. And she*

191

specifically told me she'd be here, so she lied to me into the bargain.

Once he had finished the paperwork—including a terse report on certain experimental equipment, a report which pulled no punches—he removed the force shield ring, placed it in its container, and placed the container in the special lockbox in the corner. Then Echo checked out for the day, logging out of the computer before heading straight for his quarters. It had been an exceptionally long shift, and he wanted to give Omega her ass-chewing and go to bed—assuming that was where she was.

Pretty likely, he decided. *She was yawning in Fox's office, and trying to hide it. She might already be in bed. In which case, I'm waking her up for that ass-chewing.*

So as soon as the front door was closed behind him, he bellowed, "OMEGA!" and headed for the back door.

"In-n h-here, Echo," came the distant reply.

"Young lady, you have some serious explaining to d—" He broke off as he reached the door, still half-open from early that morning, looking through as a wave of tropical heat washed over him from the other apartment.

A miserable Omega sat, huddled in mounds of blankets and shivering violently for all that, on the end of her sofa, in a sweltering apartment. India—who had removed her Suit jacket, loosened her tie, and rolled up her shirtsleeves, laying the discarded garments across a nearby chair—knelt in front of Omega, swabbing something on his partner's reddened, bare toes, before encasing both feet in Zarcorian thermal wraps. Omega promptly pulled her feet into the base of the pile of blankets, and India gently tucked the blankets around her feet.

"Better?" the physician-agent murmured to the other woman.

"Y-yeah, th-thanks," a nodding Omega stuttered, teeth fairly chattering with cold. "It doesn't s-sting and b-burn so bad now."

"So I take it you can feel 'em now?" India wondered.

"Yeah. K-kinda wish I couldn't."

"Mm. I can't give you an analgesic, hon. We can't risk it. In addition to killing pain, they also suppress vitals...and you sure don't need that."

"I kn-know. 'S okay."

"What the hell happened?" a shocked Echo wondered.

"Frostbite," India replied, clipped and succinct. "And her body temperature is fully eight and a half degrees Fahrenheit below normal, so she's hypothermic into the bargain, bordering on seriously so. Her vitals are badly depressed. I'm surprised she didn't pass out on you," India said, and Echo suddenly recalled Omega zoning out at the maglev station. "I strongly recommend a large, piping-hot bowl of her favorite soup or stew, some decaf or hot cocoa, and maybe a hot soak in the tub later on. Then into bed once she's more comfortable. And she WILL need help with ALL of that." She jabbed an index finger in Echo's direction. "Which means you."

"I d-don't need help in the t-tub," Omega protested in a weak voice.

"No, but you'll need somebody to run it for you," India pointed out. "And help getting there, and maybe into it."

"I-I can..."

"NO. I told you already. You need to stay wrapped up until you get warm, girl," India insisted, wagging that same index finger. "You're mildly hypothermic as it is, bordering on moderate to severe like I said, so if you get any worse chilled, you could be at risk for cardiac arrhythmia, which CAN lead to full-on cardiac arrest—which is not pleasant, I promise you. CPR tends to bust ribs and break the sternum; the defibrillator paddles are prone to leaving burns, the bruises...it's just no fun, girlfriend. And that presumes we're able to jump-start you again, which isn't a sure-fire guarantee, even with Division One equipment. I'm sure your partner there won't mind helping you out. Better that than having to cart you off to Medical for resuscitation."

"I-I g-guess..."

"I left some Rejuvic and frostbite ointment in your bathroom, so when you're done with that soak, reapply it, okay? Swab on the Rejuvic, then glop the ointment on top. IF the skin feels flexible, you can rub it in, but if there's ANY stiff spots, DO NOT RUB IT. Echo, the tub needs to be comfortably hot, but not scalding—be careful, or we could damage the tissues even worse. Ditch your Suit jacket and roll up your shirt sleeve, and test the water by sticking your elbow in it. If it feels good to your elbow, she'll do okay. Now, Romeo will be waiting dinner on me," India addressed Omega with a smile, "but we're staying in tonight—just for you—so if you need me, all you gotta do is yell. But I want YOU to take it easy tonight, get warm, STAY warm, and just rest. Even relatively minor hypothermia can depress the immune system, and with all of the off-world immigrants coming through, not to mention the tourists on vacation, we don't need you contracting something nasty that human immune systems weren't designed to handle, to begin with." She looked over at Echo. "This lady toughed it through at your side today. You should be proud of her. Take good care of her tonight, all right? And call or come next door and knock if you two need me for anything, and I'll come running. Pay attention, and if she doesn't get warm in the next hour or so—especially once she gets something hot in her, but seriously, if she's still cold after a hot bath—come get me right away." She grinned at him. "You get to play nurse tonight!"

And she was gone.

* * *

Echo came to the sofa and crouched down, the better to meet Omega's eyes.

"You okay?"

"I-I'm g-gonna be," she murmured, dropping her gaze. "Sorry ab-bout this."

"Hold that thought for a few minutes. Lemme go crack open a can of stew and get it started heating, maybe stir in some red wine and herbs to beef it up a little and get rid of the canned taste, then brew a pod of coffee. India's right; we need to get something hot in you. The sooner, the better."

"Oh, I can do—"

"Apparently not."

He rose and headed for her kitchen, removing his jacket and loosening his tie as he went.

* * *

In Echo's wake, Omega did a slow burn.

"Apparently not." Right! So I'm completely incompetent! I did everything he said to do. Everything FOX said to do. Kept the Ke!endarians safe, took out one of the embedded terrorists my own damn self. Got Zhaejoh into the safe car, past all the bombed-out shit, even with the middle cars blown open to near-vacuum. And I'm still getting treated like an inept child,

dammit! This ain't gonna cut it.

She sat staring at the kitchen door, waiting for Echo to emerge, whereupon she intended to ensure he was made aware of her viewpoint on the day's events.

* * *

Echo, his sleeves rolled up above his elbows, tie completely undone and hanging down his chest, collar open, came back a little while later with a TV table laden with a large bowl of beef stew, several thick slices of cheddar cheese, an equally thick slab of buttered bread, and a big mug of hot coffee with plenty of cream already stirred into it.

Omega's appetite promptly took priority over matters of informing her partner of her viewpoint of events—they had, after all, not really eaten since cobbling together sandwiches in the train kitchenette on the way down.

This lack of food turned out to be a factor which India indicated had only exacerbated Omega's hypothermia by leaving her running on low fuel. Though, Omega had tried to explain, there had been no real opportunity until they got on the maglev for the return trip, and even that got aborted by the terror attack. Zhaejoh had been extremely anxious by the time they were safe in the lead car, verging on a panic attack, so Alpha One had spent the rest of the trip getting him settled. By the time the pair were finally en route back to Headquarters, they had both been too tired to bother.

As Echo sat the portable table in front of his partner, he also snagged the cold can of Diet Coke that sat on it, moving to the adjacent armchair to sit. Omega extracted gloved hands from the mass of blankets, reaching for the mug, as Echo popped the top on the soda and took a sip.

"There," he said. "Eat up, baby. That's decaf, by the way. You'll remember India specified it. Hypothermia patients don't need caffeine. It's not good for 'em. Among other things, it can trigger that cardiac arrhythmia she was advising you against."

"Oh? You know this because...?"

"How do you think? Eat, now. Then you can sit there and digest a bit while I change clothes, then run you a hot bath in your tub."

"Thanks," Omega admitted. "I'm starved." She picked up the mug of coffee, wrapping her hands around it to absorb its warmth...and also to steady it in her still-trembling hands. She took a long, slow sip. "Ohh, that's nice."

* * *

"Good. Be careful and don't spill it, or you could burn those hands. At least your teeth have stopped chattering, which is good. Try to relax as much as you can; it'll help soften the muscles, letting the blood flow easier, and you'll get warm a little bit faster."

"Okay." Omega launched into an enthusiastic—if slightly clumsy— consumption of her dinner, making appreciative smacking sounds from time to time. Echo sat back and watched, occasionally sipping his cold drink, and mulling over what exactly had happened. Finally he decided to be direct and ask.

"So...is this why you didn't show for post-shift reports?"

"Um, yeah," she said, setting her empty coffee mug aside and scraping the last remains from the stew bowl. "I fully intended to, Echo, I swear. Only, when we got back to HQ, I was still pretty badly chilled. Then I realized I still couldn't feel my feet, my hands were stiff, and my ears weren't any better. I thought maybe I might need to have 'em looked at, so I spotted India in the Core as we went through, peeled off and told her about it. She wouldn't take no for an answer; she and Romeo grabbed me, and the pair of 'em marched me back here, practically under armed guard. I'd swear my feet weren't even ON the floor at times. India said..." Omega shrugged. "She said, if I'd let it go much longer, as low as my internal temperature was...well, I wasn't gonna warm up on my own, not without help, and I coulda lost some toes, maybe a finger." She waved her left hand. "And I'm kinda used to typing on the computer with all ten, so I sorta figured..."

"Meg, why the hell didn't you TELL me you were freezing?!" Echo wondered in exasperation.

* * *

That was the last straw on Omega's camel. The irritation, annoyance, and anger boiled over.

"I DID!" she exclaimed then. "I KEPT TELLING YOU I WAS COLD! You told me to suck it up, so I did! 'What part of "This is Antarctica" don't you get?' I got ALL of it! There just wasn't any damn thing I could DO about it!"

"But Meg..."

"Look, Echo, I'm sorry I'm not as big as you are, so I don't generate and retain as much body heat! That's just the way it works!"

"You could have worn a heavier Suit, and put on thermal layers under it. We stopped off so I could change, and I expected you to do it, too. You should've—"

* * *

"NO, I COULDN'T!" she cut him off, yelling by this point, face turning red as the Celtic temper fairly exploded. In that moment Echo was grateful for the fact that Agent quarters were soundproofed, otherwise their neighbors would be complaining...AND gossiping, because Omega was very effectively reaming HIM out. "I didn't have anything to change INTO, dammit! Quit blaming me for shit! I can't help it if I didn't have any winter-weight Suits! Supplies didn't GIVE me any yet, because it's SUMMER here! All I had was linen blends, summer weight cotton-blend socks, NO thermal under-layers of ANY sort, no clothing suitable for anything below sixty-five degrees! At least I had the good sense to layer my socks! I did every damn thing you and Fox told me to do today, to the best of my ability, and all either of you did was fuss at me, like I'm some incompetent, pathetic, brain-dead excuse for an Agent! You said hurry up this morning, so I hurried—and then you AND Fox complained about my tie! Well, you know, that damn special knot y'all do is a pain in the ASS to tie every blasted morning of the world! We'd have been another ten minutes or more leaving if I'd tried to do that damn thing, and THEN you'd have been fussing for my running us late! And don't think I didn't know that you were wondering, in the train, if you should have brought Romeo along instead!"

He blinked in surprise at that. *She knew? She read me that well? Damn.* But Omega's diatribe wasn't over.

"THEN we got to McMurdo and I was freezing half to death and you told me I was complaining! 'Suck it up,' you said! So I did! And now I got frostbite! And here you are, fussing at me about THAT! And I heard you plain as day, yelling a while ago when you came into your quarters, too, probably because you thought I skipped out on helping you fill out the damn paperwork! So just..." she flung herself back into the sofa, "shut the hell up! I don't wanna hear about it! I gave you my abso-damn-lute best today, and all you've done—ALL DAY—is CRITICIZE! If I'm not good enough for you, throw me back into the NASA pond and have done! I was good enough to make bloody damn ASTRONAUT there!!"

* * *

Echo was silent, watching her rant, realizing she was venting all the emotions from the mission...*and a few other things, too,* he thought, hearing the NASA comment...at once, and seeing the sapphire eyes glimmer a little more than usual.

She's right. Nothing about what happened today was her fault, but she caught the brunt of all of it. And that, even with taking out one of the terrorists we didn't initially know was there—all by herself, and no backup, 'cause I had my own hands full with the OTHER terrorist. And she did it with a dual wield, by the look of it, too.

And now she's injured, and I still gave her hell. She looks like she feels like crying, but she isn't. She's way stronger than that, anyway. I've never seen her cry, and I don't think I've ever even seen her tear up...before now. And if she wasn't in a world of hurt medically, she probably wouldn't now, either. But if I interpreted India correctly, Meg's burned all her reserves, and doesn't have anything left to suck up WITH at this point. He bit his lip, thinking.

Shit. I need to file an addendum to today's report. Fox needs to know about this. And we need to make sure, from now on, that new recruits get a full year's wardrobe, up front—ESPECIALLY if they're going into Alpha Line. Damn. Major oversight, and as much mine as anyone's. If I'd known she didn't have the heavy weight clothing...dammit to hell! I thought she'd changed, too. I guess it took her all that time just to tie the proper knot.

"Why didn't you tell me up front?" he finally asked when she paused for breath, keeping his voice low, and as gentle as he knew how to make it; she was upset enough as it was and he didn't want to make things worse, or in her condition, she really MIGHT end up in Medical.

198

"Because..." Omega suddenly broke off the diatribe.

"Because why?"

She drew a deep breath and let it out as a long sigh, seeming to collapse in on herself.

"Romeo asked that, too." Another sigh.

"What did you tell him?"

"That I didn't tell you because I reasoned it all out. Because I knew you needed backup, or Fox would have sent you by yourself. And you and he figured I could handle it, or you'd have asked for Romeo instead of me. Like I said, I already know you considered him, and you used to be partners, so it woulda worked okay. But I didn't know I'd only have the coat and gloves and face mask until we were on the way. I thought—hoped—maybe Supplies would give us some more clothing, mukluks and insulated gear and stuff..."

"So THAT was why you kept asking about the coats."

"Yeah. I started to tell you at that point, but then I realized if I did, you'd probably make me stay in the train. And if you did that, you...might not come back." She looked away, and the cowl of blanketing hid her face from his gaze. "I...didn't want you to get...get killed, even if it meant I lost a few toes and fingers." The blankets shrugged. "I figured maybe the medics could grow those back if I needed 'em to. Hoped so, anyway. I thought it would be easier to do that than to bring you back from the dead, especially if you had a big hole in the middle or something."

Echo sat staring at her for long moments, astounded at the revelation, and at the woman in front of him.

Damn. She was literally willing to sacrifice body parts to see that I had backup. To ensure I made it back in one piece. That...is a partner. Abruptly he rose, and she blinked.

"Where the hell are you going now?" she wanted to know, and Echo heard a kind of beaten-down tiredness in her voice.

"I'm gonna go run you a nice, hot bath to soak in, so you'll warm up faster," he said, keeping his voice quiet and even. "You've more than earned it. Is all your stuff within reach in the bathroom? Robe and junk?"

"Oh. Um, my robe is hanging on a hook on the back of the bedroom door. House shoes are by the bed."

"I'll grab 'em and put 'em beside the tub. You want bubble bath shit?"

She shrugged, apparently still annoyed. So he pressed on.

"Can I find it? The bubble bath shit, I mean."

"Yeah. It's the lavender-scented stuff sitting in the back right corner of the tub."

"You do this hot soaking a lot?" He raised an eyebrow.

"Not usually. But as hard as we work out, sometimes I get sore muscles. The lavender helps me relax. And I think it smells better than the eucalyptus and menthol stuff, which irritate my skin a little anyway."

"Oh. Okay, I get it. Stay here and just try to unwind. I'll run the tub, lay out everything, and come back and help you get in there."

It was Omega's turn to raise her eyebrows.

"What, are you planning on helping me into the tub?"

"Er, no. That's not what I sai...well, I guess it might've sounded like it, but I meant I'd help you get into the bathroom. Uh, not meaning to be over-familiar or anything, but what've you got on under all those blankets?"

"Um." She flushed. "I've still got on my trousers and shirt, if that's what you mean. Romeo grabbed my jacket, and they helped me take off my shoes and socks and my tie, 'cause I was kinda fumble-fingered. I dunno where they put 'em."

"Fumble-fingered, huh?" Echo ran a hand through his hair, concerned. "Can you HANDLE getting undressed on your own?"

"Uh, I think I can, now. My teeth aren't chattering any more and I've almost stopped shivering. It might take a little longer than usual, and I'll probably just leave my clothes in a pile in the bathroom for the time being and clean it all up in the morning, but I think I can do it myself." She grimaced. "I might pop some shirt buttons, but those can be sewn back on in Laundry, I guess."

"Good. So like I said, I'll get you into the bathroom. After that, you're on your own. But leave the door cracked open a little bit, and I'll stay just out here, so if you slip or something, all you gotta do is yell and I'll come running. Hell, if I hear a loud crash and you DON'T yell, I'll come running. You already got frostbite and junk. We don't need you banging yourself up, into the bargain. Or worse yet, half-drowning in the tub."

She rolled her eyes and flopped back into the couch as he headed for her bathroom.

* * *

By the time she'd had a long, luxurious, lavender-scented bubble bath, Omega was starting to feel better. She was WARM, for one thing, and feeling much more laid-back and relaxed, for another.

So when she emerged from the bathroom wrapped in a thick, soft, full-length black terry robe with matching fleece-lined suede house shoes, and Echo—still in the armchair, an empty soda can on the end table beside him, but now dressed in lightweight black lounge pants, moccasin slippers sans socks, and short-sleeved t-shirt—scrutinized her from head to toe, she didn't react, merely stood there and endured his inspection.

"Hold out your hands," he said then, and she understood he was verifying for himself that she was okay. So she obliged, spreading her fingers so he could see that the redness had diminished somewhat.

"You treat 'em already?"

"Yeah. I swabbed on the Rejuvic, then I glopped on some more of the stuff India left before I put on my robe," she noted. "And I kinda rubbed it in, a little." She made motions as if applying hand lotion. "Nothing was, you know, stiff or frozen or anything. Feels a lot better already."

"Good. Now let me see your feet."

"Um, okay." She leaned over and looked down at her fleece-encased feet, holding out first one, then the other. Echo snorted.

"Tired?"

"Yeah. Little bit."

"More than a little bit, I expect. You look like you're half asleep. Can you take your house shoes OFF?"

"Uh, yeah. Why...?"

"Wow. You ARE tired. I wanted to see how those frostbitten toes are doing, and I don't have x-ray vision."

"Oh. Duh." She kicked off her slippers and displayed her feet, wiggling her toes in the soft denim-blue carpet.

"Not too bad now," he decided. "India hit 'em with Rejuvic on the first go?"

"Yeah, that and about three other things." Omega pointed at one toe. "This one was almost black and the one next to it was turning kinda dark blue. They're just pink now."

"Damn. You really WERE about to lose 'em. You feel okay? No sign of blood nasties from dead tissue? What is it they call that...oh yeah. Sepsis?"

"No, I'm just tired. And I think I got good reason for that." She shoved her feet back into her house shoes.

"Yeah, you do. We both do."

"Yeah. Besides, India gave me an antibiotic."

"Aha. That lady is on her game. You warm yet?"

"Yup, nice and warm. Finally! I thought for a while there, I'd never feel warm again."

"Okay, good. So...you wanna go to bed early, or stay up and watch TV...? Read? What do you wanna do now?"

"Oh, I figured I'd watch TV for a little while, then go to bed a bit early." She glanced at the clock on the wall, noting the time. "Oh. Well, never mind about the early thing..."

"Yeah, it was past our normal crash time when we got back. You wanna go straight to bed, then?"

"No, I still wanna watch TV. I need to wind down a little before going to bed. My brain is still crankin' at maglev speed."

"With or without company? For the TV," he added.

"Are you the company?"

"Only if you want it." Echo shrugged. "I'll understand if you're still pissed off at me."

Omega thought that one over for a moment.

"I guess it depends," she considered. "Are you still mad at ME?"

"I was never mad at you. Distracted, during the mission. Irritated... and disappointed when you didn't show up for the reports. But not angry. And now that I understand what happened, I'm not even that. Any of that."

"Well...good. I'm glad," Omega confessed. "I was...upset."

"I gathered," he said drily. "And you had every right, in retrospect.

But I hope you get where I was coming from."

"I do. And even for all our training, you don't really know me well enough yet to know that I WASN'T just complaining," she acknowledged. "We haven't ever gone on a mission that...strenuous...before. So, just for future reference, if I say something like, 'I'm cold,' it doesn't mean it's a little nippy, and I'd like a sweater. It means I'M REALLY COLD, and I might be in trouble. Likewise anything else that might sound like complaining, such as, 'I'm too hot,' or 'That hurts,' or something like that. I expect a lot of myself, so I don't complain just to hear my voice, Echo. If I pipe up, it's because something is WRONG."

"Fair enough. I swear to you I'll remember that next time, and I will take it very seriously. But you gotta do something for me, too." He stood. "Want a brew? I got some in my fridge. Since you're warm now, you can risk a little alcohol, and it'll help you sleep later. Only one, though. I'm not lettin' you get sloshed, not until you're fully recovered. And I made sure the alcohol in the wine I tossed in the stew had all cooked off before you got it."

"A beer would be nice, yeah. Stew tasted good, by the way; thanks. And I prefer not to get sloshed anyway, as you oughta know by this time. Although I guess it might be easier to do right now, given my medical condition, so I suppose we DO need to be careful. Got any chocolate stout yet? I forgot to put it on my last order to Supplies, and was hoping you remembered to put it on yours..."

"Yup. Picked some up day before yesterday, down at the corner market, 'cause I saw it and remembered you like the stuff."

"What, the day I was doing the case study and you went out to pick us up some lunch at the deli?"

"Yeah."

"I take it all back. You're a prince of a partner."

"Okay." Echo snorted. "Apologies all around, I guess."

"...Yeah."

"All right. Be right back. You sit down, get comfortable, and find out if there's anything on the tube worth watching. We got satellite cable from across the galaxy, and I still have trouble finding something I'm interested in watching, dammit. If you can't find anything, I'll pull something from my movie collection."

"Okay." She sat down and grabbed the TV remote, beginning to surf as he headed through the back door. Moments later his voice floated back to her.

"Oh, while you were in the tub, I scheduled an appointment for us to meet with the maglev tube engineers, day after tomorrow, so you can ask 'em all the questions you like. To be honest, I think they were excited at the prospect. They don't generally get a lotta interest from the new recruits, let alone somebody with your background."

"Cool! Thanks."

"You're welcome. I also filed an amended daily report to include your injury, then I contacted Fox and told him personally about the Suit snafu and its being the direct cause of your frostbite. After he was done cursing a blue streak—in English, Yiddish, German, Hebrew, and several extraterrestrial languages, plus a couple I didn't recognize—he said he was dropping everything to compose a memo to Supplies, updating the policy." Clinking sounds came from the other apartment. "Hauling Tango in for tribunal and probable brain-bleaching can wait, he said. Not for long, but long enough for this."

"Really? Oh, thanks, Echo. I appreciate that. So Fox wasn't happy about it either?"

"Oh HELL no." He came back in, carrying two steins of stout, and handed one to her. "He called back a couple minutes before you came outta the bathroom. He'd called India and got the full details on your condition— she says no gym workouts tomorrow, by the way; you need an easy shift, to finish healing—and Fox said it explained something."

"What did it explain?"

"He said, when he patted you on the shoulder in his office, he was shocked at how cold you felt."

"Um, yeah. Didn't think about that."

"Then Fox called the head of Supplies directly and they had a 'comin' to Jesus meeting,' as Fox said I'd have put it. THEN he sent the memo! You'll have a complete, year-round wardrobe by the time we get off our next shift, if not sooner, and all future recruits will have a full, all-seasons wardrobe no later than the time they are finished with training."

"Geez, I didn't mean to get Supplies in trouble."

"No worries there. Frankly, Fox and I both should have ensured you had everything you needed up front, especially with you and me being the prototype Alpha Line team. And Fox told me he made sure the head of Supplies knows the blame was shared among us. We're the experienced agents, after all; it isn't reasonable to assume a rookie agent has thought about crap like this. But WE should. And we didn't. It never once occurred to me you might not have a full wardrobe. It didn't come up with Romeo, and my previous partner trained ME, so I wasn't aware of the glitch in the protocol." He shook his head in annoyance, most likely at himself, Omega suspected. She already knew he took her training very seriously, and she fully recognized that the fact he'd overlooked something that had led to her injury would bother him to a significant degree.

"Oh, okay. I get it," she offered gently. "Don't blame yourself for it, Ace. I promise I don't. Like you told me over the Ke!endarian's death, you can't prevent what you don't know about."

"Plus, Fox gave us permission to sleep in tomorrow, and come in a quarter-shift late," he went on, seeming to ignore her comment. But the look in his eyes told her it had registered, and he appreciated it, even if he didn't quite agree with it. "We're authorized to come in a half-shift late if, in my judgement in the morning, you need the extra rest—which means I'll be coming in to check on you before you've gotten out of bed, maybe even before you wake up, so be aware of that."

"Okay. Do what you need to, I guess. Should I bother with my alarm clock?"

"Nah. I'll slip in and check your vitals real quick—you know, pulse, forehead temp, and stuff—and see how you're sleeping. If I don't like something, I'll call India. If you're still out of it, I'll sneak back out and let you sleep. You can wake up when you wake up. That work for you?"

"Yeah. Thanks."

"Based on what India told him, Fox wants to make sure you have time to heal a little more before risking your having to go out on assignment again. And frankly, if something major comes up, he's probably going to send Romeo and India, anyway. Or Romeo and me, if we decide you need India here to look after you medically. Consider yourself on partial sick leave, I guess."

* * *

He plunked his stein onto the end table, then reached for the blankets she'd used earlier.

"Here. Let's cover those legs and feet up, and put the hood up on that robe. If I let you get chilled again, you'll end up in the medlab for sure, and India—AND Fox—will kill me. And I'll probably self-flagellate for a week, into the bargain." He tucked her in from shoulders to toes, studied her face to make sure she was comfortable, then sat back down and looked at what was on the television. "Oh, that'll do nicely. I like that movie."

"So do I. Hey, you said I had to do something for you."

"Yeah."

"What?"

"Practice tying that tie."

"I HAVE been," Omega protested, then sipped her stout. "Mm, that's good. No, Echo, I have been, I swear I have, I'm just not quite getting it somehow. Well, I mean, I can, it just takes time. Way too much time."

"Didn't you read the handbook?"

* * *

"I keep the damn thing open on my dresser, to that very page," Omega said, pointing to the bedroom door, before plunging her arm back into the soft, welcoming warmth of the blankets. "You can go look and see. But the illustrations for the knot just suck."

"Ouch. And that's coming from the woman who can construct a hypercube puzzle in world record time, too."

"Meh. Listen, y'all don't have a, I dunno, a video or something, do ya? It ain't like us women are used to tying those things, anyway. I need to SEE it being tied, and then maybe I'll remember the trick to it."

"Hm. No, not that I know of. But I'll put it in as a recommendation."

"Okay. Thanks."

"Remind me some morning, during breakfast or something, and I'll let you watch me tie mine."

206

"I will if I'm ever awake enough to remember. Oo, here comes one of my favorite scenes!"

"Mine too. Gotta love that actor."

"Yeah, and the car chase is awesome!"

* * *

When the movie ended, Echo turned to Omega.

"You sleepy yet?"

"Not quite yet. Gettin' there. Why?"

"Wait here."

He rose and went into his apartment, returning moments later with his electronic tablet. He placed it in her lap and swiped a finger across the screen to wake it.

"There. Some light reading material for you."

"What—?" Omega broke off, double-taking at the information on the screen. "This is a...birth certificate? For...Alexander Ian Bryant..."

"Originally of Ozona, Texas. Right." Echo waved at the tablet. "Alex for short. That's the entire file, right there. Want another cup of decaf? Or maybe some hot chocolate before bed..." He ambled toward her kitchen.

"The chocolate, please." Omega scanned through several documents in the file. "This is...but...wait. Alex doesn't begin with an E..."

"Echo was my nickname," the Agent's soft voice wafted out of her kitchen in explanation. There was a hiss in the background from the pod brewer. "Middle name was actually supposed to be Elan, which is Apache for 'friendly,' but the clerk evidently misheard. Mom was Lipan Apache; Dad was Irish-American." He paused, and a laugh emerged. "Make that Irish-Texan! Anyway, as a kid, I had a good ear for mimicry; I was especially good at bird and animal calls. Came in handy when I started learning alien languages, especially the avian groups like Ke!endarian. At any rate, the name stuck. It was sheer coincidence, when I was co-opted into the Agency, that they chose to use that particular phonetic alphabet for the first batch of code names. Or maybe my nickname inspired their choice; I dunno."

"So...this is...but you'd said..."

"I figured it was time," Echo said, coming out with two mugs of hot chocolate.

* * *

The next couple of shift days went a little better. And they were certainly quieter, rather to Omega's secret relief.

By first lunch the next day when they were to report late for duty, Omega was well over her mad at Echo, both because she was finally warm, and because his actions the night before demonstrated to her without doubt that he valued and trusted her. More, though he had yet to use the term in reference to the two of them, she now felt more secure in their friendship, over and above being partners.

The frostbite on fingers, toes, ears, and to a much lesser extent, nose, had largely healed as she slept, under the powerful influence of advanced alien pharmacology. She still had a couple of blisters and some peeling skin, but even those were healing rapidly.

India gave her a quick once-over, coming by well before Omega and Echo were due to leave their quarters that morning, and instructed Echo that, unless there was a planet-level emergency, Alpha One needed to have a slow, quiet recovery day.

"Omega's vitals are back to normal, like you said earlier this morning," she told Echo, "but that doesn't mean her blood chemistry has caught up yet. And I tagged up with Zebra already this morning, just to confirm, and she agreed. She'd like Alpha One to come by at your earliest convenience today, though, so she can run a full scan on Meg and get it into her medical records, but I expect everything will be okay. Give it about one more shift day, she and I decided. Although, girl, now I look at you, you must have burned some serious calories..."

"Yeah, I had to take up the belt a notch or two this morning," Omega admitted, and Echo raised an eyebrow in surprise, quickly scanning her up and down.

"Did you step on the scale?" India wondered. "Bet you were down at least three pounds."

"Um, six and a half."

"Okay, I get this picture," Echo said then. "No workouts, take it easy, and stuff her face."

"Right," India said, grinning. "Given your respective dialects, I recommend grabbing a big ol' Southern breakfast, for starters."

"We can do that," Echo decided, heading for his kitchen. "The biscuits'll have to be canned, but I even got grits."

"Good!" Omega declared, and India laughed.

* * *

Meanwhile, Tango was in the brig at Headquarters, her own people having turned her over, and the PGLEIA Division One tribunal agreed to convene an emergency session on Earth. Within days, she was convicted of collaboration with a terrorist agency, subversion, collusion, several counts of conspiracy to commit murder, and conspiracy to subvert a fellow agent. She would be brain-bleached and expelled from Division One as soon as a likely cover story was devised for her—though said cover identity would remain completely under Division One control, and was unlikely to be a nice position; Fox was not about to allow a convicted criminal to get the same treatment that their trusted retirees got. The intelligent and adaptable Baker had been put in charge of the McMurdo Office upon the joint recommendation of Alpha One, while an investigation was instituted to ascertain that Pip had indeed retired under his own cognizance, neither coerced nor tricked.

More, Alpha One encountered nothing of significance on their routine patrol run.

* * *

By shift's end a few days later, they were filling out paperwork, as usual. Omega initialed the last form, slapped it on the stack, stretched, and said, "There! Ohh...I'm starved."

"Me, too!" Romeo chimed in from the next desk.

"Well, at least Meg has good reason," disparaged India, elbowing him. "You're always starved."

"I am not!"

"You are too! You had to do an extra workout this week just to burn it all off!" India poked Romeo in the ribs.

"Well, maybe if you weren't such a good cook..." he leaned over and kissed her nose, then tickled her. "Damn, girl! All that Korean soul food your gramma taught you t' make? How'm I s'posed to resist that? After all,

I'm still walking wounded."

"Hmph. Sez you. And it's your own damn fault for that. Maybe if you weren't such an omnivore..."

Echo and Omega watched them teasing each other for a moment, then caught each other's eye and grinned. Omega rolled her eyes upward, as if to say, *We might as well not be in the room,* and Echo let out a brief sputter that, to someone who didn't know him well, might have sounded like a suppressed laugh.

Romeo looked up at that, from where he and India were still teasing each other.

"Whaat?!"

* * *

Echo and Omega instantly assumed bland, innocent expressions, unaware that they were near-duplicates of each other.

"What 'what'?" said Omega.

"Never mind. What say we go out for pizza?" suggested Echo. "I know this great little pizzeria just this side of East Williamsburg on Meserole Street, run by a segmented bipedal felinoid from Antares IV. Trifle makes a terrific calzone. And the kitchen-sink pizza is a killer."

"I'm with that!" exclaimed Romeo. "They got cheesecake?"

"You ever had Antarean cheesecake?" Echo asked, raising an eyebrow.

"Oh HELL yeah! Let's go!"

* * *

"Mmm! Good taste, Echo!" purred Omega, as she practically inhaled her current slice of the extra-large pizza. India was also oohing and aahing, and Romeo nearly went into a feeding frenzy. Echo gave a thumbs-up to the felinoid owner, who watched them through the kitchen door from his perch atop the refrigerator. The felinoid blinked a friendly acknowledgement, waved with a front paw, stretched, and leaped down to see about his other orders.

At this time of day, there were a few other customers in the restaurant, and more came in every few minutes to order take-out. By now, even Omega was knowledgeable enough to tell the natives from the casual off-worlders, and there was a good mix of the two in the pizzeria's clientele.

When the huge pizza had been devoured, Romeo decided he wanted dessert, and India decided he should split it with her, then decided that Alpha One—especially Omega—needed the calories. While they were at the counter ordering huge slices of Antarean cheesecake for everyone, Echo leaned over to Omega.

"So, is it any easier?" he asked softly. "Being here, I mean. As opposed to...what you'd originally planned to do with your life."

She turned to look at him, meeting and holding his eyes. She stared at him for a long moment, thoughts turned inward, and then answered.

"Yeah. Yes, it is. Thanks to Romeo and India. And Fox. And you. Especially you."

"Good. It's time to tell you something, then. I wanted to wait until I knew you were handling this thing a little bit better before I told you. You made astronaut corps, you know. The last tests were just formalities."

"I know. You don't hit the delete key as fast as you think you do." She sighed regretfully as he shot her a startled glance, before continuing, "Any chance I'll ever get to go out there in this job?"

"...I'd say yeah. It happens from time to time. In fact, I'd guess Alpha Line is more likely to go off-planet than most of the other Division One departments. Except maybe Diplomacy."

"Good. Something to look forward to, then."

"I'll tell Fox first thing tomorrow that Alpha Line is fully operational and back online."

* * *

The pizzeria was only about a mile and a half from Headquarters. It was a straight shot and a nice evening, so the foursome had decided to walk over and back. As India pointed out, it gave them a little light exercise to work up an appetite before, and allow their food to settle and digest properly after. Echo considered it good team bonding, never mind a fun social outing with friends and colleagues.

But on the way back to the Headquarters Building after dinner, Omega shook her head slightly, then rubbed at her temples. Echo gave her a curious glance, and India asked, "What's the matter, Meg?"

"I don't know. Head just feels a little funny."

211

"Probably indigestion from all that pizza we ate," Romeo said. "I feel like a beached whale."

"You kinda look like one, too. You sure you're okay, Meg?" Echo inquired. She shook her head again.

"Yeah, I'll be fine. Probably just need to pile up in bed when we get back. I didn't sleep too well last night. Weird dreams."

* * *

Romeo and India stopped off at their respective doors, but Echo walked Omega to her door and followed her inside her quarters. He closed the door, took her by the shoulders and turned her to face him, refusing to relinquish his light grip on her shoulders.

"Now, what's this about sleeping badly? Were you putting on a good face for me back at the restaurant? How long have you been having trouble sleeping?"

"No, no, Echo, I told it to you straight, I swear. I wouldn't lie to you. I'm doing fine these days. And I've actually been sleeping—well, like a rock, to be honest. Y'all keep me so busy, I'm usually asleep by the time my head hits the pillow."

"And when you wake up the next day?"

"I feel fine. Rested. Ready for anything you and Fox—or the Universe, for that matter—can throw at me."

"But—"

"But...I don't know. The last couple of days, I just haven't slept so well. Like I said, weird dreams. Nothing I can remember. They just make me...restless." She shrugged.

"Dating from when?"

"Um..." She thought for a moment. "Maybe...the night after the Antarctic mission? Not that same night—I was so exhausted by the time I piled into bed, I woke up the next morning in the same position I laid down in; I never even rolled over, the whole night. Wow, was I stiff! But the next night, not so much. So...a couple nights, I guess."

He studied her intently for a moment. Then he released her.

"All right," he told her. "But if you don't sleep better tonight, we're going to the medics tomorrow, okay? Working a Division day is hard enough on humans without insomnia on top of it. And you're only just pulling out of the hypothermia and frostbite. We need to keep you in top shape to safely do this job, and insomnia won't cut it."

"Okay. Fair enough."

He headed for the back door, then paused with his hand on it.

"Do you mind if I do something a little...unorthodox...tonight?" he asked.

"What?"

"Leaving the back door open."

"Why?"

"Call it...a funny feeling. Those seem to be going around lately. These walls are designed to be soundproof so the neighboring agents aren't disturbed no matter what we do, since we're all on various shifts. If something...happened, I could at least hear a call for help."

"You're the senior partner, partner."

"Yeah. But I've never had a female partner before. And I like to at least think I'm an old-fashioned gentleman."

"You checked on me the morning after the Antarctic mission."

"True. But this is...different."

She walked over to him then, looked up at him, and laid a hand firmly on his shoulder.

"Echo, you need to understand some things. I haven't known you long, it's true, but these last couple of months we've worked really closely together. You and Fox have been evaluating me, I know, but I've been evaluating you, too, in my own way—remember what I told you, way back, about deciding what's right for me, what's acceptable? That. So I may not have known where you're from or who you were until just the other day, but I've seen the kind of man you ARE. And...you're my partner. If I didn't think we made a damn good team, I'd have asked to be transferred quite a while back, never mind fighting to make sure my partner stayed alive. And I think you feel the same way. Plus, you're experienced—like you told me, you're one of the Originals..."

"...Okay. So?"

"So it all boils down to this: I trust you, Echo. Completely. With my life, if necessary. Do what you think is best." Then she let her hand drop to her side, continuing to meet his gaze calmly, steadily.

He looked down at her for a long moment, seeing the sincerity in the blue eyes while keeping his own expression unreadable, feeling the warmth where her hand had rested. Then he said, "Good night, Meg. Sleep well," and disappeared into his darkened apartment.

But he left the back door open.

Chapter 9

The scream woke Echo from a deep sleep, leaving him sitting bolt upright in bed, adrenaline surging. He flung back the covers, groped in the semi-darkness for his pants, grabbed his flashlight, and headed through the back door two seconds later.

He slammed through Omega's partly closed bedroom door and came to a halt for a moment, staring in shock at her bed. In the dim glow of the night light, he saw her silk-pajama-clad body lying in the bed, thrashing about wildly, convulsed in agony and crying out with the pain.

He hit the light switch, dropped the flashlight, and rushed to the bed, kneeling and trying to gather her writhing form into his arms to calm her, but her convulsions were so violent, he could scarcely hold her. She looked up at him and gasped.

"Echo! Help...me!"

He brushed back a stray wisp of white-blonde, out of her eyes.

"What's wrong? Meg, tell me, what's wrong?"

"Thing! In...in my...head! Tear...tearing me...apart! Ohh! No! STOP! ...Make it stop! AAAaaah! Echo! Make it stop! Please...make it stop!" Her hands clutched desperately, imploringly, at his bare chest, her fingernails leaving behind red scratch marks in his flesh. Tears ran freely down her face, and he knew then that it was bad: She had never cried in his presence before.

Echo scrambled for the cell phone on her dresser. He found it lying next to the handbook—open to the necktie knot-tying page—and slapped at the screen to activate the device in emergency mode and hit the speed-dial contact. A beep told him he'd connected.

"Fox!" he yelled into it. "Priority Alpha One-Black emergency! Omega is down, repeat, Omega is down! Send the Arcturan ambassador and a trauma team to her quarters immediately! That's the Arcturan ambassador and a trauma team!"

"We read you, Echo," Fox's voice responded. "We're on the way."

Echo returned to the bedside and grabbed her by the shoulders.

"Hang on, Meg, just hang on. It's gonna be all right. Fight it! Fight it, honey! C'mon! You can do it!"

Omega buried her face in his chest, muffling her cries; her fingers dug desperately into his biceps as she fought the pain, still convulsing. Echo tried to will her his strength through the physical contact.

* * *

Fox and the medical team came rushing in moments later, followed closely by Romeo and India, wrapped in dressing gowns. India took one look at the scene and gasped, amber eyes wide and horrified.

"Ah! Oy gevalt!" Fox murmured, and moved into the nearest corner.

"Oh, maan," Romeo groaned, and began pulling Echo, who still held Omega's shoulders, away from the bed to give the medics more room to work. But the instant Omega could no longer feel Echo's touch, she cried out.

"NooOOO!" she shrieked, thrashing frantically. "Echooo! He's gone, he's gone. It got him. No! Stop it! Get out of my HEAD!"

Echo pulled away from Romeo, and the trauma team parted to let him back through. He grabbed her shoulders in a firm, reassuring grip.

"It's all right, Meg, it's Echo, I'm right here, baby! Where's that blasted TP?"

"I am here, Agent Echo," answered a seven-foot-tall blue alien in the corner by the dresser, who happened to be the Deltiri ambassador from Arcturus VII, and the Division's resident telepathy expert. "It is obvious she is under telepathic attack. I am already attempting to set up a block to that attack. One moment, please."

To the worried agents huddled around the bed, it seemed like forever. But after a couple of seconds, Echo felt Omega sag in his arms, and her wild flailing and cries of agony quieted. He wiped the tearstains from her face with compassionate fingers, offered a brief, gentle hug, eased her down to the bed, and rose to his feet. She lay limply, platinum hair fanned out across the bed, her usually pale skin even paler than normal, gasping for breath, totally drained.

"What happened?" Romeo asked his former partner then, pulling him to one side.

"I'm not sure. After we dropped you two off at your door last night, I talked with her about her sleep problems, which seem to be recent, only the last few nights. My gut told me something wasn't right, so I left the connecting door open in case she...well, I wanted to be able to hear if she called me, or...or something happened. And the hell it did! I woke up to a bloodcurdling scream, and when I got here, she was like you saw. Said something was in her head, tearing her up—from the inside out."

The Arcturan telepath listened quietly.

"Let me see what I can glean from her." The alien turned to Omega and asked politely, "May I look inside your mind? I am the Arcturan ambassador assigned to the Earth Agency. My name is Zz'r'p, and I am a trained telepath. I may be able to piece together who did this. I promise I will not hurt you, nor invade your privacy. I will look only at the events surrounding this attack."

Omega looked past the Arcturan at Echo. He noticed then, with some considerable trepidation, that her eyes were not completely focused. More, she seemed—uncharacteristically—to need his reassurance.

She doesn't fully understand what's happening, and she needs to know what's the appropriate thing to do, he realized. *And that means she's looking to her mentor for advice and a recommendation.*

So he gave it without hesitation.

"It's fine, Meg, Zz'r'p here's one of the good guys," he offered. "I've known him for years. He's the Arcturan ambassador to Earth, a Deltiri— they're allies—and he's a natural telepath, a strong one, with a lotta training under his belt. Just relax, do what he says, and he'll do the rest."

* * *

At that injunction, Omega struggled to sit up. But she was still weak from the attack, and floundered a little. So India gathered up the pillows— scattered around the room by Omega's writhing form—to pile them back in the bed, and Romeo and Echo helped Omega sit up and lean back against them. Once settled, she looked at a medic and whispered hoarsely, "Water?"

Almost instantly a glass appeared in her hand, and she sipped for a few moments. Then she handed the glass to Echo and turned to Zz'r'p, as Echo sat the discarded glass on the nightstand. Zz'r'p accepted Omega's invitational mattress pat, and sat on the edge of the bed where indicated.

"Ready," she told the telepath quietly, leaned back, and closed her eyes.

* * *

A slight tremor shook her frame as the alien began probing her mind, and then the room became completely still. It seemed to India as if no one was even breathing, and she was sure Echo had turned to stone. His ashen face was certainly set like granite.

After an eternity, Omega made a sound like a dry sob, and Zz'r'p rose slowly, thoughtfully, from the edge of the bed. He turned to the medics and issued orders.

"Do not, under any circumstances, sedate her. Give her a stimulant."

Fox moved forward then, from the location he had occupied throughout, in the corner of the room nearest the door, as the medics obeyed.

"Zz'r'p, don't keep us in suspense. What's happening?" Fox demanded.

"It is not good." Zz'r'p gave the Arcturan equivalent of a shrug; it made him look like a gasping blue fish. "It was indeed a telepathic attack, intended to destroy her mind."

"And that would have left me..." came a weak voice from behind them.

"Damn those sharp ears," Romeo muttered.

"It would have left you either in a vegetative state, or deceased," Zz'r'p responded, compassionate despite the harshness of the words. "The dreams that have been disturbing you were the preliminary probes, as, I suspect, was Agent Echo's 'gut feeling.' But you are in your most susceptible state when asleep. That is why you must not sleep."

"Oh, boy. Great. And me already short on that commodity."

"I must also try to teach you how to erect a rudimentary mental block. It will be difficult; few humans can master it."

"Wait a minute, Zz'r'p," interrupted Romeo, "Why do you have to do that? You just said she was susceptible only when asleep."

"No, kiddo," countered Echo, "he said she was MOST susceptible when asleep. She was awake and aware when I came in, and has been ever since, yet she was still under attack."

"And there is more and worse, Agent Echo," added Zz'r'p. "You see, whereas Agent Omega was the victim of the attack, she was not the target."

"Explain," commanded Fox.

"It is really terribly simple. The attacker was attempting to cause pain to Agent Echo by destroying his protégé, Agent Omega."

Echo froze, paling further.

"So, man, do we like, know who this dude is?" asked Romeo.

"The identity I gleaned from Agent Omega's contact with him is—"

"SLUG," was the only word Echo said.

* * *

"So, who—or what—is a Slug?"

Romeo quizzed Echo as the agents waited in the dark living area of Echo's apartment next door, while the medics treated Omega, and Zz'r'p worked with her. The only light came from Omega's den, where Fox had switched on an end-table lamp. Its light poured into Echo's den through the back door, creating a yellow wedge in the darkness. Significantly, Echo stood just outside that wedge. India, sensitive to Echo's mood, elbowed Romeo to be quiet.

Echo said nothing.

"Slug is a name from the past," Fox supplied. "Slug is a gastropoid symbiote from the Delta Scorpii system. The Delta Scorpians look kind of like giant green snails to humans—Shell and all, they're a good five to six feet in height, and as much as eight or ten feet long, so I do mean giant. The difference is that the Snail and its Shell are separate beings, linked in a symbiotic relationship. The Snail part of the creature is a powerful telepath, and this is the means of communication with the Shell-being."

"Man, you're kidding," Romeo said in disbelief. "Are you tellin' me there's an entire planet that could be wiped out by a damn salt lick?"

Fox glared at him.

"Are they, like...mates?" India asked, curious.

"We're not sure. We haven't had much contact with them; they're an isolationist system. Such a concept may not even apply. We do know there's a very close mental link. What one feels, for example, the other feels, so it isn't JUST telepathic, it's also empathic—at least between the two members of the symbiotic relationship."

"So—how 'bout this Slug dude?" Romeo followed up.

"About...oh, I don't know...it was a long time ago, early in Division One history; I'd have to look up the year anymore. Slug was hired as a mercenary telepath by the Veldorn in their dispute with the M'Quer. They were trying to locate the M'Queran ambassador so they could kidnap it. At any rate, when we discovered we had an unauthorized offworlder, we mobilized some teams. The Snail—he wasn't called Slug then; given the telepathy, I'm not sure if we ever knew WHAT he was called—"

"Azeln," Echo's hoarse, low voice came out of the shadows. "He was called Azeln."

"How did you know that, Echo?" Fox wondered softly. "Telepathic bleedover?"

The dark head nodded once.

"Okay, Azeln...took out three of our agents before we got to him. One died outright. His entire nervous system simply ceased functioning. Burned out. The other two...well, that was before the concept of a living will caught on. We see to it that their life support is maintained, and they're properly cared for. Several civilians got in the way, too. The CDC never did figure out why the Big Apple had a rash of fatal cerebral aneurysms that year..." Fox paused, remembering. "Anyway, to make a long, painful story a little shorter, a very young Echo was the lucky one; with some good detective work, he actually located the Snail. The Snail telepathically attacked; Echo retaliated, and the Shell accidentally got caught in the crossfire."

"Aaand?" prompted Romeo.

"The neural feedback from the Shell's sudden death incapacitated Slug, and Echo was able to bring him in. Basically, it fried the circuits in the gastropoid's brain. He was comatose for a long time, and now he's... insane. He used his telepathic skills to escape imprisonment only a couple of years after we brought him in, but he never replaced the symbiotic Shell. So now he's called Slug because he's a Snail with no Shell."

"So Slug has decided to pay Echo back in kind, it sounds like," India finished for Fox.

"Sounds like it," Fox agreed. Zz'r'p entered the room.

"Agent Omega is rather unusual for a Terran. She has already learned to erect an acceptable mental shield. It is not as strong as a native telepath's would be, but it will do, except for encounters in which the assailant is physically close—the sheer power will tend to overwhelm her block, in proximity. Barring that, she will be protected from attack as long as she stays awake to maintain the mental block."

"Yes, but how long will that be?" asked a worried India. "Humans can only stay awake for so long before sleep deprivation and lack of REM sleep begin inducing psychosis..."

A sudden, spasmodic jerk from a still-mute Echo as he turned away from them, deeper into the darkness, drew their momentary attention.

"Yes, that is true, unfortunately. If she falls asleep, she will lose her mind, and if she stays awake, she will lose her mind," Zz'r'p responded. "It is ironic, but true nonetheless. She is in a...how is it you humans say it? Ah. A 'no-win scenario.'"

Echo's hands balled into fists.

"What's up there?" whispered Romeo, jerking his head at Echo's shadowed form.

"He considers himself responsible. He feels he should do something to stop Slug, to protect his junior partner, but he does not yet know how," surface-read Zz'r'p, very quietly.

"Echo? Guys?" Omega's voice came floating through the back door, then her robe-wrapped silhouette appeared in it. "Hi, guys," she greeted them.

"Hi, Meg. You doin' okay?" a concerned Romeo responded.

"Yeah, I'm fine. Really," she added for emphasis. "Where's Echo?"

Romeo wordlessly pointed into the darkness at his former partner. *Wow,* he thought, as he watched her walk past him. *There but for the grace of God. If I hadn't busted up that leg...*

"C'mon, honey," India whispered to Romeo, motioning for the others to leave. "I think they really need to talk now."

* * *

As the other Agents filed out silently, Omega stood in the darkness until her eyes adjusted. Then she moved over to the shadowy, statue-like figure. Immediately her dark-adapted eyes caught sight of the red marks on his upper arm.

"Oh, no," she whispered softly. She thought for a moment, then leaned forward. "What about your chest?" She studied his torso, then inhaled sharply. "Damn. It's bleeding too. I hurt you. I didn't mean to." She reached out a tentative hand to gently touch the wounds she'd inadvertently inflicted in her anguish, and which no one else had thought to treat. "I'm so sorry."

He turned away.

* * *

"Echo?"

He gave no answer, not knowing what to say, or how to apologize. Omega moved back around to stand in front of him again; sad, understanding blue eyes gazed up at him. He blinked and averted his own gaze, unable to meet those cerulean orbs.

"Echo, it's not your fault." Her voice was as gentle as her words, as her touch.

"Isn't it?" His voice sounded rough even to his own ears.

"Of course not. You can't control the actions of some psychopathic critter from the other side of the galaxy. Hell, you can't even control my actions. You can only control your own."

"Then maybe if I'd handled things differently all those years ago... been a little more accurate..."

"Maybe. Or maybe you'd be dead. Or the planet blown up. Or something else. You can't let it eat you up. That's exactly what Slug wants—he's messing with your head, just like he messed with mine—only he's using me to do it, which makes me madder than hell. Listen, Echo, I get what the situation is here. I know what I'm up against. I'm holding a ticking bomb. The only chance I've got is to find the bomb's maker and force him to defuse it. And I can't do that alone. I'm not good enough, and not nearly experienced enough. I need you, Echo. Don't hold me at a distance like this. I need your help; I need your support. Help me."

He turned then, finally, his face hard, jaw set. Determined.

"I'll go see Fox about—"

"NO. Not that way. I'm not a passive observer in this, Echo." She laid her hand lightly on his forearm. The touch was soft, but surprisingly strong. "I'm your partner, remember? WE will go see Fox. Together."

Echo stared down at her for a long moment, remembering a woman so determined to ensure he had proper backup that she had risked her own life and limb. *That...is a partner,"* he recalled thinking at the time, when the full measure of her sacrifice had become apparent, only a few days ago. *She's right. We have to do this together. But this time, SHE needs MY backup. And I will give her everything I've got. Just like she did for me.*

"Okay," he finally agreed, covering the hand on his forearm with his own. "Together."

"Right after we patch up these scratches," she added, towing him by that same forearm toward the bathroom. "You will utterly ruin your shirt otherwise."

* * *

Omega was tying her black tie in the mirror when she heard the knock at the bedroom door.

"Meg? You decent?"

"That's a matter of opinion..."

There was a snort from without. The door opened and Echo stepped just inside. Omega fussed with the knot, trying to get the tie's ends the right length. She undid the knot and started over, wrapping the tie about itself, concentrating on what her hands were doing in the mirror.

"Up...and through..." She looped one end over, then double-checked the handbook. "Nah, wrong way..." She backed the loop out; wrapped it the other way. Finally, she pulled the half-formed knot back out in frustration. Her hands trembled almost imperceptibly, despite herself.

* * *

Echo noticed.

"Blast and damn the irritating thing to hell and back again, twelve times over," she grumbled somewhat whimsically, in an apparent attempt to seem light-hearted. "I can calculate the gravitational lensing effect of

223

a galactic cluster; I can visualize eleven-dimensional unified fields. I can reconstruct a hypercube puzzle in twenty minutes. But it takes me an hour and a half to tie my stupid tie! I get up a half an hour early every damn day because of this thing, and every morning it's a crapshoot. You'd think by now I'd have the hang of this thing. You guys must be born knowing how to tie these."

"No more than you're born knowing how to braid your hair like that. I promised you this the other day, anyway. Here, watch," Echo said as he moved up close behind her, put his arms around her, looked over the top of her head at the mirror, and proceeded to tie her tie as if it were his own. She studied his movements carefully in the mirror.

"Slow down. Back up. Show me that loop again..."

He obliged.

"Yeah. That's where I'm going wrong," Omega said, as Echo snugged the tie up to her throat. "I think I see now." Their eyes met in the mirror.

"...There," Echo said, taking a deliberate step backward. "Think you can do it yourself next time?"

"...Yeah, I...think so. Thanks." She sounded oddly breathless. "Just... make sure you're around next time I have to do it..."

"I'll keep that in mind." He smiled slightly. "And you're welcome."

"How...how's your chest?" There was an odd, intense expression in the blue eyes.

"What about it?" The smile was still there.

"I clawed it pretty good a little while ago..."

"But you patched me up." He waved a hand in dismissal. "Glad you still had some of that bottle of Rejuvic left over. It'll be good as new by tonight, tomorrow morning at the latest."

"Doesn't it still hurt?"

"Those little scratches? Nah. Getting spit on by a Froon? Now THAT hurts."

"Oh, okay. Yeah, I guess acid saliva ain't fun. So, what did you want?" she sighed finally. Echo sobered immediately.

"I was wondering..." he began thoughtfully. "When you were...under attack earlier...I was wondering if you remembered any details."

A shadow crossed her face.

"Yeah. I remember," she said flatly.

"Had you rather not?"

"No. It's okay. You hung in there with me when I needed you, so..." she shrugged. "What do you want to know?"

"What was happening in your head. You weren't always...here."

"You're not asking for much there, are you?" she murmured softly, wincing. "Why didn't you just ask Zz'r'p?"

"I could have. And I thought about it. But I respect your privacy. Anyway, I wanted your direct impressions, not secondhand ones, even from a telepath. There could be something important in them. Besides, I thought you might..." Echo shrugged, "need to talk."

"All right. And I probably do. Need to talk, that is." She sat down on the side of the neatly-made bed and sighed, patting the mattress beside her. "You're going somewhere with this, anyhow, so I'll try. Just be patient."

"You've got all the patience I have. Which can be—and in this case, is—considerable."

He sat down next to her and waited. She leaned forward, settled her elbows on her knees, steepled her fingers, and rested her face against them.

"Okay. Let's see." Her voice grew distant, and an edge of pain entered it. "It started as a dream. We were on a mission."

"'We'? You and me?" He gestured between them, and she peered over her fingers at him.

"Yeah. Alpha One. I'm not really sure where we were, but wherever it was, it was dark. Cluttered. Almost pitch-black. We split up, trying to flank our target. Which turned out to be a really bad move..."

"Target? What were we after?" Echo asked.

"I...I don't know. Whoever or whatever attacked me, I think. Slug, I guess."

"All right. Go on."

"For a while, I could follow your location, because your white shirt showed up in the darkness, a little bit. Then you just...disappeared...and... and something...lunged out of the darkness...where you had been...be-before I could react...and...and gutted m-me..." Her voice trailed away, and she hid her face in her hands.

There was a long silence. Finally Echo broke it, very quietly.

"Is that when you screamed?"

"Yes..." in a whisper. "I felt it..."

"And it woke you up."

"Yes. I knew something was in my head, then, but it didn't stop...it kind of blended with real events, and I started having serious trouble telling the dream from waking reality. You suddenly came out of the dark; I suppose that's when you came in the bedroom?" She peeped between her fingers at him. He nodded, and she continued. "And I was lying there, with my... with..." Her voice broke. Her hands gestured to her belly then, to indicate a disemboweled state, as if her internal organs laid about her on the floor. Then she bent her head, leaned forward, and wrapped her arms protectively around her abdomen, in remembered pain. The instinctive gesture was a telling one to the experienced agent. Suddenly Omega shuddered almost violently, and opened her mouth to speak, but Echo cut her off.

"Sshh. No, just hush now. I get the idea," Echo whispered, leaning forward himself to put a comforting arm around her shoulders, which were trembling. "That's all I need to know. You don't have to go on."

"I-I'm not finished. If I'm going to tell you...I might as well tell you all of it."

"...Are you sure?"

"It might be important." She nodded, drew a deep, shaky breath, and continued. "You called the medics—which was real, I guess—and then... then the thing pulled you away from me, and I saw it...you..." She stumbled to a stop, unable to go on, then tried a different approach. "Echo, have you ever seen footage of JFK's assassination?"

"Yes. The Division—or, well, the prototype organization; the First Envoy wouldn't arrive to bring Earth formally into the PGLEIA for several more decades—didn't get there in time..."

Her voice dropped to a whisper.

"Okay, then. That's...like what happened to you next. Only there were no bullets...just...just mental...all...mental..."

Echo said nothing, merely continued holding her quivering shoulders.

"And...Echo?" Her voice was husky with emotion.

"Yes?"

"It makes no sense, but...when it...killed you, I could see the image of the killer..."

"And?"

"It was you, Echo. In some bizarre way, you killed...both of us."

* * *

Once the girl's dissected eyes had been reconstructed, this torture continued on her ears, as they too were 'enhanced.' The girl thought that surely it would end then...

...Until she felt the terrible ripping sensation as the scalpel sliced open her abdomen. Scarlet blood spurted several feet, then was seemingly miraculously stilled, as the surgery continued. Extra hands...or clamps... came in then, to hold the incision open, as wide as it would go.

She watched in horror, still struggling to scream with the pain, as one by one the organs of her abdomen were removed and laid on the surgical table about her, by those same cold robotic hands, operating under the influence of that malevolent mind. That mind was now ignoring all her mental pleas and cries for help, for relief from the dreadful agony of what amounted to a vivisection.

Each organ received its due attention from the robotic limbs, occasionally itself being dissected and reassembled, before being tucked back into her wide-open abdominal cavity, the tendons and ligaments which normally held them in place reattached. Once everything had been replaced, the remote-controlled hands closed each wound in turn, bathing them with some sort of strange light, in which glow the tissues immediately and swiftly knitted closed with no residual scarring.

Excellent, *the alien voice returned.* Now you will have greatly enhanced nutrient absorption, as well as increased resistance to toxins and infectious materials. Let me have a look at those lungs and heart...

No! *she cried.* NO! PLEASE! Please stop!

But her desperate pleas were ignored as the scalpel-wielding automaton approached her chest, slicing down between her budding breasts.

* * *

When Echo and Omega walked into Fox's office, the door was open, and Romeo and India were already there. Fox looked up at them and said, "We're already on it."

"Then what have you got for us so far, Fox?" Echo was all business now. Hard business. By contrast, Omega was unusually subdued, withdrawn.

"Couple possibilities. Look here." Fox brought up a map on the wall screen, centered on Division One headquarters. "We figure Slug has watched the two of you come and go for about a week; that's how he ascertained who your partner was, Echo. So I got the Hypothenemoid envoy in here—their planet's had more interactions with Snails than we have—and asked them to hunt up the range on a gastropoid's telepathy. It's not infinite. And it's not even very large. Fact is, to mass the kind of power we saw last night, Slug had to be within a mile or two. He can 'ping' as far as eight or ten miles out, but to attack like that, he has to be no farther than two, or maybe three at the outside."

A circle appeared on the map, centered on the PGLEIA Division One Headquarters building.

"That ain't great, Boss," Romeo murmured, concerned. "Not only does that cover a big chunk of Brooklyn, it gets most of south Manhattan, an' almost to Queens. An' that's with a two-mile radius. At three, you got all of the south end of Manhattan Island, AND part o' Queens."

"Whoa," Echo remarked, mentally calculating. "That's anywhere from a third to almost three-quarters of a million people for him to hide in."

"Yeah," India agreed. "That's a huge haystack in which to go looking for a needle."

"Which is why I discussed the effects of high population density on gastropoid telepathy, with both the Hypothenemoids AND with Zz'r'p," Fox explained. "The more people, it turns out, the tighter the range has to be—telepaths have to erect their own mental blocks against the random thoughts of so many people. And that limits them even farther."

Fox punched a couple more buttons on the virtual keyboard in his desktop; the circle shrank considerably, to a radius of only about three-quarters of a mile.

"So, to reach Omega, Slug has to be somewhere within this circle. But that's still a damn big haystack, as India notes, so we need to come up with some other factors to narrow it even more. Now then. I've debriefed Romeo and India, who told me about the 'funny head' you had last night after dinner, Omega. That had to have been a preliminary probe. So they reconstructed the route you took in walking back. Here it is." A jagged, zigzag line appeared, overlaying certain streets. "We were just trying to determine in which block the probe occurred when you two came in."

"Here." Echo leaned over and tapped the screen. "It was right here. Halfway down this block between Driggs and Bedford, this spot exactly."

"You sure?"

"Positive."

"All right, then." A glowing red square appeared underneath Echo's fingertip.

"Wait a minute, guys. I got an idea," exclaimed Romeo.

"That'd be a first, champ," deadpanned Echo.

"No, it'd be a second. Remember the saucer at the Mardi Gras," prompted Fox.

"Oh yeah. Well, go on, Romeo."

"Don't get no respect. Dissin' me...hell, I was the number one until Echo got back, an' now—"

"Go ON, Romeo." Fox was stern.

"Anyway, if this slimeball—"

"Slimetrailer."

"—Slimetrailer has such a limited range, why don't we just move Omega somewhere else until we catch 'im?"

Echo and Fox looked at each other in surprise.

"Hmm..." mused Fox.

"My turn, guys."

All eyes turned toward Omega in startlement. It was the first thing she'd said since arriving in Fox's office, and everyone had almost forgotten she was there—except Echo, who was acutely aware of his partner's silent presence.

"So, does anybody in here besides me know how to erect a mental block against a telepath?" she continued.

Four pairs of eyes looked at her blankly.

"Uh-huh." Omega sighed. "That's what I thought. So Slug already knows you're considering it."

Echo picked up on her line of thinking.

"And if he's close enough to observe that you're my partner, he's close enough to observe us taking you away."

"And to follow me wherever you take me."

"Damn."

"In fact, I've been thinking: what if that's what caused the headache at the Cape?" Omega added.

"Well, shit. Good point. So he may already be following us," Echo surmised. "At least to some extent—I doubt he followed us to Antarctica; that's way the hell outside a Snail's habitable environment. But with a small saucer or spacecraft at hand, equipped with some basic cloaking..."

"Right."

"Okay, so, okay," Romeo brainstormed, "what about this: We get that blue guy, Hiccup or Zz'r'p or whatever, and he follows Omega around with that block thing of his..."

"Good idea, Romeo, and one I'd actually already thought of because it would give her a break and some rest, but we're too late. Zz'r'p was called back to Arcturus VII this morning, right after I finished talking to him. Political crisis; diplomatic consultation with the ruling council," Fox filled him in. "Damn poor timing, but there it is. I don't suppose there's ever a good time for a political crisis."

"All right, all right, I'm not done yet. Surely we got some, like, resident telepaths?"

"Hombre, humans don't do telepathy—not like this," Echo replied. "Didn't you catch Zz'r'p call Omega exceptional just because she learned how to erect a passable block? Fox and I both trained under Zz'r'p during Slug's original excursion, and we never learned more than rudimentary stuff."

"Well, then, what about some of the other aliens on the planet?"

"What about it?" Echo turned to Fox.

"I don't know, Echo. Maybe. There's a couple of innate telepaths on-planet right now, maybe four or five. If we can figure out whose political sympathies lie with the gastropoids, weed out the ones who might have it in for you, which ones would get their kicks seeing a lowly human get wasted..."

"Yeah, yeah. I get the picture."

Romeo's shoulders slumped. Echo clapped him on the back.

"Hey, you tried, sport."

"Yeah..."

"Okay, so we're back to square one," sighed Fox. "Computer, enlarge target area."

The red square swelled to fill the screen. Now individual buildings could be seen.

"So. Let's eliminate all of the completely occupied buildings and highlight those that are empty or partly empty. Slug's not likely to let himself be seen any more than he can help. People would think a six-or seven-foot green slug unusual, even for New York City. And there's only so much mind control even he can do. So I expect crowds are a no-no."

Two buildings lit up.

"There. The four of you go check it out. And take some firepower."

* * *

A black '96 Corvette pulled up to an empty building and two couples in solid black Suits, wearing wraparound sunglasses, got out. There were barely noticeable bulges underneath the arms of each jacket, where each carried at least one concealed proto-cyclotron blaster. Further, each carried a pocket-sized Winchester & Tesla Mark II death ray somewhere upon his or her person. The driver, a man appearing to be, perhaps, in his mid-thirties, pointed a small device at the Corvette, which promptly emitted a low beep as the vehicle's security system—which was substantial, and quite deadly—armed itself.

"Ready?" Echo asked.

The other three agents nodded. As several pedestrians walked by, Echo dropped into a patter.

"...And gentleman and ladies, this piece of real estate should be a prime location for your offices. Shall we go in and look around?" With that, Echo smoothly opened the lock on the door with an electronic lockpick. Once inside, Omega moved swiftly to the building's security system, disarming it with a small silver mechanism she produced, while Romeo and India drew their blasters and fanned out to either side.

Quickly, two by two, they searched all three floors and basement. They met back at the front.

"Nuthin'," a glum Romeo volunteered.

"Same here. See any potential escape routes?" Echo enquired.

"As a matter of fact, we did. Or rather, Romeo did," India said.

"Yeah, Echo, there's like a service crawlway in the basement down into the tunnels and sewers and stuff," Romeo elaborated.

"Huh. Did you seal it off?"

"Yeah." He patted his blaster. "Low setting melts cast iron pretty damn good."

"Something to remember for the future. Good job." Echo pulled his cell phone. "Fox, Locus One is clear. Proceeding to Locus Two. Sweep the tunnels and sewers."

"We're on it, old friend," Fox's voice answered.

Echo deactivated the cell phone, and they moved on to the next location, across the street and down. As Echo picked the lock, Omega improvised for the benefit of passersby, taking her cue from Echo's earlier routine.

"Now, Mister Wright, before I rent, what can you tell me about the architecture? The structure?"

"Well, Ms. Lloyd," Echo picked up, never missing a beat, "I'm just a real estate agent. But our firm employs an architect, and I'm sure Mister Frank can tell you all you want to know." With a flourish, Echo opened the door. "Please, enter and tell me what you think."

Once inside, Omega again deactivated the security while India and Romeo provided cover. They fanned out and began searching. As they moved to the second story, Omega commented to her partner.

"We're not going to find him here, you know."

"What makes you say that?"

"The same reason I said sneaking me out of the city wouldn't work. Slug knows we're coming as soon as we know. He has plenty of time to clear out, wherever he is."

Echo stopped dead in his tracks.

"Damn. You're right. Now what?"

"You're in charge, Echo, but I'd vote to continue. We might at least uncover a clue to his actual whereabouts or something."

"Mmm. Let's see."

Omega and Echo were coming down from the top floor when they heard India's excited call, coming from somewhere below.

"Guys, come here! We found something!"

Echo and Omega pounded down to the basement. There, Romeo and India flanked a shiny patch of dried greenish goo or slime on the floor. Echo walked over and knelt down beside it, studying it. Touched it, smelled it, held his fingers up to the faint light to inspect the residue on them.

"Yep," he said, standing. "It's gastropoid ooze, all right. I don't even need a spectral analyzer for this one. If it isn't Slug, then there's another unauthorized gastropoid on-planet."

"And the chances of that happening without our knowing about it right now are slim and none," India amended.

"Right. Fox will have been all over that one."

"Look! It leads off to another manhole-thing." Romeo pointed.

Echo went over to it and began trying to pry it open, but it was wedged. With some help from Romeo, they opened it, and Echo bent down to peer inside.

"Somebody hand me a flashlight, will you?"

India handed him her light, and he shone it into the opening.

"Hellfire an' damnation!" he grumbled then, his tone bitter and annoyed...and very Texan.

"What's wrong?" Omega moved over beside him.

"This is the storm drain access, and we had that big rainstorm early this morning, so the water's high and running. The slime trail's washed away. We've lost him."

* * *

233

Back at headquarters, the four headed for Fox's office to report, but Omega hung back and unobtrusively peeled off, moving to an unused laptop on a desk in a corner of the Core.

The other three continued, unaware they had lost one of their number. As soon as they entered Fox's office, Echo launched into a debrief.

"We found a dried slime trail in the cellar of Locus Two leading into the sewers, Fox, but the Snail read our minds and knew we were coming, well in advance. He took care to see that his trail got washed away. We sealed the access, so he can't come back there, at least not easily, but we don't know where he went."

"I had the sewers swept, Echo, but we came up empty. Sorry. We'll keep our eyes out, maybe assign some more Agents to monitor the tunnels. Where's Omega?"

"She's—" Echo responded. They all turned.

"—Not here," Romeo supplied. Fox stepped to the door of his office.

"There she is, at the computer. Echo, go find out what she's up to."

"Do you think that's wise, Fox? If she's onto something, telling us seems to be tantamount to telling Slug."

"Hum. Excellent point. Oy. Let her alone, then, but tell her to notify us if she needs anything."

"On it."

* * *

As Omega pulled a prescription bottle from her pocket and popped a stimulant capsule from it, she looked up and saw Echo striding across the Core in her direction, his gaze fixed on her. Quickly, she saved her work to a cloud file and minimized it, effectively blanking the screen. She hated to do it; she trusted Echo implicitly, aside from her promise to tell him before tackling a new idea. But Slug could extract the information from the mind of anyone who wasn't shielded. And Echo, being his real target, was probably being scanned more than most.

"Whatcha doin'?" Echo asked as he walked up, then shook his head in annoyance. "Damn! I did it anyway. Look, forget I said that. Bad choice of words—it's better if I don't know what you're doing. How is it going? That's a safer question."

Omega, gratified that he understood, told him.

"I have an idea. It's not great, it's a long shot, and I'm still working on it. But if I just suddenly grabbed you and asked you to come with me, no questions asked, would you? Without knowing where you're going, or what you were getting into? Can you trust my judgment that much? I know I'm still a rookie..."

"Still a rookie? After Antarctica? Where'd you get an idea like that? Not as far as I'm concerned, not now."

"You still call me 'baby.' You know, like 'baby agent'?"

Echo stared at her blankly for several moments, then all but smeared his hand down his face.

"Well, damn. I guess it kinda got to be a thing I call you—one of those Southern things like honey or sugar, that you call family and friends. You know? You're not offended, are you? Do I need to break the habit?"

Not a teasing reminder of status, then, not anymore—it's a term of affection, of friendship, Omega thought, warmth washing over her, a welcome morale boost in the circumstances. *Family. I can deal with that. At least, I can from him. I'd probably be pissed if anybody ELSE said it, but he's my partner—and my best friend. Yeah, I get where Echo's coming from. It IS a Southern thing! 'Cause I've 'honey'ed him a couple times, too, without thinking...and he never so much as blinked.*

"I...think I can live with it," she told him with a half-smile, and he grinned for a moment, seeming pleased. "So...what about my plan? Are you willing to follow my lead like that?"

Echo looked down at her, brown eyes uncharacteristically gentle, and laid a light but firm hand on her shoulder. He smiled, and she held her breath, uncertain if his next statement would be support...or pity. *Don't let it be pity,* she thought. *Please, God, not pity. I don't think I could stand pity. Especially not from him.*

"As somebody I think highly of recently said to me, 'You need to understand something: I trust you,'" he told her, confident, and she drew a deep, relieved breath. "You've proved yourself to me, partner. The way you trust me, I trust you. And I always look out for my partner, to the best of my ability. I've got your back, Meg. I'll be close if you need me."

Chapter 10

Echo walked back to Fox's office, to find only Romeo awaiting him. "Where's India?" he wondered, glancing around. "She was here when I left to go talk to Meg…"

"Oh, she went off to do some research," Romeo replied.

"On what?"

"Er—sleep deprivation," Romeo said, somewhat apologetically. "She thought maybe there was an outside chance she could find something that would help Meg get through this a little easier. Fox agreed. That's…one reason India and I are on this mission with you two: medical support. Well, at least she is. I think I'm just extra hands…and firepower, when you need it. 'Cause the way Fox an' I figure it, you'll need it, sooner or later."

"Oh. Thanks, then, to both of you. Pass it on to India, would you?"

"Sure thing, Echo."

"And Fox? Where'd he go?"

"Said something about trying to get the Arcturans to send a replacement telepath, like, yesterday."

"Oh, okay. Probably still couldn't get one here in time for Meg, but it's worth a shot."

"Yeah, man," Romeo agreed. "Long shot, but sometimes those go through the hoop."

"Yup. Listen, hot shot, I was thinking: What say, since India and Meg are busy, we go out and check the informants? We just might find something useful."

"Kinda like the old days, huh? You an' me? Sounds like a plan."

"Good. Let's go."

* * *

But, to Echo's dismay, no one had heard anything of significance on the street. So when none of the regular informants panned out, the pair decided to change tactics.

"What about that new crazy radio station?" Romeo wondered. "You know, the one that carries that nationwide weird-stuff show, an' the paranormal shit, an' all that?"

"Turn it on," a frustrated Echo gestured with one hand at the radio while he drove. "Can't hurt. We're oh for five now."

Romeo turned on the radio and searched until he found it.

"...And now it's time for Strange News Around the World," the announcer said in an overly-dramatic voice.

"Hey, good timing," Echo decided.

"Yeah, man," Romeo agreed. "Lessee what they got."

"...First up today, the Virgin Mary has appeared in the cereal bowl of a man in Rio de Janeiro. He claims the Blessed Virgin has a special message for the Pope. He says the Virgin told him the world will end this autumn, on September twenty-third, and that the Pope should..."

"That ain't no thang," Romeo decided.

"No."

"My mama always told me, ev'rything's gotta end sooner or later, but ain't nobody gonna see it comin' when it does. An' if they start namin' specific dates, ignore 'em."

"Your mama was a wise woman."

"...Bigfoot has been captured in the Pacific Northwest by a man who was..." the radio continued.

"Huh," Echo grunted, "remind me to get Fox to have somebody break 'im out."

"Okay."

"...And in New York City, a homeless man says, 'A giant mutant sewer slug tried to eat my brain!'" the announcer declared.

"Shush!" Echo and Romeo said simultaneously, as the radio show host continued.

"...George, a homeless man in New York City's Central Park, had a harrowing experience recently when one of the denizens of the city's sewers crawled out of a manhole and tried to make an appetizer of him..."

"Bingo," said Echo. "Oh. Well, damn."

"What?"

"Meg and I were chasing a lost Dendroid kid though Central Park a couple weeks ago. Back before Antarctica. I wonder if Slug followed us there, too."

"Shit. Sure sounds like it, man."

"Let's see if they say anything else we can use." Echo pulled into the nearest open space along the street and parallel-parked so he could concentrate on the radio show.

"...'The face of Jesus appeared in my coffee!' a stunned Preacher Larry Hargreave told our reporters yesterday..."

"Nope," Romeo said. "Well, He might've, I s'pose. Depends what you believe, I guess."

"Yeah," Echo agreed. "But unless He had a message for how to get Meg outta this mess, it doesn't help us much."

"...The Bermuda Triangle claims its latest victim..." the announcer went on.

"Hell! We have GOT to get those Atlanteans to stop joyriding," Echo cursed.

"Not again," Romeo groaned. "Every time we think we got 'em to behave, they go an' pull this shit again."

"Don't I know it. Wait—hush."

"...Brighton Beach psychic Zelda Romanoff claims there's an alien assassin in New York. She says he's here to get revenge..."

"Uh-oh," Echo said, staring at the radio.

"Uh-oh," Romeo parroted.

"Exactly."

"That is too damn close, man. Want me t' dig out 'er particulars on my smart phone?"

"My thoughts precisely." Echo extracted his special glasses. "And then, what say we go visit one 'Zelda Romanoff.'"

* * *

The 'consultation room' of psychic Zelda Romanoff was a fifth-floor walk-up in a shabby old brick building just off the BMT Brighton Elevated, and on the inland side of 'Little Odessa.' It was an outré mix of decor, all calculated to produce a pseudo-mystical atmosphere in the room. A smoked mirror hung on the far wall, framed by a bronze casting of intertwined naked human figures that bordered on—or perhaps crossed over into—the obscene. The windows were draped in a shabby, synthetic faux-silk brocade in a dark burgundy, faded to a rust-brown in places; a giant pyramid structure made of PVC piping drooped listlessly from the center of the ceiling, dust bunnies swaying like Spanish moss beneath. Crystals of any shape and color imaginable cluttered every available horizontal surface. Tarot cards and a crystal ball sat on the central table, which was the only surface in the room not covered by a layer of dust. A reproduction photograph of Czar Nicholas and his family, ostentatiously framed in cheap, painted gilt, was prominently displayed over the decrepit couch along one wall. Smoke from the brass incense brazier in the corner stung Romeo's eyes, and stained what used to be pale blue walls—if the narrow stripe alongside an askew Nicolas & Co. was anything to go by—a dull olive drab.

The end result of all this was a kitschy sort of neglected neo-gypsy-moderne look, and the younger agent found the whole thing ridiculous; how anyone could take it seriously was beyond his comprehension. Romeo rolled his eyes upward; Echo's reaction to the room was invisible behind his special sunglasses.

"Zelda Romanoff?" Echo began.

"I am Madame Zelda, only daughter of the Princess Anastasia, last of the Romanoffs," a dark-haired woman at the table pontificated in an obviously feigned Russian accent. Echo held out his carte noir even as it morphed.

"Secret Service, ma'am. We read your article on the assassin..."

"Yes?"

"We'd like to know how you found out."

"It is true, then?"

"...Yes, ma'am. It's true. There is an assassin in New York."

"I had...a vision in the night."

"A dream?" Echo pressed.

"To the uninitiated, yes, I suppose it would seem as a dream."

"We'd also like to know what you found out. Who the assassin is targeting, for instance."

"Well, in my vision, I saw an image...hazy...unclear...I remember it was a couple. Yes, yes, a man and woman, very close. Dark and fair. Well-dressed, powerful, important. I think it might be the President and First Lady, perhaps..."

"Reeeally? Close, huh? Exactly...how close?" Romeo muttered with a suggestive grin, and elbowed Echo.

Echo just turned and glared at him. It was the kind of look Echo usually reserved for alien criminal trash who'd just gotten on his last nerve, and left the impression on the recipient of a supervolcano about to blow on his ass; the younger agent had once heard Fox refer to it as, 'Echo's Yellowstone look.'

Romeo also abruptly remembered the expression on Echo's face after Omega was attacked, realized the other man was in no mood for jokes, and likely would not be for some time. He promptly subsided.

"...Yes, ma'am. That's our concern, too. Go on, please," the older agent said.

"What happened next was...horrible. Their heads just...exploded... and...they fell. It was not unlike watching President Kennedy's assassination...but I saw no guns or bullets..."

Romeo looked at Echo's grim face and pulled his special glasses as he saw Echo reach into his pocket and produce an object that looked like a smart phone.

"Anything else?" Echo said.

"Yes. Could you do me a favor?"

"Certainly, ma'am. What is it?"

"Could you deliver a message to the President?"

"Yes?"

"Tell him, 'Watch yourself. Nothing is as it appears.'"

The room lit up with a multicolored flash.

* * *

As they drove away from Madame Zelda's, Romeo's face developed a deeply puzzled expression. Echo noticed, but said nothing, waiting patiently for the other agent's brain to finish processing the thought. Finally, Romeo rewarded his patience.

"I don't get it, Echo. I thought you said humans don't do telepathy."

"They don't."

"So how did this Madame Fruitcake find out about—"

"Remember, junior, humans may not be telepaths, but Snails are. Think of it like this: Humans are the radios, Slug is the broadcasting station. If the radio happens to be on the right frequency, it picks up the broadcast."

"So, Madame Zelda just sorta—caught the news, so to speak."

"Maybe."

"'Maybe'?"

"Maybe."

Romeo stared at him, but Echo didn't elaborate, busy pondering the encounter, looking for clues he could extrapolate. Finally the younger agent gave in.

"All right, I'll bite. 'Maybe' what?"

"Oh. Maybe she just picked up the broadcast—and maybe it was a beamed transmission."

"'Beamed'? What do you mean?"

"Intentional, not accidental. Maybe Slug was trying to send me a message."

"Well, I'd say it's one he's already delivered. We know he's after you and Meg."

"Not that message. The other one."

"Other one?"

"'Nothing is as it appears...'"

* * *

The bone saw cut through the girl's sternum like the proverbial hot knife in butter, and the same nightmare that had happened to her abdomen now occurred to the organs in her thoracic cavity. Her blood was duly routed away from her heart to an artificial device—leaving her washed with cold, as a nasty plastic taste suffused her mouth—while her heart was opened, strengthened, made more efficient. Her lungs were spread out, each lobe separated to be injected with she knew not what, even as she felt a drowning sensation fill them. She instinctively tried to gasp for breath, but her chest had been stilled, the oxygen she needed to survive this ordeal

241

provided by the artificial system through which her blood was being routed.

I'm going crazy, *she thought, desperate.* I can't stand much more of this.

Yes, you can, *came the chilling reply.* We are not nearly done here yet.

* * *

After Echo left with Romeo, Omega recommenced her research. For lack of any better ideas, she had pulled up a map of the city around Division One Headquarters, roughly bounded by the distance limit Fox had used. Next she commanded the computer to overlay all sewers and service tunnels, with in-building access hatches. Then she began cross-correlating those locations with empty or little-used buildings. Slowly she was compiling a list. It was a long list.

She sighed, popped another stim, and washed it down with some cold coffee. Rubbing her dry, stinging eyes, she resumed her search.

Several hours later, she glanced up, across the Core, to see Romeo and Echo returning, evidently headed to Fox's office to report in. Her partner spotted her watching, and sketched an acknowledging salute; she nodded, and waved a couple of fingers in greeting.

Echo paused, then coded, *You okay? Need anything?*

No, I'm good. Tired. But okay.

How's it coming?

Slowly, but I think I may be getting somewhere.

Good. Come get me when you're ready. I'll be in Fox's office.

Okay.

Echo followed Romeo into Fox's office; the entire exchange had occurred so fast that Romeo hadn't even been aware of it.

Fox came by a couple of hours later and informed her that he had ordered everyone not to disturb her, and not to try to find out what she was doing, but to supply her with any help necessary, no questions asked.

This included, she discovered, a continuous supply of coffee from the Hypothenemoids, a race of giant beetles with prehensile antennae which they used as hands. Having been introduced to coffee via a trade agreement with Earth, the species was intrigued at the resemblance of their own carapaces to the whole bean; shortly thereafter, it became a huge fad on their homeworld of Loterus V. The entire embassage was delighted to finally find a human who liked coffee as much as they did. Omega doubted they realized that it wasn't so much that she LIKED it as that she NEEDED it, but she saw no reason to risk offending them by pointing out the difference. They DID make excellent coffee, though, she decided.

Pretty much everyone at Headquarters knew what was happening, and no one wanted to give away the hand she was playing. Echo was even singlehandedly filling out all their paperwork for the day, having volunteered to do so. Omega was incredibly appreciative of it all.

Just then, a giant insectoid antenna appeared, wrapped around a steaming, fresh cup of coffee, which it deposited on the desk. Looking over the edge of the desk, Omega espied a grinning Hypothenemoid.

"Thanks, Irokin," Omega said, offering her own grin in return. The alien clacked its mandibles at her in an encouraging fashion, waved with both antennae, and headed back to the break room to prepare more coffee for its favorite Agent.

* * *

Omega was still at it when the shift ended. When she popped yet another stim and showed no sign of quitting, Echo walked over to her, careful to come up directly in front of her, so that the monitor screen was hidden from him, along with its contents.

"Quittin' time. You ready to go home? Romeo and India left well over an hour ago."

She looked up at him blankly.

Damn. She's having a little trouble focusing, he thought. *That seems to be occurring more and more often. I can't think THAT'S good.*

"Oh. The shift's ended already? Mmm," she rubbed her eyes for the thousandth time, "gotta remember to blink once in a while. Bad habit I've got while working on a computer. I expect my eyes look like a couple o' fried eggs."

"Well, they are kinda bloodshot, now you mention it. We can pop by Medical on the way home and get you some eye drops, if you need 'em." Echo cocked his head and studied her eyes. "I bet they'd feel better for it."

"Probably." She rubbed her fists into them. "Maybe later, though. Uh,

Echo, look, I'm nowhere near done here...and it's not like I can afford to crash anyway. You go on without me. I'll just stay here and..."

"Nope. Not happenin', baby. Save the data to the Agency cloud, and triple-passcode it. You can work on it later from your study. Right now, you—and those eyes—need a break. And food. I know I'm starved."

"Um...I'm not really very hungry."

He was a bit startled, but hid it. *Not hungry? After the better part of eighteen hours with no meal? First lunch was a long time ago, and she didn't even get an afternoon snack, let alone second lunch.* He declared with mock-sternness, "Well, you're gonna eat, whether you're hungry or not, if I have to tie you down and shove it in your face. The way we work? Hell no! You need the nourishment. C'mon, let's run by Medical and get you something for those eyes, then go home, and I'll whip up an omelet or something."

Omega acquiesced at last, and while saving and shutting down, she mulled over something—which apparently was the proposed menu, Echo judged by her next statement.

"You got any mushrooms?" she wondered.

"As a matter of fact, I do. Button and morel both. Good idea. I'm kinda partial to mushroom omelets. With Swiss cheese and some ham or prosciutto, maybe?"

"Yeah. You know," she admitted, as she fell into step with him, "that doesn't sound half bad..."

* * *

After supper, which Echo made sure was healthy, tasty, and sufficiently calorie-dense to keep Omega on her feet for a while, she disappeared into her study and logged on to the wifi in there with her laptop.

Just before Echo went to bed, he looked in through the back door, and saw the light in her study and her shadow on the wall, hunched over the laptop, working as if her life depended on it.

Which, he considered, it probably did.

* * *

The next morning when Alpha One reported in to Fox, Romeo was also waiting.

"What's up?" Echo asked, as he and Omega entered Fox's office.

"It seems we are all requested down in Medical Research," Fox noted. "Romeo, tell 'em."

"Yeah, well, after all the study and research my partner did yesterday, I think it all kinda gelled. Because India had an idea last night while we were eatin' dinner," Romeo explained, "somethin' she thought'd help Meg, so as soon as we finished eatin', she cleared out for Medical, and I ain't seen her since. Then this morning, when I'm gettin' ready for shift, she calls and says to grab Fox and you two and get you down to the research lab in Medical first thing, unless there's a boojum about to destroy Earth in the next few minutes or somethin'."

"Which there isn't, so let's go," Fox declared.

* * *

India was waiting for them in the research lab, along with a couple of colleagues, Zebra—and Zarnix, who was finally back from the alien birth.

"Wassup, babe?" Romeo asked, coming to her. India smiled.

"We think we might have something to protect Omega," she answered.

"And if it protects her, it'll protect all of us," Zebra added. "And we're pretty sure we can manufacture it in bulk, if it does. Look here."

The assistant chief of Medical led them to a nearby table, on which was a rather complex headset, perched on a plastic mannequin head. A browband circlet was connected to another circlet, canted at nearly a forty-five degree angle to the browband. A third arc connected the two intersections around the back of the head just below the crown, and a fourth connected the center front all the way to the center back. Each arc had some sort of electrodes or sensors along its length, and a tiny pack of electronics perched on the top.

"What the hell is it?" Fox wanted to know.

"Not bad," Omega said at almost the same moment. "I'd been meaning to come to y'all with some ideas I'd had about this, but you beat me to it."

"I have always been fascinated by the human nervous system," Zarnix, the only alien in the group, noted. "It has been an especial study of mine for years."

"Which helped a lot," India said. "Fox, this is our prototype mental block. It's partly based on the technology of our carte noirs, modified by some ideas I had last night. If we've got it figured right, and if the various encephalon frequencies are what we think, then once we've tuned it a little, this should protect Omega from Slug's telepathic attacks."

"And she can get some sleep," Echo realized, hiding his relief. *Maybe I'm not gonna lose my partner again after all,* he decided. *I was starting to wonder if I've become a damn jinx or something.*

"Right," Zebra confirmed with a smile. "Now, all we need to do is to get a quick cerebral scan on Omega, for a baseline."

"But you got those on me already," Omega pointed out.

"We do," Zebra agreed. "But they're your NOMINAL baseline. You've got a block up right now, don't you? One that you're maintaining continuously?"

"Yeah. Oh, I see. This isn't about my normal baselines. This is something you can use to help test the thing."

"Yes," India said, nodding, as she led Omega over to the scanner. "Since the only handy, trustworthy telepath we got is off-planet right now, we're having to come up with some workarounds. If we get a cerebral scan of you with an active telepathic block that's working, and compare it with your nominal baseline, we'll know what frequency brainwaves counter Slug's telepathy."

"We SHOULD," Zarnix corrected. "Unfortunately, the study of telepathic/non-telepathic mental interaction is still in its infancy. It is quite complex, because the two types of brain are not structured the same, and the normal frequencies are very different. We may counter one frequency, only to discover that it is a harmonic that is actually the culprit. So be prepared, Agent Omega—we are NOT asking you to drop your block at any time."

"In fact, honey, if you can, right now, strengthen it while we do this scan," India suggested.

"Okay."

Omega sat in the scanner, closed her eyes and ran through some breathing patterns, seeming amazingly serene for what was happening. When she opened her eyes, they were a clear, vivid sapphire blue, almost glowing. Echo happened to be right in her line of sight, and he blinked several times, disconcerted; that tranquil gaze seemed to pierce right through him.

Damn. Could she actually...? Fox said something about a possible mutation. Maybe she can. It would sure make for some hella interesting field comm. We could forget the damn codes. He turned his thoughts outward. *Meg? Can you hear me?*

Her only response was to smile softly at him, and turn her attention to the physicians. He blinked again, uncertain.

"I'm ready," she told them.

They lowered the scanner onto her head and initiated the scan.

* * *

While the cerebral scanner did its thing, Echo watched his partner. He was silent, but his own brain was active.

So...did she hear me, or not? he wondered, puzzled. *She smiled at me, yeah. But was that because she saw me watching her, or because she heard me? If she heard me, was she playing with me, or just preoccupied with needing to get this gadget working, so she can collapse and crash for a change? She's not a flirt or anything, so I doubt she was playing head games with me, especially not with Slug playing his own brand of head games with her. So either she didn't hear me at all, or she was too focused to try to answer.*

A loud *ding!* sounded just then, and Zarnix and Zebra removed the scanner from Omega's head.

"Got the comparison software ready, India?" Zebra wondered.

"Yeah," India said, from her position at the nearby computer. "Feed me the scan as soon as it compiles, and we'll run it."

"Here it comes," Zarnix said, watching the scanner readouts, then hitting a button.

"Got it," India said a second later, then typed a key command on the computer. "Comparison underway. Give it about five minutes, and we should be able to tune the block."

"Meanwhile," Zarnix said, pulling a stool over to face Omega, "I need to ask you a few questions."

* * *

Omega met the copper-colored eyes of the alien physician, wondering what he wanted to know. Zarnix was a Chesharilzi from the second planet of the Gliese 667C system, but his people were not unlike humans save for the bright purple hair, orange eyes, and slightly blue skin. He was highly trained in multiple medical fields and enthusiastically curious about the similarities and differences between the two species. The combination made for an excellent chief physician for the Agency.

"Fire when ready," she murmured, offering him a tired smile.

"You maintain the telepathic block at all times?"

"Yeah. I pretty much have to."

"Why? Is Slug's attack so continuous? Can you feel it?"

"I can feel it, yeah," Omega admitted. "It's like...kinda like pressure, like when you have a really bad cold and it feels like your head is gonna explode. Except instead of being around the sinus area, the pressure is around...here." She spread her fingers and wrapped her hands around her head, holding them horizontal just above her ears. "But it's not continuous."

"Is it regular, or irregular, his attacks?"

Omega nibbled on her lower lip, considering the question.

"Fairly regular, I think," she decided. "He seems to mix it up a little, so I can't afford to let my guard down. But I can pretty much count on feeling his...probes, I guess I'd call 'em...about every twenty minutes or so. Give or take," she added.

"Mm. That is good information, Agent; thank you," Zarnix said. "Now, let me take the opportunity to obtain your vitals, if you do not mind. I am concerned for your condition, given the lack of sleep, and the constant use of stimulants."

"Okay," Omega sighed.

* * *

Just then, Zebra, who had moved into a corner, where an additional laptop computer sat, signaled Fox. Fox tapped Echo, and the pair eased unobtrusively to Zebra's side.

"Keep your voices low, guys. I thought you two would want to have a look at this," she murmured. "Echo, you saw Omega's original scan, right?"

"Yeah," Echo averred. "Pretty impressive, I thought."

"Yep. Here's the one we just took."

The doctor brought up the image on the laptop screen and set it in motion. It depicted a very different brain from the bright, active, colorful image they had originally seen. This brain had a deep turmeric-yellow periphery, almost uniform in color and brightness, though none of it depicted the brilliant white flashes of cognition Omega's original scan had shown.

But within that periphery, which Echo decided showed the extent of the telepathic block, there was little to no yellow at all. Even the colors which denoted autonomic activities were muted and muddy in color.

"That...does not look like the same brain," Fox muttered.

"No, it doesn't. That can't be good," Echo agreed.

"It isn't." Zebra's voice was little more than a whisper. "Zarnix is keeping her busy, so hopefully those sharp ears of hers won't hear, but..." she shook her head. "Other than the block activity around the margins, she's one category removed from..."

"Hell. I was afraid of that," Fox breathed.

"Afraid of what, Boss?" Echo asked, suddenly fearing for the answer.

"Echo," Zebra leaned over and whispered into his ear, "your partner is one statistical box away from a dying brain. Keeping Slug at bay is taking everything she's got, and then some. This may kill her, even if he doesn't attack again."

Echo had all he could do to remain silent and still at that explanation. "It's not brain damage from his initial attack, is it?"

"No, of that I'm sure. The patterns would be very different. No, this is a fully-functioning brain, it's just...grossly overtaxed, I guess you could say," Zebra explained as softly as she could.

"Dammit," Echo grumbled in an undertone. "This gizmo better work."

"Yes, or she isn't gonna make it," Zebra agreed.

Echo turned away at that, sick at heart.

* * *

By the time Zarnix was done checking over Omega, India had the comparison run, and the trio of doctors began programming the blocking helmet. It wasn't a particularly swift process, and in the end, Fox headed back to his office, leaving instructions that he was to be called before they tested it on Omega.

"Sorry it's taking so long," India apologized. "But if it's gonna properly protect Meg, we gotta get things just right."

"Not a problem. I appreciate it," Omega replied, waving a dismissive hand as she allowed herself to merely rest in a chair in the lab, her secretly-worried partner staunch at her side, broad shoulders squared. "I just hope it does what we want it to."

"I second that," Echo declared.

"That's three," Romeo averred.

"Four, five, and six right here," Zebra said, chuckling. "And if I know Fox—"

"And if anybody does, you do," Echo added with a devilish grin, and she blushed slightly.

"...Then he makes seven," she finished. "Speaking of, Echo, would you give him a heads-up? By the time he can shake free from his work and get down here, we should be done with the preliminary tests, and ready to put it on Omega."

"On it," Echo said, fishing out his cell phone.

While he softly contacted their director, the trio of physicians finished checking out the device.

"India," Zarnix ordered, "would you outfit Omega with the sensor suite, while Zebra and I adjust the fittings? I want to have hard data of her physiological responses."

"All over it," India said. "Meg, c'mon over here, behind the dressing screen. I need to put EKG leads on you, so you'll have to peel down to skin on the top, girlfriend. Then we're gonna tie in some remote EEG leads for your noggin."

* * *

"Okeydoke," Omega said gamely, standing and following India to the changing corner.

Echo and Romeo sat in the waiting chairs and watched absently while Omega stripped behind the screen; they were both concerned about whether or not this would work, and how Omega would be affected if it didn't.

250

So they didn't think much about it when her Suit jacket and tie were tossed across the top of the folding screen. Her shirt, too, was of little consequence; those were, after all, garments the two men wore, as well. But they sat up and took notice all of a sudden, when the dainty, lace-and-silk, flesh-toned bra joined it.

"Um, uh, wow," Romeo stammered, suddenly unsure where to look—Omega was not his lover, after all; India was. Only India was helping Omega disrobe. He met Echo's eyes, and the older man could see a certain pleading desperation in his gaze.

For that matter, Echo was urgently searching for something else—anything, really—upon which to focus his attention. While he was aware that Omega possessed a very attractive, very shapely figure, and had even admired it from a distant aesthetic, it had not occurred to him that his female partner wore such incredibly alluring undergarments beneath her Suit. Let alone that Supplies had such sexy items in stock for the women Agents; the men's briefs surely didn't provide for sex appeal, and Supplies only offered the choice of gray boxers, tighty-whiteys, and black spandex bikini briefs. And he wasn't entirely sure this was a piece of information he wanted to have about the woman who did battle at his side. Worse, by that point—and being, himself, a healthy hetero human male—he couldn't help but wonder if the panties matched the bra.

But that bra was filed in the memory now, without doubt, and nothing short of the brain bleacher was going to remove it. So Echo decided to rise to the occasion.

"Um, hey, buddy," he said, extracting his cell phone again, "have you, uh, seen the new tracking app Software's come up with...?"

* * *

Both Omega and India had heard the sudden stammering and flurry of activity from the peanut gallery, and they glanced at each other, curious; then in tandem, they peered surreptitiously over the privacy screen, in plenty of time to see the wide eyes of their partners, as well as the fixed direction of their gazes—straight at Omega's lacy underwire bra.

When Echo finally managed to come up with his cell, and he and Romeo both went face-down over it, the two women crouched behind the

251

screen. Sapphire eyes met amber ones, growing wide, and both women promptly clamped hands over their mouths and noses to stifle the giggles.

"Men will never get it," India murmured through her fingers.

"Nope," came Omega's reply via the same means. "Damn, I needed that."

They leaned on each other and gasped and giggled until they were finally able to sober, whereupon India applied the sensor stickies all over Omega's torso and head, and she was able to get dressed again, albeit with shirttails hanging out around the leads, and no tie nor jacket.

* * *

Finally everything was ready, and Fox had arrived. He, Echo, and Romeo sat in the waiting chairs—"My audience," Omega called them— while Zarnix parked Omega in what he and Zebra jokingly referred to as "the lab rat's chair," then turned to India.

"This was your idea, dear," Zebra noted in a soft voice, smiling. "You do the honors."

So India lifted the helmet and gently settled it on Omega's white-blonde hair.

"Do I need to take down the braid?" Omega asked. "I guess it's good I didn't wrap it into an updo today."

"It's good it's not an updo, yeah, 'cause it fits better this way," India said, adjusting said fit. "But the braid shouldn't hurt anything. Okay, here we go." She stepped back and pulled her cell phone, activated it, and initiated an app. Instantly several small green lights came on around the brow of the helm. "Aaand it's on, and operating."

Zarnix clicked a digital stopwatch, and set it on the table.

"Can you feel anything, Omega?" Zebra asked.

"...Not...particularly," Omega said, after a moment to consider. "But I'm not sure what I'm supposed to feel."

"Nothing, from the device," Zarnix explained. "But we must wait until your adversary tries to attack again."

"He might wait for a bit," Omega pointed out. "After all, I'm sure Slug knows you're trying this."

"True. But he will have to go against it at some point, else he will not know if he can best it," Zarnix pointed out. "We must simply be patient."

"In that case, let me break this out," Fox said, producing an Agency electronic tablet from somewhere on his person. "I'm not willing to go off and leave Omega, here, but I do have work to do, to keep this place going."

"No problem, Fox," Omega murmured. "I was kinda thinking about getting back to my little things while we wait, too."

"Then I'm glad I brought my tablet along this morning," Echo said, producing the device from one of the innumerable pockets he seemed always to have on his own person. He handed it to his partner. "Have at it, baby."

* * *

They waited over an hour in relative silence. Fox and Omega sat at lab tables, working on the tablets, while the others watched Omega. Even Fox threw periodic, surreptitious glances her way. But she seemed undisturbed by anything, although her awareness of being watched made her somewhat self-conscious.

"It's been over an hour and a half, now," India murmured at last, glancing at the stopwatch. "Meg, didn't you say he tries to get at you about every twenty minutes?"

"Yeah," Omega said, looking up from Echo's tablet. "On average, anyway."

"You thinkin' it's workin', India babe?" Romeo wondered.

"Yeah, I'm thinking we might have really done i—" India said…just as Omega grunted, and put a hand to her head.

"Uhn," she said, wincing. "Ohhh, geez. Dammit! Stop that!"

"Guess who's back?" Echo said, and sighed. "Damn the creature."

"Yeah, and stronger than usual, too," Omega murmured, holding her head in both hands. "I think he's probably trying to make sure he gets through the thing."

"Damn. Hot knife and butter?" India asked, disappointed.

"More like hammer and anvil, but yeah," Omega agreed.

"Why didn't it work?" Fox wanted to know. "I was right there with India—I thought it was working."

"Shell-fry," a grimacing Omega got out around a sharp twinge. The others glanced at each other in confusion; Echo noticed that Zarnix and Zebra exchanged concerned frowns.

"What?" Romeo wondered. "What'd ya say, Meg?"

"Shell. Fry," she enunciated clearly, still holding her head. "Pounding head, guys. Work wi' me."

"Oh," Echo said then, as it hit him what she was trying to say through her pain. "I get it, baby. Shell-fry, guys—Slug's Shell got hit, and the neural feedback fried his nervous system."

"Ah!" Zarnix exclaimed. "Of course! So Slug's nervous system is no longer nominal Snail. It probably significantly altered the brain waves..." The alien doctor reached over and punched the app on India's cell phone, which lay at Omega's elbow. This deactivated the helmet, and he gingerly lifted it from Omega's head. "Is there any change?"

"No," Omega murmured, still holding her head. "Asp'rin?"

"We got better than that, girl," India said softly, going to the pharmaceutical cabinet.

"Perhaps some adjustments," Zarnix mumbled, carrying the headset to the workbench and bending over it. "If we can just find the frequency of Slug's telepathic transmissions, we can set up a counter-wave..."

"We'll keep trying, Omega," India promised. "We can probably get this working in a couple days. Just hang on."

"I know, and I'm hangin'," Omega agreed, as she washed down the alien analgesic and it took effect.

"That stop it?" Echo asked. "Your headache gone?"

"No, it doesn't stop it. It can't, just because of what's causing it," Omega admitted. "But it does ease it."

"Well, damn."

"Yeah, but look at it like this—I can actually carry on a coherent conversation now."

* * *

India bent over the device on the workbench, head together with Zarnix, as they pondered how to adjust the settings on the headset in order to block Slug and protect Omega, but it looked like taking some time. So Fox returned to his office, and Romeo went with him; the Director had a few matters he wanted the agent to check into, since Alpha One was effectively unavailable, and Romeo's partner would be assisting in Medical for the next few hours at least. Echo waited patiently, off to one side, while Zebra took Omega back behind the privacy screen to remove the EKG and EEG leads.

As she peeled the last bit of stickum from Omega's skin, Zebra found her arm caught in a gentle but firm grip.

"Listen, Zebra," Omega murmured, keeping her voice as low as it would go and still ensure the assistant chief of Medical heard, "keep workin' on that thing, because Echo, and probably a buncha other agents, are gonna need it. I've read the reports from the first go-round with Slug, and I know: Taking that monster down ain't gonna be easy. It wasn't, the first time, and he wasn't insane then. But," the junior agent broke off, looked away, and nodded her head in thought. "Okay, look, I DO have really good hearing. So I know about the scans."

"You heard us." Zebra felt like the pit had dropped from her stomach.

"Yeah. And you're right. Having to keep this block up all the time... it's whippin' my ass, as Echo would say. It's taking everything I've got to keep it up and keep going, keep working toward resolving this. And no rest of any sort, at all. I'm tired, Zebra, and no end in sight yet. And when I finally do see the light at the end of the maglev tunnel, it'll probably be an oncoming train. But...well, look. Despite what Echo told me yesterday, I'm a rookie, and I know it. On the other hand, Echo is the head of what's about to be a really important department, Alpha Line. And he's probably gonna become Director, one day. And he's a good man, a good agent, and a good friend."

"Aw, Omega, don't say what I think you're gonna say," Zebra whispered, heart joining the pit of her stomach. Omega shrugged.

"What else is there to say?" she wondered. "Y'all aren't gonna finish that gizmo in time to help me. You and I both know it. I'm too far down the drain already. But you can help Echo. And now you have the frequencies of my block to model the thing on." She took Zebra's shoulders. "Now listen to me. Echo is my best friend. I admire and respect him more than any person I've ever met. As us Southerners say, I love him to pieces. I dunno if the feeling is mutual; he's never said, if it is. Then again, that's not the way he is. So I'm not happy about what I'm gonna say, and I'd rather not have to, if we can find another way...but I'm willing to go down, if it means Echo stays alive and healthy. 'Cause that's what partners—what FRIENDS—do." She stared into Zebra's eyes, and the physician swore the agent had blue lasers for eyeballs. "So. Keep Echo alive and healthy. You hear me?"

Zebra could only nod; her throat was too tight to speak.

* * *

By the time they were done in the Medical Research lab, it was getting late. Alpha One reported back to Fox's office, and they were relieved of duty for the rest of the shift.

"Because I saw how badly Omega was hurting, and I can at least send her off to be comfortable in her quarters, tsu aldi rukhes," Fox said. "So go. Have dinner, and kick back in front of the TV or something."

"Eh," Omega murmured. "Not that hungry. Slug's little shenanigans are worse than migraines, from what Zebra told me."

"Stomach upset?" Echo wondered.

"A little. Besides, I still gotta finish what I'm doing, if we wanna have a hope of catching our personal slimetrailer."

"You can take a couple of hours off, maydele," Fox insisted. "Echo, take her home, and find something that'll stay on her stomach, then tie her to a chair in front of the television, and put something light on to watch. I want her away from any sort of work for at least two or three hours, the longer, the better."

"On it, Boss. C'mon, Meg, time to go home."

"Okay, Ace," Omega sighed.

* * *

Echo did indeed manage to get some very basic fare into his partner, converting a can of biscuits, some leftover roast chicken, and chicken stock into a quick chicken and dumplings entrée, with applesauce and steamed carrots on the side. Omega complimented him for being a good cook, he fired back a jibe, she riposted, and soon he had her laughing. It was a good sound, he decided.

Then he pulled a couple of MTP devices from his movie collection and they watched TV until it was bedtime. *Mine, at least,* he thought, internalizing the sigh as he watched her go into her study and boot her laptop.

* * *

Echo walked into Fox's office alone the next morning. India and Romeo were there waiting.

"Anybody seen Omega? She wasn't in when I checked on her this morning."

"Yeah, Echo. Omega's already out there on one of the work stations in the corner," Fox observed, waving a hand at the overlook window.

"She was there 'way before we got here," Romeo noted, concern in his voice. "Couple of the guys on the other shift said she was there, like, halfway through their shift."

"Damn," Echo grumbled. "Fox and I made her take a couple hours of do-nothing last night, so she must have decided to make up for lost time."

"Yeah, I didn't think about that," Fox confessed, and frowned.

"How's the artificial block coming?" Echo wondered.

"It got beyond me," India noted with a sigh. "Neuro stuff wasn't my specialty, but Zebra and Zarnix are both experts in it. So I left it to them, and went back to get some sleep, myself. I figured I'd do Meg more good rested and close by than worn out, down in the medlab."

Echo nodded; so did Fox.

"Well considered, India," the director remarked. "And thank you. I'm quite sure the device will prove useful, once the bugs get worked out."

"Yeah. I'm just not sure it's gonna be in time for our current need. You know, guys," India admitted, rising and moving to the bay window overlooking the Core, "I'm starting to get awful damn worried about her. She's been working 'round the clock for several days now—Division days, meaning two solid days apiece, Earth time—and it's beginning to show. And it isn't helping at all that, when this whole mess started, she was only a couple days off a pretty serious case of hypothermia and frostbite from the Antarctic mission; I can't think her reserves had got back to normal yet."

"I know whatcha mean, hon'," Romeo agreed, joining her. "Girl's startin' to look a little ragged."

257

"She's moving a bit slower today, like she's trying to conserve energy," India pointed out, as Echo and Fox came to the window as well. "Don't even look at her eyes, especially after all this computer work."

"I made her go by Medical with me and get some eye drops the other day," Echo noted. "Isn't she using 'em?"

"She is, 'cause I've seen her doing it," India noted. "But those can only do so much. Plus, I'd be willing to bet serious money that her reflexes have slowed. And she's starting to look rather gaunt."

"'Gaunt'?" echoed Echo, gaze fixed on his partner, sitting at a console in the middle of the bullpen. Just then, India took his arm and pulled him away from the window.

"Come back and sit down, guys. We don't want her to see us all staring, if she happens to look up. Thin," she elaborated, as Fox took his desk chair and the others sat in front of him. "She's getting too thin, Echo. Extremely so. It might not have been so noticeable last night, but pay attention to the hollows in her cheeks next time you look at her. Aside from the extra energy she's burning just going around the clock—and let me note that her body was still revved up from the hypothermia—now the stimulants are really starting to have an effect. By increasing her metabolism more than it already was, they're forcing her to burn fuel even faster. And stims can also tend to suppress the appetite. I've been watching her all morning. I'm pretty sure she hasn't eaten breakfast, and she hasn't even stuck her nose into the break room; if she gets low on coffee, Irokin brings her some. She's having to pop stims every couple of hours now—with that same coffee. And Agency coffee's more like espresso than anything else, in my opinion, especially that syrup the Hypothenemoids brew. It's really good stuff, but MAN is it strong! She might as well be mainlining straight caffeine. I don't know how much longer she can go."

A light bulb went off in Echo's head as he listened to India. *Damn. It definitely explains Omega's lack of interest in dinner the last few nights. At least I know she's gotten to eat one good meal in every day. I may need to consider calf roping and forced feeding.*

"As time goes on, and she starts running out of reserves, her morale is going to be affected, too," India added. "We're going to have to be as supportive and encouraging as possible, to keep her spirits up. And that goes double for you, Echo."

"How so?" Echo raised an eyebrow, throwing a concerned glance at Fox, who returned it. *Hell. This is getting worse and worse,* the seasoned agent thought, worried. *We get to fiddle while Omega burns...out.*

"Because you're her mentor, AND her PARTNER. Though you may not have realized it yet, the bond between the two of you is much stronger than her connection with any of the rest of us."

"Well, yeah—like you said, we're partners. Partners are there for each other."

"Yes, but it's more than that, in some ways."

Echo blinked in surprise.

"What do you mean?" he asked, startled. India drew a deep breath.

"I mean, I believe she considers this group," India waved her hands around at the people in the room, "as the closest thing to family she's got."

"Yeah, she has made a couple of comments like that..." Echo admitted, somewhat reluctant; he was concerned he might somehow be broaching Omega's secrets, though he couldn't remember her ever telling him not to mention it.

"Aha! I knew it! Now, the rest of us, one way or another, we've had family—either of the actual genetic variety, or in the form of close partnerships and colleagues—for years. Even you, Echo, as much as you like to come across as tough and independent and a loner—Romeo has told me how badly you grieved X-ray. Omega, on the other hand, has basically isolated herself in order to achieve her goal, her dream, of becoming an astronaut. And her actual genetic family has been dead for a good while—at least a decade or so, I think."

* * *

"So...she's been all alone, is what you're sayin', girl," Romeo mused. "Until we, um, until Echo found 'er."

"Right. For a long time. And you raise a good point—Echo IS the one who found her and recruited her. And now, all of a sudden, she's got family. Us. But more, she's got Echo. Now, Echo, I dunno how she thinks of you— I've picked up that Fox is the father figure, which makes sense; so you aren't that, and I doubt you're THAT much older than her anyway, so she wouldn't see you in that light—but you could be a brother, or MAYBE an uncle, though with the ages, it's a stretch. But I know for a fact she's called you her best friend. Or she might even think of you in a more...intimate... fashion, though I personally haven't seen any signs of that, so far."

"Ooo, you mean the lady got a crush on Echo? They got a thang?" Romeo wondered, not bothering to restrain a smirk. Echo turned that same supervolcano glare on him that he'd seen two days before—and over the same subject, he suddenly recalled—and he shut up quickly.

* * *

"I SAID, I didn't see any signs of that, but it's possible, I suppose." India shrugged. "Or maybe it's some combination of all of it, and even she hasn't sorted it all out in her head yet, or even become aware of it; that's neither here nor there, for the purposes of this situation. But my point is, of everybody here, YOU are the one she considers IMMEDIATE family, Echo. AND you're her go-to for everything about this job and this way of life, her subject-matter expert in all things alien, her mentor, her teacher, her closest pal. You're the one she always turns to, always comes to, always looks to for the answers to what she doesn't already know or can't figure out on her own. She likes you, she admires you, and she looks up to you. And she trusts you implicitly."

"India," Fox interjected, very, very quietly, "are you saying what I think you're saying?"

"I am, Fox," she said with a vehement nod. "She'd probably deny it, and may not even realize it's true, but it is. Echo...is Omega's hero."

They were all silent for a moment, watching Echo. In turn Echo stared at the floor, feeling his face heat. Finally he looked up at India.

"Okay. Slug is my problem, anyway. So...what do I need to do?"

"No, Echo, he's OUR problem. Omega's mental state...that's OURS, too, but the way she feels about you is your secret weapon."

"But we're not fighting her!" Echo protested.

"No, we're fighting Slug, and the mental state he's put Omega into," India pointed out. "And in that, YOU are OUR secret weapon. Or you can be. Look, I know it's not your nature, but for her sake, drop some of

260

that reserve of yours and reach out a little more. Let her know—I mean, actually, verbally TELL HER—that you care about her, about what happens to her, and I'd lay money it will boost her spirits more than anything any of us could consider. You can do far more than the rest of us that way, if you'll only try."

"You're saying..." Echo began, and broke off, not willing to verbalize what he was thinking. *You're saying to just drop the walls I've spent essentially my whole life building, in order to be able to do this job and still sleep at night...*

"Look, Echo," India softened her tone. "I bet I know pretty much what you're thinking right now, and I get it. I had to build mental and emotional walls as an ER physician, and I'm having to build more in this job. I understand, probably better than you realize, what it takes to do a job and be able to walk away at the end of the day and not go crazy. I get how emotions and thoughts have to be categorized and put into boxes, and put the boxes inside those walls. I'm not saying you have to destroy 'em, those walls. You probably couldn't, no matter how much you might want to—I know, because I can't. But something you CAN do, because I DID, is to create a door in those walls, and show Meg how to walk through 'em. Let her in."

Echo sighed. *Because if I don't, I'm gonna lose her. But if I do, and I lose her anyway, can I handle another nuke being detonated inside those walls? Damn. I blocked up that door after X-ray's death. But I don't think there's any other option.* He made his decision.

"All right. I'll...see what I can do."

* * *

Omega entered the office just then, holding a sheaf of papers which she was studying intently. Echo took the opportunity to observe her closely without her awareness. She was very pale, unhealthily so, with hollow cheeks and dark circles under severely bloodshot eyes. Her usual French braid was a bit scraggly this morning, instead of its normal sleek self, the silver-blonde hair dull and lifeless, almost straw-like. She did indeed move slowly, as if through molasses, although still with her accustomed grace. And the Suit, which had fit her so perfectly once, now hung loosely from

261

her shoulders and hips, the trouser cuffs dragging the floor at her heels.

She tapped a finger on the page, then groped at her breast pocket. Seeing and interpreting the gesture, Echo scooped a disposable pen off Fox's desk, and tossed it her way without thinking.

"Here, catch," he said.

Omega swiped at it, but her usual excellent coordination failed her. She missed badly; it flew past her and bounced and skittered across the floor, ending up against the far wall. Echo glanced meaningfully at Romeo and India, who returned his pained gaze solemnly, then looked away. Omega—who was too preoccupied to have seen any of the exchange—retrieved the pen without comment and began marking the papers. When she was finished, she folded them, tucked them into her inside jacket pocket, and looked at Echo.

"I'm done. Are you ready, Echo?"

Echo looked past her at India and Romeo for a long moment, questioning. They nodded, and looked at Fox. The head of the Division cocked an eyebrow, then nodded permission. Echo, Romeo, and India stood.

"WE are ready," Echo declared. "We're with you, Meg, wherever you go."

They went.

* * *

The black Corvette pulled up in front of the sixth building. From the 'special' back seat—only made possible by the inclusion of a small space warp in the highly-modified sports car—Romeo complained.

Again.

For the twelfth time.

"I can't believe you let HER drive! You never let ME drive, the whole time we were partners."

"SHE actually LIKES my car," Echo pointed out, and Omega nodded from the driver's seat as India rolled her eyes at Romeo. "You've never done anything but insult it."

"It's a cool car," Omega murmured. "Always did like 'Vettes. Long, low, lean and mean. This one more so than most."

"See? Toldja."

"Hmph! At least we coulda taken my Lexus, 'steada crammin' us into th' warp seat, back here."

"You got plenty of room back there."

"Yeah, it's the gettin' in an' out that's awkward as hell. There's still only the two doors! Besides—"

"For the last time, champ, you know if any of us drove, it would tip Slug off where we were headed. Besides, Meg drives better than you."

"Whaaaat?! How th' HELL you figure THAT?"

"Meg is a jet pilot now, for one thing. A good one. For another, SHE didn't learn to drive in a big city like SOME people I could name. Now, if you don't mind, shut the hell up about it."

"Oh, I mind," Romeo grumbled, and would have added more. But when he became the recipient of yet another of Echo's patented Yellowstone-eruption-imminent glares, he shut up. Quickly.

That's three times in a couple days. Man got some serious anger-management issues there, he decided. *Guess I can't blame 'im in the circumstances, but dayum.*

* * *

As they piled out, however, India sounded discouraged.

"Suppose we'll find anything this time?" she wondered, morose.

"...I don't know," Omega answered, hesitant. "But I have to keep trying. Look, um, I know it's late an' all. I'm sorry about that; I didn't think about what time it was when we set out, let alone how long the list was. My whole time-of-day an' day-of-week thing is pretty hosed right now. So if y'all want to go back to Headquarters and get some rest, I can go on with the list. It isn't like I can go home and crash anyway."

"Uh, no, no, I didn't mean it like that," India replied hastily. "We're with you, all the way, honey. I just meant I'm frustrated becauase we haven't found our target yet."

"I know," came the faint reply.

"Look, let's just go find out," Echo said, practically pinning India to the wall of the building with the sharpness of his glance.

Whoa, thought Romeo, worried, *that even went beyond his Yellowstone look. That 'uz more like a supernova about to blow.*

"Okay," Omega almost whispered, downcast. She headed for the front door of the building. India bit her tongue, and shot a contrite glance at the two scowling men.

"Morale, huh?" Echo muttered sarcastically. "I'm sure THAT really helped."

"Sorry," India murmured. "We're way past the end of the shift. I'm tired. I didn't think."

"If you're tired, just think what SHE is."

"Guys?" Omega called, from the now-open door. They all hurried to catch up with her.

Inside, they secured the perimeter, then headed straight for the basement.

"There!" Omega breathed in excitement, pointing to a faintly greenish slime trail, almost luminescent, and still moist. "Over to the tunnel access again."

"This time, ladies and gentleman, I came prepared." With a little flourish, Echo produced a pocket photometric chemical analyzer. "Time to get our minds into the sewer."

"Oh, joy," commented Romeo.

* * *

Once in the sewer, Echo activated the analyzer on the directional setting, and slowly turned in a circle, letting the laser scan the entire tunnel, until the gadget glowed purple.

"This way." He led the way down the tunnel.

"What a wonderful aroma we've discovered," Romeo remarked sarcastically, as they slogged their way through knee-deep sludge.

"—Aw, shit," Omega commented, and stopped dead.

"There goes that apt-descriptor talent again," Echo interrupted, but Omega didn't even smile at the good-natured jibe.

"...I am so SORRY, y'all," Omega continued, nearly cringing at Echo's additional comment. She was penitent, apologetic to the point of pain. The other agents came to a halt, astounded.

"Why, Meg? What are you sorry for?" India asked gently, as Omega turned away from them to hide her face. Her shoulders slumped.

264

"For...for..." her voice began to quiver and her Southern accent got thicker, "draggin' y'all down here, makin' you have to go through all this... this shit...literally..." She rubbed at her temples. "It's way late, halfway through the next damn shift already, and Ah know y'all are worn out an' ready to crash...an' instead of a nice, soft bed, here we go, traipsin' through th' sewers. I just wish..." She broke off.

"What do you wish, Meg?" Echo asked in a quiet voice. Her response came in a scant whisper.

"...I wish it was all over. At least I could rest, then."

Echo, Romeo, and India exchanged significant—and shocked—glances in the gloom. The sleep deprivation appeared to have gotten quite serious. They all understood what she was saying, even as obliquely as she put it: Omega was tired of fighting, and ready to die.

Echo felt the blood drain from his face. India jabbed her index finger at Echo, then at Omega's back. Echo nodded, and drew a deep, silent breath, mustering words—the gentlest, most encouraging he could manage. *Her very life might depend on my nailing this,* he thought, anxious. And suddenly, he knew what to say. He wasn't sure he could choke it out, especially in front of the others, but he was damn sure going to try.

"Hey...hey," Echo said softly, turning Omega to face him and looking down at her, searching her eyes, which glimmered a wet sapphire even in the dim light. "I think I recall somebody recently telling me, 'It's not your fault'...remember? And this isn't yours. You're my...my, best friend," he stumbled over the unaccustomed words a bit, but tried to make his sincerity as obvious as he could, while privately wondering just when it had happened, "and I'm not about to let you do this by yourself, especially when it's really all about getting back at ME. Don't give up on me now, baby. We're not—I'M not—giving up on you! We're here because we want to be, not because we have to be. All three of us. And even if we sent Romeo and India back—"

"But we wouldn't go," Romeo averred.

"Nope." India nodded vigorously.

"—I'm stickin' right here. At your side, baby. For as long as it takes."

Echo ran a gentle fingertip underneath his partner's eye; it came away gleaming wetly in the dim light, and he scrutinized her face, concerned. But somehow her expression, though still downcast, seemed a little more hopeful, and he realized that India had been right—Echo's encouragement, friendship, and caring, once expressed, reminded Omega that she was not alone and gave her strength to continue.

More, he decided, *the fact that I DON'T say stuff like that normally should mean she knows, when I DO say it, I MEAN it. Hang in there, baby.*

So he put an arm around her shoulders, squeezed her tightly against his side, and said encouragingly, "Now cheer up there, bestest pal o' mine, and let's go bag the slimetrailer who really deserves the blame. We got this."

"Yeah," said Romeo enthusiastically, "let's go sprinkle some salt on that Slug."

"About a whole truckload," India added.

Omega offered them a weak attempt at a smile, then waved at Echo.

"Let's go then," she murmured, pointing at the analyzer still in his hand. "What does that thing say?"

* * *

They moved forward slowly. Footing was treacherous, and a bone-weary Omega nearly slipped and fell twice, with Echo catching her once; even Romeo slipped several times. At each tunnel intersection, Echo double-checked the chemical analyzer, then confidently chose the direction. At one intersection, however, he hesitated.

"Hmm. There..." he pointed, "and there. Two options."

"Is there a difference?" asked Omega.

Echo pointed to the right.

"Yeah. This one's stronger. But not by a lot."

"Then it's probably more recent," said Romeo. "Sewer sludge has probably washed some of the older trail away."

It made sense.

"This way, then," said Echo, heading into the tunnel with the stronger signal. A little farther on, Echo remarked in a low voice, "Everybody on alert. The signal's getting stronger. We may be getting close."

The four agents drew their blasters and proceeded at the ready. A few yards farther, Echo crouched and spun around quickly, surveying the area.

"It's strong here, almost all over," he whispered. "But it doesn't go any farther."

"So now what?" whispered Omega. Echo raised his hand and pointed. "Up."

They climbed a ladder and pushed aside the manhole cover at the top, emerging in a rear alley. Several buildings backed onto it, with half a dozen back doors and several fire escapes opening into it.

"Now what does the gizmo say?" Romeo asked. Echo studied the analyzer a few more moments, then pointed at one of the doors.

"There. According to the analyzer, there's Snail behind that door."

Omega took a deep breath, readying herself. Romeo, Echo, and India watched her in mute sympathy as she wordlessly went through the exercises Zz'r'p had taught her—was it only a couple of days ago?—to reinforce her telepathic block.

"All right. Let's do it!" she said finally, jaw locked, a dangerous glint in her eye now.

"That's my gal!" Echo encouraged. "Romeo, shall we?"

"We shall. We most definitely shall."

Together they kicked in the door, and the four rushed in, blasters at the ready—

—As a chef in formal white jumped in surprise and exclaimed, "Mon dieu!" scattering sautéed escargot all over the restaurant kitchen.

* * *

"Yeah, Fox," a tired Echo spoke into his cell phone, "it's pretty much a wash. House specialty was escargot. They had tons of it. We were up to our eyeballs in snails. Romeo and the others are taking care of brain-bleaching the kitchen staff. But I think it's definitely time to recalibrate the photometric chemical analyzers."

"Noted. You calling it a day?"

"I think so. Shift ended a helluva long time ago, and we could all use a shower and clean Suit after slogging around in the sewers for hours. Not to mention, I think our shoes are ruined."

"All right. And I'm sliding your shifts, given the time. Even if Omega can't sleep, the rest of you need it. You can check the other sites tomorrow. Finish up there and then bring it on in."

* * *

Later that night, after he'd napped for a couple of hours to alleviate exhaustion and enable him to slide to a new shift schedule, a casually-dressed Echo, in off-duty black jeans and t-shirt, stuck his head through the now continuously-open back door. There, he saw Omega, also clad in black jeans and t-shirt, at her front door.

"Hey there. Just where are you headed?"

"Come on, and I'll show you," she responded enigmatically.

Curious, he promptly ditched his evening plans of a book and a brew, and followed her out and down the corridor to the elevator. She hit the button for the top floor, and when the doors whooshed open, she got out and immediately turned left, Echo at her heels. Opening a door into a stairwell, she started up. At the top of the stairs, in a tiny alcove formed by some girders, there was a little pile of neatly-folded and stacked pillows and blankets. Echo's eyebrow rose as Omega gathered them up, pressed her hand to a touchpad to unlock the door, and stepped out onto the dark roof of PGLEIA Division One Headquarters.

She spread a blanket on a large open area, plumped the pillows down, and laid down on one half of it, putting her hands behind her head and staring up into the night sky.

* * *

Echo, apparently uncertain of her intent, stood beside the blanket, hands in his pockets, eyes dark, staring down at her quizzically. She looked up at him, and patted the blanket next to her in an inviting fashion. Wordlessly, he stretched his length out beside her.

"When I was a little girl, growing up on the farm," Omega began softly, "on a warm summer evening like this, long after everybody else my age had gotten tired of chasing lightning bugs, I could usually be found, stretched out on a pasture hillside late into the night, looking up at the stars. I used to wonder: Did any of them have planets? Which ones? How many? Did any of the planets have living beings on them? Were they intelligent? Would I ever meet them? And would I ever make it out there?"

"And now you know," responded Echo, "there are, they do, and you have."

"Yes. But I still wonder if I'll ever make it out there."

There was a long pause.

"How long have you been coming up here?" he wondered.

"Oh, I don't know. Several weeks, I guess, off and on. Pretty much ever since my scan pattern got put in the main computers. I had to scope things out a little to figure out how to get up here, I'll admit, but I finally managed it. You're the first person to find out about it, although I expect Fox knows, on some level. It's not so bad as city observation sites go, especially so close to the river. I had been toying with the idea of asking Fox if I could set up a telescope, maybe even construct a little permanent observatory dome. Last couple of nights...well, let's just say this makes a good refuge when everyone else is asleep and I get tired of beating my head against a damn computer screen. It's...not so lonely up here, somehow."

* * *

Echo looked up, deep into the darkness.

"You know, on the few occasions I have the chance to just...stargaze," for a moment he thought of X-ray, who had been an amateur astronomer, "I always remember a psalm: 'When I consider the heavens...'"

"Yeah, I know the one you mean: 'When I consider the heavens, the work of Thy fingers, the moon and the stars, which Thou hast ordained— What is man, that Thou art mindful of him? Or the son of man, that Thou carest for him? Yet Thou hast made him a little lower than the angels, and hast crowned him with glory and honor,'" she quoted from Psalm 8.

"That's the one."

"Yeah, I like it too. Whenever I've been taking a little too much 'human slime' attitude off some of the more arrogant of the new immigrants, I come up here and remember that verse. Helps me get things back in perspective," she said. Echo nodded.

They were silent for a while, a comfortable, companionable silence, gazing upward; two dear friends enjoying the company, and the view. Then Omega's hand shot up, pointing.

"Wow, nice one!"

Echo dug around for his cell phone.

"I'd better let Fox know we've got an unauthorized incoming."

"No...no, I don't think so. Did you see the way the light intensity flared and then rapidly tapered off at the end? Then became kind of sporadic? If it was an incoming spacecraft, it didn't make it to landing. No, I think it was just a nice meteor."

"'Nice'? That bright?"

"That's nothing, Echo; I've seen 'em in the daytime. Those are rare, I'll grant you. But I'll tell you what. In a couple of months, 'long about mid-August, some night we're off-duty, we'll find us a nice big open field 'way out in the country—maybe we'll go back to Texas—and I'll introduce you to the Perseids."

"'Perseids'? The meteor shower?"

"Yeah. You ever seen 'em?"

"No. I don't get much opportunity just to stargaze, I'm afraid. And I'm not a pro at it like you are."

"Meh."

"'Meh' what?"

"My professional status. No big wup. Not around here, anyway."

"Sure it is. You know this stuff. A good bunch of the rest of us don't. You..." Echo paused, trying to figure out how to express himself. "You get how all this," he waved a hand at the heavens, then at the rooftop beneath them, thereby denoting the Division itself, "goes together, in a way the rest of us...don't."

"I dunno about that. But I try."

"I think you do a lot more than just 'try,'" he told her. She shrugged, and even in the dim light, he could see her face flush at the compliment. "So tell me about these Perseids. You were saying?"

"Oh, yeah. So. Do you know what causes 'em?"

"Used to. Been a long time. Refresh my memory." He knew she just needed to talk. *About anything except Slug,* he thought. *For that matter, I could stand a change of topic too. And this is proving interesting, in the fun sorta way.*

"Well, see," she began, "when a comet nears perihelion, it often develops two tails. One is an ion tail, composed of plasma; the other is a dust tail—comets are 'dirty snowballs,' so when the 'snow' sublimates, ionizes, and becomes the plasma, the 'dirt' has to go someplace. So the dust tail that's formed leaves a trail of debris behind the comet along the orbit. And if the comet's orbit intersects the Earth's orbit, the Earth's gravity well sweeps up the debris as we come through, and when it hits the atmosphere, we get a meteor shower."

"Any ever hit?"

"I've never heard of any impacts from a shower. We're talking small, grains of sand and dust and stuff. I guess now and again you might get something you could skip across a pond, but it still isn't gonna survive to impact. Over time, the trail of debris tends to spread out a little, and the longer it is between so-called 'comet apparitions,' the more the shower kinda disperses. But I'll tell you this from experience: If the parent comet has been through recently, then it's laid down a fresh deposit of debris, and the shower will be pretty spectacular. It's been quite a while ago now—I was a little kid; Daddy took me out to watch it—but I was watching the Perseids a year or two after the comet came through, and I was able to read by the light of some of the meteors."

"What?!"

"I'm serious. It was just freakin' incredible. Anyway, the Perseids usually make for good fireworks; I think you'd enjoy 'em. So how 'bout it? August, desert, you and me, Perseids?"

"It's a date." Echo gave her a warm smile, then pushed himself up on one elbow to study his protégé in the dark. "You know..." the man of few words wrestled for the right ones, finally settled for, "...you're impressive." He smiled again, just slightly; he was proud of her.

"Howzzat?" She returned his smile, seeming pleased.

"Well, here you are...holding, to use your own analogy, a ticking time bomb. But you're lying here calmly, even enthusiastically, teaching me basic astronomy and making a date that's two months away, like nothing else is going on. Pretty good for a 'rookie.' Which you aren't anymore, anyway. I'm...damn impressed."

She abruptly averted her gaze. His smile faded.

"To be honest, Echo, for a few minutes...I just forgot."

Idiot! He cursed himself silently. *The train of thought had changed tracks, and then you went and derailed it. What you just did, Echo, was far worse than what you nailed India to the wall for, this very afternoon. You damn fool!*

"I'm...sorry, Meg," he said softly. Even as he said it, he was stunned by the sheer inadequacy of the words.

"For what?"

He shrugged.

"For reminding you. For...getting you into all this. For everything. You're too young to be used as a pawn in some alien's idea of revenge games for something that probably happened before you even started school."

"'Too young'? 'Before I started school'? Waitaminit, Echo, how old do you think I am?"

"Pretty close to Romeo's age, I'd think." He scrutinized her in the dark. "Twenty-five, twenty-six, tops."

"Wow. Thanks! But didn't you check my records?"

"Of course."

"So what about vital stats? Age, weight, height?"

"Never bothered. You told me your weight once, but I've forgotten what it was. The numbers aren't what's important, anyhow—you're of age, in great shape, and tall for a woman. Besides, I'm a gentleman, remember? And you're a Southern belle." He offered her a half-smile.

"Why, thank ya most kindly, Mistah Echo, suh," she said, letting her full, aristocratic, old-Southern dialect emerge for a moment. He almost shivered in pleasure; it had been a long time since he'd heard the accents of his youth in so honeyed a voice. But he caught himself before it manifested, and she continued. "So tell me what you know about me. From before I came here, I mean."

"Okay: Bachelor's degree in physics, biology, geology, AND chemistry. Masters in aerospace engineering. PhD in astronomy and astrophysics. Then eight years with NASA. Published researcher. Civil pilot's license. Scuba cert..." and then more softly, "Astronaut."

She winced almost imperceptibly at that last remark.

"...Right. Now, how long do you suppose it would take to do all that? And how old would I have been when I started? Even if I were precocious... which I was, a little bit. I was barely sixteen when I started undergraduate school."

Echo paused a moment, calculating.

"...Oh."

"I'm only about two or three years younger than you, if I remember right—and you already showed me your files, so I know you're not too old, either. What I'm trying to tell you is, don't feel so responsible for me, hon. I'm not a child. I'm a fully adult, mature woman—"

The image of a certain lace-and-satin brassiere flashed into his mind's eye.

"I had noticed," he interjected drily, and shifted his eyes to the stars.

"—Completely capable of handling myself, and of facing whatever I have to. If you think astronauts have it easy when it comes to facing death, talk to the last *Challenger* crew. Or maybe the *Columbia* crew. Or hell, the *Apollo One* crew, for that matter."

He looked back at her then, and deliberately pulled a grimace.

"...Mm. Point taken."

They were silent for a few moments. Then Echo heard her soft voice.

"'Though my soul may set in darkness, it will rise in perfect light; I have loved the stars too fondly to be fearful of the night...'"

"What's that?" he asked, voice quiet.

"It's from a poem I ran across when I was in graduate school, called 'The Old Astronomer to His Pupil,' by Sarah Williams. I've got it in one of my books downstairs. I'll let you read it later. That way...well...I...always thought I'd like to have a friend read it over me, when..." her voice faded away.

"...You may not be twenty-six anymore, but you're still not exactly an old astronomer, Meg."

"No. But that's a moot point now, isn't it?"

Echo looked down at her from his prone position leaning on his elbow, his forehead creasing as he realized the meaning behind her statement. It implied, *Maybe not, but I'm not likely to get any older.* Omega glanced at his face, then gazed back into the sky.

"I'm all right, Echo. I never have been afraid of the dark."

He nodded in understanding. *Good girl. Courage and to spare. But if I've got anything to say about it, Meg, we'll be working together, you and I, until we're too old to do it any more, dammit. And then we'll retire together, and do...something.* After a few more moments spent studying her starlit profile, he rolled onto his back again.

"Okay, Teach," he said, lightening his tone, "show me how to find my way around the night sky."

"All right. Let's see. Oh, see that big curly J over there? Sort of over on its side? That's Scorpius."

"Where?"

"Lean over here. Now sight along my arm. See?"

"Oh, yeah."

"The bright red star in the center is Antares. Its fourth planet is where our favorite pizza chef's from. The star to its right is Delta Scorpii; it's a variable star, which probably explains a lot, because that's where our least favorite source of escargot originates. Now, look over here. See the outline of a teapot?"

"Yeah?"

"That's Sagittarius—the galactic core is over there..."

* * *

Echo arrived very early the next morning at Fox's office, alone again. Again, India and Romeo were already there, and again, Omega was on the main floor of the Core hunched over a laptop work station. From Fox's door, Echo noticed five or six styrofoam cups sitting around the terminal, as well as two Diet Coke cans, a pill bottle sitting among them. Omega seemed to be just staring at the screen and rubbing her temples subconsciously.

"...Couldn't sleep any more, Fox," India was in mid-sentence as Echo turned and entered the office.

"Yeah, so we decided to make ourselves useful. If Meg c'n do it this long, damn straight I can, for one night. So we hit up the informants—ALL the informants," Romeo agreed. India began ticking off fingers.

"Mack the Knife, Shakespeare, Gordo, Gertrude and Heathcliffe down at the harbor..."

Fox held up a hand.

"Right," he acknowledged. "And?" Their shoulders slumped.

"Nuthin'," a glum Romeo admitted. "They wanna help—everybody that's met her likes her—but nobody knows anything more than we do. Evidently Slug can, if he has to, mess wit' your mind to make you think you're seeing something else, even if you're lookin' right at him. He can't do it long; it takes a lot of effort to keep up so much detail. And too many people around, he can't do it. Too many minds. But we coulda walked right past him in the sewer, and never known it."

"Probably did," Echo said, and Romeo and India both shivered.

"But why wouldn't he just attack then? He could've gotten all of us," India pondered.

"Cat and mouse. He's toying with me, exacting his revenge. Trying to make me sweat," Echo supplied. "Snails are very patient, and very long-lived. They move slowly, but steadily. I've heard of Snails that planned and worked for fifty years just to achieve a single goal. No, Slug is in no hurry. The longer he draws this out, the more painful it becomes...to all of us. He knows time is on his side."

"We had another team check out the fainter sewer trace, Echo," Fox filled in. "It was an outflow. Ran out to the river. There was no sign of Slug. He must've masked his trail with the waste from the French restaurant, and gotten clean away. Well, not clean; not in the sewers. But you know what I mean."

"Yeah, I know. I saw the report on the network. I didn't sleep much last night, either."

"Echo," Fox began a bit hesitantly, "there's something I think maybe you should see..."

* * *

Fox handed Echo a small folder. Echo opened it, and thumbed through the papers inside. He did a double-take and sat down suddenly, wearing an expression of dismay Romeo had never seen before—at least, not on Echo's face.

275

"Hey, what is it?" a surprised Romeo asked.

"It's—Meg's will."

"Whaat?!"

"She gave it to me yesterday," Fox said softly. Echo began to read quietly.

* * *

"'I, Omega, an Agent of the Pan-Galactic Law Enforcement and Immigration Administration, Division One, Earth, being...yet...of sound mind and body, take this opportunity to make provision for the dispensation of my few belongings upon the event of...'" Echo paused, then continued, "'...my death.

"'To India, I leave all of my jewelry, including the heirloom pieces, with the assurance that it all goes with basic black. I also leave my gratitude that I had a girlfriend given to me here, with whom to talk about the guys.'"

India managed a wobbly smile at that; leave it to Omega to ensure that even through tears, there would be laughter. But India's lovely amber eyes were still moist.

"'To Romeo, I leave my collection of science fiction novels and video games. Think of me when you're enjoying your off-duty time, hot shot.

"'To Fox, I leave my personal photographs and mementos for the Division One archives. The Hypothenemoids will know what to do with them. I also leave the family land holdings to provide a safe house for Division agents and guests.'"

* * *

Echo stopped reading aloud, reluctant to continue, uncertain he could get through the words he saw next, and the name attached to them.

"Go on, Echo," gently prodded Fox. Echo closed his eyes for a few moments, steeling himself, then continued.

"'...And to Echo...the one who has been there with me every step of the way on my Division One journey, my mentor, my partner, and my... closest friend...I leave my most treasured possessions: my astronomy texts. I'm sorry, Echo; I know it's not much, but...may they remind you of me... whenever you see...the starry heavens.'" Echo paused briefly, struggling to get through the reading.

"'I have one final request to make of Echo: Please take...take my body,'" he choked out the words, "'aboard a spacecraft and...set me adrift among the stars. That way it can be said that...I finally...made it out there.'" Echo's voice tapered off into silence.

The room was still for a long time.

"Ohh," India exhaled softly, as a tear spilled over. Romeo turned his back to the group for a moment, struggling for control himself. Echo sat staring down at the folder, unseeing, then he slowly flipped it closed and wordlessly handed it back to Fox, who filed it carefully in his desk.

"I thought you all should know," Fox said simply.

* * *

Romeo turned back to the others and cleared his throat hesitantly.

"She knows the score, don't she?" His voice was rough despite his best efforts.

"She knows," Echo nodded. "She's known from the first."

"How is she handling it?" India queried.

"She's...holding up."

* * *

Maybe better than everyone else, Echo thought. Omega was preoccupied with fighting for her life, and so was not as aware of her steady deterioration as were those around her. *At least,* he amended, thinking about the will, *I hope not. But what was it she said last night? "Capable of facing whatever I have to. If you think astronauts have it easy when it comes to facing death..." I guess I know what she's been staring in the face, all alone, while the rest of us slept, these last few nights. No wonder she started leaving her quarters in the middle of the sleep period to come out to the Core and work; at least she wasn't sitting all by herself in the...dead silence...that way. Damn it, I should've...*

"This can't be happening," India murmured, breaking Echo's train of thought, putting her hand to her forehead and turning away. "It must be a nightmare. With all of our resources, why can't we find this bag of slime?!" she exclaimed, spinning on her heel and flinging out her arm in a violent, frustrated gesture.

"Hey, baby, be cool," Romeo soothed. "We'll think of something."

"We have to," Echo declared, racking his brains for an idea, anything that might help his partner survive.

"What ever happened to the block you were constructing in the medlab?" Fox wondered.

"It's been put on hold," India said, obvious frustration increasing even more at the question. "Zarnix has been trying to get a fix on what Slug's brainwave patterns look like now, so we can calculate a counter-wave. In fact, it's all he's been working on; he's delegated standard Medical work to Zebra. He says until we can get that data, the gadget's worthless, at least against Slug. Though if we have another gastropoid go rogue on us, it should work."

"But that's not much use in this situation," Echo noted.

"No, it isn't. I'm sorry, guys. I tried."

"Of course," Fox murmured. "And it is appreciated, India. I've already annotated your records with a commendation."

A knock came at the door just then, and Omega entered. They broke off their conversation to watch her. The last few hours had marked some sort of turning point, it seemed. She moved now like a woman well more than twice her age, with back hunched, shoulders stooped, and slow, trudging steps. Her unfocused eyes appeared to have heavy blue ink smudged beneath them. Her pale, sallow cheeks were hollow. Her once-shining, platinum hair resembled straw, and the smooth braid was now a scraggly, uneven plait; she no longer had the strength to manage her usual polished coif. The cuffs of her trousers bunched up at the ankle and dragged the floor in back: Her belt, even in the smallest notch, was now too big to keep her trousers up, and the waist rode low. Correspondingly, her shirt bloused out over the belt, the tails tending to come loose in a sloppy fashion, peeking out beneath the tails of her Suit jacket. And she no longer made any effort to keep them tucked into her trousers.

She sank wearily, painfully, down into a chair in the corner, slumped in on herself, and stared blankly off into space. She was, by now, well into at least her fourth Division 'day' with no sleep—which meant she had been going for over a week in normal Earth time. And none of them knew for sure how long Slug's probes had kept her sleepless before his initial attack.

After all, Echo thought, *just because she slept in exhaustion right after the Antarctic mission doesn't mean she was sleeping BEFORE it.* He shook his head.

"It's my job to make sure you stay alive..." His own words suddenly came back to haunt Echo in that moment.

A knife twisted in Echo's gut then. Suddenly the room seemed confining. In a few quick strides he stood just outside the office, on the balcony overlooking the Core. Romeo followed, and stood there wordlessly beside him for a few moments, patiently waiting.

* * *

"I'm losing her, Romeo," Echo finally said in an uncharacteristically low, hoarse voice. "It's a wonder she hasn't had a psychotic episode yet. She can't last much longer. And there's not a damn thing I can do about it. AND...it's my fault."

A worried Romeo was silent; there was nothing he could say, no reply he could make, to ease the pain of Echo's burden. There was a pause as Echo reflected.

"This will make the second partner I've...lost...like this. And when it happened the first time, I swore it would never happen again."

"How many have you had?"

"Just three. X-ray was my first partner, and one of the first Agents, even before me. He was part of the Agency before the Agency joined the PGLEIA. He was MY mentor, and the closest thing I had to a father, by that point; my real dad died when I was 15."

"How'd he die? Your dad, I mean. He was a rancher, if I'm rememberin' your files right?"

"Yeah. He used horses to work the ranch," Echo murmured. "His horse threw a shoe and tripped at a lope, went down with him still in the saddle...and rolled." He shrugged. "A saddle horn is a good, solid anchor for ropin' and junk. But it isn't so well placed when a horse rolls on you."

"Ow." Romeo winced.

"Yeah. But I lost X-ray during a run-in with an interstellar rogue terrorist; he sacrificed himself to ensure we finally took out Kenny. Then you were my second partner; I brought you in soon after X-ray's death.

Maybe a little TOO soon for me, in hindsight, but we needed you. And now Omega is my third." Echo turned to face Romeo then. "Romeo, you know I'm not much for...expressing myself. And we...you and I...were never as close as partners oughta be..."

"It's okay, Echo," Romeo offered, resting a tentative, sympathetic hand on the other man's shoulder. "I knew you were grievin' X-ray—Fox made sure to give me the heads-up on that, when he assigned me to ya. An' I been there, too; I lost my best buddy on a SEAL team mission—we went all the way back to junior high school, Pete an' me. So I know how much it hurts, an' I know it takes a little time f'r the pain to ease up. I figured things would change, once you worked your way through all that, an' I was willin' to wait. I just...didn't expect for Fox t' bring in India. That...kinda changed everything."

"I know. I saw it happening, and I was, and am, glad for ya, pal. She's a smart lady, a beautiful woman, and seriously on her game; she's good for you, in a lotta ways. But maybe...well, this just seems like a good time to let you know that my partners have given me some good memories, and that includes you. And it's been good to know that there was always someone at my back I could count on. With each of my partners, champ."

Romeo said nothing; he didn't dare try. Instead he nodded, swallowing hard. Finally he managed to choke out, "Same here."

Just as a strangled scream from Fox's office cut through the atmosphere of the Core like a knife.

Chapter 11

Inside the office, India and Fox were hovering over a semi-conscious Omega, who had slumped to the floor and lay there, trembling weakly.

"Was that Meg?!" Romeo and Echo sounded like a Greek chorus.

"Yes," Fox confirmed.

"What happened?" Echo demanded.

"I think she dozed off while Fox and I were talking," India explained, crouched beside Omega, checking her wrist for a pulse. "She's almost comatose, Echo. I can't get her to pull out of it."

"Oh, God," Echo groaned. It was more a fervent petition than reaction. He knelt beside his partner and began going through her pockets, searching hastily. Finally he came up with a half-empty pill bottle and glanced up at the ceiling gratefully. Getting out two capsules, he carefully lifted Omega's head and shoulders, leaning her back against his chest. "Here, Meg, take these. Come on, here we go." He worked them into her mouth. "Now swallow, honey. Come on, swallow. Swallow, baby. That's it. Attagirl." Romeo handed him a cup of water from the cooler in the corner of Fox's office. "Now drink this. Easy...easy. Good. Now just lean back against me for a minute and relax. It'll be okay as soon as the stims kick in."

No, it won't, Romeo thought, in deep pain as he watched, *but I guess he has to say that. He has to say SOMEthing, an' it has t' be encouraging, or she'll give up, right here. An' then she'll die, right now, right in front of us. Like she ain't just before doin' that anyway.* It was killing him, killing all of them, watching this beautiful, intelligent, witty woman, this determined, valued member of their team, slowly dying by inches.

* * *

In Echo's arms, Omega choked, then coughed for a few seconds. Eventually she slowly opened her eyes, tilted her head back, and focused with some difficulty on her partner's face. Her eyes were alert now, but too bright. Her skin felt slightly feverish.

Unexpectedly, she snatched the bottle of stimulants from Echo's hand, put it to her mouth, and downed most of the rest of them in one swallow. Alarmed, Echo jerked the bottle away from her.

"MEG! What the hell are you doing?!"

"The girl's lost it!" Romeo yelled.

"She's having a psychotic episode! Get the emergency medics up here, and have Zebra prepare to pump her stomach!" India exclaimed, digging in her pockets for her medscanner. Fox picked up the phone.

"Will everyone please just SHUT UP?" Omega said clearly.

* * *

When she had everyone's attention, she continued.

"I am not psychotic; I am not losing it. At the moment, I am completely lucid. I am not certain, however, for exactly how much longer. And I need to remain so for just a little while longer—whatever it takes. Regardless of the personal consequences."

At that last addendum, Echo's brown eyes narrowed in something that, to Omega, resembled deep pain.

Echo seldom showed much in the way of emotion, but he was not a robot, and over the weeks they had been together for almost all their waking hours, his savvy and observant partner had learned to read those fleeting glimpses. Omega knew he fully understood that she was likely dying, and she knew he wasn't sure if he could face losing another partner so soon. And she felt bad for that, but there was little she could do about it.

It isn't like it's my call, she thought, rueful.

What she was less sure of was whether or not she was only a partner to him. Granted, Echo had called her his best friend only the day before; but she was uncertain if that was because it was true, or because in his mind, he equated 'partner' with 'best friend.' And, unlike her declaration that he and the others were her family now, Echo had never made such a claim.

It could be because he just couldn't force it out, I suppose. But I don't know. About either one, friend or family. And chances are, I never will know, she thought, saddened. *I'll never have the opportunity to find out. But I can do this for him, at least.*

"Why?" Echo demanded to know then. "Why does it matter so much,

Meg? Why is it worth your life?"

She met those pained eyes, held their gaze, confident.

"Because I know where Slug is."

* * *

The room erupted in a flurry of activity at that declaration. Echo, Romeo, and India went to grab some high-powered weapons. Fox began arranging backup.

With his permission, swiftly given, Omega commandeered Fox's computer, which was logged into the network with Director authority, and began typing in commands to the virtual keyboard as fast as her hands would go—which, at the moment and under the influence of a significant number of stimulants, was nearly a blur. When the others came back in, they watched, astounded, as Omega appeared to be everywhere in the room at once, feeding Fox information, running to the maps being rapidly displayed in succession on the wall monitors, back to the computer to key in commands almost faster than they could see. Her pale cheeks were highly flushed, her azure eyes brilliant, almost luminous.

"Man, that is one serious buzz," Romeo observed in a soft voice.

"What he said," India agreed. Echo watched for a moment.

"'Nice meteor,'" he murmured.

"What?" Romeo asked, confused.

Omega looked up, that exceptional hearing having caught the remark, and locked eyes with Echo. If she had learned to read him, it was no more than he had done with her. And to him, her sapphire gaze held a wealth of meaning in that moment: determination, despair, anger, resignation, and caring. It said to Echo, as plainly as any words could, *If I'm going out, let it be in a blaze across the night.*

"...Nothing," Echo replied, stifling a sigh.

* * *

"Everybody ready? Let's go salt the Slug," Omega said, her blue eyes flashing with a fierce light.

"Waitaminit," Romeo paused. "How do we know he ain't just gonna move? After all, he knows that we know that you know...you know?"

"That's true. But this time it won't do him any good."

"Ooo-kaay…"

"But be careful, everybody, because that means he's cornered, and he's desperate."

"Right," Echo agreed. "If Meg's figured out how to box him up someplace, then she's on the money, on that. He isn't gonna go down without some serious argument."

"So where's my argument?" she demanded.

Without a word, Echo handed her a Mark IV Tachyon Smasher rifle. She took it and checked it out, then nodded her approval.

"I'll get the Corvette," Echo said, turning.

"No." Omega grabbed his arm. "Just come with me. Fox?"

"I'm on the curve, Omega," Fox replied, self-assured. "As Romeo likes to say, I'm all over this one. I'll have things ready when you get there."

"All right. Everybody—GO!" And Omega headed off at a sprint, taking the point. The Core looked like a stirred-up ants' nest as they ran through, and got in—

"The elevator?!" Romeo exclaimed, surprised.

"The elevator," Omega said firmly, as she pushed <SB3>.

"The facility support sub-basement? What has Fox got hidden there for us to use?" India wondered.

"Well now, let's go find out, shall we?" Echo remarked, with an odd glance at Omega.

* * *

An encouraging Omega smiled at Echo, and it was telling: He had a hunch he was starting to realize what she already knew. The elevator door opened on a dim view of Sub-basement Three; the lighting was poor, because most of the facility equipment here was automated and did not need frequent maintenance. Omega immediately dropped into a wary crouch and eased out the elevator door. Echo groaned softly.

"You're kidding, right?" he asked.

"Nope," she replied. "Never more serious in my life…whatever's left of it."

Echo winced at the remark.

"Sub-basement Three? Here? In our own headquarters?"

"We didn't think of it, did we?"

"You did," Romeo interjected.

"Not exactly. I—ooh." She put one hand to her temple, wincing. "Ow."

"What?" India wondered. "What's wrong?"

"He's—unh—here, all right." Omega rubbed her temple. "And he knows we're here, too."

* * *

Echo took over then. He waved Romeo and India off to one side.

"Go through that door, then turn right, into the corridor. At the end of the corridor is another door. Go through it. It'll put you at the far end of the basement. Start working back this way," he whispered. "We'll shoot for a pincer move." They headed off, into the gloom.

Echo returned his attention to Omega, and promptly bit his lip in concern. Her forehead was deeply creased with a frown of pain, her face pale and slightly drawn. The flush that had colored her cheeks in Fox's office was gone.

Damn. Is Meg even gonna be able to do this? Maybe I should leave her here, or more, send her back—assuming I can get her to go. Then again, can I take this bastard out without a partner to back me up on this end? I just sent India and Romeo to the far side of the building. I probably can; I basically did it before. Meg will be pissed as hell if I try, though. But if Slug has Meg in this much pain, how can she concentrate on helping me take 'im out? Well, only one way to find out. How she reacts...or IF she reacts... to this will tell me what I need to do next.

He jerked his head toward the cluttered, dark area before them, his meaning plain—to her.

Omega nodded, brought up the tachyon smasher. He hefted his as well.

Huh. Maybe she CAN do this. Maybe WE can.

He motioned her to the right, then turned to the left himself. Suddenly her eyes widened in horror.

"NO! Don't! Come back here!" she whispered hoarsely, vehemently, reaching for him, grabbing at his arm and hauling on it with a strength he wouldn't have credited to her in her condition, seeming almost desperate.

285

He turned back toward her.

"What?!" he whispered.

"It's the dream, Echo! This is it!"

"Slug's attack? This is what you saw?"

"Yes! We mustn't split up! That's what he's counting on! We have to work together! It's the only way! Don't leave me, under any circumstances, or we'll both be killed!"

He nodded, trusting her completely, and returned to her side. Cautiously, using whatever was available for cover, they moved forward, Echo taking the point.

* * *

The layout of the sub-basement was complex. According to Echo, this was where most of the Division One headquarters facility support equipment was located, and this included air cooling units for the computers, water heating and cooling, waste water treatment, pumps, and electrical equipment, as well as some other complicated—and obviously extraterrestrial—machinery that Omega could not immediately identify and Echo had never bothered to find out about. Omega strongly suspected it pertained to generating, sustaining, and manipulating the space warp with which the building was equipped.

In addition to all of this, the dimly-lit sub-basement level was the lowest floor in the building, and was partitioned off by a number of thick structural walls; space warp or no, there was significant WEIGHT to be supported here. Searching such an area for an interstellar criminal would be slow, tedious work. And more than a little dangerous. And that was WITHOUT said criminal's telepathic camouflage ability.

Advancing silently, by now intuitively knowing each other's moves, the Alpha One team slowly worked their way over to a kind of bottleneck corridor between two structural walls. The far end of the bottleneck was pitch-black.

Behind Echo, Omega had begun to pant inaudibly as she struggled against the telepathic assault raging around her head. The mental block Zz'r'p had taught her kept out most of it, but there was no doubt in Omega's mind that Slug was someplace really close. And it remained to be seen how close she could get to the alien being before her block failed.

After that, she fully realized, *I'm dead meat, and Echo's on his own. One way or another, I'm not walkin' away from this one. But Echo might, if I play my cards right. I gotta push it as far as I can.*

Echo moved noiselessly to the left edge of the opening, while Omega simultaneously took the right, both of them out of sight of anyone at the other end of the bottleneck.

Omega leaned against the wall momentarily and closed her dry, burning eyes. The concrete blocks felt cool against her fevered cheek; it helped ease the pounding in her head, at least a little. She fought to suppress the gory memories of Slug's nightmare attack that forced their way into her thoughts, consequent to the current attack.

Omega looked up in time to see Echo glance around and down the ersatz corridor, then at her. She raised her left hand slightly and nodded: It was her turn to take the point. Hefting her weapon, she took a deep breath and sidestepped around the corner, crouched to rush to the far end—

—And staggered back, gasping. Her hands released automatically, and the Mark IV tachyon smasher rifle clattered to the floor. Omega clutched her head, then grabbed for the wall, in an effort to find a point of stability. She doubled over then, holding her belly against the pain of a mental evisceration, no longer able to hold off the grisly images that flooded her mind.

"Nuh—No! Dammit! Nuh—not...not now...not that! Too—too close—too strong! Echo! Get out! Get OUT! GO! RUN! I can't...can't keep...block..."

* * *

But instead of running, a determined Echo lunged forward and put an arm around her waist, prepared to drag her back behind cover. She turned toward him then, a wild look in her unfocused eyes as she apparently strove to maintain coherent, independent thoughts, and clutched the lapels of his Suit jacket. She pointed down the corridor, one hand still grasping his crumpled lapel.

"I'm com...no, he's...coming for you, Echo! Hates...you...not content... to hurt you. He...I...HE wants...both of us! He—aaaAAIIIII..."

Her voice rose in a piercing scream as she grabbed at her head with both hands, and then fell like a freshly-chopped tree.

* * *

From the far side of the huge sub-basement, Romeo and India heard the reverberating scream and looked at each other in horror and dread.

"That was Omega!" gasped India.

"Yeah, but which damn way?! It echoed all over!"

They sped up the search.

* * *

A fiercely angry Echo stood protectively over his prostrate, unconscious partner, one foot firmly planted on either side of her crumpled form, shoulders squared, tachyon smasher snugged into his hip and aimed down the corridor.

"That's it, Slug," he called out in a voice colder than interstellar space. "Come out and show yourself! I've had enough of you!"

Oh, have you? came a voice, loud in his head. *Well, I have had MORE than enough of YOU, monster!*

Echo staggered back at the mental onslaught. When he regained his equilibrium, he looked up; there, at the end of the bottleneck, moved a giant, iridescent green, slug-like figure. Its bulk filled the narrow corridor, and it advanced slowly with a soft, wet, squelching sound. Slug had no eyes, no ears, and no visible mouth; his food-ingestion orifice was underneath his skirted foot. Two short, soft, bulbous-tipped antennae waved above his head, serving both as sensory apparatus and telepathic amplifiers.

Still standing, monster? came the silent voice again. *Well, let's see what we can do about that...*

"AAaah!" gasped Echo at the telepathic blast which followed, and he stumbled back again in spite of himself, hard into a cooling unit. He bounced off and fell; quickly he scrambled back to his feet, grabbing for the tachyon smasher rifle. He moved left, trying to flank the gastropoid.

Oh, please! Do you really think it will do you any good to get behind me? My ability to see is not limited to lines of sight like you pathetic creatures.

"Huh-oof!" This time Echo slammed into the cinder-block wall, sliding down the rough surface to the floor, scraping the bare skin of one hand bloody as he tried to catch himself. He struggled to his feet and doggedly brought around the tachyon smasher.

* * *

Clattering, crashing sounds, accompanied by occasional male grunts and gasps, echoed through the sub-basement, reaching India and Romeo.

"You hear that?" Romeo asked, worried. "That's Echo! He's in trouble!"

"Yeah, but you know what I don't hear?" India noted, equally anxious.

"Uh-huh. Meg. She screamed, an' there ain't been another peep outta her. That's...bad."

"Probably. She's either unconscious, or..."

"Yeah."

"Can you tell where Echo is?"

"Yeah, this way..."

They turned and followed the sounds as fast as they dared—without risking an unexpected encounter with their enemy.

* * *

"It was this 'pathetic creature' that took you down last time," Echo reminded the gastropoid. He fired.

And missed.

An air cooler developed a large hole; he hoped the computers were backed up, because they were going to overheat fast, with that unit down for the count. He picked himself up from the recoil, rubbing his suddenly-cramping arm, and kept circling.

Your perceptions are so limited, Slug noted with disdain. *Control over your own body so crude. I can cause your arm muscle to—twitch—just as you fire, spoiling your aim.*

Déjà vu.

"Muscle...twitch..." Echo mumbled, as his mind drifted back in time.

* * *

The gastropoid lashed out telepathically, and Echo staggered back and fell, his lanky body splashing water from puddles as the rain poured down around them. He scrambled doggedly to his feet, plucking his laser pistol out of the mud, and glanced around in something like desperation.

'Where the hell is my backup? Where's X-ray?' he thought. 'Maybe one of the more experienced agents will know what to do with this...Snail.'

My name is Azeln, *came the incensed telepathic response.*

'Yeah, yeah. Azeln. Like I care what a murderer's given name is. Where's X-ray?' Echo wondered, continuing to keep one eye on the gastropoid, and a lookout for the other Agents with the other eye.

But no one else was in sight; it was up to him. He brought the laser pistol around and drew a bead on the Snail's head.

Do you really hope to harm me with that? *resounded the alien voice in Echo's head, as he squeezed down on the trigger.* Don't you know I can reach into your mind and make your muscle—twitch?

Echo felt a painful spasm in his bicep, just as he fired. The laser pistol jerked, and the beam sliced through the Shell on the gastropoid's back, carving a gaping, ugly wound into the Shell-being as its bodily fluids spurted several feet away. The remainder of the Shell's flesh and nacre tore under its own weight and it released, falling from the back of the gastropoid in two huge hunks of raw, bleeding meat encased in broken fragments of carapace, twitching in obvious death throes. Echo heard a kind of mental scream...

* * *

NO! YOU LIE! It was you! YOU did it! YOU killed her! Slug screamed, insane with anger and grief, as he relived the event through Echo's thoughts.

"No, Slug! YOU did it!" Echo insisted. "Your little mind games threw off my aim, just like you did now, and caused the Shell to be hit! You did it yourself!"

NOOOOO!! YOU did it! You must be PUNISHED! You are a MONSTER! The monster MUST be destroyed! With frightening speed, the nearly hysterical gastropoid calmed. *I will...I can...ahh, yes, I know...I shall make you feel the pain of a nonexistent blow.* The voice was cold now, murderously intent.

"Whoof!" Echo doubled up with the force of an unreal—but nonetheless powerful—blow to his solar plexus. Pain cramped his belly.

Stubbornly, he brought the weapon around to try again. Suddenly, the sub-basement seemed to distort: warping, flowing, changing, morphing. Echo's senses went haywire as he felt the cold, malevolent contact of an alien mind. He staggered despite himself, spinning about in an instinctive effort to locate some part of the huge, dark room that was familiar, or at least stable, that he could use as an anchor. Failing that, he raised the tachyon smasher rifle and turned back in the direction he had been facing—at least, he thought it was the direction he had been facing—and laid his finger on the trigger. But as he looked down the weapon's sight, instead of Slug, he saw Omega's crumpled form in it.

I can make you think your partner is me.

Echo stopped then, finger on the trigger, remembering Omega's 'dream.' Should he take the chance? Where WAS Omega? Was the figure in his sights Meg, or was it Slug? He glanced around quickly, searching his constantly-changing surroundings. Slug—wherever he was—seized the momentary distraction.

"Uff!" A nonexistent punch to the jaw sent him spinning, falling—right on top of—another Omega.

Well, that's something, he thought. *If she's HERE, then I can fire THERE. At least, I THINK she's here.* Slug interrupted his thoughts.

But what if you're wrong? What if that's really me you're leaning against, and Omega you've got in your sights there?

The thought that he was lying against the psychopathic alien was cringeworthy, but Echo was tougher than that; he did not give in to the temptation.

He did pause, however, suddenly unable to trust his own perceptions. There had to be a way to tell the difference between reality and illusion. There had to be. Didn't there?

Vertigo built nausea in the pit of his belly as the room continued to shift and change, like layers of hot wax melting, then swirling into a vortex. He brought up the nose of the tachyon smasher rifle. He had to try, had to do something to stop this creature.

How does it feel, human? To be prepared to kill your OWN partner?

He studied the two apparitions of Omega, one partly underneath him, the other across the unstable room. *There has to be a clue...*

As he concentrated, trying both to analyze his situation and to maintain equilibrium, arms wrapped around his chest from behind. Automatically, he struggled away.

"Echo, it's me," the Omega beside him seemed to whisper hoarsely, hanging on to him weakly with one hand.

"How do I know?—unh." Another illusory blow landed. "The whole place has gone crazy. Can't trust any of my senses. And there's two of you."

"Oh. Well, you don't know, I guess." The husky voice held an edge of pain. She laid a hand—or some sort of appendage—on the back of his shoulder. "You'll just have to trust me."

"What—uh—did you have in mind?" *Maybe there'll be a clue in what she says,* Echo thought.

"Let me get my arms—" she slipped them around his prone form, pressed her cheek hard into his right shoulder to get the reach, "—there. Support the gun for me, but let your arms move. Okaaay..." she adjusted the settings on the stock of the gun, slid her face down his sleeve. "Drop your elbow a little. No, here." She pulled down on his left arm slightly.

He looked down at her hands on his arms. *So thin,* he thought, *almost bony.* The chronometer on her left wrist flopped loosely. *The CHRONOMETER...*

"Aah!" Echo grunted as the unseen Slug suddenly rained a flurry of telepathic blows, apparently designed to distract him. He battled to focus on the Omega figure across the room. *The chronometer...on the RIGHT. The breast pocket...*

"Mirror image," he murmured. "Of course."

"There! PULL!"

"Meg—If I AM wrong, I'm sorry, baby..."

His finger depressed the trigger, the tachyon smasher blasted, and the rifle's recoil blew them both back hard into another concrete wall, just as two more discharges came from the side. A mental burst from Slug caused Echo to black out for a second.

When Echo's vision cleared, Romeo and India were covering Slug's limp body, which was now missing both antennae and the top of his head—

—And which had a neat, round hole in the midsection, where the heart used to be.

* * *

Slightly dazed, Echo staggered to his feet and over to the body. He could tell Slug was dead, because the incessant jackhammer inside his head was gone, and the room stayed still. He poked Slug's tail with his foot. He was not gentle.

"Good riddance," he muttered, and turned—

—To see a small, black-clad form crumpled against the far wall, and lying very, very still.

Without knowing exactly how he got there, he found himself kneeling beside his unmoving partner. He reached for a pulse in the wrist, and prayed.

Nothing.

Echo dropped her wrist, loosened her tie and collar, and gently probed her throat. A trickle of blood ran from the corner of her mouth at his touch. Her ears and nose were bleeding as well.

Nothing. Oh, damn.

With mounting dread, he pushed her jacket aside, undid her tie, ripped open the top of the shirt to expose part of a lacy wisp of flesh-toned undergarment, and laid his head directly on her chest, pressing his ear down just above the upper left breast—

THERE. Weak. Slow. But there.

"India, get over here. NOW!"

India came running.

"Oh, no. Is she—"

"There's a heartbeat. Barely."

India knelt beside him and began checking Omega.

"Romeo, you still on the horn to Fox?" India called. Romeo looked up from the cell phone.

"Yeah?"

"Tell him to get the medics down here stat. Code Black. Agent down."

"Code Alpha One Black," Echo amended automatically, watching India as she obtained vital signs on Omega.

"Oh, maaan. Shit. Did you hear that, Fox?"

"Tell him to feed them these vitals," India interrupted before Fox

293

could reply. "Respiration, eight and shallow; pulse, thirty-seven, extremely weak and thready...pupils dilated and uneven, minimally responsive. She's badly shocky. Hemorrhaging from mouth, nose, and ears; possible internal hemorrhaging, but I can't be sure without more equipment. Airway clear. Muscular reflexes active, but slow. No sign of fractures, at least that I can find with no equipment, though possible busted ribs..."

Romeo relayed the medical data as India continued the examination and Echo knelt, watching.

"Is there anything you can do?" Echo managed to choke out; for some reason, his voice didn't want to work.

"Not right now, hon," India replied, voice soft and understanding. "All I got is my med scanner. I don't have any medications or anything. The best I can do is to monitor her condition. The emergency medical team should be here any minute, and then we can roll."

"Is she gonna...?"

"I...don't know yet."

The three agents fell silent, watching over their fallen comrade. Finally they heard the elevator in the distance.

"Hey! Hey, guys! Over here!" Romeo called, waving.

Fox, along with the mop-up team, trailed the emergency team through the facility machinery. Once the emergency team arrived, they swiftly began establishing life support and loading Omega into a basket stretcher.

* * *

"Well, farkakt," Fox remarked, looking at Slug's lifeless form as the mop-up team went to work on it, "looks like we've gotta clean out the cellar. Then we gotta find out where all the pests are getting in. Good thing Omega had me completely seal off the sewer access tunnels, and every other access we could get our hands on."

"So that's why th' girl wasn't worried about Slug gettin' away this time," Romeo realized. "She had 'im boxed in."

"Yep," Fox responded. "Once she detected where he was, and with her block back up, she had him trapped before he knew what she was about."

"Uh, guys," India interrupted, pointing at a pale Echo, who was impassively watching Omega being carried away, hands shoved deep in his trousers pockets, lips tightly compressed. "We have more pressing matters..."

Romeo and Fox looked at the floor in something approximating shamed embarrassment, then nodded. Romeo moved over to Echo, and put an encouraging arm across his shoulders.

"C'mon, man. Let's go to the medlab."

* * *

In the medlab waiting room, the doctor on duty, Whiskey, who had begun Omega's first Agency physical before handing over to Zebra, walked up to them.

"Which one's India?" he asked.

"Me."

"Oh! I remember you now. What've we got?"

"Extreme sleep deprivation, bordering on psychosis; telepathic mental trauma. Hemorrhaging from cranial orifices. Forced stimulant abuse. Contusions, hematomas, some edema. Probable concussion. Possible internal injuries, possible broken ribs. Dehydration and malnutrition, likely."

Doctor Whiskey whistled in concerned shock.

"How serious do you think the head trauma is?"

India started to answer, but she caught herself just in time. Glancing around, she saw a silent Echo, Romeo, AND Fox focused on their conversation with all the intensity they would normally give an intergalactic murderer. She took the doctor's elbow and steered him over to the corner of the room, where they continued the conversation in hushed tones.

* * *

Romeo shot a look at Fox behind Echo's back and shook his head at India's behavior. *Not good.* Suddenly a medtech burst through the door from the lab.

"Doctor Whiskey, Zebra says you better come quick. We've got cerebral swelling. She needs extra hands, stat."

With an exclamation, the doctor broke off the conversation with India and ran back into the lab. Echo's face tightened.

"Hey, look, Echo, dude...I'm sure that's somebody else in there,"

Romeo tried to reassure him. Echo nodded.

"Yeah."

Not very damn likely, Romeo thought, *all things considered. I'm lyin' through my teeth, here. But...the lack of expression on Echo's FACE, combined with the pain in his EYES...he cares about 'er, a lot. He just can't admit it out loud. I dunno, man. I gotta say something. I just wish India and Fox would throw me a bone an' help out. But...I guess they know the score too, an' they don't wanna lie about it.*

* * *

India had examined Echo and pronounced him fit except for a few bruises and scrapes, particularly his knuckles and the back of his right hand. She had swabbed those down with a bit of Rejuvic, given him an analgesic for the residual headache, and pacing had set in amongst the agents when another medtech emerged and hurried over to Fox.

"The doctor—uh, Zebra said to ask you if the Arcturan ambassador is planetside, or, well, any friendly Arcturan, really."

"'Fraid not, son. Tell her that he's back on the homeworld. Government crisis. And his substitute hasn't arrived yet, and won't, for two more days."

"...Oh. Well, crap." The medtech hurried back into the lab, calling out, "That's a negative response on the Ambassador, Doc!"

From the back they heard Zebra's voice call, "Then get me a corticostimulator! STAT!"

"Yes, ma'am!"

India moved to the door and cracked it a bit to look in. An unconscious Omega was lying there on a gurney in a black medical jumpsuit, white as death. IV lines hung suspended beside her, running into both arms. Monitors were attached to sensors on her chest and head, displaying heart rhythms and encephalographic readouts, neither of which were in normal bounds. Medtechs were attaching a large, modular gold device to her head. Suddenly the heart monitor hiccupped, flatlined, and a shrill tone rent the air.

"CARDIAC ARREST!" Zebra shouted, beginning CPR. "WHISKEY! Get me a crash cart over here STAT! And somebody finish getting that corticostimulator hooked up!"

"Oh, my God..." India heard a low, fervent male voice at her shoulder.

India spun, and Echo was standing behind her, pale, immobile, his dark gaze fixed on the sight beyond the door. She closed the door quickly, grabbed his arm and pulled him back into the waiting room, where she made him sit down. She seriously considered forcing his head down between his knees, but he hadn't shown evidence of dizziness or lightheadedness so she refrained, knowing he would fight it.

In the background, she could still hear the piercing shrill of the heart monitor. Faintly, she heard the doctor call, "Clear!"

* * *

After a few moments, the medical alert sound stopped. Everyone froze, then, waiting to discover why.

Is Omega...? Echo wondered, breaking off the thought in intense dread; he found, for the first time in his life, he couldn't make himself finish it. She was his third partner, and the one who, at least in his estimation, was the most like him, the most relatable, the most understandable. The closest friend he'd ever had, though he'd never admit it to Romeo, lest the other man feel offended. *And yeah, she IS family, somehow. When X-ray died*, he thought, *even though I tended to think of him as a father figure, he wasn't quite, 'cause I had Dad until a couple years before I met X-ray. So when he died, the grief was still that of a pupil for his mentor. And it was bad. But...* He broke off. Finally he completed the thought. *This...will be worse. A LOT worse. It almost feels like part of me is in there, dying with her.*

An aeon later, the other doctor—Whiskey, Echo remembered—came out and motioned for India. As she crossed the waiting room, Echo heard the doctor speak.

"We've got her stabilized, for the moment. Now..." their voices trailed off into a soft murmur.

Echo relaxed fractionally. He got up and began pacing again.

* * *

The conversation finished, India turned.

"Guys? I'll be back in a little while. I'm gonna throw my weight in on this one, for whatever that's worth, so I need to go scrub up." She turned to follow Whiskey through the lab door.

"India?"

"Yes, Echo?"

"Is there anything I...?"

"No," she answered gently. "Just...pray."

India turned and left the room quickly after that. She didn't want to see what Echo's expression might be.

* * *

A weary Romeo slouched in a waiting-room chair, watching his former partner wander around the room, and wondered what was going on in the lab beyond. He hated hospitals and doctor's offices. But he had to admit, having India around, even if she was a doctor, could definitely be useful in an emergency. Hell, having India around any time was a good thing. She made a good partner and a good teammate, completely aside from their romantic relationship...or maybe BECAUSE of their romantic relationship. They understood each other, and he was glad to have her around. He wondered how he'd feel if he were in Echo's shoes right now, and that was India in there, fighting for her life. How would he handle it?

Probably not half as well as Echo's doing, Romeo thought, considering the other man as Echo continued to pace. *The man has coolness in his genes.* Yeah, sure, he was pacing a bit, and he was obviously concerned: Echo was no robot. But Romeo felt sure that, if the roles were reversed, Fox would be leading him off to a rubber room by now. Romeo was already as tense as a violin string, and Meg wasn't even his partner. *Then again, ain't like they got a romantic thing goin' like India and me. Still, it ain't easy.*

The bad thing is, Romeo thought, *Echo blames himself for this. As if he could have read the future or something. Probably one of the few things the man can't do.*

* * *

Fox sat patiently in the waiting room, and sighed noiselessly. He had attempted doing some administrative work on his tablet, but that hadn't lasted long. He simply couldn't concentrate, knowing what was going on in the emergency lab, and remembering that the agent victims of Slug's last Earth rampage lay, on life support, only a few doors down.

This sort of thing didn't happen often. But when it did, it never seemed to get any easier. His agents were good. The top of the line. They didn't get to be agents if they weren't, especially not field agents. But theirs was a dangerous business, and sometimes they just...lost someone. Times like these were the only thing Fox really hated about being Director. *Well...that and the damn paperwork,* he amended.

And it's almost always the rookies, he thought, morose. *The junge leutt, the ones with promise, who never make it to the fulfilment of that promise.*

He glanced at Echo, who wandered around the waiting room, absently studying the artwork on the walls.

Damn, but this is tough on him, Fox considered. *Bad enough it's only been a few years since we lost X-ray, but he really identified with this one. Hm. I might want to see about setting up some sort of clandestine psych eval on Echo, just in case. We don't need our top agent getting his head all wrapped around the notion that he's responsible because two outta three have died. Damn bad luck of the draw, is all. Still, I know what he's thinking. He's second-guessing everything he did in her training, wondering if he forgot something, anything that might have given her an edge on this. Because it's what I'd do in his shoes.*

Fox knew Echo strongly identified with Omega in some ways, partly because of the way they had both ended up in the Agency, and partly because they shared certain idiosyncrasies of personality, such as the same slightly warped sense of humor, and the same drive and sense of duty. Echo had thought VERY highly of the woman. He had worked hard to train her right. And she had proved him right. His faith in her had been fully justified: Omega had done what was necessary, no matter the cost, and without flinching. Every time.

Now, Fox supposed, with another wordless sigh, he'd better start preparing the details. Even if she lived, it sounded as if she would be—how had Zz'r'p put it, only a few days ago? Damn, it seemed like forever..."in a vegetative state," was what he'd said. And when Omega had formally given Fox her will, she had expressly requested of him that, in such an event, she wanted life support terminated, even appending a specifically-worded do-not-resuscitate order onto the will—which order he had NOT shown Echo.

It hadn't even been in the folder when Fox had handed it to him.

No, he didn't—doesn't—need to know about it. It's my responsibility to handle that, Fox thought. *I'm sure as hell not loading it onto Echo's shoulders, or giving him even half a chance to try to assume it on his own. He'll have enough of a burden, trying to blame himself for all this mess. But damn, that is gonna be one hell of a hard order to give.*

And then the funeral, and the will, and disposing of her effects. And the spacecraft launch, with full Division One honors, of course. He'd send along India and Romeo, and maybe one or two others, to help Echo; it would be better that way, and a little easier on his Alpha Line director.

And then...new recruits.

Fox sighed again.

* * *

India, gowned and scrubbed, her short black hair stuffed up under a surgical cap, worked alongside Whiskey, Zebra, and a significant percentage of the Medical department staff as they fought together to jumpstart Omega's nervous system. Unfortunately, Zarnix was off on an emergency call from the Gorthonian family with the newborn, so their most knowledgeable resource wasn't available. Still, they had all the skills and resources they needed; India just wasn't sure it was going to do any good.

You've taken some damn serious punishment this time, girlfriend, India thought as she worked. *I don't see how on Earth you managed it. But then, you're like Echo. He just keeps going no matter what, too. You and Echo kind of go together, I guess. You make good partners. You're both strong-willed and determined. Stubborn. Tough. I just hope that this time, you're tough enough, girl.*

Her mind drifted back to Echo reading Omega's will, even as her hands worked frantically to make the re-reading unnecessary. Omega had some elegant, understated pieces of jewelry, it was true. But India preferred Omega's fast friendship over all the jewelry on this, or any other, planet. She had far rather see the baubles on Meg at one of the big interstellar balls that the Agency sometimes had to host. *Provided, of course, we can keep you going long enough for another one of those to roll around.*

She wondered what Romeo was doing right now. *Probably sitting out*

300

there worrying Fox and Echo half to death, she thought affectionately. She hoped he was at least distracting Echo. *That man is more considerate of us,* she suspected, *than he will ever let on. And it is simply impossible,* India thought with a hidden smile, *not to be fond of Omega. Meg is...was...IS... that unique individual: Someone who really cares, with everything she's got.*

"Hang in there, girlfriend," India told the unconscious form.

* * *

Echo glanced at his wrist chronometer as he wandered around the waiting room, trying to find something that would take his mind off of what was transpiring in the emergency medlab. He wasn't finding anything. His mind's eye kept flitting back to the image of that still form, half-hidden in shadows, lying so quietly on the floor of the sub-basement.

I'm supposed to be the senior partner, he thought, berating himself. *The mentor. I'm supposed to have trained her better than this. Supposed to keep things like this from happening.*

But then, that was Meg: independent and strong-willed. What had she told him so gently that time? "You can't control me." If it needed doing, and she could do it, she didn't ask permission, she simply did it.

He looked at his chronometer again. It had been over three hours since Omega had arrived in the medlab. And still the doctors were saying nothing. Was there anything to say? Was there anything left of the woman who was his partner? Or was she now merely an empty shell? He winced at the irony of that.

Maybe Slug has had his revenge after all. What if...she IS only a shell? Echo closed his eyes for a moment, thinking of the agents on life support only a few rooms away, put there by Slug's last visit. *No,* he thought, *I think I'd rather she was...gone...than like that.* He couldn't imagine those bright blue eyes—the ones he'd seen so many times now, sparkling with intelligence and warmth and wit—dull and vacant. *And I sure as hell don't want to try.*

* * *

Omega floated in a misty white dream world, completely disoriented. Wherever she was, Slug was not there, of this she was certain; the telepathic pounding from without had, thankfully, ceased. For that matter, she realized, she was experiencing no pain whatever. Given how much she had been hurting before, this was a distinct relief.

She was, however, alone. Very much alone. *Where is everyone?* she wondered, confused. Romeo, and India, and Echo. Especially Echo. He should be there. They were partners, after all. It wasn't like him to just go off and leave her, especially during a...what had they been doing, anyway?

She thought hard. It was difficult because she was so tired and confused, and really all she wanted to do was to lie down and sleep for forever, but she made herself concentrate; she had a mission to complete, after all. And the last thing she remembered was...the battle with Slug. Echo had been there; she was positive of that. They had been working together. They were partners, after all. There had been a loud blast, a scream, an impact, and then darkness. A scream...

Oh, no. Echo. Please, God, not Echo...but if he isn't with me, where is he? What if he's injured, somewhere in this fog? Or worse? The explosion must have thrown up a cloud of steam in the sub-basement.

Echo? Echooo... she called. There was no answer.

She drifted about, searching in the mist. She had to find him! They mustn't be separated, under any circumstances! He might need help. She would have to be careful; Slug might still be lurking somewhere about.

A brilliant white light, almost like a door, or perhaps a tunnel, suddenly shone out ahead of her. A figure stood in it, almost glowing, wrapped in the shining mist. Instinctively, she moved toward it.

Echo...? Is that you?

* * *

Hours later, Echo found himself back in the elevator. He had worn a path in the waiting room floor, watching grim-faced doctors and medtechs enter and exit the emergency lab. The prognosis didn't sound good. There was Omega's already severely weakened condition, twice over as she was still recovering from the Antarctic mission...followed by Slug's second mental onslaught in just over a week...then the tachyon smasher recoil—a double insult to her frail form, since her body, behind Echo's, had absorbed the full impact against the wall for both of them.

He closed his eyes for a long moment, leaning against the elevator wall as his entire frame sagged in guilt-ridden despair. By now, he readily understood how she thought, and he knew what she had done: She had intentionally cushioned him, knowing full well the force of the recoil on that setting—because hadn't he insisted they trained with it in simulations often enough?—knowing too, that she could do little more in her condition, but that an unharmed Echo could finish the job, if necessary.

But he—the experienced agent, Mr. Badass—had not realized what she was doing until it was far too late.

Idiot, he thought, and decided the word wasn't nearly strong enough. *Damn imbecilic fool doesn't even cut it. I'm not the badass, here. But she sure as hell was.*

Then there was also Slug's telepathic death scream, powerful enough to make even Echo black out, at least briefly.

"Well," he'd overheard the doctors telling Fox, "IF she lives, it isn't certain that she'll...be the same. Or even, for that matter, BE." And as their eyes met, he and Fox had both remembered the agents a few rooms over, on permanent life support, nervous systems shorted out.

Echo had to get away then. And he knew where he was going. He picked up the little pile of pillows and blankets in the nook at the top of the stairs and stepped out the door onto the roof, into the midsummer night. He spread a blanket on the roof, stretched out on it, and gazed up at the nigh-eternal stars. *Might as well be eternal, compared to us tiny, fragile humans,* he decided.

Mentally, he began identifying all of the objects Omega had taught him, the objects she loved so much, so...fondly. There was Scorpius, and the red star Antares; there, Sagittarius, toward the galactic center with the hidden maw of its supermassive black hole, not so very unlike the much smaller bottomless pit into which he and Meg had dropped Klu!vit kre Molcren. Lyra, with the bright star Vega. *When I consider the heavens...*

A meteor swept by overhead, flared brightly, and was gone. It made him think again of that last look in Fox's office. *Nice meteor...*

"I'll see to it you make it 'out there,' Meg, I swear," he vowed quietly into the darkness.

I'll keep that date with you, too, he thought. *In the desert with the Perseids.* Even if it was only with her memory.

He'd never lost a partner like this before. It was, after all, his fault for not preparing her better, and his fault for allowing her to be targeted by his old enemy. He owed her that much.

* * *

He had been there for some time, alone with his brooding, somber thoughts, when the stairwell door opened, and Fox's voice floated through the darkness.

"Echo? You out here?"

"Yeah, Fox," Echo responded wearily. "I'm here. How did you find me?"

"Good. Somebody wants to talk to you."

There was a crunching sound as feet stepped out onto the roof. Romeo's voice said softly, "Hi, Echo."

"Hiya, hot shot. Listen, sport, I appreciate your concern and coming to see about me and all, but I don't really feel like talking right now..."

"I'm sorry. After everything that went down, I just needed to see for myself that you were in one piece," said a frail voice coming from the thin form that Romeo laid, ever so gently, on the blanket beside Echo. A shocked Echo sat up quickly as Romeo and Fox withdrew, disappearing through the door in the roof.

"Meg?!"

"Hi, Echo. I thought you might be up here, when nobody could find you."

"What happened? The doctors said...I thought you were...gone," he finished in a low voice.

"Romeo says it was a winning combination of human ingenuity, alien technology, and a stubborn, ornery Agent who just wouldn't give up. I never thought you were ornery. Or maybe he meant me." She grinned weakly.

Echo just gazed at her, still stunned, and leaned closer.

"How are YOU?" she asked then.

"Me? Oh, fine. Little headache is all. Couple bruises, some barked knuckles. Nothing big."

"Good. Slug knocked you around a little bit."

"Takes more than that to stop me. You know you took out Slug?"

"Me?" Omega asked in surprise.

"Yeah."

"That's strange. Strikes me that it was YOUR finger that pulled the trigger, and your hands holding up the gun. I couldn't do it."

"Yeah. You aimed it, though. You done good."

"Thanks. So did you."

"I suppose."

"Then I guess it was a partnership, huh?"

"Yeah, I guess so. Pretty damn good one, if you ask me."

"Yup."

They were silent for a few moments, content to look at each other. Omega smiled slightly.

"How did you know?" Echo asked then, curious.

"Know what?"

"Two things, I guess: Where Slug was, and where to aim. Romeo remarked in the waiting room that you must have x-ray vision; you hit the heart exactly. According to the coroner's preliminary exam report, there wasn't enough left of the heart to fit in a damn pill box."

"Same answer for both: A telepathic link can be a two-way street, especially for somebody with enough wits about her to pay attention to little details, and desperate enough to make use of 'em." She shrugged. "How did YOU know?"

"Know what?" Echo replied.

"Which one was the real me."

"Smoke and mirrors."

"What?!"

"Snails don't have eyes. They don't 'see' like we do. Slug had no idea what you really looked like, so he pulled his image of you from your own mind, and it was a mirror image, because that's how we humans are used to seeing ourselves."

"Oh! Good catch."

Echo lay back and they gazed at the stars in companionable silence for a while. Then he felt a slight vibration next to him. It suddenly hit him that she was shivering.

"Hey! What—oh! You cold, baby?"

"Yeah, a little. This jumpsuit thing from the medlab works good for the purpose, even if I swear it IS made mostly of velcro so they can get to IVs an' stuff! But it's pretty lightweight, and the breeze is stiff up here tonight. An' I don't have quite my usual amount of natural insulation."

He sat back up, removed his jacket, and spread it over her, then tucked it in gently.

"There. How's that?"

She snuggled down underneath his jacket, still warm from his body heat, and sighed.

"Much better."

He leaned back and they watched the stars again in congenial quiet. Suddenly, he pointed a finger at the sky.

"There goes a nice one." He glanced at her to see if she'd seen it.

She was asleep.

Chapter 12

She awoke in her own bed. Omega indulged in a long, delicious stretch and groggily swung bare legs out of the bed, stood up, and raked her loose hair back from her face with her fingers. She adjusted the men's pajama shirt—which alone comprised the full extent of her current sleepwear—and yawned prodigiously. Sleepily, she padded on bare feet out into the living area.

"Well, well, if it isn't our very own Sleeping Beauty."

Echo's long, lean, muscular form, casually clad on his day off in black t-shirt and black jeans, was now stretched out comfortably on her leather couch, as he watched her. The television was on, with the volume turned down low, in obvious deference to her sleep. Her doctoral dissertation lay open on the coffee table next to a half-empty Diet Coke can. Confused, she raked a hand through tousled platinum hair.

* * *

"What are you doing here?" Omega asked him.

"Fox told me the medics wanted someone watching you, in case any delayed reactions occurred. I got the job." He didn't tell her he'd asked for it.

"And were there any?"

"Nope. You slept like a baby, baby." He grinned, then paused. "I did catch you sleepwalking to the bathroom several times, and I always made sure I was waiting for you with a glass of water when you came out. Didn't want you getting dehydrated. But you never woke up, even when you were drinking the water."

* * *

Omega paused a moment, thinking.

"The last thing I remember is the roof...How did I get here?" she mulled.

"How do you think?"

Her eyes widened as she took his meaning. She looked down at her pajama top in realization and felt her cheeks flame.

* * *

"...Oh. Sorry."

"Meh, it's okay. You were entitled. Besides, India was happy to help." He turned his head so she wouldn't see the slight smile.

* * *

Omega stared at him doubtfully, wondering just how much India had really 'helped.' Finally she decided not to pursue the subject, because she wasn't sure she wanted to know anyway. She trusted Echo and knew he would never have taken advantage of the situation, whether India had helped or not; she was merely embarrassed—intensely so—that he might have found it necessary to handle matters regardless. After a moment, she regained her wits enough to continue.

"How long have you been here? No—the real question is, 'How long have I been asleep?'"

"About a day and a half—Division time. Close to three days, regular Earth time. You were out of it, baby."

She absorbed that, and ran her hand through her hair again. It kept falling across her face.

"Besides, after all that shit you just went through?" Echo continued. "You not only needed it, you EARNED it." He shrugged.

"Well, I needed it, anyway," she murmured. "Not so sure about the earning part."

"Hey—in this job, trust me, we earn our keep. So...how are you feeling?" Echo continued.

"Fine, I think. Stiff, a little sore, slight headache," she amended. Her stomach growled. Loudly. "And hungry. Really, really hungry."

"That, we can fix," Echo said, getting up and going into the kitchen.

* * *

Once Omega had eaten a largish breakfast—Echo wouldn't let her stuff her face, lest she get sick—she showered and dressed. Then Echo took her back to Medical for a once-over.

After about half an hour of "being poked and prodded," as Omega was wont to put it, Zebra pronounced her in relatively decent shape, all things being considered.

"But I don't want you reporting for duty for AT LEAST three more Division days," a stern Zebra told her—and her partner. "You're lucky you're not dead. You have had one hell of a past two weeks, and what you need right now is REST. Follow hard on the heels of that with plenty of good, nutritious food—no junk shit—on a regular schedule whether you're hungry or not, LOTS of fluids, and MAYBE some light exercise by the third day. But only if you have the energy for it. If you're still tired, DON'T." Zebra glared at Omega. "I want you to sleep as much as you want—go to bed early, sleep late, take naps, whatever. Getting out for a little fresh air and sunshine won't hurt, either. I'm going to give you some medications and supplements to help you recover, and I want you to take them regularly, don't miss a meal, and eat a few snacks while you're at it."

"Yes, ma'am," Omega murmured, uncharacteristically meek. Zebra spun to Echo.

"And as for YOU," she told him, "as I told Fox this morning, your job until further notice is to look out for her, see that she follows my orders, and report to me right away if you spot anything out of the ordinary. Oh, and take her for the odd walk in Central Park or to a museum or something. I don't care what you do, just take her on some non-mission outings that she'll enjoy—preferably that BOTH of you will enjoy, because this hasn't done you any favors either, Echo, and don't think Fox and I aren't aware of that. But if anything happens, if she passes out or you can't wake her up, or ANYTHING like that, you bring her back here immediately. Straight to me."

"As fast as I can get her here," Echo agreed.

"Good. Bring her back here every day at this time, or as close to this time as her sleeping schedule allows—meaning don't wake her up just to bring her here, if she's happily zonked—so I can keep track of her healing. I won't certify her to return to duty until I'm satisfied she'll be okay. Got that?"

"Got it, Zebra. And for whatever it's worth," Echo added, "as the head of Alpha Line, I was gonna impose much the same restrictions on her, anyway. But I was gonna see if she wanted to help me design the setup for Romeo and India to test for Alpha Line, while she recovered, just to give her something to do. Would that be okay?"

"Mm. What does it involve?"

"Nothing physical. Some creative brainstorming about variations on training scenarios, maybe walking through the obstacle course while it's offline to figure out where to put stuff. And I wanted her input on how effective she thought her training was, so we can improve for the next Alpha teams."

Zebra pondered that for a few minutes.

"Okay, I'm all right with the first two...IN MODERATION. Which means, for now, you can do this for no more than a couple of hours each day. But I think...let's wait until she's a little stronger before you start doing what amounts to a debrief of the last several months, all right?"

"Yeah, good point. So it sounds like Alpha One is basically on indefinite sick leave."

"That's about the size of it," Zebra agreed.

"Aw, crud," Omega muttered. "Sorry, Echo."

"Hush that," he said mildly. "You did good, babe. You did everything we expected of you, and then some. AND you managed to survive it. Consider it a well-earned 'staycation.' When's the last time you had a vacay, anyway?"

"Um, dunno. Been a while."

"Good." Zebra smiled. "Echo, go show her around the Big Apple a little, why don't you? I bet she hasn't even had a chance to properly play tourist."

"I haven't," Omega admitted. "And I'd never been here before I got recruited, either."

"Then let's go," Echo said, grinning.

* * *

In the end, it was just over a full Division week before Echo and Zebra, with some assistance from India, got Omega's weight back to something

Zebra considered acceptable, and her sleep cycle beginning to stabilize to her previous shift norms.

During that period, Alpha One had a lot of time off. They wandered through Central Park, visited museums, took in a couple of Broadway shows, checked out the Statue of Liberty and Ellis Island, wandered the boardwalk at Coney Island—hot dogs in hand, though they didn't tell Zebra about THAT—and even went to a baseball game. In short, they did anything and everything that two best friends, exploring New York City together for the first time, might do. Omega's color returned to normal, and her strength—mental as well as physical—began to return.

After each outing, they ate, then returned to their quarters for her to take a nap. And at least once a day they brainstormed effective training methods for Alpha Line teams. Omega proved quite good at it, to Echo's delight.

"No, it isn't bothering me," she avowed to Zebra, when that physician expressed concern. "Actually, I think it's kinda fun to do. And it helps Echo; he's been a little busy looking through applications for the new department...from pretty much across the Agency, I gather. And since I come in relatively fresh to the whole concept, I sometimes manage to come up with stuff neither he nor Fox have thought about. Not often, but once in a while, I come up with something new."

"Yeah," Echo agreed. "She's damn good at it, if the truth be told. Once the whole Line is up and going, I'm seriously considering making her the head of Training for it."

Omega grinned, then shrugged.

"Be careful what you wish for, Ace," she warned. "I will not be easy on the trainees. And you're talkin' to the gal who ran through Antarctica on frostbit feet."

"I know." Echo returned the grin. "Alpha Line will be in damn fine shape. Or frozen, one."

"Oh, hell," grumbled Zebra. "I better go tell Zarnix now to get a special ER ready, just for Alpha Line."

"You do that, Zebra," Omega chuckled, then sobered. "Actually, if my last couple missions are anything to go by, that might not be a bad idea, anyway."

"What she said," Echo agreed, equally somber. "I'd been thinking about that myself. We ARE supposed to take the front line and all, Zebra."

"I was joking," Zebra protested. "But...you two do make a good point. I'll get with Zarnix and Fox. And you two, if we need any additional info."

"We'll be around," Echo pointed out.

"Every day, until you release me," Omega appended.

"And I know where to find you, after that," Zebra averred.

* * *

Fox stood on the balcony outside his office, and motioned all four Agents over as they walked into the Core, nearly a Division week and a half after Slug's demise; it had taken that long before Zebra would release Omega to return to full—but only light—duty.

"Good morning, everyone," the Director said as they entered his office. "Good to have you back, Omega."

"Thanks, Fox. Thanks, everybody. Good to BE back."

"What's up, Fox?" Echo asked.

"Nothing major. Vlaxon, the Zumbirian from Beta Ophiuchi 7, is up to his usual 'coming out of the closet' antics again."

They all groaned.

"Not again," Echo grumbled.

"Why does he keep tryin'?" Romeo wondered.

"Oh, he wants to make sure the whole damn planet knows there are aliens among us, whether the Council thinks Homo sapiens is ready or not," Fox pointed out with some disgust. Omega inhaled and opened her mouth, and the Director knew what she was about to ask, so he answered before she could speak. "Now, of you four, only Echo went through the entire Klydonian invasion—Romeo, we brought you in at the tail end, but you didn't see nearly the action, or coordination, that he did. So Echo, did YOU think humans were ready to find out?"

"Oh HELL no," Echo asserted, firm. "Most of the civvies wanted to run screaming as soon as they encountered ANY alien, and the military just wanted to blow 'em ALL up, friendly or not. I used more brain bleach in the wake of that invasion attempt than I used in all the years I worked in the

Agency before that, dammit."

"What he said," Fox noted. "Listen to Echo. The man has experience. I wanted you younger and/or less-experienced agents to have a real-world grasp of WHY we're secret. Make sense?"

"Yeah, Fox, I can see that now," Omega murmured. "Thanks for elaborating, y'all."

"Okay, Fox, down to details. Who's he talked to?" Echo inquired.

"Some reporter over at the World Orbit newspaper, for sure. One of the cable stations too, we think. But we've already covered the current editions of the paper and come up with nothing, and nobody really believes that cable show anyway. So either the reporter's blown him off for a nutcase, or she's trying to put together a feature, maybe a series. The first option would be fine; the second, a disaster in the making. Echo, Omega: You take the reporter. Find out what she's got, and get it, then rearrange her memories."

"Consider it done."

"Romeo, India: You hit up our favorite UFOnut to see what else Vlaxon put out."

"Jerry the Packrat? We're all over it, Boss."

"Go, then."

* * *

Once the girl's chest cavity was closed—again, with no residual scarring, and no trace it even happened that Earth-based technologies would ever find—another round of painful injections took place, all over her body.

There. Circulatory system...done, *came the chilling, disembodied voice again.*

The girl's head swam as her blood pressure abruptly dropped, then stabilized. The robotic arms exchanged the empty syringes for another set, and repeated the process; suddenly she was intensely hot. Her naked form broke a profuse sweat for several minutes, then finally cooled.

Metabolic enhancements...done.

It took several seconds for the effects of the third round of injections to hit. But when it did, she tried to writhe as searing pain filled her body. It seemed to her as if it would never end, and her head pounded. Dimly she 'heard' the disembodied voice again.

Nervous system enhancements...very good. Oh, very, VERY good. I could not have wanted better. Yes, girl, you were a fine candidate. You will make an excellent tool.

Are you... *She broke off, finally able to pant again, as the agony subsided to a dull ache, then faded entirely.* Are you done yet?

Not...quite, *came the answer.*

And the scalpel-wielding artificial hand moved toward her head.

Oh, dear God, help me! *the girl thought fervently.* Make it stop!

I doubt it, *the alien answered, callous.*

* * *

Jerry the Packrat was a wizened little human male, flaky as a bowlful of granola in Romeo's opinion, but useful because he so diligently read and archived so many magazines, newspapers, and even websites. Romeo and India preferred to tag-team him whenever they went to see him, and had developed a useful strategy, India 'distracting' him in the next room—making sure he kept his hands...and other appendages...to himself, though she still found the drool disturbing—while Romeo leafed through his archives. So it went today.

But this time, Romeo came up empty. No recent listings had Vlaxon in the equation. As Romeo replaced the bulky, awkward scrapbook on the shelf, another tumbled off and fell open on the table with a loud thud. Muttering expletives to himself, he picked it up and was about to slam it shut when the yellowed article caught his eye. He scanned it rapidly, muttered another expletive, and tore it out, shoving it in his pocket as he ran for the door, yelling.

"INDIA! Come on, honey! We gotta roll! NOW!"

* * *

The passively-cloaked Lexus tore through the city high above the streets, narrowly missing billboard signs, water tanks, and communications antennas, as Romeo took the shortest possible distance to his destination.

"Do you think we'll be in time?" India asked, worried.

"We'd better be," was Romeo's only answer.

* * *

Echo and Omega had finished interrogating the reporter. As 'FBI agents,' they had managed to gain access to all of her evidence by offering to copy it, then verify it for her at the FBI lab. Now, Echo shot Omega a single quick glance, and simultaneously they slipped on their special glasses, as Echo pulled out his brain bleacher, on the pretext of "taking notes on the smart phone app." Omega smiled to herself; after about the twentieth time, she was finally starting to get the hang of this 'rearranging memories' stuff.

At least, she thought, *with the special sunglasses on, I don't get those damned spots in front of my eyes for ten minutes.*

* * *

But the smile on her face faded as the brain bleacher's polychrome flash went off and Echo began re-creating the woman's memories.

"Now, Ms. Kent, the man who kept the appointment with you the other day was obviously mentally unstable; in fact, you can tell your editor, Mr. White, that you discovered he had managed to slip out of his nursing home..."

Behind him, an expressionless Omega calmly removed her sunglasses and tucked them in her breast pocket, then reached underneath her jacket and silently drew her proto-cyclotron blaster. She calmly leveled it at Echo's head.

* * *

Romeo burst into the room then, India close behind. Taking in the scene at a glance, he acted immediately.

"Echo! DUCK!" he yelled. "NOW!!"

* * *

Without question, Echo lunged forward, carrying the reporter down with him, just as the discharge from the blaster shot over his head, leaving a scorched hole in the far wall; the building opposite could be seen through it. Rolling, he looked up to see Omega bringing the blaster around again.

"MEG?!"

India made a running leap and tackled Omega, taking her down hard. Romeo ran to Echo.

"Your shades are on. You use the brain bleach?" an urgent Romeo asked.

"What?" Echo tore startled eyes away from where his partner struggled with India, to look at Romeo.

"The brain bleacher! Did you use it just now?"

"Yeah, on the reporter," Echo responded, bemused. "Of course. Why?"

"Oh, boy...think fast, Romeo, my man..."

Just then, India went flying across the room as, with almost inhuman strength, a blank-eyed Omega threw her off, grasped the fallen blaster, and began rising to her feet.

She moves stiffly, a distracted Echo thought, a sense of outré horror creeping through him as he watched. *Strange. Meg is usually so graceful.* He didn't understand that. At the moment, he didn't understand any of it. Why was his partner suddenly trying to kill him??

* * *

Within moments, the girl knew the exquisite agony of being scalped, as the laser scalpel sliced open that cranial sheath, and mechanical fingers stripped it back, away from the skull. Blood gushed briefly down the back of her violated head, before being mysteriously staunched.

Another, automatic and instinctive shriek tried to escape, but could not, and suddenly she found that she was no longer allowed to even think.

The girl lay unmoving on the table, staring blankly at the metallic ceiling, as the top of her skull was sliced open and removed, then easily half a dozen probes entered her brain, doing she knew not what. Phantom sensations riddled her body: flashes of light, auditory hallucinations, tickling, stabbing, nauseating tastes and scents. Abruptly her nipples erected, and her loins clenched; her barely-pubescent body was immediately gripped in powerful orgasmic contractions. The brief moment of unexpected pleasure was followed and immediately overlaid by searing pain. Sudden bright, blinding lights flashed directly in her face, like lightning. She tried to tense for the concussion of the thunder, but there was none. And she could not, in any case.

Simultaneously she grew dizzy, and bile rose in her throat, but she was helpless to swallow...or anything else. It seemed to go on forever, and blind, unthinking fear rose as it felt as if she might drown in her own vomit.

Suddenly the bile receded and all sensation ceased.

Am I dead? *she wondered, despairing.* Please, let me be dead...

Hardly, child, *the cold voice returned.* My equipment is now closing your cranium, and there is but one more thing to be done.

Then are you going to kill me? *she wondered.*

Oh no, *came the answer.* You will live for many more years, become an adult, find the man upon whom I shall have my vengeance, work with him. And THEN I shall kill you.

* * *

In desperation, Romeo whipped out his special glasses and his brain bleach, setting it for only a few seconds.

"If it turned her on, maybe...India! Shades!"

Running across the room, Romeo stuck the brain bleacher directly in Omega's face, just as she raised the blaster at Echo, who was now prudently diving for cover. A prismatic flash lit the room.

Omega froze.

Romeo took the blaster out of Omega's locked arms and handed it to Echo, who stared at it with intense distaste. Behind them, India scrambled to her feet.

"I don't get it. I thought the brain bleach didn't work on her," India wondered.

"It doesn't," observed Echo. "Look at her stance, her expression. She's not brain bleached, she's paralyzed." He turned to Romeo. "What's going on?"

Romeo pulled out the article he'd 'borrowed' from the UFOnut, and handed it to Echo.

"Says here that around eighteen or twenty years back, a girl in her early teens went missing for about twenty-four hours while stargazing from a farm near Huntsville, Alabama. Neighbors reported UFO sightings in the area the night she disappeared. Afterward, all she could talk about for a couple months was the 'silent lightning'—and snails. Look at the picture, Echo."

* * *

Echo studied the faded color image. It was a girl, maybe as much

317

as twelve or thirteen, awkward, no longer child, not yet woman, with a long, silvery-blonde French braid and wide blue eyes that sparkled with intelligence and wit. The light bulb went off for the senior agent.

Damn. 'Nothing is as it appears...'

"Meg," he breathed, the light dawning. "She's a sleeper agent."

India was already on the horn to Fox, detailing the situation and requesting containment. Echo moved over beside her.

"Let me talk to him a minute."

India handed the cell phone to Echo.

"Fox? Echo. Has Zz'r'p returned yet?"

"You're in luck, Echo. He arrives on the next transport, and hands off with his substitute—the one that arrived too late to do anything—at the gate."

"Good. Tell him to stand by and prepare for an in-depth mind probe. And, if my hunch is right, probably some serious deprogramming."

"Will do."

* * *

While Zz'r'p explored the mind of a still-paralyzed Omega next door, Echo sat down at a currently-unused medlab laptop and began accessing the records of Megan McAllister that he'd routinely downloaded into PGLEIA archives before deleting the originals. He was curious. After only half an hour of work, he turned to his supervisor.

"Fox, come have a look at this."

"What have you got?" The head of Earth's PGLEIA division came and looked over Echo's shoulder.

"I took a shot at cross-correlating people in Meg's past with our rosters of aliens, legal and illegal. Look. None before the age of, oh, roughly twelve, but four teachers in junior high were aliens, and three in high school. Then add these to the list: her undergraduate advisor, her graduate supervisor, one member of her dissertation committee, and even a couple of NASA managers—including the superior of the one who hired her."

"Hm. And all of them from races having some connection or affiliation with the Delta Scorpii system. Some coincidence. Not."

"I thought of something else, too," Echo continued thoughtfully.

318

"What?"

"She was in Houston for a few years at JSC before we encountered her..."

"So?"

"Cartman's race, the Teludal, has an alliance with the Snails—and Kenny was his brother. I wonder if Megan McAllister was observing somewhere in the desert the night X-ray died."

"Are you saying—"

"That, if my suspicion is correct, it looks to me like Slug planned and worked for a long time to get Meg's path and mine to cross. And wasn't hesitant to do whatever it took to do it, including sacrificing allies...or risking entire planets. Hmm..."

"What?"

"Fox, what if even the accident that killed her family was no accident?"

"Well, damn. I think we need to do some additional investigations, Echo."

"I agree, Boss."

"You stay here and keep me posted on progress...assuming there's anything to be reported. I'll see to this investigation." And Fox headed out to check everything related to Agent Omega and Dr. Megan McAllister that he could find.

* * *

Young Megan McAllister hovered in midair, upright, unmoving, unblinking, seemingly frozen. Her blank gaze stared across the cabin of the alien spacecraft at the seven-foot-long, giant slug-like being as its antennae waved gently in her direction. She had been there for over twenty-four hours, and it was nearing the second dawn since she had been abducted. But Slug was not finished with her—not quite yet.

He addressed the girl directly, in her trancelike, altered state.

This is Level One of your programming, *the giant slug said.* You will continue upon your plan to become an astronaut, obtain your desired degrees, and more. You will accomplish whatever you set out to do. Once you are accepted into the astronaut selection process, you will move to Texas, and obtain permission to set up your telescope and observe on an abandoned ranch outside Ozona, in west Texas. You will do this each free weekend, until you encounter a Division One agent code-named Echo. When he uses the Cerebellar Holographic Mnemonic Re-Encoding Induction System on you, it will initiate Level Two...

* * *

The Director of Division One came back some time later, grim of face. Echo took one look at him, and something inside his gut clenched tight.

"So you found more." It wasn't a question.

"Yes, Echo, I did. Unfortunately."

"Damn. How deep does the wormhole go?"

"Pretty damn deep, I'm afraid."

Fox pulled a couple of folded printouts from an inside jacket pocket and tossed them to Echo. The Agent skimmed down through them, then did a double-take and read through them again, slower. He felt the blood drain from his face, his eyes blurred, and his head swam for a moment. When his vision cleared, Fox was crouched next to him, his expression alarmed.

"Are you all right, old friend?" Fox whispered, holding Echo's shoulder. "For a second there, I thought you were going to pass out, just now."

"For a second, I thought I was, too. This...is bad."

"Yes, it is. I wish the damn DNA analysis ran faster. We might have seen this coming, might have been able to do something about it."

"If she's unaware of all this—and I can't believe she knew about it, not consciously—she's NOT going to be happy. And I don't blame her, 'cause I sure as hell wouldn't be, in her shoes. I know her closely enough by now, Fox, to be able to tell you that she's not gonna take this well. Not at all. Not to mention, the backup terrorists on the maglev."

"Just the one backup being, it looks like, though the lead assassin— the being that the two of you managed to toss down the bottomless pit— was, too, according to the Coalition police currently breaking up the cult. We finally got the offworld coroner to have a look at the bodies you brought back. That's what took me so long to get back to you. Once he found the implant on the one, it gave the Coalition the idea to try to find out whodunit, and who else they'd done it to. And then that uncovered several more on the

320

homeworld, and the whole mess just kept snowballing."

"So two of the three terrorists here on Earth had long-range telepathic implants, tuned to Snail brainwaves? Fox, are we SURE?"

"As we can be, Echo. Two of the Ke!endarian assassins sent to Earth were working directly with Slug."

"But WHY?"

Fox shook his head.

"We'll never know, at this point, since all of the perps are dead," he said. "But if I had to speculate, I'm thinking that this was another of Slug's levels of planning. And THEY probably thought Slug had joined their cause, without realizing that Slug was using 'em for HIS cause the whole time. He probably never expected the Ke!endarians to actually take you and Omega out..."

"But he wouldn't have cried a river if they had," Echo amended.

"Probably not. It would have suited his vengeance nicely, I expect. But I went back and studied the external security video from the maglev train, and it gets interesting. And not in the good way."

"How so?"

"Well, because the terrorist that Omega took out? One Throtlama kre Meorn, if memory serves? I think I met it several years ago, at an offworld PGLEIA function..."

"Yeah?"

"The video shows that, just before Omega shot it, it froze...just like our old videos of Slug's first attack, where he locked up the agents' nervous systems. Omega could have beaten that Ke!endarian to death with her bare fists, and it wouldn't—COULDN'T—have flicked a feather."

"WHAT?!"

"If my hunch is right, Slug probably was intending to raise Omega's worth in your—and my—eyes, in order to make the psychological torture of his end game that much more acute."

* * *

Echo's shoulders slumped, in the closest representation of utter despair Fox had seen in him since he was first recruited.

"So she was only set up to look like a good agent..." he murmured,

321

staring at the floor. "She's going to be miserable when she finds out all of it. I wonder how much of the rest of it he faked for her."

"No, Echo, she really was a good agent," Fox corrected, wanting to offer some solace to one of his oldest human friends, and glad to have something legitimate to offer. "She took out that Ke!endarian, no question."

"With Slug holding it still for her."

"Well, he did—but it wouldn't have made any difference."

"What do you mean?"

"I mean that Omega was already in action. She analyzed, lined up and shot BEFORE Slug could lock up the Ke!endarian's nervous system. If Throtlama was lucky, all Slug accomplished was to anesthetize its death."

"Damn. You're serious? Meg was faster than a telepath?"

"This time, she sure was." Fox nodded in firm affirmation. "Part of it probably had to do with the long-distance relay, so I can't say she could do it every time, but this time, without doubt, she anticipated the Ke!endarian's actions and popped him before Slug could even get a good read on what was happening. I slowed down the video and went through it frame by frame. Omega targeted and shot split-seconds BEFORE kre Meorn was immobilized. There's no doubt in my mind—and I had Forensics verify my mind. And they concurred."

An unusually-agitated Echo ran a hand through his dark hair, standing it on end.

"Well, good for her, but...damn. So Slug was willing to take out anything and anybody to get his revenge."

"He surely was. Including any and all allies. When that realization hit me, and given her behavior and who she was working with, I immediately sent a team to locate the former agent Tango, who we'd brain-bleached and sent off to a rather miserable little 'retirement'..."

"Aw crap. He didn't."

"He did. She's dead. Murder victim in a bizarre murder-suicide."

"Let me guess: where the suicide showed no prior symptoms of mental disorder or derangement."

"You got it. More, I pulled out Tango's file and studied it a little closer. None of her earliest psych evals indicated any tendency toward narcissism or deceit. When she came aboard about eight years ago, she was a smart, straightforward if introverted, somewhat mousy little accountant with no sign of either deception or narcissistic tendencies, let alone the kind of kinky sexual escapades her quarters revealed—which reminds me. If you haven't seen the pictures yet, you shouldn't."

"...Too late." Echo scrunched his face in patent distaste. He also unconsciously crossed his legs, and Fox wasn't sure whether to be amused or worried for his old friend.

"Mm. I was afraid of that. Well, just keep this in mind, then: the eval conducted as evidence for her tribunal indicated both strong deceit AND narcissism, which means both traits had a VERY sudden onset."

"Which isn't normal. Somehow, Slug got to her, too."

"That's the way I read it. I figure part of what Slug was doing while the four of you were hunting for him was taking out 'loose ends.' And the time frame for the 'murder-suicide' fits that hypothesis, too."

"When did her personality change?"

"Oh, a couple years ago, judging by the responses to inquiries I put out. Remember that big reception that got held here for the signing of the Sydys Concordat?"

"Yeah?"

"She was here for that, and things got hinky with her right afterward, according to the reports I'm getting out of McMurdo."

"Shit! You mean Slug has been living under the same roof with us for TWO YEARS?!"

"No, I don't think so, Echo. Otherwise, I expect he'd have bumped you off back then, instead of going through all these machinations just to get to you. After all, given the psychic attack on Omega that first night..."

"True. It would've been easy enough, if he was here long-term."

"And consider that, while it wasn't Omega, you DID have a new partner in training at that time, in that Romeo had just come aboard. If he had been under our roof the whole time, he could have executed essentially the same plan, only substituting Romeo for Omega. And you'd both be dead, along with who knows how many other agents."

"You might not wanna tell Romeo that theory."

"Yeah, I thought about that, and I won't. There's no point in him hashing over might-have-beens. We get enough of those moments in this job, in any case. Anyway, I don't think Slug was any more comfortable with the idea of staying within Division One Headquarters than you are about the notion he might have. Over that long a time? Remember, we were making some upgrades and renovations to the building and the internal warp along about then, too, so there was an awful lot of coming and going in the sub-basements. No. The risk of discovery would have been just too great. He might have been insane, but Slug wasn't stupid. So I'm quite certain he didn't stay any longer than he had to. Besides, he'd have had to come and go a good bit anyway, just in order to tie up matters with the Ke!endarian cult. From what I can tell, that's probably about when he figured out how to get into the sub-basements, though."

"Ugh."

"Yeah. I'm working on closing that particular little loophole in our security, don't worry. It should be taken care of by the end of the day today. But there's more. I fired the idea past my political advisors, and...well, remember how nobody could ever figure out how such an extreme cult as the Naese!en!Re could have formed in Ke!enda!ar culture to begin with?"

"Aw, damn, Fox. You're not saying..."

"I surely am, alter khaver. The notion of a highly-skilled telepath, especially one with a malevolent intent and outlook, influencing those members of the population who were already outliers in matters of religion and politics...well, it all really made a hell of a lotta sense to MY advisors. Especially with as many years as Slug had to lay the groundwork." Fox paused, and met Echo's eyes. "We now strongly believe that 'the renegade Snail called Slug may well be responsible for inciting the current unrest in the Ke!endarian Coalition by means of the cultic politico-religious group known as the H!nar kre Naese!en!Re, via mental manipulation of the group's leaders, at the very least,' as my report to PGLEIA Galactic Central put it." Fox ran a hand through his salt-and-pepper hair. "I...did recommend that, if possible, they be treated as mentally ill, and skilled telepaths be brought in, in an effort to deprogram them. Much like Zz'r'p is currently attempting with Omega, I guess."

"Damn. We've skirted disaster by the skin of our collective teeth, several times over. If we'd lost any of the ambassadors or their staff..."

"Right—Earth wouldn't be here right now, and astrocartographers would be mapping out a new asteroid belt."

* * *

The police found young Megan McAllister near the edge of her parents' farm, wandering dazed and confused, her clothing disarranged. They promptly took her to the emergency room in Huntsville Hospital, insisting she be examined and checked for sexual assault and rape. Her parents, Jonathan and Robin McAllister, were notified and arrived at the hospital as soon as they could. Moments after their arrival, the ER physician, Murphy by name, came out to talk to them and the waiting police officers.

"No, there's no sign of rape, or any other kind of attack," Dr. Murphy told them reassuringly. "She appears to be just fine. We're not sure WHAT happened, and neither is she."

"She was missing for over TWENTY-FOUR HOURS!" an upset Robin McAllister exclaimed. "How can you say you don't know what happened?! Let me talk to that girl! She had some sort of meeting arranged with a boy! I just know it!"

"Honey!" Jonathan McAllister said, shocked. "Calm down! You know better than that. When has Meg ever lied to us? She hasn't even started noticing boys yet! She's still all about exploring space and becoming an astronaut!"

"...And horses," Robin added softly, slumping as she calmed. "You're right, of course, Jon. I'm sorry."

"I know. It's okay. We'll just have to be patient with her, and maybe eventually she'll tell us. Something obviously has her too upset to talk about it."

"Well, somehow I doubt it, Mr. McAllister. We've even had a psychologist come in and work with her," Dr. Murphy pointed out. "Not even regression hypnosis gave us anything. We may never know WHAT happened to her while she was missing. It's possible she experienced some sort of dissociative fugue state, but the shrink says there's not even any psychological evidence of THAT, except for the fact that she doesn't

remember what happened, or where she was. My guess is, she got lost and disoriented in the woods, maybe fell asleep and lost track of time, then finally made her way out to where she was found. She had very low blood sugar when she was found, according to the lab workup, and that could lead to confusion, especially at her age. The important thing is that she's okay, she's not been molested, and she's safe now."

"I...I guess so," Robin murmured. She sniffled once, then turned into her husband's shoulder and wept.

"Honey, you gonna be okay?" Jonathan wondered, concerned.

"Yeah. Gimme a minute."

"I'll go have the nurse put your daughter to rights, then I'll send her home with you," Dr. Murphy said, soothing.

"Doc, you get that rape kit for analysis?" one of the policemen asked.

"I did, and it's already off to the lab, but it isn't gonna give you anything, because she wasn't raped," Murphy replied, brusque and almost cold, giving the police officer a hard stare over the bluntness of his request, then glancing in concern at the distressed parents. "Insofar as I can tell, not a hair of her head has been touched, by anything or anybody. She's just fine."

* * *

Zz'r'p emerged from the medlab examination room then.

"I fear it is as we suspected, Director. Agent Omega was indeed abducted as a child by Slug. And while captive, she was subjected to certain wide-ranging...modifications."

The agents gathered around with a sense of simultaneous curiosity and dread.

"What sort of modifications?" India voiced what they all wanted to know, but were afraid to ask.

"Aside from the extensive mental programming which made her a sleeper agent, she was...permanently...physically AND mentally..." Zz'r'p searched for words, shrugged, and settled for, "...enhanced. Particularly mentally. It was these enhancements which were responsible for things such as her extreme giftedness in hyperdimensional physics, her unique capacity to learn mind-blocking techniques—though I think that was an unintended side effect—and her immunity to the brain bleach."

They looked at each other, dismayed.

"So, Slug gave her her smarts?" Romeo asked. Echo winced.

"No, not at all," Zz'r'p corrected the agent. "She was already well above average in intellect for her species, and possessed of an extremely high intelligence quotient. That seems rather to have been one of his selection criteria, as was her giftedness in hyperdimensional physics, which she also already had. He simply took those innate abilities and increased them. His intent was apparently to engineer the perfect Division One agent candidate using whatever methods were available—ethics be damned, as you humans would put it—install a 'time bomb' in case it was needed, then bring her across Agent Echo's path. She was his bait...and his failsafe. And you were right, Agent Romeo, the brain bleacher's flash was the trigger for her own attack, but not until the twenty-first flash; Slug seems not to have bothered with programming for the twenty-second. He apparently assumed Echo would be dead by then, and it would not matter what happened to Omega."

"Because his revenge against Echo would be complete," India murmured, thoughtful. "Echo's own partner and protégé would have killed him. Face to face."

"Precisely." The telepath sighed.

"Well," Fox glanced at Echo. "Much though I hate it to hell, all the evidence points that way. Your hunch was right, Echo."

"I have VERY carefully searched her mind," Zz'r'p continued, "and 'deleted' all of Slug's programming. She is conscious, and now remembers all of these events, including the memories of the abduction, which Slug deliberately suppressed...but which she and I both suspect may have partially manifested as part of her 'dream' scenario during Slug's recent attack." The alien paused, and a look of pain crossed his face. "Most notably, she believes the 'telepathic evisceration' of which she told you, Agent Echo, was in fact a flashback to Slug's original and VERY extensive surgeries upon her body—performed, I might add, while she was awake and unsedated, with no anesthesia whatsoever."

All the agents winced, even Fox.

"Do you think it was wise to return ALL her memories, Zz'r'p? Couldn't the abduction memories cause her psychological problems, in either the short-term or the long run?" India asked, worried. "They sound pretty hideous."

"I understand your concern, Agent India, and it is a consideration, certainly; but I did not feel that the way to heal such manipulation was by more manipulation."

"Of course. I'm sorry."

"I would, however, recommend some counseling...if you can convince her to accept it. She is not in an especially...amiable...frame of mind, at the moment."

"Which is completely understandable, in the circumstances," India added.

"No shit," Echo murmured, glancing at Fox.

"Indeed," Zz'r'p agreed. The alien gave a wry half-grin, if fishlike faces could be said to grin. "I am, frankly, surprised we have heard no loud crashes coming from the examination room as yet."

A weary Fox sighed.

"Right. Do I need a shield?"

"Not unless Engineering has fixed it," Echo declared. "Take a trash can lid. It'll serve you better. I'm serious."

"Uh, yeah, no thanks; I'll pass. I'm going to go in and tell her the rest. Back in a while."

* * *

"You're joking," Omega said, voice flat.

"No, I'm not," Fox told her, earnest. She shook her head, disbelieving.

"I don't see how I can. I don't see how HE can. It's not..." she broke off. Fox shrugged, and they were silent for a moment. "What about you?" she finally asked.

"I agree with his assessment."

Omega raised a skeptical silver eyebrow. It was query enough for Fox to respond.

"Look, Omega, I know you—"

"Obviously not as well as you thought you did," she pointed out.

"...True. But I've known him a lot longer. And he knows you even better."

"Still not well enough."

"He TRUSTS you, Omega."

"And I appreciate that. More than either of you will ever know. But..." She paused again. "No. Just...no."

"You don't trust his judgement."

"No, it isn't that."

"You don't trust HIM."

"No, I trusted him from the first. I'll admit, in the beginning that damn obstacle course gave me a few doubts and second thoughts for a bit, but no. That's not it, either."

"What is it, then?"

"Fox, I don't trust...myself. Not...not any more. I'm...I'm worse than Frankenstein's Monster ever was."

"But Zz'r'p..."

"'But Zz'r'p' what?"

"He removed all your programming, Omega. It's gone. As for the rest of it, none of us care; it isn't something that troubles us. You are NOT a monster. You are not an alien. You are unique, yes, but that isn't necessarily a bad thing, especially here. What—who—are you? You are Omega, you are an Agent of Division One, Alpha Line, and most importantly, you are our friend. It's okay. You'll be fine now."

"Are you sure? Are you absolutely sure?" she demanded. "That there will be no repercussions?"

Fox had no answer for that.

* * *

Echo found her where he had suspected he would: her favorite refuge, the dark roof. As he stepped out, he saw the pillows and blankets flung heedlessly to one side, as if in frustration or anger. As his eyes adjusted, he saw her dark form standing at the far end of the roof, instead of lying on it nearer the door. Her back was toward him, her head thrown back, arms out stiffly at her sides, hands balled into fists, glaring at the sky.

"Omega?" he queried softly as he approached.

"Don't call me that," she answered in a low voice.

"Why not?"

"It's not who I am."

"What about Dr. Mc—"

"No. She's 'unacceptable', too."

"Then who are you?"

"That's...what I'd like to know." Suddenly, spasmodically, she flung her arms upward and shouted to the heavens in a kind of righteous indignation and suffering, "WHO AM I?? My whole LIFE has been a lie! I've been programmed, manipulated, used, and tinkered with! Have I ever made one single decision on my own, one career decision, one choice of hobby? Or was all of that made for me, too?! Or should I say DONE TO me?? How far back does it go?! Was Slug influencing me as a child, even before the kidnapping? Dear God! Everything and everyone I ever cared about has been taken away now! After all Slug did to me, am I even human any more? Or, God help me, am I just a puppet, Slug's little automaton—a machine? Or worse, a murdering alien monster, created by another world's version of Frankenstein?"

Her agony was palpable; instinctively, Echo reached out to put a compassionate arm around her, but she stiffened and pushed away from his touch, backing across the roof.

"Don't," she warned him. "Don't touch me. Don't get close to me. It's not good for people to get close to me. They seem to wind up dead. I'm surprised, after everything that's happened, you're even willing to be on the same planet with me."

"Aw, c'mon, Meg. It's not like you knew what you were doing."

"NO! You're as wrong as you can possibly be, Echo. I knew exactly what I was doing—I just couldn't stop! Don't you understand? I tried to shoot you! I don't know if I can EVER forget the image of your head, lined up in my sights, while my finger tightened on the trigger despite my best efforts to stop it! I KNEW I was about to blow your head off, and there was nothing I could do about it! NOTHING!" Her increasingly-wobbly voice finally broke. She put her hands to her face. After a moment, her muffled voice emerged. "I was never so glad in my life to see Romeo burst in! When he hit me with the brain bleacher and my body froze, I...I was hoping...the paralysis would be permanent."

Oh, Lord, he thought fervently, in carefully-concealed horror. *She was aware of everything, the whole time. Trapped inside a body that was obeying orders that weren't hers. That explains why she moved so stiffly—she was fighting Slug's programming every inch of the way...and losing. Dammit! And that last bit...shit, she didn't mean that...did she?* He looked her up and down, studying her expression and body language. *Damn. She did. She was that desperate to ensure it all stopped before her programming managed to kill me.*

He stepped toward her again, hand outstretched. She moved away, deliberately turning her back on him, bowing her head and wrapping her arms around herself. It was the same motion, Echo noted, with which she'd reacted to the telepathic evisceration. *And in some ways, it is...and maybe worse,* he considered.

"Echo, please. Just go away. Stay away from me. I couldn't live with it if I killed you. And I have no idea what might trigger the programming again."

"Meg, you don't have to worry. Zz'r'p removed the programming, remember?"

"Did he, Echo? For sure? Are you one hundred percent certain he removed all of the programming? Can Zz'r'p provide a guarantee?"

Echo hesitated, unable to truthfully answer yes, then said matter-of-factly, "I'm willing to take the risk."

"I don't think I am."

* * *

Omega, clad in black jeans and T-shirt, long platinum-blonde hair flowing loose, walked through the Core toward Fox's office. Her Suit was slung over one shoulder. As she progressed, a wave of silence fell over the Core, as all eyes turned toward her, and the lighting dimmed in response... except for the concurrent halo of dark blue light that followed her, and her alone.

She heard the progressive silence, saw the shift in lighting, felt the stares, and it took all the willpower she could muster not to visibly cringe.

She could easily imagine the whispers that would follow in her wake.

"Look, there goes the traitor, the one who tried to kill Echo—her own partner. Her teacher. The legend. One of the last of The Originals."

She flushed a deep brick-red with shame.

And kept walking.

* * *

Behind her, out of hearing of even her sharp ears, one agent murmured to his partner.

"Damn. She's really quitting."

"Yeah. They say it's tearing her apart," his partner responded, sotto voce. "Every bit as bad as the telepathic attacks were doing. Maybe worse."

"They say...they say he didn't believe it, even when she was pointing her blaster at him."

"He didn't. He knew immediately that something was wrong. Her whole posture, movement, even her body language was...like it had been replaced by someone else. And I guess it had, when you think about it."

"I guess so. But how'd you know all that? You talk to him?"

"Yeah, I did. Wasn't sure but what I'd get told to go to hell, but he was actually willing to talk. Ya know, normally he wouldn't say shit about it—you know how he is—but this time, he seemed...I dunno, it seemed important to him, that, that the rest of us should know the truth."

"She sure isn't talking..."

"No. And I don't blame her. Did you see her flush, after the whole place got quiet? She knows everyone's talking about it, about her. And she probably figures we're blaming her for it."

"Ow. Embarrassment, humiliation, and shame, all in one lump package. Economy-sized, at that."

"Yeah. But hell, it's not like it was her fault. Not even Echo thinks that. He was really clear on that point. 'It wasn't her doing it, so it sure as hell wasn't her fault,' he said. 'She's my partner, the Arcturan ambassador fixed matters, and I still trust her.' That's what he said. And you could tell—he meant every word. He TRUSTS her. As much as he ever did, maybe more."

"Damn. But, you know...I don't think it matters what he thinks, at this point. Or what ANYbody thinks, for that matter. Because SHE thinks that."

"Yeah. And now she's acting on it."

"Well, you wouldn't expect her to do any differently."

"Nope."

"Damn."

"Yeah." The agent drew in a deep, thoughtful breath. "It's a pity. Once she got up to speed? I've never seen any agent better suited to partner with Echo than she was. Not even he and X-ray were as...well-tuned, I guess you could say."

"Yup. Then again, she WAS programmed to be the best partner for him possible."

"You can't program personality. OR determination. Or caring."

"True..."

The two agents sighed sadly.

* * *

They were all waiting for her in Fox's office—Fox, Romeo, India... and especially Echo. Wordlessly, she walked up to Fox's desk and carefully, regretfully, almost reverently, laid the Suit across it.

"I have to go, Fox."

"Why?"

"I'm here under false pretenses, for one thing. I don't belong here—I was put here. I'm," she broke off to swallow hard, "I'm an enemy infiltrator."

"Do you regret killing Slug, then?" Fox asked bluntly. "Now that you have free will, would you side with him?"

"NO! I'll never be so glad of anything that demonic monstrosity is dead!"

"Then, while you may have been embedded BY an enemy, you are not yourself an enemy infiltrator," Fox pointed out. Omega sighed.

"C'mon, Fox. You know what I'm trying to say. If it hadn't been for Slug, I wouldn't be here at all. I never should have been a Division One Agent, let alone a member of Alpha Line. And a prototype member, yet! And probably not even an astronaut, to boot. No, I don't belong here. I need to leave."

* * *

"The brain bleach still doesn't affect her, Fox," Echo interjected

333

quietly, hoping to influence the direction this was taking.

Omega blinked in shock at the remark. She stared at Fox, then at Echo, with an expression of hurt so deep that Echo winced despite himself.

All that Slug did to her, yet I have never seen pain like that in her eyes before now. And I caused it. Dammit. I only wanted...

"You have my word," she declared then, interrupting his thoughts, "for whatever it's worth after all this, that I will never betray Division One, or the Pan-Galactic Law Enforcement and Immigration Administration."

"We know, Omega." Fox waved a dismissive hand. "Echo was just..." The Director shrugged. "We want to stop this, to get you to see what we see. He was just trying to delay your leaving, to give us the time we need to convince you."

"Okay. I get it. And I appreciate it, but—look, y'all—I NEED to go away," Omega tried to explain, seeming almost desperate for them to see her point of view. "To find out who I am, what I am. I seem to have lost myself. Or maybe I never had me to begin with—not the REAL me, assuming there IS a real me, I guess. I just don't trust myself anymore! Please understand! I can't...I don't...until I can learn to trust myself again, to learn who and what I really am...I won't be good for anything. And this job is...EVERYthing."

She met their eyes in turn, her own expression earnest. She met Echo's eyes last, and held them for a long moment before speaking again.

"It's...really bad, guys. I'm second-guessing myself about everything—even when I was trying to run through some katas last night in my bedroom. In less than five minutes, I couldn't even DO any katas, because I couldn't relax enough to let the muscle memory flow. It was like I'd forgotten everything, even though I could still see it in my head."

Echo blinked in surprise, and shot a concerned glance at Fox, who returned it. Omega continued.

* * *

"...So I'm a mess, y'all," Omega reluctantly confessed. "I'll get somebody killed, like this. Even if Zz'r'p really DID get rid of all the programming. And I don't want that! I'd rather jump off the roof. Please... let me go. Before things get worse, and one of you really DOES die, because

334

of me."

She looked around, desperately willing them to understand.

Romeo met her eyes, then glanced aside at India. India looked up at him, then at Omega, her gaze thoughtful. Finally India took Romeo's hand, squeezing it tightly, and they nodded simultaneously. They turned to Fox, who took a deep breath, then nodded as well.

All eyes turned to Echo.

* * *

He stared at Omega for a long moment, expression veiled, even from his partner.

Damn, he thought, struggling with the pain and misery he was hiding from the others. *I've lost her anyway. All that, all the fighting to keep her alive, and I've still lost her. Only this time, she's chosen to walk away from the Agency. To walk away from me. There's nothing I can do to stop it...not one damn thing. And if I care about her at all—and I do—I have to LET her. Then watch while a piece of me walks out the door with her.*

Finally he let his gaze drop to the floor. He sighed noiselessly, and his usually-straight shoulders slumped in reluctant acquiescence. The others glanced away, and Omega turned back to Fox, expectant.

"All right. I'll set it up for you," a regretful Fox agreed.

"Thanks, Fox." She ran a distracted hand over her hair. "Time to say goodbye, I guess."

* * *

Omega took a step toward Fox, but he waved her off.

"I'll be seeing you off and on for a week or so yet, most likely," he decreed. "I want to make sure we get you set up properly, so whatever cover you eventually decide to adopt will hold, and not give us away."

"Oh. Right."

India and Romeo, who had remained silent throughout the exchange, came up to her now.

"You were right about me, India. From the beginning." Omega hung her head, ashamed. "I WAS too good to be true."

"No, I wasn't," India whispered, then hugged her. "Can't we work this out somehow? Do you really have to go?"

"You know I do."

Romeo put his arms around both of them.

"Hey, pretty lady. Whoever you turn out to be, you'll be cool."

"Thanks, Romeo. Coming from you, that means a lot."

When it was Echo's turn to say goodbye, no words needed to be said, nor would they have been adequate. He and Omega just stood there for a long moment, blue eyes locked with brown ones. Then she simply turned and walked out.

Echo's anguished gaze followed her all the way out of the Core.

* * *

After Omega's official departure from the vehicle hangar on the outskirts of the city—which, upon his own orders, only Fox attended—the head of the Agency returned to his office overlooking the Core, feeling particularly melancholy. The whole affair with Omega had not gone according to prior planning and standard procedure, from Echo's very first encounter with her, right down to her reluctantly-approved departure. A pensive Fox paused on the balcony outside his office and looked out over the Core, wondering what they'd done wrong, and what—if anything— they could have done, should have done, to derail the chain of events that had led to this point.

Nothing, that I can see, he concluded. *It presumes abilities that even our resident telepathic ambassador doesn't possess. We none of us can read the future. And if we'd known, I can't think of anything we could have done differently...except maybe to deprogram her before it came to the trigger. Medical sure as hell can't undo what was done to her. A kholere oyf dir, Slug! Geh in drerdt!*

He sighed and turned to his office, allowing his retina to be scanned to unlock the door. He turned the knob and entered.

Echo was waiting...inside.

"I won't even bother asking how you got in," a tired Fox muttered, rubbing a hand across his face. "I'm not sure I really want to know, anyway."

"Nothing you need to worry about, Boss," Echo replied, unusually subdued. "After that little incident with the Garadonian last year, when you designated me your successor and it was approved up the chain of command,

Facilities went ahead and added me to the security lock. I...needed to talk to you about something in private, so I let myself in and waited."

"Must have been important."

"Kinda. To me, anyway." Echo paused. "She get off okay?"

"Yeah, no problems. Look, Echo, I've got some recruits lined up, and a couple of 'em look promising..."

"That's sorta what I wanted to talk to you about, Fox. Listen..."

* * *

The woman with no name, no past, and no discernible future left New York, headed vaguely west. Fox had generously supplied her with everything she would need to get by for a while, including a vehicle, a temporary ID and persona, at least until she figured out what to do with herself.

Maybe a cross-country trip, she thought. Surely, by the time she reached the West Coast, she'd have worked out a plan for the rest of her life. She would take her time getting there, explore a little...or a lot...along the way. Maybe even learn something about herself—the real self, not Slug's version—in the process. *Maybe.*

* * *

The first leg of her trip found her working her way through the Midwest, driving through seemingly endless fields of wheat and corn in the car Fox had provided.

She detoured on a whim and dipped far south, watched an SLS launch, drove by the old farm in Alabama, crossed the Mississippi near Memphis. She explored the diamond fields in Arkansas, then followed the meanders of the Mississippi south, where she checked out the Big Easy and the Gulf of Mexico. Oklahoma saw her hooking up with a team of stormchasers, and racing tornadoes across the prairie states.

She avoided Texas.

She hiked Pikes Peak, prowled through gold mines near Cripple Creek, helped a miner hunt for aquamarine on the mountaintops, panned for placer gold in the Painted Desert.

She climbed over Devil's Tower. *Talk about close encounters,* she thought in heavy irony. Yellowstone, with its intricate geology and beautiful scenery, fascinated her as she hiked its trails. Continuing westward, she found delight in Big Sky country—at night, the stars seemed close enough to touch. She regretted, then, that she would be unable to stop by Kitt Peak National Observatory when she headed into the desert Southwest, but it was far too risky: Someone might remember Megan McAllister there.

She kayaked down the Colorado through the Grand Canyon; explored the Petrified Forest. Helped excavate a newly-discovered kiva in one of the ancient Chacoan pueblos. Retraced part of old Route 66...

But always, always something missing.

She kept moving on.

* * *

The first thing that Echo did after Omega's departure was to put India and Romeo through their paces. With the Alpha One team broken, Division One needed a team capable of filling their shoes, and it was the consensus of both the Director and the Head of Alpha Line that Romeo and India were the most likely agent team to be able to quickly step into the void.

So Echo used the plans he and Omega had created while she was on sick leave, and ran the pair through testing.

As soon as that was over—after testing was successfully completed, but before either agent could be formally declared Alpha Line...

...Echo vanished, headed out alone on a classified mission.

* * *

Over the ensuing weeks, Romeo didn't see a lot of Echo; he seemed to be very busy on various restricted missions that took him away from Headquarters. Once or twice, though, Romeo encountered him at one of the laptops in the Core, with a Division One geosynchronous satellite tight zoom view pulled up on it. All Romeo ever saw, before Echo blanked the screen and turned to say hi, was a little black sports car traveling down various roads. Once, he saw cornfields in the background; another time, mountains.

"Checkin' up on your old girlfriend?" Romeo asked him once.

"What?" Echo asked, startled.

"You know, Chase? Wasn't that her name? What exactly happened there, Echo? I figured you were gone for good, when you took that sabbatical..."

"No." Echo looked away. "No, I'm not checking up on her. There's... nothing to check up on. That was over a long time ago. Nothing is as it appears, champ. You should know that by now. And so should I."

* * *

She had gotten as far as exploring the American Southwest, southern Nevada to the immediate east of Death Valley to be specific, when she saw the incoming that night. She jumped into the little black sport coupe Fox had provided when she left, and burned rubber as she peeled out, headed down the empty highway at speed, chasing the ion trail.

She pulled up at the impact site in a cloud of dust ten minutes later, and jumped out of the car, running over to the crest of the smoking crater rim. There in front of her was not the black, fusion-crusted meteorite she had half-expected to see, but a familiar, gleaming, if badly-damaged, saucer-shaped spacecraft, half-buried in the bottom of the crater. She stared down at it, ticking off fingers, then glanced at her watch.

Oh damn, she thought, glancing around, *this WAS the regular inbound transport to the Area 51 landing site! Something must have gone seriously wrong during re-entry. And no Agency team in sight. I better check to see if everybody's okay inside. That was a damn rough landing.*

She scrambled down the rim of the crater toward the battered saucer. The hatch, twisted by the impact, refused to open more than a couple of inches. But as she attempted to brute-force it open, she inadvertently leaned the heel of one hand against the hull. There was a hissing sound, and she jerked back with a cry. Looking down at her palm, she watched in pained fascination as blisters rose rapidly beneath the burned skin.

AH! You stupid idiot! This puppy just came screaming through the atmosphere fast enough to half-bury itself in the back side of the desert. Of COURSE it's hot, dummy! Mm. I'm gonna have to improvise for this one.

She ran back to the car, scrabbled in the trunk, and came back with a tire jack, with which she proceeded to jimmy open the hatch. It took some time, and necessitated fetching a towel from the car to pad her injured hand. Nobody inside the craft came to help, either, which told her that within, things were decidedly off-nominal.

Once she got the hatch pried open far enough, she used her powerful legs to kick at it, then started jumping on the lower door, forcing it farther and farther open until she could safely enter.

Ducking into the darkened interior, she was glad to see that there were only a few passengers, still strapped in, alive but apparently unconscious. She unstrapped two, grappled them, and quickly began maneuvering them out.

Once out, she dragged them up the crater lip, and over to the far side of her car; she had already concluded they were safer there if the propulsion system blew. She ran back for the other passenger and the pilot.

She had just laid them down beside the other two, and stood over them with a feeling of intense satisfaction, hands on her knees, breathing hard from exertion, when a deep, familiar voice came out of the night.

"We seem to have a habit of midnight desert encounters."

She whirled to see a tall dark figure wearing black sunglasses walking toward her.

"Echo?!"

"Hi."

Neither said anything for a moment. Then Echo waved a hand at the downed saucer, and spoke.

"Thanks for the rescue there, by the way. We knew it was coming down, 'cause the pilot radioed a mayday, but we couldn't triangulate and get a team here fast enough. It's a little bit off-course."

"Did I ever mention you have a talent for understatement, sir?"

"Once or twice." The faint hint of a grin graced the partly-hidden face. "Anyway, appreciate the assistance."

"No problem. I was close by, and saw it re-enter. I could help, so I did."

"As usual."

There was another silence. Echo removed his special glasses.

"Well, at least you've got a ready-made explanation for this one," she said matter-of-factly.

"Oh? What's that?"

She pointed up. He looked up into the diamond-dusted, velvety black sky just as a brilliant streak illuminated it. Golden spangles trailed in its wake, and hung there for a few seconds before fading.

"Perseids," she finished.

"Oh." He shot her a quick glance. "'Nice one.'"

"Yeah."

Suddenly a voice from across the crater rang out.

"TAKE COVER! IT'S GONNA BLOW!!"

Without thought or hesitation, Echo pushed her down, landed on top, and spread out to cover her, as the remains of the spacecraft lit up the desert night.

When the fireworks were over, he got up, dusting himself off as she sat up, and offered her a hand to rise. As he pulled, she inhaled sharply and instinctively jerked her hand away, shaking it as she hissed in pain. He crouched beside her, very gently took her wounded hand in his, turned it palm up, and surveyed the burn.

"Mm. Ouch. Accidentally grab the hull?"

"Yeah. Stupid, huh?"

"Nah. Happens all the time. Done it a couple times myself; you get intent on rescue, on getting the damn hatch open, and you just forget. I keep telling Fox that hatch needs a redesign, but nobody listens. Come on over to the Corvette. I've got something for it."

He led her partway around the crater to his sleek black car with the special 'improvements' and opened the passenger door, pointing at the seat inside, while he fished the first-aid kit out of the trunk. She sat on the edge of the passenger seat and held out her hand as he knelt before her and carefully cleaned the burn. Then he delicately applied a special burn ointment from the Division One-issue medikit, topped that with some Rejuvic, and began expertly bandaging the wounded hand. As he did, she looked around at the activity while the mop-up team went to work.

"Romeo and India?" she asked, searching the swarm of agents with her eyes.

"Off on a mission. The Prime Minister of Braxitar fell into a coffeepot during resumed negotiations between the Caltorians and the Ulyffon Alliance—Braxitar's a member of the Alliance, by the way. They needed

India to filter him out. So Romeo went, too.”

“‘Cause that’s what partners do, huh?” She grinned, allowing a mischievous glint in her eye. “Especially THAT kind of partners.”

“More or less.” Echo shrugged. “But extra security’s always useful when a planetary leader’s indisposed.”

“Oh. Well, never mind, then.” She continued to search the agents expectantly. Finally she got up the nerve to ask the question she dreaded. “Where’s...um, where’s your partner?”

He glanced at her sharply as he completed the bandage, and raised a knowing eyebrow.

“MY partner left some time back to go find herself.”

She blinked in shock.

“And you didn’t...you haven’t, you know, replaced...her?” she wondered.

He simply stared at her, saying nothing; the hard, reproachful look in the brown eyes told her all she needed to know. She had the good sense to stay silent in the face of that gaze.

“So, have you?” he asked then, leaning back and looking at her with a more benign expression.

“Have I what?”

“Found yourself.”

Instead of answering, she stood and walked to the rear of the Corvette. There, she gazed out over the crash site, as medics tended to the spacecraft occupants, and the mop-up team steadily made all evidence of the crash disappear.

Just then, the pilot of the wrecked spacecraft sat up slowly, conscious once more and looking around. The woman murmured something to the attending medic, and the medic pointed across the crater at the pair who stood apart from the rest of the agents, just the two of them watching the operation. The pilot smiled, waved, and nodded vigorously, then gestured at the passengers of the downed craft, who were gradually starting to wake up; it was an expression of deep gratitude. So she smiled back and waved, throwing the pilot a thumbs-up; the pilot returned it with both thumbs and a huge grin.

She felt her face heat with embarrassment...and more than a hint of pleased pride...at the gesture of praise. Glancing down, she found the fender of the Corvette under her good hand, and rubbed it affectionately.

Then she looked up at Echo, who had come to stand beside her.

"Yes," she told him then. "Yes...I think I have."

Epilogue

Romeo, India, Echo, and Omega sat at their favorite table in their favorite pizzeria, the one run by the Antarean felinoid, teasing each other and laughing. A large kitchen-sink pizza on the table before them was rapidly disappearing. Occasionally, a 'normal' customer would come in and curiously eye the four in their identical black Suits. But they ignored it, for the most part.

Until a nosy, rather arrogant older woman in a couture jogging suit at the counter looked them over with upturned nose, and nasally intoned loudly to the largely empty room, "A bit over-dressed for a pizzeria, don't you think? WHO on Earth are THEY?"

Conversation at the table abruptly ceased. Without a word or a glance, four pairs of special wraparound sunglasses came out simultaneously. One hand hovered over an inside jacket pocket. Four pairs of shaded eyes stared unsmilingly, intimidatingly, at the woman until, uncomfortable, she picked up her order and hurried out. When she was out of sight, four pairs of sunglasses were removed and placed in breast pockets. Four grins appeared.

"We," Romeo said proudly, "are Division One."

"Now—" said India.

"—And always," added Omega.

"Amen," invoked Echo.

And they all remembered the words on the plaque Fox had formally dedicated in the Core that morning:

The Pan-Galactic Law Enforcement
and
Immigration Administration
Division One
hereby commissions
Department: Alpha Line
The Division One special forces front line
Alpha One team: E, Ω
Alpha-Two team: R, I

Author Notes

First of all, there are the usual suspects to thank: My parents, Steve and Colene Gannaway, and my husband, Darrell Osborn. They are always supportive and helpful, and Darrell is great for brainstorming.

But speaking of brainstorming, there are a few other people to thank — my beta readers, Dr. James K. Woosley and Larry Bauer. Much brainstorming with them on this entire series is making for a lotta fun. An additional brainstormer includes fellow author Mark Wandrey.

I'd also like to thank Sgt. Terry Minton, head of the Clarksville (TN) PD's CSI team. As usual, he was invaluable in providing insight into how to conduct a proper areal search for a missing child.

Nitay Arbel of Tel Aviv and Red McCord of Tennessee are both fluent Yiddish speakers and they'll be helping me get Fox's Yiddish comments right through the series! Thank you both!

And just so you know, the word "Ke!endarian" is not a typo. For this "alien language," I borrowed from one of the more exotic Earth languages, the !Kung of the Kalahari Desert. The exclamation mark represents a sound for which most other languages have no letter, an alveolar click. In the case of the Ke!endarians, who are avian, it is intended to represent a beak clack. (And no, it is NOT a language that humans are readily able to reproduce!)

~Stephanie Osborn

Huntsville, AL

August 2016

About the Author

Stephanie Osborn is a former payload flight controller, a veteran of over twenty years of working in the civilian space program, as well as various military space defense programs. She has worked on numerous Space Shuttle flights and the International Space Station, and counts the training of astronauts on her resumé. Of those astronauts she trained, one was Kalpana Chawla, a member of the crew lost in the Columbia disaster.

She holds graduate and undergraduate degrees in four sciences: Astronomy, Physics, Chemistry, and Mathematics, and she is "fluent" in several more, including Geology and Anatomy. She obtained her various degrees from Austin Peay State University in Clarksville, TN and Vanderbilt University in Nashville, TN.

Stephanie is currently retired from space work. She now happily "passes it forward," teaching math and science via numerous media including radio, podcasting, and public speaking, as well as working with SIGMA, the science fiction think tank, while writing science fiction mysteries based on her knowledge, experience, and travels.

For more, go to http://www.stephanie-osborn.com/.

A sneak peek at *A Small Medium At Large*, Book 2 of the Division One series, by Stephanie Osborn!

"Okay, I can see it," Echo decided. "His small stature, his stage abilities, all of it. So how much of what Houdini did on stage was standard Glu'gu'ik quantum foam manipulation?"

"That, I couldn't tell you," Fox admitted. "The Glu'gu'ik race could do most of that without much difficulty. But probably some of it was easy enough for Ho'd'ni that he didn't need to. Especially when you consider that Glu'gu'ik are smaller than humans, so all he really had to do was slip out of his disguise, exchange it for a different one, and presto."

"Wait," Echo interrupted. "Are you saying his wife Bess…"

"He didn't have a wife named Bess. Humans and Grays aren't compatible sexually; I thought you knew that, Echo."

"I do," a slightly sheepish Echo admitted. "I'm just still trying to wrap my mind around the notion he was a Glu'g'ik."

"Ah, all right. Well, 'Bess' was most likely a different disguise, something ginned up with his brother to enhance their cover—and then they realized the potential use onstage."

"Sonuva—" Echo began, stunned.

"But how does that have to do with things now?" Omega wondered. "Surely any direct descendants of his family are long dead by this time."

"Well, they are, but that doesn't mean there isn't family back on Va'du'sha'a," Fox pointed out. "In fact, there's a cousin, and she's coming here today, with the intent to hold a séance tomorrow night."

Alpha One pondered that for a few moments.

"I'm still not seein' it," Omega admitted.

"Yeah," Echo agreed. "Holding séances for Houdini on Halloween is just what you do, in some circles."

"Except that Glu'gu'ik can manipulate—" Fox began.

"The quantum foam, yeah, I know," Echo finished for him. "So theoretically, this cousin could actually contact Houdini."

"You're kidding," Omega said, staring at him.

"No, he's not," Fox averred.

"But so how is that important to us?"

"Because the reason they fled Va'du'sha'a was due to massive civil unrest. According to their historians, the entire planet was in a huge civil war. Think of it like a massive, planetary War of the Roses—their history indicates something like half a dozen or better claimants to the throne, with the Hou'd'ni clan right in the middle—they were special stewards to the throne. What sort of special, I don't know. There were skirmishes, and hundreds of people were killed, but there wasn't an outright war...yet. What I do know is that, right on the brink of a planetary war—which would likely have involved a nuclear exchange—was when the Hou'd'ni family came to Earth...and the whole civil unrest thing fell apart," Fox explained, "apparently due to something that they brought with them."

"What?" Echo asked. "What did they bring, and how did it relate to the civil unrest?"

"That, we also don't know. But the cousin may. According to my intel, the cousin wants to get back at the 'other side,' and thinks that she may be able to find out where this...kheyfets...is, if she contacts Ari Ho'd'ni. More, GALINT indicates that this is one of the more powerful factions that existed then."

"But I thought they were a democratic republic now," Omega protested.

"They are. And the majority of the population is happy about it—but not everyone agrees," Fox explained. "And evidently there is a big enough faction—or factions, GALINT suspects more than one—who want to go back to the rule of royalty, that they're willing to risk another full-out civil war to do it." He paused. "But since then, the Zeta Reticuli system has joined PGLEIA and added a LOT of offworld connections and treaties. So then you have to start factoring in who's allied with whom, from what system, and how many of them aren't as stable as we'd like them to be...and the whole mess just grew exponentially."

"Crap," Omega grumbled.

"Exactly," Fox agreed. "And—"

"And Zeta Reticuli is now in Division One," Echo realized, finishing for him.

"Oh, damn," Omega murmured, a look of comprehension spreading over her face. "So the Zeta Reticuli problem is..."

"Ours," Fox finished. "Right."

"Well...shit," Echo said, with feeling.

Don't miss any of these highly entertaining SF/F books by Stephanie Osborn!

Burnout: The mystery of Space Shuttle STS-281 (ISBN: 1-60619-200-0) by Stephanie Osborn

How do you react when you discover the next shuttle disaster has happened...right on schedule?

Burnout is a SF mystery about a Space Shuttle disaster that turns out to be no accident. As the true scope of the disaster is uncovered by the principle investigators, "Crash" Murphy and Dr. Mike Anders, they find themselves running for their lives as friends, lovers and coworkers involved in the investigation perish around them.

~ * ~

Sherlock Holmes: Gentleman Aegis series by Stephanie Osborn:
Sherlock Holmes and the Mummy's Curse

Sherlock Holmes and the Mummy's Curse (ISBN: 1-51888-312-5) by Stephanie Osborn

Holmes and Watson. Two names linked by mystery and danger from the beginning.

Within the first year of their friendship and while both are young men, Holmes and Watson are still finding their way in the world, with all the troubles that such young men usually have: Financial straits, troubles of the female persuasion, hazings, misunderstandings between friends, and more. Watson's Afghan wounds are still tender, his health not yet fully recovered, and there can be no consideration of his beginning a new practice as yet. Holmes, in his turn, is still struggling to found the new profession of consulting detective. Not yet truly established in London, let alone with the reputations they will one day possess, they are between cases and at loose ends when Holmes' old professor of archaeology contacts him.

Professor Willingham Whitesell makes an appeal to Holmes' unusual skill set and a request. Holmes is to bring Watson to serve as the dig team's physician and come to Egypt at once to translate hieroglyphics for his prestigious archaeological dig. There in the wilds of the Egyptian desert, plagued by heat, dust, drought and cobras, the team hopes to find the very first Pharaoh. Instead, they find something very different... (First book in the Gentleman Aegis series)

Sherlock Holmes and the Mummy's Curse is a Silver Falchion Award winner.

~ * ~

Displaced Detective series by Stephanie Osborn:
The Case of the Displaced Detective: The Arrival
The Case of the Displaced Detective: At Speed
The Case of the Cosmological Killer: The Rendlesham Incident
The Case of the Cosmological Killer: Endings and Beginnings
A Case of Spontaneous Combustion
Fear in the French Quarter

The Case of the Displaced Detective: The Arrival (ISBN: 1-60619-189-7) by Stephanie Osborn is a SF mystery in which brilliant hyperspatial physicist, Dr. Skye Chadwick, discovers there are alternate realities, often populated by those we consider only literary characters. Can Chadwick help Holmes come up to speed in modern investigative techniques in time to stop the spies? Will Holmes be able to thrive in our modern world? Is Chadwick now Holmes' new "Watson" — or more?

And what happens next?   [First book in the Displaced Detective series]

The Case of the Displaced Detective: At Speed (ISBN: 1-60619-191-0) by Stephanie Osborn

Having foiled sabotage of Project: Tesseract by an unknown spy ring, Sherlock Holmes and Dr. Skye Chadwick face the next challenge. How do they find the members of this diabolical spy ring when they do not even know what the ring is trying to accomplish? And how can they do it when Skye is recovering from no less than two nigh-fatal wounds?

Can they work out the intricacies of their relationship? Can they determine the reason the spy ring is after the tesseract? And — most importantly — can they stop it? [Second book in the Displaced Detective series]

The Case of the Cosmological Killer: The Rendlesham Incident (ISBN: 1-60619-193-4) by Stephanie Osborn

In 1980, RAF Bentwaters and Woodbridge were plagued by UFO sightings that were never solved. Now, McFarlane, a resident of Suffolk has died of fright during a new UFO encounter. On holiday in London, Sherlock Holmes and Skye Chadwick-Holmes are called upon by Her Majesty's Secret Service to investigate the death.

What is the UFO? Why does Skye find it familiar? Who — or what — killed McFarlane?

And how can the pair do what even Her Majesty's Secret Service could not? [Third book in the Displaced Detective series]

The Case of the Cosmological Killer: Endings and Beginnings (ISBN: 1-60619-195-0) by Stephanie Osborn

After the revelations in *The Rendlesham Incident*, Holmes and Skye find they have not one, but two, very serious problems facing them. Not only did their "UFO victim" most emphatically NOT die from a close encounter, he was dying twice over — from completely unrelated causes. Holmes must now find the murderers before they find the secret of the McFarlane farm. And to add to their problems, another continuum — containing another Skye and Holmes — has approached Skye for help to stop the collapse of their own spacetime, a collapse that could take Skye with it, should she happen to be in their tesseract core when it occurs. [Fourth book in the Displaced Detective series]

A Case of Spontaneous Combustion (ISBN: 1-60619-197-7) by Stephanie Osborn

When an entire village west of London is wiped out in an apparent case of mass spontaneous combustion, Her Majesty's Secret Service contacts The Holmes Agency to investigate. Once in London, Holmes looks into the horror that is now Stonegrange. His investigations take him into a dangerous undercover assignment in search of a possible terror ring, though he cannot determine how a human agency could have caused the disaster. Meanwhile, alone in Colorado, Skye is forced to battle raging wildfires and tame a wild mustang stallion, all while believing that her husband has abandoned her. Who — or what — caused the horror in Stonegrange? Will Holmes find his way safely through the metaphorical minefield that is modern Middle Eastern politics? Will this predicament seriously damage — even destroy — the couple's relationship? And can Holmes stop the terrorists before they unleash their outré weapon again? [Fifth book in the Displaced Detective series]

Fear in the French Quarter (ISBN: 1-60619-202-7) by Stephanie Osborn revolves around a jaunt by no less than Sherlock Holmes himself — brought to the modern day from an alternate universe's Victorian era by his continuum parallel, who is now his wife, Dr. Skye Chadwick-Holmes — to famed New Orleans for both business and pleasure. There, the detective couple investigates ghostly apparitions, strange disappearances, mystic phenomena, and challenge threats to the very universe they call home.

It was supposed to be a working holiday for Skye and Sherlock, along with their friend, the modern day version of Doctor Watson — some federal training that also gave them the chance to explore New Orleans, as the ghosts of the French Quarter become exponentially more active. When the couple uncovers an imminently catastrophic cause, whose epicenter lies squarely in the middle of Le Vieux Carré, they must race against time to stop it before the whole thing breaks wide open — and more than one universe is destroyed. [Sixth book in the Displaced Detective series]